Praying for Rain

Emma Gates

Wells Street Press

Praying for Rain

ONE

"RESOLVED: that Saudi girls be allowed to drive."
Leila's sharp chin lifted in challenge as she stared
at her classmates.

"Against," stated Feiruz. "I don't like. In London, it
frighten me on the road. I won't like to drive here ever!
The Riyadh traffic is *excruciating*." She glanced at Arden to
underscore her choice of the day's adjectives. They were
on E, five days into Intermediate English Conversation at
Riyadh University Womens' College.

"Against," Princess Khadijah said. "I don't want
strange men see me. And if I am covered I can't to drive
because I can't to look out."

"No infinitive." Arden paced the half-circle she'd
arranged. "I can't drive, I can't look out." She still wasn't
used to the brush of skirt against her ankles.

"Tell Miss Armstrong why we cover," Leila prodded.
"I know the Americans women think this is *extraordinary.*"

"Only men of my family can see me," Khadijah
replied. "If any man sees me uncovered, he can to say,
"oh, she is pretty" or "oh, she is ugly." It is not for him,
how I look." She ran a hand over her glossy French braid.
"My face is for me."

Arden kept her own face still. In the teachers'
orientation session, they'd been warned not to bring up
veiling, driving, religion, sex, or politics of any kind, in
class discussion. How hot could she let this water get
before she turned it off?

1

"He won't say you're *very* ugly, ya Khadijah." Eyman's teasing smile tightened black cloth against her round cheeks. She alone wore a headscarf. The others shed their robes and face veils once past the two sets of steel gates sheltering them from the city. They preened in class, showing off perfect makeup, primary-color jewelry, strappy high heels and tight tops under the strict green school uniform.

Arden felt gauche next to them. Her limp purple Indian-print dress was the only long style available back in the Columbus mall, and her hair was a mess since her dryer didn't work here. But she enjoyed the girls' beauty and their perfumes scenting the half-circle. They were a garden in gorgeous full bloom.

"Maybe he will say you are *exquisite*." Feiruz leaned into Khadijah's shoulder, batting eyes. Khadijah laughed and batted too.

"Do you *all* feel this, about the veil?" Arden asked. Khadijah was an Al Saud, one of the royal family: maybe her view was unique?

But most of the students nodded.

Leila scolded, "You silly girls. You don't see how the hijab is a way to keep us simple. If we cannot see, cannot drive, cannot work with men, we can never have power to make the own life. We are *excluded*."

"Good use, Leila," Arden said. She stopped herself from adding "good point."

"I feel sorry for women who have power to make the own life," said Feiruz. "In London they work all the days. They send their babies to strangers and they don't have time with their family or any friends. They don't have time cook good food. They are all peoples there so tired! Nobody in England look pretty. They should cover also. I don't like see their tired face." She slumped in her chair and flapped a slim hand, slowly, waving away the grim English.

"Faces," Arden corrected, latching onto the conversational thread she could control. "I don't like *to* see their *faces*. They *are all so* tired." She flashed on her

2

mother's face after a working day, during the lean years, one hand stirring a pot on the stove and the other holding her sister Annie's spelling homework. She pushed away a pang of homesickness.

"Some of the English boys look pretty," said Khadijah, with a sly smile. "But not as pretty like our Saudi boys. They are *exemplary*."

"Good use, Khadijah! But, not as pretty *as*. And for a boy we say handsome, or attractive." This was hot water too, but the girls waded in eagerly. She hoped their enthusiastic comments would not carry into the hallway.

"Don't you think our men are too attractive, Miss Armstrong?" Feiruz asked.

Saudi men were frightening white blurs dominating the dun-colored landscape. *Extraterrestrial.* She was tempted to examine them more closely but eye contact was forbidden. "I am here to teach and to learn from you, not to look at men."

Khadijah gave her approving-princess nod.

"Our topic, again?"

Leila spoke. "Resolved: that we have a night driving lesson at my house, in our brothers' thobe and ghutra, so the police don't to see we are girls, and we show the solid? With our aunts who went driving during the war against the Iraq?"

Arden knew about the 1991 equality protest, when organized Saudi women took to Riyadhi roads in the family Cadillacs. Those women were jailed, their husbands fired, their families disgraced. "Not a serious resolution, Leila."

"Miss Armstrong, you know how to drive?"

"That's not relevant—"

"Resolved: that Miss will come my home to teach us driving."

She let their laughter go awhile as she circled behind them. Teaching them to drive would be a hoot. She pictured their glee, swathed in headdresses and floor-length white shirts, sporting aviator sunglasses ... or no, not sunglasses, not at night. Not in Riyadh.

"You know this can't happen." She spoke briskly, not letting her regret show.

"It is debate." Leila's black eyes widened. "We do nothing. What is that word, Miss, show the loyalty, the support for the politics idea? Solidity?"

"Solidarity. Political ideas," Arden muttered. The water was now boiling over. "This is a subject your families—"

"Is idea, only," Leila argued. "My topic. Resolved."

"Can I ask, what would happen if I took you out driving?"

Leila's long eyelashes quickly shuttered her bold stare. She didn't answer.

"You will be put to prison." Feiruz sounded almost smug, but when Arden checked the girl's face, it was as bland as the others' were, in the suddenly silent room. Arden felt her shoulders tighten, but she continued her slow pacing.

"And what would happen to you?"

"We don't come to university more. We stay at home," Feiruz said softly.

"So, then, no driving lessons. Thanks for the tip." Arden snapped her note cards into a neat rectangle. "Any more responses?"

"For," Eyman said. "When I am doctor, how I get to hospital? Why I have to wait for my father or my brother to drive me?"

"The hospital can give to you his driver." Khadijah's soft voice was a drawl, Arden thought, the drawl of unending comfort. Or boredom.

"Hospitals should give money to equipment, not to driver for women doctors. I want drive my own car for work."

"*Excellent* observation," Arden said.

"How will you drive if your face is covered?" Leila asked.

"I can use the dark glass, so nobody look inside to me."

"Miss Armstrong, what is your position, on the topic?" Leila, again.

"I'm your guide on how to conduct a debate. I don't take a position."

"But in the true, what do *you* think?"

Arden paced faster, not wanting them to see how uneasy Leila's insistence made her. She peered out the latticed third-story window, but saw only the feathery tops of palms from the nearby wadi and, closer, a strip of road bordering the steel gray gates that walled off the College like a moat. Feeling cornered, she turned back to the class and asked Leila, "Why do you want to know about me?"

"You just arrived. We are curious what do you see here."

As if realizing this anew, every girl stared at Arden.

"Leila, it's not my place to judge."

"But I am interested to your idea. Is talking only, you don't judge."

Talking only? More like treading water while sharks circled, slow and sure. "I don't want to start my year here by disagreeing with your society." But if she expressed her opinion, they would know it was safe in class to express theirs. She smoothed her dress with clammy hands. "However, since you ask, and this is just my own view … I think it's common sense for young adults to be able to drive. In case of emergency. Like swimming. Everyone should know how."

The prolonged silence that followed this statement, and their sober faces, told her she'd probably fucked up. She tried a weak smile and then, to further distract them from her blurted opinion, she walked to her case and took out the banjo.

"I promised I'd play for you." She pushed back her long hair, strummed a loud chord, and launched into a funked-up "Camptown Races." It was funnier and more complex than her usual new-student "Oh Susannah." Finally, they started laughing when she explained the meaning of "bob-tailed nag," and made her sing it again so they could learn the words. Doo-dah, doo-dah.

When the bell rang, Leila approached. "We can to discuss driving again next week, Miss Arden? *Extenuating?*"

"Next week we're using F words." Uh-oh. "I mean, we'll see."

She walked down with them to watch them file in an uneven procession out of the building. Students threw on the black garb once their names were barked from the guardhouse intercom. Drivers waited beyond, where scarlet bougainvillea spilled over the outer gate, the only splash of color on the street.

TWO

MELANCHOLY wailing woke Arden from her nap later that afternoon.

Evening prayer call. The singer sounded like the only other person awake in the desert somnolence. His wistful cadence made her throat ache. How would she replicate this lovesick plea on banjo? Slow. Quiet. Minor chords.

She fingered apart window blinds to peer toward the campus mosque. A sparse line of men, summoned to prayer, walked up the nearby hill. A slight breeze billowed their white robes and headdresses. The sky was the deep blue of near sunset. Landscaped palms threw elongated shadows onto the neatly kept campus pathways.

She wanted to feel the breeze. She pulled on her long purple cotton dress, slipped into flip-flops, and snatched the black scarf to fling over her head as she ran down the outdoor concrete steps to the courtyard.

The warm air stirring her skin was a welcome change from artificial indoor cold. She followed the hillside walkway curving past the mosque—a low white structure with a perfect Dairy-Queen cone of a minaret, topped by a quarter-moon shaped crescent, studded by a loudspeaker. No singer stood in the cupola.

The men inside knelt, heads touching the floor, headdresses spilling. A few wore lacy caps, like yarmulkes. The humility of their posture contrasted with the arrogance Saudi men seemed to display elsewhere.

She stopped behind a cluster of palms below the path, to be invisible. But the men at prayer mesmerized her.

7

Their balletic poses reminded her of yoga. Their rising and falling murmurs were hypnotic.

Something hard slammed painfully into her shoulder, yanking her scarf awry. She whipped around. A soccer ball!

She swooped to catch it before it bounced away.

A robed boy, from a small pack in the parking lot, started running toward her. She clenched the ball, drew a deep breath into her shoulder's sting, trying for a dignified pose even as her scarf slid further and her hair loosened in the breeze.

"Sorry miss!" He grinned as his laughing buddies caught up to him. They were young, no more than twelve or thirteen, but she didn't like feeling surrounded.

"That *hurt!*" She frowned at the ringleader, forced authority into her tone. "You should be more careful!"

"Sorry," he repeated, black eyes glittering. "We play, only."

"What if it had gone inside!" She jerked her head toward the mosque.

"Is nothing. Miss not angry."

Brats! She felt as if they'd aimed for her like a deliberate target. Maybe they'd seen her peeking into the mosque, a now-bareheaded female infidel, and wanted to teach her a lesson. She felt like striking back. But how?

The boys studied her as keenly as she'd studied the men in the mosque: too curiously for comfort. One boy jostled closer, touching her arm, his face alert with an unfriendly eagerness. She smelled his excited sweat. The others giggled at his boldness.

Men's voices broke into their standoff. The faithful were now outside the mosque.

Arden hiked up her dress and gave the ball the hardest kick she could manage with her flip-flopped foot. It stunned her toes, sailed into the nearest parking lot and sprang over several shiny cars to rest, rocking as if alive, on a Mercedes hood.

"Go get it, tiger." Now her foot throbbed as much as her shoulder.

"Miss, you good football." The ringleader shot her a rueful look.

She watched them running as she limped down the hill. She'd have stopped to massage her foot, but there was nowhere to sit, and she wanted to get back to the guesthouse before the men from the mosque caught up to her.

But she couldn't walk fast enough to outpace one of those men. His robe fluttered into her dress. She slowed down, hoping he'd pass, but his sandaled feet matched hers, and she finally glanced up, afraid of what she'd see.

Mottled green eyes were unusual against his dark complexion but even more surprising was the direct way he assessed her. His white headdress framed a face whose curved lines held a history of sun and smiling. But he was not smiling now.

"Did they give you a hard time?" He tilted his head toward the soccer boys milling around the Mercedes. His voice was low, with the clipped accent of an Arabic speaker who'd studied in the States.

Arden shook her head, sure if she spoke it would be a delayed-reaction yelp. The breeze lifted a thin lock of her hair. His gaze followed its passage skyward and down to her elbow, then fixed on her eyes.

"They aren't used to seeing uncovered women." He made it sound more of a friendly tip than an admonishment, but heat prickled her skin. She tugged at her slippery scarf. She found her voice but couldn't prevent its defensive tone.

"Their stupid ball knocked my scarf off! Anyway, I've only been here a week. I'm still adjusting."

His face creased into what looked like the beginning of warmth. "Me too. *Ahlan was ahlan,*" he murmured. She knew that meant welcome.

"You just arrived?" He looked like a Saudi except for the eyes. "But you're not a student," she guessed.

He shook his head. The moving air ruffled his headdress, and he adjusted one long end onto his shoulder with a graceful flip. "I teach archeology."

He glanced behind him at the men approaching from the mosque, then once more at her. She got a fleeting impression of a smile, or at least a flash of white teeth as he turned away. "Great kick, by the way," he added.

"What's your ..." She spoke to his back as he reached the main path. He did not sway like his countrymen. He strode, and his robe and long headdress seemed to fly behind him. The other men passed, a ponderous flock of white Sunday school figures.

Arden walked down the darkening hill. Lights now illuminated the palms on the jewel-green lawn of the courtyard. A few black-shrouded clusters of women sat on the playground benches, and, newly conscious of her thin dress and sloppy headscarf, she imagined their gazes following her.

In the guesthouse Kate, the teacher with whom she'd been paired after their arrival, was in the living room. "Arden, we're invited to dinner with the other new faculty. You should have told me you were going out—I'd have liked to walk around."

"Next time." She didn't know Kate well enough to relay her misadventure of spying on the mosque, confronting the boys, talking to a strange Saudi man.

"We're to pick roommates tonight. But I'm requesting a single." Kate, on sabbatical from the University of Massachusetts, was teaching the Modern British Novel.

"You think they'll let you?" Single women weren't allowed to live alone.

"There are always exceptions to rules." Kate smiled, adjusting her headscarf over short red hair. "I'll take it up with the Womens' College Director."

They walked outside. Now the palm-lit courtyard was crowded with strolling families. Men's white robes glimmered and women's black disappeared as they trailed behind. The archaeologist could be any of the ghostly male figures, all standing or walking in groups, some holding hands. No one was alone.

"Just think," Kate said quietly. "These black bags might be our married students, with their faculty husbands. We can't tell." Her blue eyes stood out in her pale face—the only woman's face Arden could actually see.

"They're not looking at us." Curious to be surrounded by people, yet feel invisible. "If she saw me, Leila would come say hello."

"She might be unmarried, living at home. And these men aren't *supposed* to look at us, if they're respectful. Remember, last week, the way the admin guys seemed to ignore us? I had to remind myself they were being polite, not arrogant."

The archaeologist, looking right at her, wasn't disrespectful. He was human. She wished she'd had the wit to get his name.

THREE

"**L**ADIES!" Ben Mimoun, the stylish Moroccan-American they'd met during orientation, came to clasp their hands and hold on. And on. "Did you remember the wine?" He chuckled. Everyone knew alcohol was prohibited in Saudi Arabia.

Arden yanked her hands from his.

Kate joked, "Did you remember the hashish?"

His smooth face brightened. "Do you *know* my poetry?"

"Maybe," Kate said carefully. "Why don't you remind me?"

"*Pita, Hashish and Sahara.* U Conn Press. Lit students *love* my work. They all want to visit the Middle East, even now." Six years after Desert Storm, the area was still considered unstable, in spite of the sanctions against Iraq.

"Were they *travel* poems?" Kate's sarcasm, Arden noted, seemed lost on Ben.

"More like memoirs," he crooned. "I had a wonderful childhood in Marrakesh."

"*That* I believe," George, a British engineer, put in from the living room.

"I came here to rediscover my roots in the desert," Ben went on. "I've already been inspired to write two more poems. My Arabian cycle. I'll give a reading."

Kate rolled eyes at Arden.

The teachers drank "Saudi Champagne," a mixture of apple juice and Perrier, as they got to know each other. A new woman had arrived that afternoon—Evelyn, a petite blonde English Romantics scholar from London.

Arden discovered, to her surprised discomfort, that she was the sole Midwestern American, the only one not from a name university, who had never before traveled outside her home country. She was also, at twenty-four, the youngest by at least five years, with no academic rank: her three years of teaching community college English as a Second Language in Columbus were meager compared to the credentials of tenured faculty in Ben's living room.

The university had obviously suffered a last-minute deficit of ESL teachers. Arden's interview in Houston five weeks ago, by a fine-suited guy who never once looked in her eyes, was the most perfunctory she'd ever experienced.

She kept quiet.

Ben moved next to her.

"You have an unusual name, Arden. Is it from Ohio too?"

"It's an old family name." Her family name, from the West Virginia side, she'd inherited with white-blonde hair and Great Uncle Munro's banjo.

Ben leaned close. "What's a cute girl like you doing so far from home?"

She shifted away. "Getting out of debt." Her salary was twice what she'd made in Columbus, plenty of incentive to bear the inconveniences of Saudi life, as long as she lifted her student loans completely off Mom's back.

"Too right!" George chimed in. "Only reason to come to this godforsaken place."

Arden thought of the men at prayer. "It's not godforsaken."

"No booze, no sexual adventures—I've been warned as no doubt we all have—not even any decent telly!" George exclaimed. "Nothing but desert for miles around. And hot as bloody hell. It's going to be a *long* year."

"So why are you here?" Ben asked him.

"Two greedy ex-wives and a house in Wiltshire."

There was a knock at the door.

"No more money talk now," Ben said. "I invited Sayeed." Sayeed Al Quraishi was the Orientation Director who had gotten them settled during the last weekend.

"Good, I want another look at his Rolex," George said.

"Behave yourself," Kate told him quickly. "Quraishi is a prominent family here."

George gasped, mocking awe.

The way Sayeed Al Quraishi carried himself, the pristine state of his robe and his subtle scent, changed the air. Even George sat up straight. Sayeed's smile was shy under his neat black mustache. "Thank you for including me."

"It wouldn't be a party without you, *ya sadiki!*" Ben cried.

"What did you say?" asked Kate.

"*Ya sadiki?* Oh my friend."

"Tell us more," Grace said. "Some greetings."

Ben complied. *"Asalaamu aliekum. Marhaba. Hayakallah."* Arden felt like one of her own students, wrapping her mouth around the unfamiliar syllables, reduced to childhood by the process. Sayeed's lips twitched as the teachers repeated Ben's phrases.

"All right, now how do I ask for a lager?" George shot a glance at Sayeed.

"We have non-alcoholic beer, George, it's not bad." Sayeed's tone was dry.

They ate from fragrant platters of hummus, cool tabouli, meat pastries and tart pickled vegetables. "Gorgeous food," said Evelyn as the rest dug in. "Lebanese. Makes me miss Beirut. I taught there last year."

Evelyn's comment turned the talk to Middle East politics and changes to the region since Desert Storm. Sayeed was asked his views on Saudi politics.

"We do not use the expression Desert Storm." Sayeed lowered long eyelashes to the circle of beads he was rolling through well-manicured fingers. "Other than saying that, I won't discuss our internal situation with you."

There was an alert silence.

"I remind you, don't speak to your students either, about political matters." His black eyes evaluated each of them. Did he somehow know Arden had voiced her opinion on driving, in class? She dropped her gaze, studied her hands as they knitted together.

"How about we just stick to yes-no questions, then?" Kate asked sweetly. "So as not to put you on the spot. I'm sure we're all curious about your society."

"I will talk about anything besides political condition."

"Maybe we should make it Truth or Dare." Evelyn eyed Sayeed. "For you."

"Why do you want to know about me?"

Arden heard herself asking Leila the same thing, in class, that afternoon.

"You're our key to the Kingdom, *ya sadiki,* you're the only Saudi we've met so far, except our students," Ben explained. "You're supposed to orient us."

"To the Orient," George added, straight-faced.

"Perhaps another time." Sayeed rose in a fluid white column, straightening his headdress in a nimble way that reminded Arden of the archaeologist's similar gesture. He bowed his head slightly. "This evening was a pleasure."

"Aren't we supposed to stay up until all hours drinking tea?"Arden wondered aloud, trying to interject a note of humor to lighten the atmosphere. Her two Saudi students in Columbus had told her that late nights were the norm for Arab parties.

"You're not Saudis," Sayeed reminded, eyes narrowing in amusement. "You're Westerners. You're driven by the clock."

Kate nudged Arden. "We're leaving too," she said.

Once outside, it seemed natural for Sayeed to accompany them across the dark quiet courtyard. It seemed natural for them to walk next to him. Just as naturally, he distanced himself, pulling slightly ahead. His smile, at the guesthouse, was polite.

Kate put her hand on his arm. "Won't you stay for a bit? I'd like to ask you about so many things here, we could have some tea, and talk. It's not late."

He drew away from her touch, looking down. "That is kind, but I must go."

"He refused tea," Kate said irritably, once inside. "That's an insult here."

"But maybe women don't ask men?"

"He's supposed to make us feel at home," Kate continued. "It's his job."

"Oh well." Arden yawned, peeling off her sticky scarf and fanning herself with it. She was glad Sayeed hadn't come in to observe them. Who needed that kind of scrutiny? "Welcome to the patriarchy."

FOUR

"FORMIDABLE," Khadijah offered, peering into her English dictionary but using the French intonation. "The party at my cousin's house was formi*da*ble."

"Tell us how?" Arden asked.

"Every woman wore new dress. We celebrated my cousin to have a baby boy."

"That is impressive. For*mi*dable!" She gave it the English emphasis.

"*Frenetic*," said Feiruz. "Traffic in the Kingdom is frenetic with too many drivers going all the place. We need a public transport for the workers."

"Great observation!"

"*Fundamentalist*," Leila said. "We take too much care to the fundamentalist."

"Good word choice, Leila, but your sentence isn't clear."

"I am talking about the very religious, the ones who want put more mutawas to the streets, make more troubles to everyone who are just living the simple life."

Arden strolled behind the half circle, giving herself a moment out of their sight. Mutawas were religious police, notable for long carrot-red dyed beards, charged with getting men to pray and women to cover. The one outside the Womens' College looked like a cartoon, but his menacing bark was real. She heard it just this morning, when she was caught still quickly whipping on her abaya, the black graduation-gown like robe women were obliged to use in public. Sayeed, who was riding the bus with

17

them for the first two weeks of class, gave her a ferocious scowl; it bothered her to remember now.

"You know this isn't a debate day," she told Leila, facing them again. "And, to be perfectly honest, I've been advised not to talk about religion in class."

"We are in college to think what is the right, to our society. This is the place."

"This is the place to improve your English speaking skills."

"When we speak about the interesting ideas, then we speak better."

Of course Leila was right. At community college, with ESL students from all over the world, political discussions were the liveliest. Sometimes too heated, depending on the topic and geography, but easy to guide. At least, in Ohio it was easy.

"Would you like to take a vote on free discussions in this class?"

The girls murmured their assent.

She faced them. "Three conditions, ladies, and you all have to agree on these. One: we use your daily vocab words."

They nodded.

"Two: you don't talk about this outside of our class." If they were as sensitive to controversy as the university officials, they would censor themselves. She hoped. She surveyed each face: sweet Eyman, glamorous Khadijah, the ones in the middle who did not speak out, and Feiruz and Leila on opposite ends of the semicircle, whose gazes were locked intensely to hers in separate but equal fervor.

"And three: I don't give my opinion. I am only a conversation guide."

From the center, shy Maha spoke. "How we know we don't talk, out the class?"

"You must trust each other, and me." She looked into Maha's brown eyes, behind their fashionable spectacles. "You can trust me."

"Do you give time to decide, Miss?" Maha's face reddened with the effort of expressing herself. "Please to let us talk in the class alone."

"Of course." She walked to the door. "The choice is yours, ladies."

Outside the room, heart pounding, she scanned the closed doors down the hallway. She *didn't* know the risk she might be taking, for herself or for them. Talking might be as dangerous as acting. But what was the point of being here if she was just going to shut them up?

In Columbus convo class was like conducting a choral group. You had the sopranos, altos, tenors and basses. You had your divas, prima donnas, bashful beauteous solos, cutup clown attention-seekers. It was a matter of delicate balance, and firm control, to let all have a turn in creating a magnificent work.

She sank, resting on her heels against the wall, letting her head drop and closing her eyes. She was slowly, finally adjusting to the time zone. Was she ten hours ahead of Columbus or behind? Ahead, yes. Definitely ahead.

After about ten minutes Maha peeked out. "We decided, Miss, we want try."

FIVE

WHEN ARDEN HURRIED out of the last gate the mutawa lifted his stick when he saw her, gesturing to her head and barking in Arabic, a sickening flashback of this morning's confrontation. In her haste to be on time, she had not tied her hijab on tight, and ends of her hair were fluttering out.

Sayeed spoke to the mutawa, obviously trying to appease, but the argument continued as Arden boarded the bus. Sayeed looked exhausted when he finally got on and sat in front, his back to them.

"Oooh, Arden, bad girl," teased Evelyn as the bus groaned away. "You got our *sadiki* in trouble with the Prevention of Vice and the Promotion of Virtue Committee." She held up a hand to ward off their unbelieving remarks. "It's quite true, ask Sayeed, if he ever speaks to you again. You offend with your tarty hair."

"Oh Jesus."

"And you *can't* say that," reproved Evelyn, grinning. "If you must swear, use some British words. "Bloody hell" will do, and it's inoffensive here." She pursed her lips. "We're to behave like Girl Guides. One half expects a secret handshake."

"Fuck." She leaned on the window and closed her eyes.

Kate shook her awake.

The driver had gone, but Sayeed stood in front, waiting for her to pass. She kept her eyes down as she

20

stopped to say, "Sayeed, I'm sorry I caused a problem for you with the mutawa."

His sandaled feet shifted. "You have to be more careful, Miss Arden, with covering. This happen to you two times I see. Maybe more I don't see."

She glanced up and his eyes met hers for one cool moment before he dropped his gaze and tilted his headdress toward the bus doorway. "We cannot stand alone here."

"Alone?" she repeated. He was uncomfortable being with her on the *bus*?

"It is not possible to show the same friendship inside and outside."

Inside and outside?

"Men and women are not outside friends here," he continued. "I am sure you know this." He waved his hand to the door. "Go."

"Okay, okay!" She shoved past him and clomped down the steps.

He followed, and called out to the group, "Ladies, a moment please." They turned. "I need to know what you have chosen so far, for housing. Have you decided?"

"I'm in a single," Kate said. She produced a memo and handed it to him. "Dr. Zafeeyeh okayed it." Zafeeyeh was the Womens' College Director.

"We're together." Evelyn indicated Grace.

The European, Arab and Indian women teachers had also coupled. Arden was the only one left alone. Hurt took her by surprise.

Sayeed wrote in his notebook, counted. "Miss Armstrong will remain in the guesthouse." Until we figure out what to do with you, his tone implied.

"I can stay with her awhile," Kate told Sayeed, as if from one parent to another.

Arden moved away. "I'm good alone."

Sayeed ignored them. "I will have these changes made tonight."

"And will we see you for dinner?" Evelyn asked him. "We can manage a takeaway meal at our new place."

Sayeed studied his notebook. "Thank you. I may be busy."

There was a lump in Arden's throat as she followed Kate to the guesthouse. She wished for a cold beer, good music, friends' faces, lounging on the front porch.

Kate turned in the narrow hallway. "Arden, I hope you don't take it personally that I don't want a room-mate. You won't be lonely. Single women are a hot commodity here. We should have a great social life, if we're careful."

Commodity? No thanks. "I didn't come to meet expats. But I did think I might get to know the Saudis."

"I'd like to know them too. They're enigmatic." Kate smiled. "We'll compare notes! Wild Western women exploring the mystifying Orient."

"Whoa. Sounds like one of Ben's poems."

In her room, Arden stripped and lay down. She was *so* tired. No wonder having to live alone seemed alarming, in spite of what she'd told Sayeed and Kate.

Again, prayer call woke her.

She hadn't heard such compelling devotion since she was eight, in West Virginia, singing the century-old shapenote Harmony, swaying in unison, each section taking turn. She always tried to cajole from her banjo those same trancelike notes.

At the Episcopal church they'd joined in Columbus, after they left West Virginia, the heartrending moments seemed to come from contemplation of another's Easter outfit in comparison with one's own, not from any love of God. By age fifteen she could no longer accept the virgin Mary, sweet Jesus, wise God stories.

Mom, who was sorry she'd quit going to church, went weekly to the genial service, and Arden went with her on Christmas. The sermon was always timely, amusing, delivered by a worldly clergyperson, but it never rekindled absolute belief in the charismatic Jesus she'd loved so passionately as a child.

Now, hearing the call, tingling spread through her. Were Saudis the real deal? Did they *live* their beliefs? She wasn't about to spy into the mosque again. This time she'd go to the source. She rummaged in her bags for the English copy of the Koran her two Saudi students had given her in the States, when she told them she'd be coming to their country. They'd said the Kingdom had better weather and friendlier people than Ohio, but that she should be careful. Of what, they didn't specify.

The first chapter of the Koran began with Moses asking for a cow to be sacrificed, a reference, she supposed, to the Meccan idolaters that Muhammad was persuading to embrace monotheism. The message didn't resonate. She closed the book.

Maybe she was deluded, trying to understand Islam after just a week in the Kingdom ... wasn't there a phrase about when the student is ready, the teacher will appear? Maybe Sayeed, or Dr. Zafeeyeh, would be willing to discuss religion. She'd heard Muslims welcomed inquiry. It might be a road to friendship. She wouldn't ask her students; they might feel obliged to proselytize.

In the kitchen, Kate smiled at her, stirring sugar into two glasses of tea. "Have a good rest? Feel like going for a walk?"

"Sure. I like waking up to prayer call. It's so moving."

"It's a recording."

"What?"

"There's a company in Mecca that records it. You know, in case the community is too busy to have a muezzin go up to every cupola in person."

"Wow." *But he sounded so sincere!* Arden tied on her scarf. "It's certainly effective."

They walked to the courtyard where a few children ran in the sprawling wooden play structure. Sprinklers set deep in the cultivated lawns made a soothing rainlike noise. Shaded flower beds sheltered yellow marigolds, white daisies, and orange tiger lilies from the brutal late September sun. There was a congenial feeling in the cooling scented air, a sense of hastening evening that might hold any number of delights. Kate and Arden sat on a bench and nodded to the hijabbed women nearby.

The tea was strong and sweet. Kate opened a package of shortbread, some English brand Arden didn't recognize. A tiny boy with avid black eyes materialized to watch them eat. Arden offered him a biscuit and he took it eagerly.

"Samir!" One of the black shapes detached herself from the rest and came to sit next to them. "Sorry, he hungry for sweet, all the time." Her voice was low and musical, the kind of voice sure to produce a contagious laugh. She chided the boy in Arabic.

"Thank you," he piped in English.

"He's cute," Kate said. "How old is he?"

"He has just four years now. He always very busy." Samir raced to the playground. She tilted her head. "You, doing the English?"

Arden answered. "Yes, Kate teaches literature—stories—and I teach how to speak good English."

"You teach to me?" Arden thought she could see a smile through the veil. "I study only English the high school. I like speak with you more."

"Maybe," Arden said. "What's your name?"

"Rowda Al Awais. And you, please?"

"Arden Armstrong."

"Kate McNulty."

"Arm-strong?" Rowda touched Arden's arm. "Is strong?" She *was* smiling.

Arden laughed. "Very strong."

The ladies on the other bench drew closer. Arden said, "Rowda, I teach you English, if you teach me Arabic, okay? *Ya sadiki?*"

The ladies laughed, a melodic chorus.

"Is good idea, Ahden Arm Strong. But I am not *sadiki*—that is for man! You can call me *sheikha,* is like name for lady friend."

"*Sheikha* Rowda."

They carried on awhile, heavy on goodwill and light on grammar. When the loudspeaker broke into their chatter, the Saudis gathered their children. "Is time make the small dinner now," Rowda explained, pointing uphill where a crowd of thobes was emerging from the mosque. She took Arden's hand in a warm clasp. "Is good meet you, *ya sheikha.*"

The men ambled into the courtyard, finding their women and children.

As she and Kate walked off, she felt someone watching her and she turned, thinking it was Rowda's gaze, strong behind her dark scrim. But the eyes she saw were mud-green as Columbus's meandering Scioto River, out of place in this dry climate, perfect in his sunworn face. She felt they were alone in the black and white clouds enveloping them. She smiled, aware of sending a taboo message, but encouraged by his regard. His heavy lashes lowered when another man grabbed his elbow, but she saw how his long lips held a little curve, how he glanced back at her as he walked away.

SIX

SAYEED AND HIS ASSISTANT were waiting for them outside the guesthouse. She was struck by Sayeed's expression as he leaned against the wall, laughing at something the other man said: the humor in his face was a contrast to his earlier coldness. But his ease vanished when he saw them. He straightened, took his clipboard.

"Ladies. Good evening. We're ready to move you now, Miss Kate."

Once alone, Arden wandered the guesthouse, noting the differences between this formally furnished beige and white apartment and her place in Ohio, in a big old funky Victorian just outside Columbus's small arts district called Short North.

Her room there, colorful with comforter, wall hangings and pillows in her favorite rose, lavender and shots of bright orange, had faced the welcoming wraparound porch. In summer the porch was a bower of trailing ivy, perfect for strumming tunes while leaning on the railing or sprawled in white wicker rocking chairs, and in fall it offered a panorama of brilliant trees. Her housemates were scraping by, nobody on a fast track, deadlines a little more serious than collegiate and wardrobes marginally better.

Right now in Columbus the leaves were starting to turn. At this time of evening, everyone would be getting home from work. Sometimes they cooked in the retro kitchen. They'd watch TV, play video games, wander down the street to the local bar.

She'd had an easygoing relationship with third-floor Paul, a long-haired, sleepy-eyed poet who worked part time in a print shop. They hung with an eclectic crowd, going to cheap alternative music concerts, getting high. She would miss pot more than alcohol here. Life in Columbus was simple.

But she'd been spooked by the sensation of time closing in, options dwindling, as the years lengthened past her college graduation. Advancing in the ESL academic world meant grad school and more student loans when even her BA, co-signed by Mom, still wasn't paid off. No promotion was worth that.

Her sister Annie, soon to marry Kyle, had offered what she obviously thought was a happy suggestion. "You and Paul should get married too. Our kids could be close in age."

"Yeah, like we could really support a family on a poet's salary." Or a weed dealer's, she did not say. Paul supplemented his meager income that way.

"He should be managing that CopyShop! He's smart enough."

"When he shows up to work. He's smart enough not to want to get married."

"Did you even ask him?"

"No, Annie, because *I* don't want to get married! I'm too young."

"Twenty-four isn't young. Look at your friends, they're all settling down."

True. Arden had stood up in so many weddings she could have filled her Saudi wardrobe with floor-length bridesmaid dresses, had they not looked ridiculous. But she was leery of marriage, especially to someone as chronically insolvent as Paul.

Her dad hadn't been much of a provider. Arden remembered their parents' breakup, her mother's and her own sadness, and more financial trouble after the divorce, in a way that Annie, four years younger, did not. Mom's Uncle Munro and Aunt Patty kept them stable, hosting the family in West Virginia before Mom got the Ohio job.

"I don't *want* to get married," she'd repeated. "Not yet, anyway. I haven't seen anything of the world except some of the Midwest and West Virginia!"

"So what's to see?" Annie shrugged. "All Walmarts look alike."

It was useless to try to explain to Annie, or to anyone else: she just wanted to color outside the lines before it felt too late. Even if those lines ended up being the impenetrable-seeming steel gates barricading the Womens' College.

Annie was furious that Arden would miss her wedding, not least because Arden's band, "No Requests," was scheduled to play the reception. Arden's insistence they could perform without her had not mollified Annie. Mom, too, had tried to persuade Arden to put off the Saudi job. But every time Arden went home to Mom's, the wedding preparations seemed more stifling and her own future more proscribed. Talk of flowers, food, and dress filled her with claustrophobia. The whole thing was an insane waste of money. She'd been relieved to get the Riyadh offer letter, a ticket to financial freedom and a chance to see something completely new.

Everyone tried to dissuade her. Mom worried about safety in a part of the world she thought of as scary, full of terrorists like those who'd tried to collapse the World Trade Center in 1993, just four years ago. Her friends, like Annie, didn't know why anyone would want to leave Ohio. Her fellow ESL teachers couldn't believe she would take a job in the Middle East so soon, relatively, after Desert Storm. *Muddle* East, they sneered. Why not Japan, Eastern Europe, China or even poorly paying Latin America?

But the real money was still in the Arabian Gulf.

Right now, she wondered if she shouldn't have looked a little harder before leaping. She didn't like that endless emptiness of desert out the window, nor the pristine condition of the canned-air apartment. How long before she felt at home? Felt connected? She thought of her archaeologist, of the acknowledgement passing between them as clearly as words just now in the courtyard.

Maybe his look *should* be construed as disrespect, here, where decent men didn't look women in the eye and couldn't befriend them. Maybe the archeologist just thought she was a wanton American.

She worried this suspicion for a moment before catching herself with an exasperated sigh. This was only the second week! She would manage just fine! She would learn Arabic and be a good teacher and unveil, somehow, the mystery the natives kept around themselves, and make friends with women.

And right now, she'd put on music and make herself dinner. She looked out at the stark beige sand—no, the *fiery* orange sun setting on the *wild* purple-gray dunes, she edited firmly. Inspirational.

She changed into an old Ohio State U tee and cutoffs, comfort clothes wisely packed. She unearthed her battered CD player and set it on a table in the living room. She looked around for an outlet to plug into. The socket was funny-looking, but she'd brought an adaptor, so she jammed the prongs in and turned on the player. Nothing.

"Fuck!" None of her stuff worked here: clock, phone charger, hair dryer: she looked like a witch without blow-drying, her hair a mass of kinky curls. No wonder those soccer boys had leered.

She blinked back stupid tears. *Could really use some Phish right now.*

At least her banjo didn't need plugging in. She could make up new songs: American bluegrass for a Saudi sunset. She strummed a feisty "Union Maid." Although the maid in the song never was afraid, her own voice echoed against the stone floor and walls, making her feel even more lonesome.

Deep breath. Dinner. She marched into the kitchen. There was one packet of biscuits left, several triangles of cheese, and a half-used can of condensed milk. She and

Kate had meant to shop this evening at the campus grocery.

She banged the teakettle onto the cooktop.

She turned off its shriek when she heard knocking. She went to peer through the peephole and saw white cloth, a turning face. Sayeed! Alarmed, she opened the door, imagining some emergency. He pushed past her quickly, glancing behind at the empty hallway with a furtive look, as if he didn't want his entry to be witnessed. She folded her arms over her braless tee.

"But you said, Sayeed, you said we weren't supposed to be alone?"

"We are not in the public now." This close, she realized how tall he was, how fragrant, how imposing in his blinding white. "We can be friendly, inside."

What the hell does that mean? How could she befriend him, seeing how his behavior changed with his surroundings? She backed up. "Why are you here?"

"I came to take you to Evelyn and Grace, they are having a dinner, and they told me to bring you to them, so that you know the building where they live now." He glanced at her bare legs and looked away. "But you must cover. And, when we go, we cannot walk together. You will follow me, but we won't speak."

"You'll pretend you don't know me."

"I don't know you." He kept his eyes down.

Sensation was filling her, energizing her, as she looked at him. It took a moment to recognize her anger. He assumed he could stop by any time, and be obediently accommodated. He'd been adamant, on the bus, they shouldn't be alone together; yet here he stood not three feet away. And she was barely dressed.

"I don't feel like going. I was just settling in for the night."

"It's not good, be all alone to dinner, you don't have your friend Miss Kate now." He frowned at the floor. "I can't let you like this."

"You shouldn't have come to see me," she told him, making her tone cold. "It's against your *rules.*" But instead of taking offense, he nodded.

"Any man should never come to you. But I am supposed to watch you." He must mean "watch out for you," surely? "All of you Westerners."

"I can take care of myself."

"Perhaps in America, but not in the Kingdom. You are *my* responsibility here."

"Why can't a woman take care of us here?"

"They can't drive, and there are arrangements all the time."

He had, indeed, been smoothing the way for them at every turn. Recognizing their dependence on him irritated her further. "I don't need you now." She added flippantly, relegating him to servitude, "Unless you can fix my CD player."

To her surprise, his nod was resigned. "The electric. This happens every year." He put down his keys and cellphone. "Where is it?"

She pointed, and watched as he knelt to unplug it, noticing the elegance of his movement in the long thobe, like the fluidity of the men bending to pray. She walked away and stood at the front door waiting for him, arms still crossed.

"You have other things, the iron?" He waved a hand around his head. "The dryer? I will tell a mechanic to bring the right adaptors. How many?"

"I'll take three. That's nice of you, Sayeed. Thanks."

"Welcome." He picked up his phone and clicked in some numbers. "Miss Evelyn, this is Sayeed. I asked Miss Arden to join you, but she is—"he eyed Arden—"she is going to sleep." He listened. "No, thank you, I'm going to my home now." His courtesy sounded forced and his eyelids looked heavy. "That is kind. Thank you again." He handed the phone to Arden, without touching her fingers. "She want speak with you."

"Arden, bring him," Evelyn said. "He'll come if you do!"

31

"Sorry, I'm beat."

"Spoilsport!" There was laughter in the background before Evelyn hung up.

She gave Sayeed his phone and he slipped it into a pocket.

"Tell me—what will happen to me? Can I still teach here without a roommate?"

"Of course, you will teach. Your contract is signed. There are still teachers, not yet arrived, who might need a roommate."

"And if not?"

He sighed. "Then, I don't know. It didn't happen before like this. Maybe we can find a family that would accept for you to live with them."

He thought she was a kid—but he wasn't much older. She tried to sound reasonable. "I'm used to living alone. You can trust me."

"You cannot live alone here."

"Well ... Kate's living alone."

He frowned. "She got a permission from Dr. Zafeeyeh. It was not my choice."

"So, let me ask Dr. Zafeeyeh about this, and I'll let you know what she says."

"You are too younger than Miss Kate. We will never allow it."

She clung to her composure. "I'm older than I look."

"I know you are twenty four, and if you were a Saudi girl you would be married by now." He actually disapproved of her being single. She might as well be back in Columbus, arguing with Annie.

"I'm not a Saudi girl," she said evenly. "I'm an adult, a competent teacher, that you've entrusted to be a leader for your young women."

He nodded. "That is why you will not live by yourself." For a moment his scrutiny was searching. His eyes were so dark she saw no pupil. "This is not my decision only," he murmured. "We will wait." He opened the door and looked out, as if to ensure no one would see him leaving. "Goodnight."

"*Masah al khair.*" She repeated one of the Arabic phrases Rowda had taught.

"*Masah al noor, ya* Miss Arden." His wan little smile did not cheer.

SEVEN

THE NEXT MORNING, while they waited for the bus, Grace and Evelyn bemoaned Arden's absence at their dinner and were curious about her time with Sayeed. Evelyn had decided he was flirt-worthy.

"All we did was talk about gadgetry." Arden shrugged. "He was there maybe two minutes." She was not about to disclose the anxiety his visit had provoked, nor the uncertainty he'd expressed about her living situation. She decided not to worry it today.

"Wasn't there a bit of—frisson, being all alone with him?" asked Evelyn.

"You need to meet some *available* men," Arden advised. "There was this oilman on the plane, he told me to call if I needed a drink—"

"We *all* met his type," Grace drawled. "I think they're on every flight."

"Really?" Arden remembered the looming, armpit-stained Oklahoman, confiding that he could arrange a good party for her—'with booze.' "Enterprising."

"A *hawaja*-collector," Evelyn said, grinning. "What's a *hawaja*?"

"A foreign woman."

"*All* women are foreign to guys like that!" Arden laughed.

An unfamiliar older woman joined them. Although her light gray eyes and pale skin indicated a Western background, she was dressed like one of the Arab teachers, in khaki floor-length hijab and scarf. "Late bus again, I see," she said.

"Too right, Ruth," Evelyn said. "What would we do if it never showed up?"

"Call the Womens' College."

"I'd call Sayeed." Evelyn smirked.

"I'd hitch-hike," Arden joked.

"I'd hitch with one of *them*." Grace indicated the far parking lot, where a regular procession of immaculately thobed faculty got into their luxury vehicles and roared off to the highway in clouds of dust. "Pretty nice rides over there, gals."

"I saw one who was absolutely gorgeous," Evelyn said. "He was choosing spuds right next to me, up at the shop. I nearly dropped my turnips!" The others exploded with laughter, but Ruth frowned. "Of course I forced myself to look away, like a good girl, and my chance passed. You saw him, Grace, that chap with the green eyes."

There could only be one green-eyed Saudi in this compound.

"*Very* hot," Grace agreed. "But that robe could hide a multitude of sins."

Evelyn smiled slyly. "Or talents."

"Please don't talk about men like this in public," Ruth said. "I know you're new to this society, but it just isn't acceptable." She jerked her head toward the Arab teachers walking up to the bus stop. "Would you want them to hear you?"

"Lebanese women were open about sex," said Evelyn. "It was good fun, talking with them. Not like you repressed Americans." She raised a challenging eyebrow.

"We're already considered immoral because we're not Muslim," Ruth said, impatient. "If you openly ogle Saudi men the community will judge you very harshly."

"But we need to remember our own backgrounds, in spite of living in a restricted environment," argued Kate. "Think *Heart of Darkness*."

Arden had not read it. She'd studied Communications, not literature.

"One of the main characters goes native and goes nuts, basically. I'm teaching it this term, in part because I want to see the students' reactions. The thing is, it would be so easy to lose ourselves here. We have to resist the urge to accept all this—" Kate gestured to the surrounding desert, the cluster of robed women standing silently behind them, the last of the white Mercedes leaving the compound—"as if it's normal. It's *not* normal, for us. It's totally fucked up. I thought a lot about this before I accepted the job."

"If you feel that strongly, maybe you shouldn't have come," Ruth said. "This is a powerful culture. It has its own reality."

Kate faced her. "The key to my success here, which means giving my personal best to my students, is to stay true to who I am. True to the culture that made me."

"I'm trying to keep my mind as open as possible, though, to learn from my students," Arden told her. "If I insist *my* society is normal, and theirs *isn't*, I'm just judging without considering their point of view, and I learn nothing. And, with that attitude, how do I gain their trust for them to open up to me too?"

"You can acknowledge their customs without accepting them," Kate said.

"But we *have* to accept them here," Ruth said. "That's exactly my point."

"All we really *have* to do is give the *appearance* of acceptance." Kate's smile indicated a satisfied conclusion Arden did not share.

Easier said than done. She suspected she was venturing into territory the others were not: her class pact to discuss anything they liked, no matter how controversial; the men at prayer, the soccer boys; the archaeologist she'd thought of as hers, who was now public property to drool over; Sayeed's curiously intrusive visit.

Evelyn, perhaps unwilling to contemplate such depth so early in the morning, broke into the silence that followed Kate's statement. "Cor, all this over the green-eyed spud stud at the market!"

EIGHT

AFTER CLASSES THAT DAY, Arden was opening her mail, sorting through the flurry of missives sent by the university housing department, the English department, and announcements on travel planning for the upcoming Haj holidays. Arden threw away most of it, but one was puzzling:

> *Miss Armstrong:*
> *You are requested to the office of Dr. Khalid Al Issam at the main university on the thirtieth September at two o'clock to discuss your curriculum.*

She didn't recognize the man's name, and she wondered why he, rather than Dr. Zafeeyeh, needed to see her lesson plans. Maybe the university cared more here, than did its bored Houston official, how little academic credential she had. She put the letter onto her desk and massaged her temples. She'd better get cracking on making the plans look as erudite as possible. September 30th was tomorrow.

The next afternoon, she took the university bus over to the main campus, sitting alone in the women's section in back. She hadn't asked anyone else if they'd gotten a similar summons; she didn't want to advertise that she had the quickie ESL certificate, perhaps requiring official Saudi scrutiny.

The men's offices were as daunting as she recalled from her arrival. Not one man looked at her as they swept past, cologne drifting behind them, and she had to peer at the Arabic numerals on every door to see which was Dr. Al Issam's. Finally she found it and knocked.

"*Yullah.*" Enter. The voice was terse. She opened the door. A heavyset, bespectacled, bearded man sat behind a desk that appeared, at first glance, as big as her kitchen. He frowned, consulting his watch.

"Miss Armstrong." His frown deepened as he studied her. "You may sit."

She perched on the edge of the armchair facing him.

"We oversee curriculum standards for the Womens' College. It has come to our attention that you are allowing your students to discuss controversial topics in your classes. Consider this a warning, of the most serious kind, that we are being forced to consider revoking your contract."

She felt herself shrink from the top of her tightly wrapped scarf to the bottom of her abaya. Her arms tightened around her lesson plans.

"We don't *want* that, since you seem to be an effective teacher and well-liked by the students. But our standards are for the students and of the university itself. We struggle with academic freedom in ways you have never encountered in the States." He paged through a pristine file that sat on the polished surface of his desk, stopping at one point, adjusting his eyeglasses. "Debates on driving?" He opened his hands as if in appeal. "Tell me how that started."

The image of Leila's cheerful grin unfroze her heart, pounding inside her cloaked chest. "Nothing to tell, Dr. Al Issam. You're absolutely correct in reminding me of the best way to guide class discussion. You won't have any further need for concern."

"Did a student mention Salman Rushdie in your classroom?"

Just this morning.

Leila wanted to read *The Satanic Verses*: Rushdie's banned novel of the devil's viewpoint on the Koran. Arden had said, a bit tartly, wearied of Leila's constant envelope-pushing, that it wouldn't be available in the college library.

Hot dampness in her palms made the lesson-plan folder slick. She forced her voice steady, to look him in the eye and lie, "No. That was my error entirely."

He folded his hands. He looked at her.

Low sunlight caught on the golden numbers of an ornate clock on the paneled wall behind him. She had never been so grateful to hear the prayer call sounding. "An error you will never allow to be repeated."

"No sir."

"You are responsible for protecting your girls."

"I understand."

He nodded. "Thank you, Miss Armstrong. You may go."

She got herself out of his office, but adrenalin-stoked fear pushed her against the wall where she leaned, shaky. The dim hallway echoed like grade school, outside the Principal's office following punishment, an entirely new feeling for her. The gold clock numerals from Al Issam's office seemed to be still blinding her eyes.

When the door to the office across from Al Issam's opened, sunset flooded the hall, compounding her blindness. Her files slid and made a sound like a sigh of relief as they skittered onto the polished floor. A white shape swooped down to collect them.

"*Tal*—" he broke off speaking in Arabic. "Are you okay?"

She looked up. Oh God, it was her archaeologist, witness to her chastisement. The kindness in his voice made her lips tremble and she pressed them tight.

"If it's a censorship issue, maybe I can explain."

"Censorship?"

He tilted his head to Al Issam's door. "He heads the Censorship Board. Everyone comes from his office looking as rattled as you do." He motioned to the office he'd come from. "Would you like to sit, have some water?"

Sit with him? Alone?

He closed the door behind them, indicated a pair of chairs in front of a desk more lived-in than Al Issam's, covered with papers and books. He poured cups of water from a tall bottle on a credenza in the corner and sat next to her, handed her a cup. His scent emanated, faint yet crisp. Something vaguely citrusy.

She kept her head down as she drank, too aware of being alone with him in the off-limits men's campus, afraid of how she would stare into his eyes if she looked up.

His neutral silence allowed her to speak. "I thought it would be okay to let the students speak freely, if we kept the discussions to ourselves. I was wrong."

"I think I mentioned when we first met, I'm new here too. I understand how confusing this issue can be."

"But you're ... a Saudi."

"I spent most of the last eight years in California. I'm still adjusting."

There was, she thought, a hint of humor in his voice, enough to let her feel easier about talking so openly to him.

"It isn't that I don't understand the policy on controversial subjects being discussed in class—I just never got in trouble before."

"If you were in trouble, you'd be on a plane or in prison." He said this so casually that its truth rang even more forbidding. She felt her shoulders tighten again.

"Hey." He leaned into her vision and smiled, a lively smile that lit his sharp features and brought out those cheerful lines. "Al Issam's just doing his job. He's obliged to conduct these reviews. He does it to all of us when there's a crack-down."

"A crack-down?"

"When the mutawas raise a fuss about women's education or ... other things." His smile creased, wry. "There's interest in how you behave in your class, what your students read, what they write about."

He rose to pour another cup, and she watched him drink. He turned, and she was caught in his green gaze for what felt like a long time. "We're all monitored. Not just you. So ... be aware."

"I thought I was being careful."

"What department are you with?"

"English."

"Let me guess. You didn't get much orientation, and you really weren't prepared for life in the Kingdom."

"Probably not," she confessed.

"So this is all kind of a shock."

She nodded.

She wasn't expecting his sigh. "Well, if it makes you feel any better, I'm not used to it yet either." The prayer call sounded again, louder, from down the hallway. He glanced toward the sound as if toward an alarm clock.

"You've been very kind. I appreciate it."

"I'm happy to talk to you." He stood.

She offered her hand at the door, wanting connection in spite of the usual restrictions, not caring if this made her seem reckless to him; even more reckless than perhaps she already appeared. "Thanks, Mr. ... ?"

His handshake was warm and confident. She didn't want to let go, and his amused expression told her he was letting her hang on longer than was proper. "Faisal Al Ansary. And you?"

"Arden Armstrong."

"Nice to meet you, Arden." *Slow smile mellow as the river in his eyes.*

She brought out the last of her courage. "I hope to see you again, Faisal. I could use a friend like you in the Kingdom."

Light flared in his eyes before he modestly lowered his lashes. "Maybe we'll be that lucky, Arden Armstrong."

She got herself out of the building, where every man was now rushing toward the mosque in the far courtyard, to the street where she waited for the bus, drenched in sweat as if she'd been swimming, with one other lone hijab-hidden woman.

THE NEXT DAY she delivered a little speech to Intermediate Conversation.

"We have to be more careful about what we discuss. The university censorship counselor warned me yesterday, and I don't want any of you to get in trouble."

"How they know what we saying, in this class?" Maha eyed her classmates accusingly.

"I don't think it matters, Maha." Arden didn't want their trust in each other to erode. "Someone might have carried the debate home, or chatted with a student in another class. And I still think we can explore ideas, just in different ways."

"How we do that?"

Arden picked up her banjo and fit her picks onto her first finger and thumb.

Oppression wasn't unique to Saudi Arabia; bluegrass sobbed with tales of social injustice. And who could object to discussions about harmless folk ditties?

At break, she took Leila aside. "*Don't* mention Salman Rushdie again. He's probably worse than driving, as a topic here."

The girl nodded dejectedly. "Is always the same."

Arden patted her shoulder and tried to sound encouraging. "You can *think* as big as you like. Just ... maybe not out loud."

Leila looked up with a pale version of her cheeky grin. "Is what my brother tells me, Miss, that same thing."

"Well, he's right. He must know his society pretty well."

NINE

CENSORSHIP DID NOT DAMPEN their enthusiasm for class discussion. The folk anti-tyranny songbook was deep and strong, and she got a kick out of hearing them master lyrics, even though they preferred sentimental songs. All were fodder for lively commentary. She learned how to play a few of their favorite Arabic songs too, and on song days their laughter rang out louder than the banjo's strum.

She was more relieved than flattered when Dr. Zafeeyeh recommended Arden as a reliable choice to run TOEFL tests for prospective U.S. grad school-bound Saudis at the U.S. Information Agency. It was a way to earn extra money but also, she hoped, a nod of approval by the college, meaning she did not have to worry further about Al Issam and his Censorship Board.

The teachers analyzed the learning curve they were coaxing the girls through. When they declared English as a major, junior year, they were expected to write as well as college freshmen in the States. Evelyn's British standards were higher; she chided the Americans' lack of rigor in education. Arden retorted one day with Feiruz's remark about the English needing to cover their ugliness. It made for a good laugh.

Arden felt satisfied as her balances-due lowered. She learned more Arabic from Rowda and used it on befuddled shopkeepers at the souks on shopping days. She wrote in her journal, trying her hand at poetry to capture her nostalgia for remembered autumn. But she also tried to describe the soft light on the shifting desert she studied from her south-facing window. It was not the monochrome dullness she'd first assumed. Its contour changed every day. She sent long e-mails to her mother and sister and those friends who had her address, being sure to keep her messages bland: the censors' scrutiny was common knowledge.

Paul did not write. She hadn't really expected him to, and found she did not miss him, but she missed being touched and missed male companionship, especially the guys from her band; emails could never replace the joy of jamming at farmers' markets and fair gigs. Too bad none of the expats played an instrument or sang.

The enforced segregation seemed increasingly strange even as she grew used to it. Saudi men were mythic creatures: gliding, whiteclad, elusive. She'd have liked to see Faisal again, but even if she did, how could they develop any kind of relationship here? They weren't even supposed to look at each other. He'd braved severe judgment, probably, just by inviting her into his office that day.

One evening George gave a dinner party at his apartment in the city, a reprise of their first gathering at Ben's. Arden was struck by how colorless the Western men seemed; washed out in their limp khakis and pale faces, leached of vibrancy in comparison to white-clad strong-featured Saudi men. George had driven out to the university housing compound to collect the women, cautiously maneuvering through the racetrack-like traffic.

It was not a lively party. Flamboyant Ben had been tempered by life in the Kingdom. He made Turkish coffee and read their cups, but his fortunes were harmless. His flirtation appeared perfunctory. Even George didn't have much to say once he'd queried everyone to see if they'd found alcohol sources.

The new male English teachers were equally morose; shell-shocked by their busy schedules, the enormity of Saudi bureaucracy, the monotony of scenery, and the difficulty of accomplishing daily tasks like shopping and cooking. Even washing clothes was aggravating—the harsh water chewed fabric. To a man, they denounced the horrible traffic. Arden thought maybe Feiruz was right, not wanting to drive here. Most of all, however, everyone admitted to being cowed by the sheer severity of Riyadhi society.

"The culture's just too powerful," one of the men said, with a bewildered look on his face. Arden recalled Ruth saying this. "There's a sense of—suppression—that I never felt, teaching in the Emirates. It's stifling."

Kate nodded. "Like being held hostage."

"Are we identifying with our captors yet?" Ben's sneer was grimmer than Arden expected, from him. "Anyone fallen for a *native*?" He made it sound like an insult.

"What happened to your desert roots?" she asked. "Your Arabian cycle?"

"A mirage. This culture's too inaccessible for foreigners."

"You don't find any familiarity, with your Moroccan background?"

"I feel as much a prisoner here as you all do. Saudis are *nothing* like Moroccans, they're so fucking arrogant! And I hate the way they never smile!" He hadn't lost his tendency toward hyperbole.

She didn't feel like a prisoner. More like a nun. "My girls smile," she said. "We laugh all the time."

"The boys all seem depressed, or more likely *re*pressed," Ben kept grumbling. "Religious fanatics, what can you expect."

"If I start wearing thobe and going to mosque, wake me up," George growled.

Kate said sagely, "I told you, it's *Heart of Darkness*. We must resist."

The television news was on—the first Arden had watched, since she didn't buy a set—showing arrivals and departures of various Arab leaders at various Arab airports. Cheesy background music was the Monty Python comedy theme. Evelyn wondered if there was some wag, in the network's music production staff, chuckling to himself, but they concluded Saudis did not know Monty Python: the musical irony was unintended.

In early November, a break in routine was offered by the weeklong holiday allotted for Haj, the annual pilgrimage to Mecca. Saudis and foreigners alike left Riyadh, but Arden and some of the others chose to save money and stay put. The first weekend morning of the break, the Womens' College arranged transportation for a local museum tour. Arden was eager to see more of the city besides the souks.

TEN

"MUSEUM OF ANTIQUITIES," said Kate, en route to their field trip. "Sounds old."

"Sounds restful," Arden yawned, imagining dry dioramas behind glass cases.

The museum was open to ladies, on certain days, and a small group of Westerners sat under a covered walkway. They introduced themselves as the Riyadh Women's Club. Arden was surprised by how strange they looked to her, wearing Western clothes openly. She'd worn jeans and her favorite green cowboy boots today, but covered with her abaya and scarf. *Dang I've been here too long.*

The building was ornately landscaped, with a lush-looking lawn where fountains played inside flowered circles and filigreed benches beckoned, strategically placed under leafy palms. How good it would be to beg off the tour and wander the grounds, roll in the grass. She was that parched for green.

A guard inside the domed lobby greeted them. "Welcome to Antiquities Museum," he said. "Dr. Ansary is guide today. Wait inside, he will come."

The dimly lit theater was so plush and comfortable that everyone sank down, joking about popcorn and production values.

"Hope the good doc is an easy grader," Arden said, closing her eyes. Their guide entered the theater so quietly she didn't hear him. But she heard Evelyn's hiss.

"Grace! Our spud stud!"

Arden jerked up, stared.

"Good morning," Faisal said, clipping a small microphone onto his thobe. "Thanks for visiting our museum. I'm Faisal Al Ansary, with the Department of Antiquities. My specialization is the Ubaid culture. I'll address recent finds with you today." He clicked a button on the lectern, and a screen slid down behind him.

"Mmm-*hmm*," murmured Kate.

Seeing him again reinforced how striking he was, but, Arden realized, it was his open expression that made him so attractive, not just his symmetrical features and unusual eyes. He looked at his audience frankly, unafraid of eye contact, unafraid of smiling. His face was animated as he talked about what was obviously his passion. She listened to the sound of his low, soft voice. She had to force herself to hear his words.

"The most important archeological discovery for the Kingdom, in recent years, has been Eastern Province evidence of a link with the Ubaid culture of southern Mesopotamia. The Ubaid period represented a crucial step toward mankind's first urban civilization. You probably know the early people here were nomads, so for them, this represented impressive progress.

"Our evidence shows that Eastern Arabia participated in the Ubaid era of international movement, which was a significant component in Mesopotamian development." The slides depicted elaborately painted panoramas of the Kingdom, with stylized animals, dunes, surf beaches and oil wells.

"The period of Ubaid settlement in Eastern Arabia coincided with a rare moist interval in the region. The end of that period shows a decline and change of settlement here, caused by growing drought.

"Last year, I was privileged to take part in excavations at Eridu, Abu Khamis and Dosariyah. I'm conducting an excavation this winter in Ain Qanass with a group of students and other scholars." His excitement was clear as he paced in front of them, with an energy that was palpable in the quiet room, a physical energy in sharp contrast to the languidness of most of his countrymen. Arden recognized his stride.

He motioned to a slide showing a collection of broken pieces of patterned pottery. "Ubaidi sherds. We got them just a few months ago, in this Eridu cave." The next slide pictured him with a group of men crouched in front of a cave opening, surrounded by rubble, grinning in what looked like sweaty triumph as Faisal held aloft a cracked pot.

A little ripple of amusement ran through the theater—the men were in shorts, bare-chested, although their heads were wrapped. Faisal, in the slide, revealed muscular, tanned torso and arms, and long curls escaping from his red checked headdress. His white teeth gleamed and his eyes narrowed in laughter. This image of his wild physicality reverberated deep inside as Arden's hands tightened on the chair arms.

He turned to see why they were chuckling. "Oops. This slide got past the edit. Just pretend it's National Geographic, okay, and don't tell the mutawas."

The next slide was a colored map. "These represent the Arabian, southern Iraqi, and Iranian sites associated with the Ubaid."

He stood in front of the screen to point out different areas, and the projected colors washed his thobe in red, purple and blue. He turned toward them briefly and his face shone as golden as the yellow sands portrayed behind him, in upper Mesopotamia. His green eyes were brilliant in the light. As Arden watched him, the music to her favorite Ben Harper song, "You look like gold to me," swelled loudly in her head. She leaned back, letting herself stare.

"Down here, near Bahrain, is one of my most productive areas of research." His hand and sleeve turned red as he outlined a region comprising part of Saudi Arabia's Eastern Province and Qatar. "We share digging rights with the oil exploration people, but it's cool, since they discovered a lot of the original sites. And they fund our work, after all." He flashed a quick grin that mirrored his expression from the unedited earlier slide. "Along with everything else around here."

A few women laughed, startled by this flip comment.

He leaned over to click on the next slide, and when he looked back up, at the audience, his eyes met Arden's.

For a few seconds as they looked at each other there was only the sound of the background music in the room, and it wasn't Ben Harper, she realized, it was an eerie lilting stringed instrument, presumably played by ancient people.

Straightening up, Faisal touched his forehead as if to push through hair, but his fingers ran into the cloth of his white headdress. He stepped out of the light.

"So ... where was I? Ain Qanass. The kids in my senior seminar are really pumped about our expedition. If we're lucky we'll find some more sherds, maybe some awls and borers, like these. We're looking for evidence of pearl fishing." The borers reminded Arden of Native American arrow-heads.

Faisal turned off the projector.

One of the Riyadh Women's Club members, a smartly coiffed blonde, spoke up.

"Faisal, hello again." He smiled in brief acknowledgement. "When you were here last year, doing your internship, we heard your lecture and I remember your discussion of the richest site you'd seen yet. Why aren't you going back to Eridu with the students?"

He looked down for a moment before replying in a low voice. "Unfortunately, for archaeology, it's been declared off limits by our government, at the Americans' request."

"Why?" asked the woman.

"Military significance. Strategic proximity to Iraq." He let this dry statement resonate, surveying his mostly American audience with a bland expression. Then he turned. "Come, follow me to this next area—I'll show you examples of the varieties of Ubaid pottery we found in Eridu."

"I'll follow you anywhere," whispered Evelyn. "I'd love to see your varieties." She and Grace stifled their chuckles, but they trailed obediently into a softly lit hallway after the group.

"Dr. Al Ansary?" Kate began.

"Please, call me Faisal."

"We're with the Womens' College, and I can't help but wonder—are girls allowed to go on these expeditions with your group?"

"That's ... difficult," he admitted. "I teach part time at the university, and I've given lectures to the Womens' College through videoconference. The girls always seem interested in the Ubaid period, probably because it's the area of most recently uncovered sites." Videoconferences were one-way when presented by men. The male lecturers could be seen by, but were allowed only to hear, their female audience.

"Couldn't possibly be the professor who's the attraction," Evelyn muttered. Faisal's glance flicked to her. Arden hoped he had not heard.

"I tried to talk some of the women from my doctoral program at Berkeley into teaching archaeology here, so girls could do excavations too," he continued. "But, as you know, life here can be a challenge for active Western women. So far I've had no takers.

"If a girl really got into archaeology, we'd have to convince her father to let her go on digs, some with men, some outside the Kingdom ... it's tough." He shrugged.

"Can we at least bring them here for field trips?" Kate asked.

"Sure. Dr. Zafeeyeh can arrange transport for you."

"I'd like to bring my team as soon as possible," Kate said. "This seems such a wealth of real history. And the excavation work is so exciting." She smiled at him.

"We're pleased with it." He reached toward a display to continue the lecture.

"Will you be here if I bring them?" Kate interrupted him.

He turned to consider Kate. His gaze moved from her to Arden, lingering briefly, before taking in the rest of them. "But you must know by now, Saudi girls can't see men they're not related to. That's why I don't give them lectures in person. I'd arrange for a lady guide, for your classes."

"But you just admitted there aren't any women archaeologists here."

"We've trained the guides very well."

"But how can you expect the girls to share your enthusiasm, without the personal touch, when it's your unique passion that makes all this so compelling?"

He frowned slightly. "Do you give *all* of us a hard time about the segregation?"

"Pretty much," Kate conceded.

His smile was quickly hidden as he looked down. "It won't do you any good," he said lightly. "We're experts at ignoring complaints."

The prayer call echoed within the museum, interrupting the indigenous music but just as muted and melodic. "I must go," Faisal told them. "The tour is over. Give the guard in the lobby some time to pray, please, but after twenty minutes you can ask him to page your drivers."

"Won't you come back, after the prayer?" asked Evelyn. "I really wanted to hear more about your Ubaid research." She nudged Grace but kept a straight face.

"Not today, sorry." He gestured to the wall. "All the Ubaid excavation work is documented in this hallway, though, you can read up on it. If you want another lecture, you can get a guide through the Department of Antiquities—or, for the Womens' College, ask Dr. Zafeeyeh. She knows us."

"What about coming out to Bell this week?" one of the clubwomen asked. Bell Helicopter had a huge compound north of the city.

"I'll be on Haj, but you can get another guide. Call Antiquities." The last verse of the prayer call sounded.

"Goodbye and thank you. I hope you'll be frequent visitors."

As he left the hallway he passed close to Arden, close enough for her to catch the faint scent of his cologne. His bright glance confirmed his recognition as he whispered, "Arden. Hello again." Then he looked down, like a proper Saudi, but she saw him smile as he took in her green cowboy boots. The low chuckle she heard as he walked away tilted her onto her boot heels. She let the wall prop her up.

The college group remained as the other ladies went into the next gallery.

"Oh, my." Evelyn collapsed onto a bench, fanning herself. "There is a God."

"Or at least a Paradise." Grace laughed at her.

"Girls," Evelyn said seriously, sitting up, "we have *got* to find some fun men. If I don't get away from the convent soon I'll commit a crime. In fact, hold me back, or I'll run after this luscious archaeologist and attack him in the mosque."

Kate smiled. "That didn't work with Sayeed." Evelyn's campaign to seduce Sayeed proved so fruitless that it had become a joke.

Evelyn continued, "While we're on break let's find a party. With all the expats in Riyadh there's bound to be one. We'll ask the university fellows too."

"They're so ... *dull*," Grace opined doubtfully.

"But we need reliable transport. And let's meet the sheikhas from this club—maybe they'll have some ideas." Evelyn hurried after the group that had gone ahead.

Arden stayed behind.

She stared at the one intact Eridu pot inside its glass case. She imagined Faisal's hands lifting it gently out of the rubble, saw his strong brown fingers whisking away dust with those little brushes she thought archaeologists used, saw him blowing, lips pursed soft as a whisper, onto the clay, saw his easy smile as the colors emerged. She wished she could meander the bright Ubaid gallery all afternoon to soak up the atmosphere, where every piece reverberated with his discoveries. He must have touched this and that one. He must have chosen the music, decided how to illuminate the simple tools, how the captions should be written.

She thought she'd be absorbed in the experience of the larger culture here; that *men*, by themselves, wouldn't be such a distinct group. But theirs were the only Saudi faces seen in public, in the Kingdom, even though she tried not to look at them.

It was like telling yourself not to think of a tiger: of course you then saw tigers everywhere. Contact was forbidden because they were dangerous; yet they were inescapable, always in the foreground of this landscape, blocking other vistas. She wondered if they knew how arresting their white robes were—whether male plumage designed to catch attention or simply the logical color to deflect the harsh sunlight; she wondered if they knew their avoidance of eye contact was strangely challenging. She wondered if she could make herself blind to them, as they seemed blind to her.

In the States she'd been used to men's interest. Her height and coloring—dark brown eyes, wavy platinum hair—made her noticeable.

It still felt like a liability unless she was performing.

AT THIRTEEN, just coming into bloom, feeling her way through freshman year, she'd played a high school talent show that drew the attention of her secret crush, a senior football player named Steve. He'd asked her to a party, which in her naïveté she thought was sign of affection, but which turned out to be a disgusting scene of kids mostly throwing up in the back yard. He'd pulled her into a bedroom, locked the door, and commenced an exciting kissing session she'd have been thrilled to prolong until he yanked her jeans off and threw himself on top of her. When she resisted penetration, he'd grabbed her hair in his fist to force her head down for a blowjob.

"You gotta get me off, blondie, wavin it in my face like you do."

She'd fought to break free but he was strong. She'd clenched her teeth against his slimy erection until he finally gave up and slammed out of the room.

Arden ran all the ten blocks home. Her mom had wanted to call the police or at least Steve's parents, but Arden knew enough about high school politics to resist. Later she thought she'd been a wuss; should have gotten the jerk in a pile of trouble. She'd made sure to let Annie know how to deal with horny boys.

But the ugly episode put her off dating for several years. Ousted from the cool crowd by her rejection of Steve, she'd become a loner, a shy dreamer playing folk on her banjo every spare moment; uninterested in sports or scholarship, without funds to hang at the mall, uncaring about clothes or makeup or modern music. There hadn't been close friends, then, to belittle Steve and offer comfort. She'd downplayed her looks with baggy clothes and no makeup, adopting the grunge look with relief. Once she'd regained confidence, she only went out with the sweetest boys, avoiding those whose blatant sexuality seemed threatening.

HERE IN THE KINGDOM, the total lack of male attention, a disconcerting novelty, gave her the leeway to look at men, albeit discreetly. Only Faisal looked back—a reminder she wasn't invisible. But he was perilously off limits, out of her reach, his adventures unknowable. *I can't even come back to his museum by myself!* Not since the first week had she felt so locked out of the society she'd imagined she would be allowed to know.

She'd left fingerprints on the glass case. She wiped them off with a corner of her scarf, and turned away from the exhibit. She supposed she could at least find distraction with the rest of the group, her fellow inmates, wherever they were allowed to seek it.

She caught up with them talking to the smart-looking blonde who'd asked Faisal about his last excavation site; telling them about an upcoming party. "We always welcome singles. And a new liquor shipment just came in, don't tell anyone."

"Can we tell the fellows who we'll beg to drive us? It's bound to be an inducement." Evelyn must be thinking of George.

"Sure. What I mean is, don't tell any Saudis."

"No fear." Evelyn sighed, glancing back at the hallway Faisal had left. "We don't know any, aside from our students. More's the pity."

"When's the party?" Grace asked.

"Later this week. You're in luck."

ELEVEN

SEVERAL DAYS LATER, Arden wandered through the cavernous Bell Helicopter Rec Center, illegal Scotch in hand, bemused by how many rooms there were and how loud the music was, some kind of industrial-techno-rave she couldn't relate to but which was nevertheless compelling, more so with every sip.

It seemed every Westerner in Riyadh was here tonight—diplomats, journalists, military, businessmen, all drinking furiously and chattering away. Kate and Grace were somewhere back in the first rooms, surrounded by a crowd of American Air Force men happy to see new Western women.

Bedraggled Halloween decorations were placed here and there. A red-checked headdress was draped over a plastic skull in a way that struck her as grotesque. She hadn't drunk alcohol in so long she forgot how to pace herself. She didn't even like hard liquor, but there weren't any wine coolers.

She came into a small Oriental living room, all carpets and big pillows, no standing furniture. She tossed her bag and sank onto cushions, stretching her legs in their now-unaccustomed jeans, and finally heard a welcome change of music: U2.

A door opened at the other end of the room and a group of men came in.

They were Saudis, *ohmigod,* what could they be doing here? Attuned to flinching at their white robes, she shrank into her corner, folding up her legs, wishing for her abaya in her bag across the room. There were two wizened fellows like the ones she greeted in the spice souk during shopping expeditions on Thursday mornings, and a sleek youth who stared as if she were one of the creatures in the old Star Wars bar scene. Well, that was apt: she felt like E.T. in their Kingdom right now.

Evelyn entered with a tall Saudi who bent over to address the youngster. "Oh hello Arden, meet Prince Ali," Evelyn said. The tall man nodded. Evelyn gestured to the youth. "And this lad is Prince Nawaf, with his loyal retainers. They're decent chaps." She smiled at Arden's bemusement. "It's all right, they're royals, the usual restrictions don't apply, we can do whatever we like and not get into trouble. Enjoy!" Was there some special rating system that governed interactions here? Evelyn and Prince Ali went through the far doorway.

Prince Nawaf pulled out an object Arden recognized: a water pipe, into which he tamped down a healthy-sized chunk of hashish.

"A familiar cultural artifact," she told them, but since she was speaking English, slurring actually, they merely glanced at her and bent to the business of lighting up. Prince Nawaf sucked in deeply. He was the only one smoking, she realized. Vaguely aware of her manners, she ventured in Arabic,

"Masah al khair." Good evening.

"Masah al noor," replied one of the old men. Prince Nawaf squinted at her through smoke.

"Keef el hal?" How are you? Arden asked the old man.

"Alhamdulillah." God is praised. *"Wa enti, keef halik?"* And you?

"Alhamdulillah."

"Zawj fee?" Are you married?

She considered him. He was old enough to be her grandfather; he must simply want to account for any unaccompanied females. It seemed to be a national pastime: women were errant sheep, and men their natural shepherds.

"La." No. Her Arabic wasn't good enough to say, if I were married do you think I'd be hanging out at this rave,

alone? But she wouldn't have the nerve to say that to a trio of Saudi men.

The two old men left the room. Prince Nawaf extended the pipe toward her. She studied it. What imperative ruled in this kind of situation? If she didn't smoke, what hospitality law would she be violating? She looked at him. He appeared barely twenty. He smiled, encouraging, and she thought, *what the hell.* She hoped Evelyn was right about royal protection from Kingdom laws. She took the pipe, took a hit, held it. Let it out slowly and took another.

Who knew they had such *great* hash here in ... the Magic Kingdom. They really should advertise in the Ministry of Information brochures. The music expanded and Bono's voice boomed through the room, so strong it sounded flame-colored. The guitar solo soared, racing around the walls and sinking into the brilliant carpets.

She set down her Scotch glass. It took a long time for her to hand the pipe back to Prince Nawaf, who seemed to be sitting at the other end of a telescope, and whose smile, as she watched him, seemed to grow flirtatious and conspiratorial.

He sucked in, and the water in the pipe bubbled hilariously, chuckling like a woodland creek from the West Virginia countryside of her early childhood. Stoned, smiling, she lay back on the cushions. He leaned toward her and asked softly,

"Who are you?" She understood his Arabic perfectly!

"I'm a teacher at the Womens' College of Riyadh University." Her Arabic was flawless!

"What do you teach?" His voice was so low she could hardly hear it, so she moved a little closer to him. He handed her the pipe again.

"English." She sucked in, held.

"You like teaching our girls?"

"Very much. Saudi girls—excellent." She was having a real conversation, in Arabic, with someone who wasn't Rowda or a shopkeeper!

"What do you think of my kingdom?"

"I love the Kingdom. The country is interesting. The country is ..." she searched for a more descriptive word in Arabic, but failed—"big." She gave the pipe back.

"What is your name?"

"Arden Arm Strong." She'd learned how to say it in Arabic, and flexed her arm, watching his face relax into friendly amusement. Why, he was a darling boy! Her girls would love him. Maybe, as a prince, he was related to Khadijah. She tried to find the words to ask but her Arabic melted, as quickly as it had just flowed, as she swallowed smoke. She laughed, caught by the merriment of hash.

He laughed too, leaning amiably close, lolling on the cushions, a sultry sheikh of the old Arabian Nights. He lifted the pipe to her lips, like any guy at a party, and she sank further into the cushions, taking another hit. She could have been back in Short North, with stronger hash. She closed her eyes as the *Batman* theme blared, U2, overwhelming with a throbbing refrain about thrilling and killing.

Suddenly Prince Nawaf was snaking an arm underneath, pulling her against him, kissing with an avid open mouth, running his free hand down her body. Alarm and arousal shot into her simultaneously as his clever fingers wandered here and there. She hadn't been touched in such a long time! His warm tongue tasted like hashish. Forgetting herself, she kissed back, clutching him tight for one delicious moment, excited by the unfamiliar feeling of his headdress in her hands.

But his headdress reminded her of where she was, and that he was a total stranger, and of the number of severe taboos they were breaking. She struggled up and pushed him away, stifling stoned giggles that rose, unbidden, superseding her fright.

She told him in Arabic, fighting to find the right words, "You are sweet. But no."

He didn't argue—he was staring, wide-eyed, at something behind her.

She turned to see a uniformed American approaching, looking as though he'd like to drill holes into both of them with steel blue eyes. He was what her friends in Ohio called a straight edge: blond hair in a crew cut, clothing pressed into sharp lines, expression so grim she felt afraid, although she didn't know enough about the military to guess his rank or his service branch. He hauled Prince Nawaf to his feet.

The pipe fell. Water and smoldering weed ran together in a fragrant little rivulet on the beautiful red, green and blue patterned carpet. Arden stretched one leg, to stub out the smoke with her boot.

The soldier berated the prince in what sounded like excellent Arabic, but the youth shrugged him off with a sulky grimace.

"Let's get you outta here." The soldier had a strong Southern accent, in English. He grabbed Prince Nawaf's arm and marched him to the door. "Hurry up," he snapped over his shoulder to Arden, still slowly moving her boot on the carpet, absorbed by its intricate pattern. "Come on!"

Jolted by his authoritative bark, she snatched her purse and followed them. The American set a hasty pace out of the compound and into the parking lot. He practically threw Prince Nawaf into the tinted back seat of a black Grand Cherokee, motioned for Arden to follow, and leaped into the front.

"Wait, wait just a dang minute, wouldja." She pushed aside crowded sensations, trying for a shaft of rational illumination. She sucked in a lungful of suddenly cold evening air. She shivered, dug out her scarf and abaya, wrapped them around her. "Why should I go? Who are you?"

"I'm Johnny, and you're about two minutes away from gettin busted. I don't have to tell you that's no joke here."

"But they're royals, right, it doesn't matter?" Was Evelyn wrong about this?

"It matters to the mutawas!"

"My friends are inside, what about them?"

"Depends what they're doin. Drinkin, well, they're honkies right? No biggie. Night in jail. You were smokin—with *him*! and you better believe I'm gettin him out before they start with the drug tests. You comin or you wanna get deported?"

She climbed in beside Prince Nawaf, whose sly smile and black eyes beckoned. She was tingling, still, with excitement from kissing him, still dizzy high from the Scotch and smoke. He slid his hand up her thigh, and then higher, entirely too practiced for such a youngster. She pushed him away, knowing she had to dissuade him but feeling childishly bonded, too, as if they were both criminals in the back of the cop car.

Johnny sent them a sharp look in the mirror. "Cut it out, wouldja, we're in public. You can wait till we get to the palace."

She sat up straight. "I'm not going with him."

"No short-term marriage for you?"

"What?"

"Buncha gold bracelets or necklaces?" The sneer in his tone was unmistakable. "Marry him, for a night, it's okay."

"No." God no. Never in a million years, no matter how stoned she was. She *needed* this job. All the admonitions came flooding back, now that she'd committed a drug crime here. She wasn't about to add fornication. Prince Nawaf seemed to be falling asleep on her shoulder. She moved him, gently, so he rested against the far window.

Johnny drove as recklessly as a native, careening around traffic circles, peeling through stop signs. The streets were deserted; she looked at empty cityscape, blocks of elegant unlit buildings. The pavement was so black it looked wet, like a TV show she'd seen of Venice in flood, when viscous Grand Canal water lapped, greedy, all the way up to the desolate second floors of mansions lining its banks. She pulled her abaya close.

Johnny turned up the music. Pink Floyd sang of a look in the eyes like black holes in the sky: "Shine On You Crazy Diamond." Pink Floyd couldn't have intended it, but their tense little dirge captured Saudi Arabia tonight, for her. They drove past a behemoth of a power station whose gleaming wires hummed with electronic life, more vivid than the walled-off stucco homes of the sleeping neighborhood. To her amazement, in her hash-induced awareness of atmosphere, the next song was "Welcome to the Machine" which fit the power plant perfectly.

Johnny, eyeing her in the mirror, let out a short laugh.

"You're hooked! I know that look. Fuckin ragheads."

What was he talking about? Only the crudest expats referred to Saudis that way. She frowned, but he wasn't paying attention to her anymore. He turned up the music until it was deafening. Prince Nawaf stirred.

"No, Johnny, no Pink Floyd," he said in English. "Put Khalid." He straightened, adjusted his headdress, muttered in Arabic, took out a little rope of worry beads and began clacking them rhythmically. Only when he shifted them from one hand to another did he notice Arden, huddled in her corner. His young face wrinkled, perplexed. "Are we ... together?" he asked, in heavily accented English.

His hesitancy would have been comical had her skin not retained an imprint of the arousal he'd awoken, unwelcome now. "Absolutely not."

Johnny snorted. "Coupla necklaces, maybe, some earrings ... you might wanna rethink." He slid in a Khalid CD. Arden knew the singer from her students; he was a kind of Arab Ricky Martin, innocuous but catchy. They rode along not speaking until Johnny wheeled, tires screeching, into an enormous circular drive in front of a tall gilded gate, guarding a classical structure that looked like the Smithsonian.

"I can't to fly tomorrow," Prince Nawaf announced. "My head is a ball."

"You gotta deal, man. I ain't coverin for you."

"I will tell to my father that I am so sick." He got out and stood at the open door. "Thank you, Johnny. You are always true friend, you escape me from my bad self." He bowed slightly to Arden. "Miss, good night. I wish for you all the best in my kingdom."

TWELVE

NAWAF MOVED SILENTLY over the wide brick drive to touch a security box by the side of the gate, which swung open, and his lithe white figure disappeared. His departure was so gracious that Arden was compelled to speak.

"Who *is* he?"

"Seventh in line to the throne. You missed out bigtime, babe. Coulda been a real Cinderella story."

"Will you stop insulting me!"

"And he's a helluva fighter pilot," Johnny continued. "Best of the best. I look out for him. I don't wanna see him busted for a little weed, a little pussy."

"Jesus!"

"Come on, you were into it."

"So what!" she snapped. "So he's a good kisser, does that make me a slut?"

He laughed. "You only got as far as kissin, hon, you must still be horny."

She had forgotten how direct a certain kind of American could be. She pinched her lips over unbidden amusement and stared, stone-faced, out the window at the palace.

"Last chance," he taunted, revving the engine. "He's generous, one night'd set you up for a long time …"

"You think I'd have sex with him for money?"

"Jewelry. Not money."

"You're so vulgar!"

"And you're Alice in Wonderland. Plenty of gals go with him, for plenty of reasons, why not you?"

"I don't like your assumptions."

"So don't." He shrugged. "Where do I take you, anyhow? Back to the party? Mutawas're gone by now."

She forced herself to think clearly for a moment. She'd call Kate on her mobile, let her know she had a ride, tell her to look out for Evelyn, who was presumably still with Prince Ali. She was lucky Johnny had gotten her out of the mutawas' clutches. He seemed like a good guy in spite of his crudeness. He reminded her of the West Virginia cousins she'd met, at Uncle Munro's. "Can you take me home?"

"With me?" He smirked in the mirror, showing her a deep dimple on one side of his mouth. "This is so sudden, sweetheart, I'm not sure how I *feel* about you."

"To my home, if you wouldn't mind?"

"Where do you live?"

"I don't know the exact directions from here, it's in the desert, the university housing compound, it's off the only highway going due west …"

"You don't know where the fuck you live?"

"It's confusing, not driving," she defended herself. "And my map's kind of vague." She gave him the folded city map she always kept with her, from her orientation packet. It was in Arabic—and French, for some reason, quaintly labeled "Plan de la Ville." He frowned at the spot her finger indicated.

"Damn, this is way fuckin out. But okay. Lose the robes and get in front."

"No way!" Unmarried couples never rode in front together.

"Do it," he said impatiently. "If they see me drivin a covered gal I'll get pulled over for sure. If you're a honky, next to me, it's none of their business."

She scrambled into the front and peeled off her scarf and abaya. He floored the engine and they flew onto the desert highway. He put on "Wish You Were Here," making her wonder if *she* could tell a smile through a veil as the music leaked, poignant, into the unoccupied-looking planet they passed.

Arden clasped her arms and stared out at the darkness. She hadn't seen, before, the night desert, its absence of color as cold as deep space. She had not known black had such depth. The man beside her seemed part of the bleak landscape and, to break her mood, she asked, "So, what kind of soldier are you?"

He shot her an incredulous look. *"Pilot."*

"You're at that air base—the Prince Sultan."

"Yes ma'am."

"You're here to protect the Saudis."

"We're teachin em to protect themselves."

"I'm a teacher too."

"Yeah?" His tone was disbelieving. He gave her a quick once-over. "Just what are *you* teachin em, babe?"

She sat up straight and put on a cool tone. "I teach English to university girls."

"They let em go to school?"

"Of course, they're progressive. The girls are getting their degrees. They're very intelligent young women."

"Unlike their teacher."

"Hey! That's not fair. I went to that party with friends, we were invited by people from the Riyadh Women's Club —"

"And you end up smokin hash and makin out with a raghead royal. In *public!*" He leveled the steely look at her again, heavy with contempt. *"My* squadron leader!"

"I didn't know who he was!"

He laughed, sarcastically, and after a moment she had to laugh too, at the absurdity of her reply. Her high resumed, shooting through her, and she bent over, consumed in harsh gasps of laughter.

"You okay?"

She tried to collect herself. "I, I just …" She howled.

"Yemeni Black? Oh yeah."

"You should have joined us!"

"One, I'm on duty." He gestured to his shirt, stiff with insignia. "I'm in uniform, guess you were too wrecked to notice. Two, I was savin his butt from the mutawas. Saved yours too. Three, I'm not so stupid, to smoke with him in public. When I wanna get high I go to his place. When we're both off duty."

"It was a private party—"

"Anytime you're mixin Saudis and Westerners in a honky compound it's public. Bell can't keep ragheads out, busted every couple weeks. My Nawaf loves parties."

"Isn't he your friend?"

"Mor'n a friend. Brothers in arms. We'd die for each other."

"But you call him a *raghead?*"

He laughed again. "What do you think they call us?"

"They don't call me at all," she quipped, but her tone was unintentionally wistful.

"Poor Alice, where's Wonderland now?" He grinned. "I can hook you back up with him, babe, ya want. Or, tell ya what, *I'll* call you. Never dated a teacher. We'll go out, catch a movie, hit the newest restaurant, go to a club, plenty to do around here." His smile twisted. There were no movies or clubs. There were no restaurants not sexually segregated. There was no bowling, no amusement park, no racetrack, not even mini golf that unmarried men and women could visit together. "Or maybe we'll just drive into the desert, listen to Pink Floyd."

They did, for several miles, in a silence that now felt companionable. The lights of the university housing compound grew clear as they rounded the final hills. She pulled on her covers again, and he glanced at her.

"Why are you doin that? Who's gonna see us?" Then he frowned as he saw the gatehouse, around the last bend. "Someone's checkin ID, I'm not goin in." He pulled over and cut the lights and music. "This a Saudi school?"

"Yes."

"Damn." He ran one hand over his practically nonexistent blond hair. "So, what do you do, when you come in alone with a guy?"

"This is the first time."

He turned to give her a cold stare. She could see the fighter pilot in him. She imagined him and Nawaf streaking overhead, above the sound barrier, avenging angels eager to strafe Iraqi planes if the Kingdom were threatened. "I'm not goin in," he said again. "I can't risk it. I'm supposed to be invisible here."

"But there's not usually anyone there. When we come in, the bus driver uses the passcard—we all have one—to raise the gate." She took out her card.

"Let's see."

Her gate ID was a simple plastic sliver.

"Might work, but—" he got out, and rummaged in the trunk, until he pulled out a red-checked headdress and a sportcoat. "Maybe." He put the headdress on and flipped the ends, expertly she thought, buttoned the sportcoat over his uniform, clapped on a pair of incongruous sunglasses, and jumped back in the driver's seat.

"We'll go in fast. This late, they're probly not checkin. Get in back, and cover your face with that thing. Act submissive." He laughed suddenly, without humor. "I had Force plates on, this'd never work." Fear and excitement clashed as she pulled the scarf over her face. *Wullahi,* as her girls would say, *ohmigod!*

They approached the gatehouse, where to Arden's horror there *was* a guard. Johnny coolly wiggled the card in front of the scanner, greeting the man in Arabic. The guard barely looked at them. The gate lifted. Johnny accelerated through.

Arden directed him to her apartment, and he braked in front sharply. "Stay covered and get out fast before anyone looks too closely." She glanced around at the deserted complex. "You think they don't look? Alice. Get out."

"Okay." She opened the door. Hesitated. "Thanks, Johnny. I know you took a big risk for me. I appreciate it."

"Here." He pulled a card from his pocket, and handed it to her with her ID. "You need to be rescued again, call me. What's your name?"

"Arden."

"Sounds like a cracker name."

"Takes one to know one, Johnny."

"So long, Arden. Be careful now."

As soon as she shut the door he roared off. She saw his tail lights winking beyond the courtyard. Suddenly exhausted, glad to be alone, she mounted the stairs to the apartment. She drank in the welcome quiet and did not turn on the lights. She put Johnny's card on her nightstand, stripped and lay down, head swimming. The evening, each scene trippier than the last, flashed wildly past her eyelids.

THIRTEEN

THE NEXT DAY dawned like a winter Sunday in Ohio. Gray clouds covered the sun, and the landscape looked so different that, even hungover, Arden felt compelled to go out in the courtyard to experience the new atmosphere. She inhaled, deep, the earth-scented air, and felt a rush of hash aftereffects which colored the gardens and made her neighbors' robes velvet black and phosphorescent white. The men's faces, smiling as they played with their children, exuded pure gentility as their voices were muted in the thick air. Noticing so closely felt dangerous. Their smiles might leak into her. Arden dragged her gaze away and sat on the bench farthest from the playground.

Rowda's voice, when she came up to Arden, was rough with pleasure. "We very happy to the rain, Ahden."

"Is it raining?"

"You are funny today! Of course, the rain will come later." Her veil moved as she sniffed. "You can smell the breathe."

"The air."

"Yes, air. The air is filled with water. It is a blessing of Allah for the Hajjis who return from Makkah today."

"Is it exciting, going to Makkah?"

"It is the most exciting." Rowda's grin widened, stirring the wispy cloth over her face. "We all thousand the same in front of Allah, all looking to the peace of Allah. We feel freedom, more than the usual life. Everyone good mood."

"It sounds ... wonderful."

Rowda looked at her closely. "Are you missing your religion?"

What a weird question. "No."

"Then you are lonely today? You like come to my home?"

Rowda had not invited her before, but Arden was afraid of seeming too needy. "Not today," she said quickly, "but can I come soon? I want to see your face."

"I think you are lonely," Rowda concluded. She patted Arden's hand. "You go to your sheikha friends, if you don't come to me. You can't to be all alone."

Nawaf's words to Johnny echoed, and she repeated them to Rowda. "You are a true friend." She closed her fingers firmly around Rowda's soft palm, relishing the touch, not wanting to let go.

"And you." Rowda glanced up as a young man came close to them. "Ahden, please to meet my husband, Sharif."

Arden knew she could not look at him or offer her hand. But his cologne beckoned as if enticing her to stare, to reach out. "I honored meet sir," she said in her bad Arabic, lowering her head. "You wonderful family."

"Thank you for the time you're taking with Rowda, ya miss. She enjoys your English lessons."

"I like too."

Arden shoved her hands into her hair, rumpling her scarf, as they walked away, trying to clear the flood of sensual awareness washing through her. Maybe it was the unaccustomed hash-Scotch hangover, maybe it was kissing Nawaf, maybe it was the dramatic moisture in the air, but the distance between herself and these people was shattered, leaving a fierce yearning to get closer.

Her Arabic had improved so much in these two months, through the weekly classes the university offered, she was sometimes dreaming in language, and could read whole paragraphs in the newspaper, and had phrases linger in her mind. She liked its musical syllables, its strict pronunciation, the way confident references to Allah's omniscience were woven into every quiet Saudi voice.

She'd taught ESL long enough to realize her Arabic comprehension was tantalizingly imminent.

She heard snatches of conversation from the families around her, and though their words were mundane, of breakfast and errands and family obligations in preparation for the post-Haj Eid holiday, there was magic in this morning; in the promise of rain and in her clear understanding of every word they said.

"Arden!" Kate was crossing the courtyard. "I knew I'd find you here."

"I know what they're saying!" Arden exclaimed. "I mean, *everything*. I love it. I *love* them!"

"Who?"

Arden nodded to the small group of families gathered in the playground.

Kate took her arm. "Are you hungover?"

"No. Or maybe, but it feels like homesickness, but for *here*. I want to *belong* here. I *know* them now. I *understand* them!"

"You're *definitely* hungover," Kate concluded, with a wry smile. "Me too. Come on, the others are already at my place." Kate took her arm. "I'm glad you left the message on my mobile. I wondered where you went when the mutawas showed up."

"Was Evelyn okay?

"More than okay. She's got herself a boyfriend, finally!"

In Kate's living room, Evelyn was holding forth, lounging on the couch with the air of a tired yet satisfied courtesan.

"I'm simply transported," she was saying languidly. "He was absolutely …"

"Don't tell us, we can't stand it." Kate passed around a plate of fruit slices.

"I want every detail," said Grace. "Give us a vicarious thrill."

"His skin, his hair, his eyes," Evelyn said slowly. "He's heavenly. D'you know, I've been fancying these chaps since I saw them at the airport? Their sexy aloofness, those lovely robes, their ever-so-discreet sidelong glances, their marvelous cars and watches, the way they smell of designer colognes ..."

Her words threw the amorphous longing Arden had experienced in the courtyard into stark relief.

If it'd been Faisal, not Nawaf, she wouldn't have heeded taboos last night.

But it wasn't his cologne or car or watch. Faisal was as vivid and unique as the soccer ball striking her shoulder that day they met, not some ... native archetype.

Evelyn was leaning back, staring dreamily at the ceiling. "But the most intoxicating aspect was that he was so ... hungry for it, you know? He was ravenous. And yet, so gentle. Reverent, really, that's the word."

Arden bit her lip.

"Of course, I was hungry too, God, no sex for months. It's unnatural. I mean, you'd all agree, there's no substitute." She sighed, hugely. "I'm in love."

No one could think of what to say to this. They looked at her silently.

She swung off the couch. "I told him I'd call him as soon as his driver dropped me off here." She went back to Kate's bedroom to use the phone. They heard her speaking in Arabic, low, with a few heady giggles. It was like high school, except that with high school sex the worst that could happen was disease, or pregnancy, or parents finding out. Public lashing, for the sin of fornication, hadn't yet occurred to the average American community—nor the British, Arden guessed.

She and the others looked at each other, bewildered, wondering what the appropriate response to Evelyn's joy should be—delight or fear?

Evelyn re-appeared, radiant with infatuation. Arden couldn't help but warm to her happiness. "So when's the wedding?" she teased.

"Actually, he told me we *are* married. 'Short-term,' he said. A good Muslim can't just fool around, you know, I had to agree to it."

"I don't believe it!" Kate laughed.

"Is that legal?" Grace asked.

"I've no idea," Evelyn replied, her airy tone signifying it was of no concern.

Kate frowned. "Are you sure you know what you're getting into?"

"Completely." Evelyn turned cool. "I've been looking for the right fellow here, and he's it. This is a rational decision."

"So he's worth the risk."

"There *is* no risk, that's why I picked him, aside from his looks. He's a prince. He can't be touched. In any case, he said we're married."

"So it's *legal?*" Grace repeated.

"Legal or not, I truly don't care." She looked at them with a challenging lift of her chin, swinging her long hair back, obviously enjoying what she perceived as her elevated position in the group. Arden noticed a new necklace adorning her graceful throat—a string of diamonds. "Now, about dinner at the palace tonight. It will be fun. He's inviting several friends."

"Any of those cute American pilots from last night?" asked Grace.

"Saudis only," Evelyn answered. She glanced at Arden. "Prince Nawaf will be there. I heard he was quite taken with you, Arden."

"That's nice," Arden said warily.

"He wants to see you again, he told Ali."

"How kind. But I'm not really interested."

"Why not, if I may ask?" Although she claimed to be rational, Evelyn looked as if she might easily take offense if others did not follow her path, and Arden imagined whatever she said would be repeated, so she framed her answer carefully.

"Prince Nawaf seems ... sweet! I really enjoyed meeting him. But I'm not dating here. I have a serious boyfriend back home." As easily as this lie came, it seemed a little strange, suddenly: the sheikhas had not traded this kind of information as to who they had been, pre-Kingdom. The most they shared, at least with her so far, was pedagogical theory. As if they were all born fully grown at Riyadh International Airport. Maybe if she had a roommate it would be different.

"Suit yourself, dear, we just don't want you to be lonely."

"I'm fine."

LATER, SHE WONDERED if she shouldn't have gone with them, or accepted Rowda's invitation. The guesthouse felt even emptier after the spate of sociability.

She sat in the living room, drinking tea, watching the palest pink of the unusually wan sunset creep across the living room wall. At least her hangover was fading. She put on one of her U2 CDs and Bono's voice brought last night back vividly, sending a little shiver through her. She was right to avoid Prince Nawaf—she sent the wrong signal by smoking with him. Stupid impulse, letting herself forget where she was. And kissing him—lunacy! Even if he was immune to punishment, she was not. She was lucky Johnny had shown up, or she might be in jail tonight.

She was well out of it.

But ... would she have any kind of social life if the expat sheikhas were all going to be royal groupies? Who else could she make friends with?

Maybe she'd just get used to being alone.

As if to contradict her, the phone rang.

"Hello?"

"Miss Arden? I'm Leila, from your Intermediate Class—"

"Leila! Of course I know you!" Hearing her voice made Arden aware of how much she missed the girls, these long days away. And Leila was her favorite.

"I call to invite you to my home for our Eid party tomorrow night. I was asking some of the other students, and I was thinking you will like to come to us."

"I'd love to come!"

"Do you have a nice vacation?"

"I miss my classes, Leila, I'm happy to hear your voice."

"You are a very good teacher. Very—dedicated." Arden smiled—it was one of their vocab words.

"I hope I will have dedicated students too."

"So you will attend, thank you Miss Arden. I will come to you with my driver after the last prayer call. Maybe I bring some one of the other girls, they like to see the new campus."

Arden's mood was transformed. Certainly, the secret to a happy life here was to hang out with the women and ignore the men, just as they'd been advised. She changed U2 to Sheryl Crowe.

FOURTEEN

SHE FELT AS EXCITED as a six-year old going to a birthday party. She wore a long black velvet skirt, borrowed from Evelyn, and a white satin blouse, borrowed from Kate. She twisted up her hair and carefully put on makeup. She'd examined every conceivable gift item in the little campus grocery shop, dissatisfied at the selections but unable to go to the city because there was no shopping bus during the Haj vacation; finally she picked out an enormous tin of Danish butter cookies and wrapped it in glittery purple paper with a lavish bow. She held it on her lap, waiting for the doorbell to ring.

She opened the door to three black-shrouded figures.

"Leila?" she asked hesitantly.

"Of course, Miss, don't you know us?" Then she knew Leila's voice. Maha and Eyman were with her, their giggles recognizable. Arden followed them out of her building to the courtyard, where families were congregating.

"They keep this garden beautiful with good water," said Leila. "It's nice everyone can come here."

"I take walks around the campus every evening about this time, usually with the other teachers. It's a good way to get some exercise."

"I like too," Leila said. "My brother is a teacher, I visit him here sometimes."

"Next time come to see me too, Leila. I'd love to have you."

The girls looked around in what seemed like awe at the men and women mingling freely together in the courtyard. Arden heard Johnny's voice in her head, "Damn, these gals don't get out much."

"Shall we take a walk now?" she asked them, wanting to prolong their enjoyment. Their heads turned to each other.

"Just a little, Miss. My driver is waiting."

She led them on the winding path past the lingering families and throughout the courtyard gardens, where in-ground sprinklers were just coming on in the dusk, and up the palm-studded hill past the mosque. Hanging in the milky sky above the minaret was one evocative early star next to a slice of moon. The moon and star configuration was the symbol of Islam. *"Allahu akbar,"* Eyman said, pointing it out, God is great.

"Allahu akbar," echoed the girls.

They walked on. The air was heady, humid although it still had not rained, scented with the flowers planted in neat rows by the walkways. They moved in a slow procession, the girls picking their way on tiny high heels, lifting their long abayas to give their feet room to move. "This is beautiful place," Maha whispered.

"I think so too," Arden said. "I love it." She was surprised to hear herself say this. "Please come back to visit me, girls. I'll be happy to have the company."

"Thank you Miss."

At the top of the hill they stopped to look over the small cluster of buildings, lit against the darkening caramel of the surrounding desert. More stars appeared as they observed, diamond chips in the purpling sky. The fragrance of jasmine surrounded them, borne on a freshening damp breeze. Arden realized she had never studied this particular view—she and the sheikhas were always pounding around their route, trying to work up a sweat and achieve specific aerobic goals. She was glad to share her first real appreciation of this beauty with her girls.

"It's like poem," said Maha wistfully.

"It's painting, painting from Allah," said Eyman, and the girls all murmured *"Alhamdulillah."*

They immediately associated natural beauty with a God they believed was directly responsible. She felt a stab of envy—she'd lost that so long ago. But she didn't want to ask them about the comfort they derived from Islam. It seemed too personal a subject. And she didn't want to reveal herself as a non-believer.

The sky seemed to close down, and the lights on the path brightened accordingly. Leila said briskly, "We must to go."

They moved as quickly as was possible in heels, long abayas and veiled faces.

"Isn't it hard to see in the dark?" Arden ventured.

"Is hard. I only go out to the souk at night, not on a long walk this way." Maha pulled the veil tightly across her eyes, trying to see more clearly.

"Take it off."

Maha laughed. "No! Miss, we can't to do that."

Arden didn't know what possessed her, but she repeated, "Go ahead, take it off. Nobody will see you up here."

They giggled, but each, carefully, peeled back a sliver of veil, and then they laughed as giddily as if they were skinny-dipping for the first time on a moonlit summer night in the lyrical lakes near Columbus. Arden giggled too, knowing she was being a poor influence, but loving their delight. She ripped off her scarf and waved it around her head. The girls ululated a soft exuberant chorus around her.

A white-clad figure moving up the path had them quickly hustling back into covered propriety, falling silent as the man passed, eyes averted. "Sorry, girls, my bad," Arden hissed after he was safely behind them. The girls just laughed again, recklessly. She went on, "I don't want to offend your religion."

"It isn't religion! " Leila exclaimed. "This hijab is not part of Islam, it is just a, what you say, a corruption. It has nothing to do with real Islam. Muhammad, peace be upon him, says nothing in the Quran about covers to women's face."

"Then why—"

"Saudis are obligated to pay attention to this idea, because the royal family—"

"Leila!" Eyman admonished her, in Arabic too quick for Arden to understand.

"Girls," she told them, mindful of their surroundings, "I am very sorry I began, that I explored a difficult subject. Please, let's forget about this, and we'll enjoy our time together for Eid."

"Yes Miss," they chorused. Arden regretted her spontaneity in telling them to take off their veils. She wouldn't have to live with the consequences of a rebellious fling, but they would. She'd be leaving next June. They'd be staying for life. Sobered, she followed them down the path to Leila's waiting vehicle, a gold Lexus SUV.

They piled into the back, Leila gave curt instructions to the driver, and they caromed away out of the campus, weaving as wildly as Johnny had the other night. The ubiquitous Khalid was on the CD player, and the girls hummed along, crooning the vaguely R&B lyrics just as girls in the States did.

"What's he singing about?" Arden couldn't make out much more than 'Sweet, sweet, I love you, my heart.'

"He is very romantic," Maha told her. "He loves his fiancée too much, he can't wait to marry her. But she is far away and he can't to see her."

"Does she love him too?"

"Yes, we can hear her voice, do you hear?" Sure enough, a light voice was ululating wordlessly in the background. "She is in his dream."

"These are silly songs," Leila said crossly. "I don't like Khalid. He's so stupid." The others shushed her.

"Who's your favorite, Leila?" Arden asked, amused.

"Rage Against the Machine."

"No way!" The band was controversial even in the freewheeling West because of their extreme political views and violent language. Their singing was more like screaming. "How did you ever hear of them?"

"My brother brings me new every time he comes from States. All the music. Nirvana, Smashing Pumpkin, Red Hot Chili Pepper, Pearl Jam, Green Day. Then when we find a band we like too much, we buy their other CD at the souk." There was a booming black market in bootleg music, reproduced in South Asia; Arden had augmented her own CD collection thereby. Naturally, none of the musicians Leila mentioned were ever heard on the radio here or sold in regular CD stores. Even Khalid was considered racy with his endless moaning about boy-wants-girl. Of course, he was Egyptian. No Saudi artist who wanted airtime in the Kingdom would bother creating overtly romantic love songs. Even instrumental music was severely curtailed by the mutawas.

"Does your brother understand what Rage is singing about?" Arden asked.

"Of course, we both understand, it is the call for our generation to show, how to say, our political will? That we have the power to change the life."

How had this repressive environment produced siblings of such outspoken fearlessness? Arden wondered again about the family she would be meeting tonight. "Leila, please, be careful about the way you express your views here."

"I know. My brother says to me same, that I am free to think anything I choose, but to be always knowing that the others here don't agree with me. After I finish college here he will take me to States for graduate school."

"Do your parents agree?"

"My father and he are arguing all the time, they never agree about anything, but he is very proud of my brother. My mother is not alive."

"Leila. I'm sorry."

"She was too sick, many years ago. My father's third wife Aisha isn't caring about ideas like this. She has my husband to worry about."

"You're *married?*" They'd all been single when school started. It was hard to imagine Leila married to a conventional Saudi man.

"No, but I have to make my engagement soon, before I am, how to say about the girl who waits too long time?" Leila grinned under her veil. "Before all of the best men of my cousins are promise to others."

"To prettier girls, Leila, who know how to be quiet," Maha teased. Leila pushed her playfully, and Eyman pushed back, and soon they were shrieking with laughter and the driver was peering at them narrowly in the rearview mirror.

FIFTEEN

AFTER PASSING THROUGH a tall gate set in high stucco walls, they drew up to a sprawling villa. The driver brought them around the back, where they joined other veiled women streaming inside.

Once unveiled, Leila was the immediate center of excited attention.

Arden realized she was underdressed; everyone was wearing ball gowns in rainbow colors and shimmering fabrics. Every jewel she had admired at the gold souk seemed to sparkle on their necks, wrists, fingers, hair and ankles. No doubt she paled in comparison. She put her package aside and covered it with her scarf and abaya; nobody else had brought a present.

She followed the crowd into an elegant gold and white salon where chairs lined the walls and a long table in the center was loaded with platters of lamb, rice and salads. A separate table held tea, coffee, fruits and sweets. Eyman and Maha led her to a seat and brought her a plate of the fragrant, sweetly spicy food.

"Shouldn't I say hello to Leila's family?" she asked Eyman and Maha.

"No, Miss, you can't to see her father," said Maha.

"Of course not, he is in the other side with the men, and his wife is still in Jiddah with her parents," added Eyman.

"How can I thank them for having me?"

"It isn't necessary. You are Leila's guest, only." Eyman took Arden's plate as soon as it was empty, and went up to the table to fill it again.

"How come Saudi women aren't fat?" she wondered, savoring the delicious rice.

"We don't eat very often like this one."

"Tell me exactly why we're celebrating Haj."

They told her of the long trek that every pilgrim followed in Makkah, echoing the first time that Haggar, Abraham's second wife, had run seven times from hill to hill, searching for water, and of her joy of finally finding the well of Zam Zam, revealed by Allah, and the ritual devil-stoning they re-enacted.

"I remember reading about this in the Koran," Arden told them, happy to recognize the story. "It represents the stones Ishmael threw at the devil, who tried to tempt him from his fate."

"*Allahu akbar!*" exclaimed Maha, grinning. "Miss Arden is understanding the history of Islam."

"What I didn't get, how come Ishmael is the sacrifice? I thought it was Isaac."

"We believe Ishmael was the first-born son of Ibrahim."

They told her about the mysterious Ka'aba, the megalith black stone discovered by Adam, around which Muhammad had gathered the disparate pagan tribes to create one community as monotheistic believers. The cube was now covered with drapes in the center of Makkah where the Grand Mosque stood. None of the girls had yet made their required Haj, but all of their fathers and most of their brothers had.

Leila joined them. "My brother just returned from his Haj," she said.

"The Rage Against the Machine brother?" Arden smiled.

"Yes, my only brother."

"Now that he's a Hajji, will he still listen to that kind of music?"

"Of course. He says Muslims are free to think about any ideas. He says our intelligence is what Allah cares for, that Allah gives us a big mind to think about anything."

"I'd like to meet your brother. He sounds so smart!"

"No, Miss, you can't to see a young Saudi man," Maha chided.

Leila looked at Arden speculatively. "Perhaps it will be possible, since you are Western and a teacher. You are not like us, we have to hide ourselves away, but you are free to meet a man if you like."

"Not here." She couldn't let them think she was too free. She grimaced, recalling her behavior with Prince Nawaf. What a horror if they were ever to find out! She could just imagine the respect in their eyes turning to contempt.

"Don't you like men, Miss Arden?" Leila was watching her curiously. "One of the English teachers last year, she liked only ladies."

"Leila," warned Maha.

"Miss Linda. They sent her back to England when they found out she had relationship with, who was it Maha? I don't remember her friend's name, from the Medical College?"

"Leila!" Maha turned to Arden. "Sorry, Miss, we don't talk about this thing."

"One of the Yemenis. They sent her out too," Leila finished carelessly. "So, Miss Arden, if you like ladies, you must be very careful."

"I like men, I just don't think about them here," Arden lied.

"Why not? You are young, beautiful, you can think about them. We all do."

Leila was enjoying her discomfiture, Arden realized, and she made her answer light. "I'm here to be your teacher. I'm not looking for a man. Besides, I don't ever see any. Except Sayee—Mr. Quraishi, when he gives us all directions."

"Then I will bring my brother to you. He is friendly, not like Mr. Quraishi. He likes Americans. Maybe you met him already, I told you he lives on your campus—"

"Leila, stop, you will make problem for Miss Arden. She isn't allowed to make friendship with Saudi men."

86

The discussion was broken by Leila's duties as hostess. She led them into another room, with carpets scattered on the floor and plump cushions leaning against the walls. She invited them to sit, with their cups of tea and coffee, and listen to the band that would play as a celebration of Eid. Of course, she told them, anyone who wanted to dance should feel free. Arden forgot the dangerous ground of Leila's talk once the band came out. They were a group of five small, round women, uncovered, in bright robes and barefoot, each with an instrument unfamiliar, and therefore fascinating, to Arden.

The ferocity of their wild dark faces stirred her to lean over to Eyman and whisper, "Who are they?"

"Bedawi." Bedouins.

When they began to play Arden felt a grinding sensation deep in her pelvis. The noisy drumming wove an intense rhythm around the room, and the strings laid a hypnotic melody on top, a melody that made Arden think of the view out the guestroom window, the untouched desert hills undulating endlessly off toward the Rub Al Khali, the great "Empty Quarter," where nothing but timeless sand dunes lay for a thousand miles.

She stared at the musicians, seeing in their eye-closed, swaying, foot-tapping movement painfully strong passion. Her fingers itched for her banjo as she felt how this could be played. Minor chords like the prayer call, some droning, some wailing, all hammering out an irresistible beat. Maybe she could arrange to play with these women? Slowly, one party guest after another rose, shaking off her shoes, stepping from side to side while hips circled and arms waved and long unbound hair swung back and forth.

When Maha pulled Arden up into the dance she laughed, trying to imitate them, and they laughed too, showing her how it was. She stepped from side to side, swung her hair. The music grew louder, the laughter of the women wilder, giving voice to a high-pitched ululation, a much louder version of the sound the girls had made on the mosque hilltop when they'd slipped their veils aside.

Finally the band stopped, allowing the guests to sink, gasping for breath, down into the cushions, mopping their faces with napkins, refreshing their cups with more sugary tea and sharp yellow cardamom-spiced coffee. The scent of keyed-up perspiration mixed with the scents of Chanel, St Laurent and Givenchy. Arden laughed in exhilaration. "This is one of the best parties I've ever been to," she confided to Eyman, who grinned as she twisted her heavy hair away from her face.

"Leila always gives the good parties," she said. "Don't mind her speaking, Miss, she is a good girl and we all love her even after she talks too much."

"Yes, I see that. You are lucky to be such close friends."

"*Alhamdulillah.*" Thanks be to Allah.

"*Alhamdulillah,*" Arden repeated quietly.

"Do you speak Arabic now?" Eyman asked her in Arabic, smiling.

"*Shway shway.* Only a little," Arden responded in Arabic. "But I understand more every day. I love the language of the Kingdom."

"It is the language of the Prophet, peace be upon him."

"Yes. The Prophet. Peace be upon him."

"We should give to you the Quran in Arabic, so that you can read in our Prophet's voice," Eyman said in English. "Do you like to read Arabic, or is it very difficult to you?"

"It's pretty hard," Arden admitted. "I get a headache with Al Hayat." The newspaper she struggled through every day, reading paragraphs as dry and unyielding as the Empty Quarter, was strangely unproductive work, since for all the effort she rarely learned anything of real interest. Al Hayat was a government mouthpiece.

"I'll give to you some ladies' magazines, they are more interesting than Al Hayat, and I will give to you the Quran."

"I'm already reading it in English. My Saudi students gave it to me in the States."

"Tell me, Miss Arden." Eyman leaned toward her confidentially. "How is the life for Saudis in United States?"

In Columbus, Arden had not considered her students' lives outside of the classroom. "I only had two Saudi students, and I didn't really get to know them."

"But we hear ... Americans don't like Muslims. After your Oklahoma City bomb, we hear Americans are putting the fault on Muslims."

"I remember." Not that she'd given it any thought. There hadn't been any Muslim students in her class that term. She felt the weight of her ignorance.

"My uncle studies in Washington. American University?" Eyman said this as if Arden ought to have known him. "He tells he afraid to go outside of his apartment in the night. He tells there are too many dangerous criminals."

"It's a big city. I'd be scared too, in D.C."

"Riyadh is big city, but nobody feeling afraid here." Eyman grinned suddenly. "Except when Miss Arden tells us take off our hijab." They shared a laugh, sweeter for bringing this difficult topic back into their small space. Arden had never before wondered how confrontational American prejudice might seem, to people who were as proud and reserved as Saudis seemed to be. Eyman touched her arm, worry in her face. "Miss Arden? Is not your fault, the bad cities."

"No." Arden forced a smile.

Then the music began again and everyone was carried away with the thrill of dancing until, amazingly, it was past three o'clock in the morning. Yawning, the band packed up. The remaining guests picked listlessly at the fruit left on the table and sipped final desultory glasses of tea. Leila materialized at Arden's side.

"You sleep here, Miss Arden."

She didn't protest. Leila left her in one of the villa's many dim bedrooms. She stripped off her sweat-damp clothing and climbed gratefully between cool jasmine-scented sheets. She fell asleep right away. Bedouin drumming permeated her dreams.

Sixteen

ARDEN WOKE THE NEXT MORNING feeling wonderfully tired as after a rigorous workout. She stretched to her fullest length, smiled at the ceiling and the simple heavy Moorish furniture. In the adjoining bathroom she lathered with sweet-smelling soap and used mysterious French shampoo, enjoying the sense of a spa getaway. How many others had spent the night? Maybe they'd brunch together before returning home.

"Miss Arden?" She heard Leila outside the bathroom door. "I bring for you a robe, it is my brother's. My clothes are too small to you. I leave for you on the door."

It was a man's finely tailored, soft cotton thobe with a small satin monogram on one pocket. It felt pleasantly illicit sliding over her nakedness. Leila's brother was tall— the cuffs fell past her wrist and the hem brushed the floor.

She rolled up the sleeves and looked in the mirror. She twisted a lock of her hair under her nose to make a moustache and frown sternly. "*Hayakallah*," she told herself in a gruff mock-male greeting. All she needed was a headdress to cover her hair—without blow-drying, it stood out in a wild mass, and she tried to push it into some kind of shape. She had a brush in her purse, which she'd left downstairs with her abaya.

Leila met her on the landing. She wore an embroidered cotton dress and her hair was also loose. They smiled at each other. Arden showed her mustache to make Leila laugh. "Leila, I need my brush if we're going to meet all the others."

"There is nobody. You stayed only, because it was too far to ask our driver to go, last night. We will make our breakfast now." She led Arden through a rotunda graced with Italian statuary. It was so quiet their bare footsteps echoed on the marble floor.

"Your house is magnificent, Leila."

Leila shrugged. "Is too big. My brother and me don't like it, since he came back we stay always in the small room near the kitchen, to watch videos and play games."

They came into a sunny kitchen, equipped with every trendy appliance; gleaming surfaces and stainless steel everywhere. The delicious scent of American coffee made Arden inhale with deep pleasure.

Leila glanced at her uneasily. "Miss Arden, it is my brother who makes this coffee, he must be here. I didn't know. I thought he will be at the mosque with my father. I am sorry, I don't want to put you in difficulty this way—"

A male voice came from the next room, exclaiming in Arabic as the sound from a television rose. Some kind of sports. Leila giggled nervously. "He likes the football—"

Arden clutched the flimsy thobe, feeling her total nakedness underneath, as the voice suddenly changed, coming nearer, speaking to Leila, full of laughter. The speaker came into the kitchen, still talking. He stopped short when he saw Arden.

"*Wullah!*" His hands flew up, his green eyes opened wide and he stepped backwards, bumping into the doorjamb.

Leila spoke quickly. "Faisal, this is my teacher that I told you about her, Miss Arden. Miss Arden, my brother Faisal, that I talked to you about him. Please, excuse for the—for my mistake. I didn't know you will meet in this way."

Faisal stood still as one of their sculptures. His uncovered hair fell in shiny curlicues to his collar. His open-necked thobe showed smooth brown throat. He looked as wild as in the slide of his last excavation. Heat—and apprehension—shivered through Arden. She rolled her sleeves down and lowered her gaze to his bare feet.

"Hello again, Arden," he said slowly, in his soft voice. "Thank you for your friendship to Leila. Welcome to our home."

"Thank you," she murmured. "Happy Eid, Dr. Al Ansary."

"Call me Faisal." She glanced up. His wide eyes were fixed on her.

"Miss Arden, you have to tell us *'Eid de kum mubarak,'* that is how to say it," Leila told her, as if trying to lighten the atmosphere.

"*Eid ... de kum,*" Arden began, immobilized by his stare. She felt a hot flush rising through her body. She wished for her abaya to cover her arousal in front of him. She shifted her feet, looked at the floor, let her hair hide her hot cheeks.

Faisal took a deep breath and let it out in an agitated-sounding whoosh. "Please, sit. I was about to make pancakes. A weekend tradition." He moved to the stovetop, turned on the flame under the griddle, uncovered a bowl of batter on the counter.

"Chocolate chip?" Leila asked, as she and Arden took chairs at the island.

"Of course." Faisal put cups of coffee in front of them. "How did you like the party, Arden?"

"It was wonderful. I especially liked the music."

"She was dancing all the night, just like us." Leila grinned. Arden knew they were both doing their best to put her at ease. "She's as good as Bedouin."

"You must have been to a lot of these parties, then," Faisal said.

"This was my first."

"How are you liking the Kingdom, now you've been here awhile?"

"I love it."

"*Love* it," he repeated, his emphasis sounding ironic. He poured batter, waited, flipped. His economy of movement was satisfying to watch. He probably showed the same physical confidence in everything he did. And what a kick, to see a Saudi man working the stove. "What exactly do you love?"

"My students. Ordinary people. The desert. The language. The prayer calls. Everything. It's beautiful."

When Faisal turned, with a plate of delicious-smelling pancakes, she had to look away from his scrutiny. "You're unusual, Arden." He was probably remembering her bareheaded, confronting the soccer boys. Or the way she boldly clung to his hand that day in his office like a breathless bimbo. "In my experience, most Westerners can't stand it here." He put the plate onto the island, and sat next to Leila.

"Eid de kum mubarak, ya helwa," he told his sister. Happy Eid, sweetheart. His smile was tender as he rubbed Leila's back. They must hear how her heart thudded, seeing his sweetness. Get a grip, she told herself fiercely. She forced a bite of pancake.

"Tell about Haj, ya Faisal," Leila said. "I like to hear you speak English to me."

"You do, huh." His laugh was the low, familiar-sounding chuckle Arden remembered from the museum. She leaned forward. "Haj was the best experience of my life. Or, at least, as good as the Eridu excavation. I'm really glad I did it, Leila. Seeing everyone going around the Grand Mosque—" He nodded slowly. "It was *awesome*. I know you didn't want to make the trip this year, but next year you just have to go."

"That will be good, *ya Hajji* Faisal."

"*Hajji*." He grinned. "I like that." As he took a sip of coffee his eyes, still smiling, met Arden's for a moment. Both glanced quickly away.

"The renovations on the highway outside Makkah were finished, Father said."

"It looked good." He frowned. "Except for all the American troops on the road. I can't get used to seeing them everywhere!" He shook his head. "Like we're occupied. It doesn't feel like the place I used to know."

He sent Arden a quick look. "I like your people, *ya* Arden, but I don't like your soldiers. They don't belong here."

His soft voice became flat. "And I learned in Makkah that Eridu is permanently closed to further excavation." He stared into his coffee. He spoke in Arabic then; it sounded like swearing, to Arden's intuitive ear.

Leila interrupted him, with a glance at Arden. "But Yahia and Mamoud? Were they good, in the travel? Did they bring money or did you have to give them as usual?"

"They haven't changed at all. But it was okay, we got a chance to catch up on the old days." As he and Leila kept talking, Arden studied him. This close, she could see shining glints in the blackness of his hair, and sparkles of a color like gold in his irises. His long lips seemed to kiss his cup. His gesturing hands were nimble. His thobe was identical to the one she was wearing. She imagined his arms inside it, as if encircling her, his heart beating just where hers was.

"Coffee?" Faisal held out the carafe, and, at her nod, reached over to pour some into her cup. His gaze skimmed up Arden's long sleeve, trailing onto her fingertips, to the monogram on the breast pocket. "You took one of my shirts again, *ya* Leila." She felt, suddenly, how her nipples were pressing stiff against the thin cloth as she leaned toward him. Hastily she sat back and crossed her arms.

As hastily, he stood, pushing back his chair and glancing at his watch. "Ladies, I'm back to the soccer game. It was good to see you again, Arden." He walked into the room off the kitchen.

He might have stayed with Leila, had she not been there.

He seemed restrained: maybe because he knew now that she was his sister's teacher; maybe because he was newly religious, having just made his Haj; maybe just because he was a Saudi man. And he was obviously distracted by the bad news about his excavation site, so maybe it was that she was American. Just as well he wasn't friendly anymore, she told herself sadly as she helped Leila clear the island: no relationship between them could be developed here.

"I wash the dishes when Faisal makes pancakes," said Leila.

Arden's pulse slowed as she helped Leila with the small task of loading their huge German dishwasher. She wiped her brow with a shaky hand.

"Faisal will bring you back, Miss Arden. Our driver does not work on Eid. I cannot come with you. I have another Eid party to attend."

Arden would rather walk back to campus than have to sit alone with Faisal for the long drive. How could she share space with him and make light conversation? "But isn't it—not allowed—for me to be alone with a Saudi man?"

"He is doctor with the museum and a good Muslim. Any mutawa don't worry about him. But nobody will be outside today, anyway, nobody work on Eid."

"I'm sure he's busy, Leila. I'll get a taxi. Don't bother him about me."

"Of course you cannot take taxi! That is not permitted. Faisal will do whatever thing I ask." Leila dried her hands and called to Faisal in Arabic. There was a low expression of assent, and Arden must have imagined the reluctance in it, for Leila nodded with satisfaction. "He will be happy to take you. He has to go anyway, he stays there when he has work for university. Is good. In this way you can know him now."

She gave Arden a bag for her last night's sweaty party clothes, and found her abaya and purse. Arden gave her the cookie package. Leila hugged her briefly.

"*Eid de kum mubarak, ya* Miss Arden, I am too happy you stay with us."

"Me too, ya Leila," Arden sighed.

SEVENTEEN

STILL CLAD IN FAISAL'S THOBE, Arden covered herself in her abaya and scarf. She was sure her heart could be seen pounding through the two light fabrics. She waited as a Land Rover came around the long circular drive to the center villa. Faisal jumped out to open the back door for her. He was dressed formally now, aloof, in crisp headdress and an embroidered beige cloak.

She got in and they drove away. Pearl Jam's "Vitalogy" was blasting from the speakers. Faisal was the only careful Saudi driver she had seen; he stopped at the lights and used his signal and merged when it was his turn. They drove for some blocks in silence, except for Eddie Vedder's lilting growl. Faisal switched lanes as they entered the highway, and sped up then so quickly that she was pushed back against her seat. Now they were on the outskirts of the desert, dun colors flying past in a blur.

She noted the absence of sunshine, again.

"Will it rain today?"

"Maybe a sandstorm today, rain in a couple of days. We might get another holiday this week. A day off to pray for rain."

"A *rain* day!" The idea tickled her.

His lips curved. "The King does it every year about this time."

"*Alhamdulillah.*"

"Your accent is good."

"I just imitate what I hear."

"But you probably don't get much practice here. Everyone speaks English."

"Speak in Arabic to me," she told him, inspired.

"What do you want me to talk about?" he asked in Arabic. He sounded different, intimate, but she knew he could have announced traffic signs and it would have sounded intimate to her.

She leaned forward, thinking of how to respond, wanting to know all about him. "You and Leila," she began, speaking carefully. "Your eyes?" She didn't know how to say 'unusual.'

"Leila and I have different mothers," he explained. Arden was used to that from her girls—entire families were created by serial marriages. Modern Saudi men seemed not to take simultaneous wives, as was the stereotype, but sequential ones. "My father's first wife, my mother, is American. Leila's mother died years ago."

"Very sad. Leila—very little girl." She could not, in Arabic, adequately express her sympathy. "I am sorry."

"You like my sister."

"I like her much."

"She's talked about you. She thinks you're a good teacher."

She felt a pleased flush spread on her face. "Thank you, for that nice talk." Her Arabic was so rudimentary that she had to laugh a little as she said this.

"She likes the way you play music in class."

"My banjo, yes, to teach songs to students. I like play with Bedouin women from party of last night."

His laugh was startled, genuine. "*Ya salaam*, that might be hard to arrange, but I could get their number, you can call them."

Arden had to resort to English to respond. "I'd love that. I really miss my band."

"You have a band? A banjo band?"

"Bluegrass, yes."

"Like … country? Or folk?"

She launched into 'Wildwood Flower' but it wasn't the same without strings.

"You sing very well."

"I sing better with my band. Or even just with my banjo."

"What was your band called?"

"No Requests."

He laughed again. "Why didn't you want to play requests?"

"The audience always wants the same numbers. We don't get the chance to do much new music if we take requests." She was using present tense, she realized. It was surprising she could talk to him like this.

"Who was in your band?"

"Dave on guitar, Ellen on base, Doc on fiddle and sometimes washboard or spoons. He's real versatile."

All bluegrass bands seemed to have a member called Doc. Probably after Doc Watson, one of her banjo heroes and a legendary bluegrass figure.

"It must have been hard to leave them behind."

"I don't think I knew how hard."

He nodded. Was it hard for him to leave California, she wondered, had he left something dear behind? Maybe someone?

Faisal switched from Pearl Jam to the Chili Peppers. The scenery rolled into the long stretch of bare, hilly desert. After a time she asked, "Have you done digs here?"

"There's so much new construction, it's hard to recognize. Sometimes I look at the ruins around Dirraiyeh. That's where we live, you know, where the new campus is being built."

"I didn't see any ruins."

"They're pretty far from the housing. It's the site of Ibn Saud's first fort. I could take you over there some time." After a moment he added, "With some of the other teachers, of course."

Of course.

He knew they were not supposed to be alone. He probably knew how much of a risk this ride would be, on a day of normal traffic and vigilant mutawas.

She expanded on their common ground. "You should know, Faisal, one of the reasons Al Issam questioned me, that day you invited me to sit in your office, was to ask who in my class was interested in Salman Rushdie."

His gaze shot to hers in the rearview mirror. "I think I can guess who."

"Leila needs to be very careful at school."

"But ... you didn't name her."

"Of course not!"

"*Alhamdulillah*." A moment passed before he said, "Thank you for that, ya Arden, I'm grateful. It was risky for you to protect her."

"She doesn't deserve that kind of scrutiny. It seemed so creepy."

"There are spies everywhere." His shoulders rose as he hauled forth a long disgusted-sounding exhalation. "It never ends."

Never ends? "So ... how do you deal with it, in your classes?"

"I stick to basic scientific facts. But I had to learn again, this year, how to keep quiet here. The students know. They tend to censor each other." He glanced at her again. "Don't you notice that?"

She nodded, thinking of Princess Khadijah and her subduing effect on the girls, even before Arden's cautionary speech, and of Feiruz' ever-watchful yet sleepy-seeming eyes.

Her sigh came deep, and louder than she was ready for. As loud as his.

Faisal laughed briefly. "It gets to me too. I forgot, in the States, how repressive we are. And you teach English composition, so you probably want more freedom of expression." He shifted gears to accelerate again, and she touched her seatbelt, seeing the blur out the window intensify.

"Sometimes I feel it's wearing me out. I try to keep things fresh, keep the girls active, but it's hard." Admitting this made the oppression seem more real, and even harder to combat. "I mean, we concentrate on writing, some reading. We discuss different topics. And I play lots of songs that stimulate discussion. But there are no more Salman Rushdie mentions, for sure."

A slow smile lit his face, and she saw clearly, in the lines of his features, how much it was his customary expression. "Have you read *Satanic Verses*?"

"No." In her Columbus life? As if!

"I thought it was pretty slow going. Long-winded."

"You … didn't think it was heresy?"

"It's fiction." He shrugged. "One man's imagination. How could it insult an entire faith? If the faith is strong?"

"Then why do you think there was such controversy over it?"

"Controversy can provide a useful distraction."

"Distraction from what?"

His eyes met hers for a moment. "Well, perhaps, from other sorts of issues. Maybe. It's just a thought."

His suddenly cautious tone discouraged further exploration. She settled back, disappointed. The conversation had just gotten interesting, the first of its kind she'd had with a Saudi, the open kind she'd hoped to have with him. They roared on through the desert. How fast could a Land Rover go, anyway? He had seemed safe in his neighborhood, but now the vehicle was vibrating beneath them. The speedometer was edging toward 200 kilometers.

"Do we have to go so fast?" she blurted, and immediately regretted it. Any Ohio guy, driving, would diss her nervousness.

"Sorry." He slowed. "I know this road too well. I could drive it blind. I usually try to make it in twenty minutes." On the bus it took an hour.

"There are so many accidents."

"We don't have many driving restrictions."

"Just women restrictions?"

"Actually, I take Leila out driving sometimes, at night. She puts on my ghutra, and she flies! Driving fast is a great way to let off steam here."

Leila, driving in Riyadh, in Faisal's headdress! She couldn't contain a laugh. "Isn't that against the law for women? Against Islam?"

"Nothing to do with Islam! The driving thing is just more of our nonsense."

"So then why ... "

"Do you know the Quran, Arden?"

"I'm reading it." She quipped, sure now that he wouldn't take offense, "There's nothing in there about driving!"

His lips twitched. "No, you won't find any suras referring to cars. Or even oil."

"Thanks for cluing me in," she told him, grinning. "I've been wanting to find a Muslim to check with."

"There are lots of us here." He flicked her a wry look.

"I mean, someone who isn't one of my students," she said seriously. "I'd like to learn more about Islam but I haven't met many Saudis to really talk to."

"You haven't met Saudis in Saudi Arabia?" he asked, with obvious irony. "Do you just hang out with the other Westerners?"

"I don't seem to have a lot in common with the expatriates," she confided. "I thought I could make Saudi friends. But it's not easy. So far I only met one woman on campus who could be a friend. She's teaching me Arabic, except we usually speak English." She thought of Rowda's recent overture. "She asked me over, but it felt a little awkward. But I'd like to go. I'd like to see her face."

"You should visit her." He glanced again at her in the rearview. "Otherwise your life here could get lonely. I remember feeling alone in the States, when I first went to college, even though I'd visited my mother there for years. It's hard being in a different culture, if you don't like the other expatriates and you can't get close to the natives."

His openness allowed her to admit, "It has been a little lonely. I was so excited to be included in Leila's party."

"Come anytime. Maybe I can give you a ride." He frowned suddenly. "Or maybe not. You know how it is here. But I'm really glad you're Leila's teacher."

"Thank you." His easy acceptance was so welcome that she had to stop herself from reaching to pat his shoulder in gratitude. "So you and Leila, did you know each other well, when you were young? Since you had different parents."

"Very well. We're my father's only children. Leila was born when I was eight."

"Did you live here all your life?"

"Yes. When I was about twelve I started spending summers in California, in Big Sur, where my mother lives. Sometimes Leila came too. I went to college in the States, finished my doctorate at Berkeley this last summer."

"So you're here to stay?"

"This is where my work is. How about you? How'd you choose the Kingdom, of all places for a young American woman?" The lines around his eyes crinkled. "I mean, I grew up here, and *I'm* having a hard time getting used to it again."

"I wondered about that," she began hesitantly, wanting to ask more, unsure if she was free to. "How does your country seem to you, after so many years in America?"

His face smoothed. He flipped his headdress back. When he finally answered, it was with a deliberation that sounded rehearsed. "I love the Museum of Antiquities. Every summer during my doctorate I came to promote archaeology here. Our committee worked so hard to get approval to show the exhibits."

"Approval?"

He glanced once. She waited for him to continue.

"Our finds are pre-Islamic. So we needed permission to present them, and we had to tie their significance to progress in the Kingdom. I think we've done ... rather well."

She tried to gauge the feeling behind his careful words. Did he resent having to get approval to show his work? But she shouldn't expect him to express any resentment. After all, she was a stranger to him, a Westerner whose judgment would not be welcome. She'd seen that attitude in her students whenever she pressed close to an analysis of their society. They could analyze; she should not.

"The exhibit is marvelous," she said finally.

"You didn't tell me, Arden, what brought you here, so far from your band?"

"I thought it would be an adventure." She confided what she would never have told another Saudi, wanting to make him laugh, "And I *really* needed the money."

"Ah! The money." He chuckled. "So, it's good?"

"Yes. *Shukran.*" Thank you. She grinned, and their eyes met in mutual amusement.

"And ... an adventure? I guess it must be. You said you love it."

"It's very interesting." *Especially this afternoon.*

"I never heard your name before. Arden. It's pretty."

Now we're getting somewhere. "It's from West Virginia."

"West Virginia." He squinted as if trying to see a map. "South of ... New York?"

"I thought you were half American!"

"That half is geographically challenged. Of course." He shot her a teasing look that was just like Leila's, when she was trying to rattle the class. "So you're from West Virginia?"

"Ohio. It's one state over. To the west."

"You reminded me of California, when we met."

"You remember that day?"

"Sure I do. I'd just arrived from San Francisco. I came out of the masjid and there you were, looking so out of place with all your hair loose." His low laugh made this a friendly comment. "I liked seeing you blow off the kids with that kick. You're fearless."

Heat rose in her as their gaze held. His face slowly, sweetly creased into the smiling pattern that now seemed so familiar. She wondered how he would react if she put a hand on the seatback, just to rest casually near his shoulder. She could run one quiet finger down a fold of his long headdress. He might not even notice, if she moved carefully. Then he turned his eyes to the road, breaking their moment. She looked again out the window. She saw that it had grown darker, that there seemed to be mist in the air.

"Is it raining now?" Maybe rain looked like mist here?

"No. This is a khamseen. Sandstorm." He flicked on the windshield wipers and they made a grinding noise. "I'm pulling over. It's safer if we stop."

EIGHTEEN

THEY CAREENED OFF the highway and bounced over to stop into a small dip of dune. "There's a stake and hammer in the back, Arden, could you pass them?"

She turned around to find a thin, pointed metal pole with a red flag tied on its tip, and a thick wooden mallet. He whipped off his headdress and wrapped it around his nose and mouth, fastening the ends securely, turning himself into a bandit. Wild ringlets sprang out around his head.

"I'm going to mark the road," he told her in a muffled voice.

He peeled off his cloak and got out with the pole and mallet, slamming the door, but not before she heard a fine whistling that rose with the mist. It grew darker. She could barely see the white of his thobe, bent against the wind, as he made his way to the highway. She caught a glimpse of him, between gusts of what looked like smoke, pounding the stake down into the sand, then struggling back to the Land Rover. The wind wailed when he opened the front door.

He unwrapped his headdress, using the ends to wipe his eyes, and she saw it was as caked with dust as his face and hair. "Hand me a water bottle?"

There was a case of plastic water bottles in the space behind her, as well as a container of what she realized were emergency supplies: cans of food, chocolate bars, flashlight, road flares, blankets, tarps.

Arden's concern at this find must have shown when she turned back to him with the water bottle, for he said, after taking a long drink, "I've been through so many of these, it's boring. You saw how fast the storm came up? They pass just as quickly and then it rains, a miracle from heaven, *Alhamdulillah*. The biggest risk is having someone drive into you by mistake. That's why we're well away from the road."

But there was the increasing noise of the wind, and the growing blackness outside, and the thin line of sand creeping up the windshield. She hated violent weather, ever since a tornado blew through Columbus three summers ago and flattened half their block. This storm was alien and terrifying and so freakishly sudden. The sky was a bilious green. They might have been on Mars. A sudden gust rocked the vehicle, smashing sand against her window.

"*Ya* Arden. Don't be afraid." He leaned his arm over the seatback to address her. His voice was as steady as his gaze, as solid as touch. She tried to find, in his filthy face, a light out of the howling darkness around them. "This is bad, but I've been through a lot worse. We'll be fine. I promise you."

He reached into the glove compartment and brought out a well-used pack of cards. "Crazy Eights, come on, you deal." He handed them to her cold fingers and she fumbled to open them, remembering what a card game was.

They managed a game, trading cards over the seatback. The rigidity in her spine lessened as she was forced to concentrate and count. And Faisal kept her busy taking things from the back space—a box of dates and a bar of chocolate they shared, a water bottle he insisted she drink, a flashlight they used when it grew too dark to see.

He told her about his worst khamseen, during an excavation, when his team had collected all their finds in one place and covered themselves with a tarp, crouching over the pile. "We didn't want to lose one sherd! We cared more about those old broken pots than about being able to breathe!" His humor let her relax a little more.

Finally, after what seemed like hours had passed, the shrieking of the wind died down. As the sky lightened the sand subsided, and she was amazed to watch the first raindrops hit the windshield and gather strength, carving little rivers into the accumulated sand. The water seemed truly a miracle.

"*Bismillah a raman u rahim.*" Faisal turned away, poured a little water onto his headdress, which he used to clean his hands and face. He lowered his head and murmured in Arabic, a low rapid chanting that she realized must be prayer. She shuffled cards quietly so as not to disturb him. The rain intensified, its force as strong as the sand had been, its power washing off the windshield completely. She could see the stake now, its red flag flapping like a beacon. Water poured down in gusty sheets.

"Will there be a flash flood?" she asked, when he stopped praying.

"No. The desert drinks the water right away. I'll show you, afterwards." As they watched, the rain lessened to a thin patter and stopped. "I'm going to dig us out."

He wrapped the headdress around his face again, climbed out, fetched a shovel from the trunk and began to chop at the wheels. The sight jarred in Arden the memory of winter. She had shoveled herself out of a drift many a time back in Columbus; she could help. She could prove she was more than a shrinking violet.

She took her shoes off and got out, and immediately sank in loose sand up to her ankles. The wind was still blowing sand around and a gust of wet grainy dust flung itself into her face. Her abaya twisted around her head in the rising wind, and she tried to flap it up so she could see where the bumper was. Now she understood why he'd taken off his cloak. She peeled off her abaya. The wind billowed it away, and whipped sand into her cheek, stinging like a slap. She covered her face with her hands and sank to her knees, thinking she could avoid the loosest sand by staying low, where the ground was damp, but the curling wind swirled another wave at her.

Arden stumbled to her feet, reaching for the Land Rover, but she was lost in the maelstrom. She gasped for breath and sucked what felt like fine needles straight into her lungs. Panic struck as instantly as the sharp pain. She coughed, fruitlessly.

Then a strong arm encircled her waist. "You're right next to the door," Faisal said in her ear. "I'm opening it for you."

He pushed her into the seat and climbed in beside her. The water he splashed quickly into her eyes, and wiped off with his fingers, took the worst of the sand from them. He snatched her scarf off her head, poured water onto it, and mopped her face, scrubbing her nose, mouth and ears as if she were a child. The sand scraped her skin and she jerked away from his cleaning. She covered her face, coughing into her hands, feeling the sand creep down her throat with every breath. Gently he pried her hands away, to tilt water into her mouth.

"Don't swallow. Just rinse, and spit." The kindness in his voice turned her cough into a sob, but the tears helped clear her eyes and nose. She spat sand into her scarf and doubled over, clutching her knees. He wrapped one arm tight around her back and rocked her against him, firmly, until her gasping slowed.

Faisal let go then. "What were you *doing* out there?" His soft voice barely contained the urgency of his question.

She sat up. "I thought I could help." Her voice was still sand-clogged.

"But it's too dangerous, you're not used to this. Khamseens can kill. The dust gets in the lungs, and suffocates. We lost a guy once, a Danish researcher, when he went out uncovered. He didn't go far, he was away from us only minutes. He died here." He spoke to himself, low, in Arabic. Then he looked at her, and reached out a hand, before he let it fall. "I'm so sorry, *ya* Arden. Are you okay?"

She nodded.

He looked out the window. "I'm going out again. *Don't* follow me."

She huddled against the window, still feeling shaken, and now humiliated. He thought she was an awful ninny. Her throat was raw and her face throbbed. It hurt to breathe. She wondered if they would ever make it out of here. If the sand covered the road completely? Could Faisal, for all his skills, shovel a path through dunes from here to campus? And the engine might not even work. She stared at the keys, thinking to lean over and try the ignition. They had enough water to last them a few days, what then?

But he'd hammered down the stake. He'd brought supplies. He'd cleaned her up with a relaxed, routine expertise. He'd probably saved her life.

Faisal opened her door and she peered outside.

"Come out," he said. "I want to show you something." The air was soft now, clean, still, but she could not move. He insisted, "Come on, don't miss this. You won't see it often. It'll make you feel better about the desert." He reached out a hand. She took it and followed him, covering her mouth with her other hand, to the top of the shallow depression they had parked in.

"Now look over there, Arden."

There was a golden glaze on the sand in front of them, as if the sun were setting, but when she peered closer she saw that hundreds of miniscule yellow flowers had risen up from the bare ground not far from where her wet abaya lay, arms flung wide like a black snow angel. Sand angel.

She knelt down, studying the flowers closely, leaning to see if they had a scent. A faint, delicate fragrance emanated toward her. She ran her hands lightly over them, feeling their dew, and brought her hands to her face. Their fragility made some of the tiny petals cling to her palms. She breathed in their cleanliness.

A final soft sweep of raindrops pattered, pasting his robe to her skin. She laughed, feeling the shiver of cool wet that confirmed she had outlasted the storm, feeling as triumphant as the first bird bringing proof of land back to the Ark.

She rose and turned to Faisal.

As she staggered toward him in the humid sand, damp robe dragging at her feet, his expression seemed to mirror her own wonder at the phenomenon of the flowers. She held out her hands, wanting him to see her petaled palms.

"Look," she told him. "Look what stayed on my hands."

He looked.

The drizzle streaked his face to dusty stripes and dripped from his grimy hair in gray trickles onto his thobe; his once-white headdress hung limp around his sand-encrusted neck, but all she saw was his beauty. She came closer, wanting to touch him, thinking that she would; she could use their survival as a reason to embrace him; surely that was permitted, even in this rigid culture?

"*Ya* Faisal." She stepped into him and slid her arms around his waist, intending a quick hug, but her pretext of gratitude instantly scorched into desire and she tightened her embrace. His throat warmed her cheek. She could almost taste the rain on his skin. She felt their hearts' thudding separated by thin cloth.

His chest heaved against hers in a sharp intake of breath, and he stiffened so abruptly that she was pulled even closer to him, momentarily. She felt his hands tighten, briefly, on her waist, but in her excitement she could not tell if he was holding her for balance or in correspondence.

Then he firmly grasped her elbows to push her away. He stepped back. He did not look at her, but his eyes were wide with something even deeper than shock. He turned and walked swiftly toward the open desert. She could barely see him as he sank into the sand several ridges away.

How did he know it was prayer time?

She dropped her hands, crushing the few remaining petals into fists. She watched him, chastened by the self-

contained white heap he made, then unpeeled her abaya
from the sand and made her way back to the Land Rover.

NINETEEN

S HE SHOOK OUT HER ABAYA, scraping off sand. She used her brush to get some order into her hair. She scrubbed off the sand still clinging to her lips, from his neck, and put on lipstick. She covered the robe, stuck to her like a second skin, with last night's crumpled satin blouse. Then she arranged her abaya, tying it tight around her. She couldn't wear the ruined scarf. She was still grubby, but at least she felt pulled together, able to put on a cool face in front of him.

Craving, mixed with despair, pooled in her pelvis and shortened her breath: unwanted flame licking from inside out. She clenched her hands into fists again and pounded her knees, trying to beat it away, but she felt it sinking into her skin like the worst case of poison ivy.

She had no right to be drawn to him, no matter how intimate their time in the khamseen, no matter how smart, kind, interesting, and beautiful he was. And now she had blown any chance of friendship with him, and perhaps even sullied her reputation as his sister's teacher. Why had she dared to touch him? *I know better! I do!*

Her throat closed with anxious tears. She swallowed. Her esophagus burned.

But he'd handled her too; he'd crossed that prohibited line first, grabbing her out of the storm, cleaning her off, rocking her in the car like a baby; he'd offered his hand to encourage her outside. Those could be construed as signs of—of familiarity, so how could she be rejected for assuming a quick hug would be okay? Why should it offend him so? *What a prude he is,* she told herself, miserably, knowing there had been no lust in his gestures; *what a hypocrite.*

She took a shaky breath, and tried to find solace in the changing light on the desert, a glorious panorama now of gold, rose, cream and gray. She could not tell what time it was. Late afternoon? No other vehicles had yet passed. She looked at their red-tipped marker and wondered again about the condition of the road, whether they'd be able to drive out of here. She eyed the keys dangling from the ignition. Maybe she should see if she could start the engine.

He returned before she could even try the stick shift. He simply opened the door, waiting for her to exit the driver's seat. When she reluctantly got out, he stepped well away from her. Unnecessarily. *I got the message, ya mister,* she thought in irritation, as she climbed once more into the back, *I'll never lay a hand on you again.*

"You'll have a good sandstorm story to tell the folks back home," he said when he got in. His tone was light. Obviously they were not going to discuss her hug. He did not look at her. A sprinkling of petals clung to his shoulders where her hands had clutched.

She had not thought of 'folks back home' in weeks. "This is home now." She listened to the way that sounded. "Thanks for showing me the flowers, by the way. They were really cool." She made her tone match his in lightness.

"That's a sight all visitors should see. It happens in the States, too. I've seen it on the Mojave, in the Joshua Tree area."

"You must have found Native American archaeology pretty interesting." Good; she was managing to sound very calm.

"Fascinating. Great design, in tools, weaving, household objects—everything, really. Very intricate." As he spoke, he stared out at the road. "Mexico, Guatemala and Peru, too, incredible cultures in the Americas. I loved my visits there."

"Did you learn some Spanish?"

"*Un poquito,*" he said in an accent so cute she had to laugh. He opened his window to peer outside.

"What are you looking for?"

"The plows. Shouldn't be long." He twisted out, looking behind them. "Yeah, here they come."

A fleet of three groaning, clanking trucks, with John Deere-style bifurcated plows attached to their front bumpers, were lumbering up the highway from Riyadh. Arden watched, astonished, as they scraped the sand drifts to both sides of the road. Sparks flew from the friction of steel on sandy asphalt. The noise was excruciating, she could feel the vibrations grating in her still-gritty teeth, but the sight was welcome.

Faisal walked to the marker and yanked it out, pulling with both hands, but she would not let his easy strength impress her now. He waved to the first plow driver, who waved back. He brought the stake back to the Land Rover and threw it into the trunk.

As soon as the last plow passed, he drove over the series of small bumpy sand ridges to the road. He sped up until they were right behind the last plow. Just what she did after a snowstorm. Following closely in its wake prevented new drifts created by the plow, on both sides of the highway, from blowing back into their path.

"This reminds me of Ohio in winter."

His smile was a faint imitation of before. "We import the plows from John Deere—isn't that in Ohio?"

"Illinois, I think."

"I've skied in snow. Never driven in it, though."

"It's probably not as treacherous as sand. The weight of the car pushes the snow down, and after awhile it melts under lots of traffic." She saw her street in Columbus, after a snowfall, the trees hung with heavy white grace; she heard the quiet whisper of small clumps of snow dropping under their own weight. Sudden homesickness gripped her as tightly as the sand still gripped the back of her throat.

The plow in front of them slowed to a stop. Faisal lowered his window and peered out. The plow driver leaped down and ran ahead to the first plow. Faisal got out, snatched a water bottle, and sprinted after him, thobe flying.

Now what? She examined, through the window, the sand on the ground immediately outside, gauging its ability not to whip up and suffocate her again. But the wind had died, and the men hadn't covered their faces, so it must be safe. She got out, cautious, covering her nose and mouth with her hand, and padded up barefoot to where they had gone.

In front of the first plow a car was stalled.

The men clustered around it, apparently advising the driver, but the engine sounded dead to her. When Arden approached, the plow drivers turned, then stared as if she had appeared out of thin air like an Arabian *djinn,* or evil spirits. The outrage in their faces almost looked like fright. Faisal, conferring with the car driver, turned to see what they were exclaiming over. When he saw her, his eyes opened as wide as theirs.

He spoke to them rapidly, then motioned her over to the back door of the car.

"*Ya* Arden, would you help this lady and her baby to our Rover, and give them some water? They're dehydrated." As she approached, he said quietly, "I told them you're a doctor. That's the only excuse for you to be outside like this. Take them back quickly and stay there. And please, *ya salaam,* cover your hair!"

Who did he think he was, snapping at her in that clipped tone? He'd been the one to wreck her scarf, telling her to spit in it, she wasn't about to put it back on. But she leaned in to the shrouded woman in the back, reaching to take the baby she was holding. She hoped his mom had supplies. Even Boy Scout Faisal would not have diapers stashed in his cavernous trunk.

The men turned away as the woman climbed out, stumbling in tiny heels in the thick sand. She clutched a baby bag. Arden held out one of her own bare feet, wiggling it slightly to indicate this was the only way to walk under the circumstances, and the woman slipped her shoes off and carried them. They made their way back to the Land Rover. Arden climbed in front so the woman could have some privacy in back to nurse, and some space to change the baby.

"What's his name?" she asked in Arabic.

"Hamid."

They got acquainted. Asia and her husband Musa were on their way to an Eid party at the campus where his brother lived. The khamseen had stranded them, and she was very grateful to Allah, and to the other men, and to Arden's husband. Their showing up was a gift from Allah. She thanked Allah for his mercy, and so forth.

Arden let the 'husband' assumption stand, for propriety's sake.

"Does Hamid look sick to you?" Asia asked anxiously, holding him up for Arden's view, peering intently through her veil.

"I don't know," Arden answered, startled. The boy was gumming intently at his pacifier, looking as darling as a cherub, obviously content and dust-free.

"But your husband said you're a doctor."

"Not a doctor for babies." *No, I'm a bloody brain surgeon. Anyone need a lobotomy?* "But he looks fine to me," she added quickly.

Faisal returned, grease-smeared from head to toe, only recognizable by his eyes. His headdress was a blackened shred falling off his shoulder. Musa had obviously not joined him in trying to fix the engine—he was still pristine. Once back on the road, they passed the couple's forlorn car, pushed to the side by a plow and looking worse for it. Faisal and Musa chatted quietly, ignoring the women.

The campus was no more than ten minutes' drive down the highway. A haze lingered, the final flurry of khamseen. The few buildings looked flimsy, easily swallowed by one blast of the wind she'd seen on the highway, and she wondered what would be left for future archaeologists, Faisal's progeny, to unearth from the rubble. Some perfume bottles, maybe, a few Khalid CDs. This Land Rover, probably. Dust to dust.

"I want to invite you and your husband for dinner soon, to thank you for your great kindness," Asia told her quietly.

"Oh."

"I like to have interesting friends come to my house, and you are an unusual couple," Asia continued. "You are American, but your husband is Saudi?"

"Well…"

"And you're a doctor, that is very good. You are a strong woman." Asia looked at her. "Your husband is a … mechanic?" Her tone was doubtful. Educated Saudis were not mechanics, and did not, as a rule, do any physical labor.

Arden shrugged. She didn't know how to say 'archaeologist.' She didn't know how to correct Asia's conclusions without more explanation than she could muster.

They stopped at Musa's brother's apartment. As Faisal got out to say goodbye to Musa, his glance seemed to snag on the sight of Arden, holding little Hamid out to Asia. A few final words were exchanged, and the couple went upstairs.

Faisal stood watching them go, seeming unwilling to get back into the vehicle with her still sitting in the back. Fine, she'd get out. Her apartment was around the corner. She grabbed her purse.

"Thanks for the lift, ya buddy," she told him, climbing down. "Thanks for saving my life, too. See you around." She started toward her building. Then she thought of a parting shot, and turned back. He was leaning against the Rover, arms folded, staring at the ground, looking wiped out, muckier than a chimney sweep.

"Faisal, if that nice couple follows up on their dinner invitation to us, you tell them I can't make it. I'll be at the hospital, delivering babies."

The corner of his mouth tilted, but he did not look at her, nor answer.

Afraid to keep talking, she turned and walked away.

TWENTY

S HE WENT STRAIGHT to her bathroom and turned on the shower. Her face in the mirror was streaked with dirt, her eyes sunken holes, her hair plastered into thin strings, her skin red as if sunburned.

Horrible! No wonder he doesn't want me.

She sniffed fiercely and peeled off her clothing, stiff with dust, wondering how she could even wash it without wrecking the machine and the fabric. Part of her wanted to keep Faisal's thobe, because it was his, wanted to fold it under her pillow so she could dream of him every night.

She tossed it in the trash along with her scarf and abaya.

The hot water soothed her aching muscles and scratched skin. She closed her eyes and let it pour over her, remembering the feeling of light cool rain out there on the highway, the wonderful sense of revival she'd felt then as it covered her. She could keep that sense. She could be glad to be alive and not have to share the feeling, could recall the wild blossoms and let the memory bring its own joy. She would just delete him, and her reaching for him, and his withdrawal, from all those scenes.

She wrapped herself in a towel and stepped into her bedroom to dress. As she pulled on clean underwear, she saw, with utter clarity, the bag sitting on the floor of his Land Rover with her bra, panties, and skirt from last night. *Oh great. Just the kind of souvenir a religious fellow will appreciate. God dammit.* She would have to retrieve them somehow, get Leila aside and ask discreetly for their return. If it were just her stuff she wouldn't care, but Evelyn would want the velvet skirt back.

As if reading her mind, the phone rang. It was Evelyn, in fact, telling her that there was to be a splendid Eid party at Ali's palace, to which Arden was invited, of course, but could she please get her skirt back right away? The little dry cleaner on campus was closed for Eid and Evelyn's other long party skirt was locked inside.

"Well, it's awfully wrinkled," Arden warned, stalling for time.

"Velvet doesn't wrinkle, dear, I'll just hang it in the shower. It will steam fresh."

"The truth, Evelyn, I left it in the car of this guy who gave me a ride back."

"Oh." Said with about five rising and falling syllables.

"I mean, I took it off last night, and then brought it back but I forgot—"

Evelyn was arch. "No need to go into details, Arden. *Been* there."

"I didn't take it off on purpose, not what you think, I mean—"

"So is it lost to him forever?"

"He lives here on campus. Maybe I can get it."

"Thanks Arden, there's a love, and anyway it'll give you another chance to say hallo to him. Want to bring him along tonight?"

"No! It's not like that! He's a good Muslim."

"They all are, darling! You can tell me about it when you bring the skirt round."

Arden sighed, dressed with care in one of her formal suits, put on the headscarf she'd brought with her from the States, and went into the living room where the bilingual campus directory was kept. He was right there in the A's. He lived in the next building! She'd just go over and check out the parking lot. Saudis never locked up anything—she could probably get her bag from the Rover without him even knowing she'd been there. Or she'd knock on his door, ask politely for his keys, pick up her bag, get out of his hair forever. Simple.

She was at his door in minutes after a frustrating stop at the parking lot: he was enough of an American to lock his Rover.

Faisal opened the door, talking on a mobile phone. He had just showered, too—a towel was draped over one shoulder and his hair hung in shining curls that dampened the collar of his clean thobe. His eyes widened when he saw her.

Her mouth and hands felt suddenly dry, then wet.

"I'll call you back," he told the phone in Arabic. He clicked off. He looked around her, into the empty hallway, then motioned for her to enter quickly, and shut the door behind her. "Arden, you can't visit me alone. Do you know what my neighbors would think of you?" His soft voice was an astonished hiss. He backed away from her as if she frightened him. "Are you out of your mind?"

Yes. She turned, to the living room, and sank boneless onto the one space on his couch, probably where he usually sat, that was not covered with papers and magazines.

"This is really risky. This is ... like going out unprotected in the khamseen." He put his phone onto a table, glaring at her. "Are you always so impulsive?"

"I just need my bag."

"Your what?"

"I left my bag in your car." She couldn't bear to watch him anymore. "Just give me the keys and I'll get it, and I'll leave you."

"You had to come to me, alone, for this? You couldn't call, or ask Leila?" He seemed to be getting more irritated with everything she said.

"My friend needs her skirt."

"Skirt?" He flung a hand. "Never mind. I don't want to know." He threw the towel onto a chair and walked down his short hallway. She heard him muttering in Arabic, then a jangling of keys. He came out with his head dressed.

"You stay here. I'll bring the bag." He did not quite slam the door.

Arden drew a shaky breath and looked around. His apartment was bursting with energy and color. The magazines were in English, Arabic, French, German, other languages she didn't know—with covers showing caves, pottery, bones, pyramids. The floor was overlaid with a thick vivid carpet and there were blow-up framed photos on the walls, more caves and pottery. Books were piled everywhere.

The Smashing Pumpkins, from hidden speakers, sang about cool kids in 1979. There was a wonderful view of the desert out the windows, just now ablaze with sunset, the dust still in the air lending crimson shades of brilliance that lit the sky. Another miraculous gift, brought to you by Allah: no getting away from Him. The radiating sight stung her eyes and she blinked water out of them. She leaned her forehead onto her clasped hands, as if in prayer, and Faisal found her that way on his return.

"Here." He tossed the bag at her feet, and stood by the door, holding it open.

Getting off his couch seemed to take all her strength.

"Are you ... all right?"

She nodded, looking at the floor, rubbing her burning eyes.

Faisal must have thought she was crying. He closed the door. His sigh sounded annoyed. "I know this afternoon was traumatic for you." He ran a hand up into his headdress and, with an impatient gesture, pulled it off and dropped it onto the chair where he'd thrown the towel. "I meant to talk to you, anyway, about the khamseen. Sit down, please. I'll bring you a drink."

She leaned back and loosened her scarf, which felt too tight around her neck. She heard him clattering in the kitchen. His apartment was identical to hers, to everyone's; she knew exactly where everything was. The fridge door opened, the milk came out. The kettle was lifted, the tea poured. He took a tray from the cupboard nearest the window. Of course, the ubiquitous tin of biscuits. She stacked papers at one end of the coffee table and cleared the couch. The Pumpkins sang about Chicago.

Faisal set the tray on the table and sat next to her. He took a remote out of his pocket and clicked it toward the CD player, turning the music down.

"I'm sorry I was rude when you showed up." He poured her tea from a small red pot. Pushed the tin of biscuits toward her. "It's just, you *have* to think before you act here. The way things are perceived, an unmarried man and woman alone, you know what it means in this society? Didn't they tell you before you came?"

Arden nodded, sipped. She kept her gaze on the table, but she felt his on her.

She watched his hands pick up the pot and pour into his own cup. His nails were scrubbed free of grease. The fine, sparse black hairs on his hands and wrists looked soft next to crisp white sleeves. She noted again that he wore no watch or rings. His cologne was unique; she recalled its scent from his passing her at the museum.

She pushed her cup away. This close to him, she couldn't swallow.

If she were to reach for a biscuit she could touch his hand, as if by accident, just brush lightly against his fingers. She clenched her hands together to keep them still. Keeping her head bent was making her scarf slip off her hair, but she didn't reach to tie it.

"You know how I admire your courage, how grateful I am for your loyalty to Leila." He picked out three biscuits from the tin, dipped one in his tea, munched it. "You have a strong spirit." He pushed her cup back toward her. "Drink."

She unwrapped one hand to take the cup.

"So, what I wanted to say. Arden. After the storm, that was ... reaction." *He thinks that's why I hugged him.* "Just weather. You understand that, right?"

She finally looked up. One corner of his lips lifted. His gaze was as steady as it had been during the storm, when he'd diluted her anxiety just by looking at her. She got lost in the shadowy greenish depth of his iris, wondering what such a color was called, seeing his pupils expand as she watched. Couldn't she stay, just for awhile? They didn't have to speak. She wouldn't threaten him with another touch. Her breathing slowed and her hands unclenched.

Faisal blinked slowly. His eyebrows pulled together as a confused cloud seemed to cross his face, erasing his composure. His gaze moved from her eyes to her mouth, following the fall of her now-uncovered hair down her shoulder and breast, traveling over the rest of her body, and then slowly back up to her eyes.

She felt unearthed, one of his excavated finds; felt herself flowing toward him, encompassed by his scrutiny. The couch sank as he leaned closer, almost imperceptibly, as their stare deepened.

His shoulder had just barely touched hers when he straightened up.

"See what I mean," he said quietly. "This is just, after a khamseen." He took a breath. "It's easy to get confused." He pushed a hand into his hair. "But this is not going to happen between us."

He collected their tea on the tray, quickly, and stood up with it, like a rude American instead of his hospitable countrymen. He went into the kitchen and she heard him putting things away.

She pressed her lips tight, willing herself to stand, pick up her bag. She turned at the door to look at him. He was standing by the kitchen, holding the tray in front of him like a shield. "If we'd met in the States," she began, hesitantly.

"We're not in America." He kept his head down.

"But we can at least be friends?" She reminded him, "You were friendly, before."

"I know," he said, low. "That was my mistake. I ... forget where I am when I'm with you." He leaned into the kitchen, slung the tray onto a nearby countertop.

He turned back, folded his arms, leveled his eyes on hers. "I never expected to meet someone like you in the Kingdom."

"Someone like me?"

"Or even in the States." A hint of smile flew across his face. "I wish I could know you better, Arden. I like your open mind, your curiosity about this culture—you're so unusual! I'd like to hear your music. But you have to understand, it's impossible for men and women to be friends here. Excuse me if I gave that impression."

Just what Sayeed had said. She glanced down so he couldn't read the disappointment she felt welling in her eyes.

"About the khamseen. You breathed in a lot of dust. It might make you sick, like a fever, you ought to see the campus doctor if you feel strange. Get some antibiotics."

Of course she felt sick and strange, of course she was feverish. The khamseen had nothing to do with it. Antibiotics wouldn't help her.

"It's serious. You need to pay attention over the next few days, and take it easy. You have a friend, a roommate? Someone who can watch out for you?"

She shrugged. He looked at her for a moment longer. She allowed herself one last look, to memorize his face, but she could not smile. He didn't either. "Goodbye, Faisal."

"Be careful here, Arden," he said. It was definitely a warning. "Don't take risks."

As if it mattered. She shook her head, and left.

TWENTY-ONE

EVELYN ANSWERED THE DOOR in her bathrobe. Arden handed her the folded skirt.

"Brilliant—you brought it." She hurried Arden inside. Clothes were piled in colorful heaps around the living room, and Grace was trying on a crimson ball gown, turning in front of the mirror at the end of the hall. Makeup and perfumes were scattered on the coffee table.

"Doesn't look like you need it." Arden eyed the array of dresses, feeling sour.

"Oh these are for Grace, from one of Ali's friends. And you, if you like. Ali's driver will be here in a few minutes." Evelyn took the skirt to hang in the shower.

"I'm not coming."

"Of course you must come, we're all going, it's just like Cinderella's ball. It will be an experience for you."

"I don't need any more experiences," Arden muttered.

"Please come, Arden," Grace said. "You know Evelyn and Kate will run off with the princes, and I'll be stuck alone fending off all the other guys."

"It sounds sucky."

"I'm kidding! There will be lots of other women, and the men are nice, and fun. The food will be great. And they'll have wine, they promised! Come on."

"Wine on Eid? This is a Saudi party?"

"Sure, they drink too."

"Not the good ones." She was sure Faisal didn't drink.

"Jeez, you sound like Ruth."

"Just pick out a dress and get ready before the driver shows up," Evelyn called from the bathroom.

There was a knock on the door, but it was Kate, not the driver. She was beautiful in a shimmering, beaded white caftan, under her abaya. "Arden! Are you coming too?" There was a hint in her tone, Arden didn't quite know what, but she could tell Kate didn't want her with them. Perversely, this decided her.

"Yeah." She grabbed the plainest-looking dress, a dark blue shift with lace edging at the long sleeves and hem. "Where did you say these came from?"

"One of Ali's other women sent them over when she heard we didn't have party clothes. She's Iraqi, they're a bit bigger than Gulf Arabs, so she thought her things would fit tall sheikhas. Not me, obviously." Evelyn was petite.

Other women? Hadn't Ali just 'married' Evelyn, supposedly out of desperate hunger? More information than she wanted right now, Arden decided, as she went into the extra bath to change. The dress had a hint of spicy perfume. She shook out her hair. Its light yellow looked nice against the blue cloth. Maybe they could stop at Faisal's so he could see what he was missing.

But that kind of thinking was idiotic. This wasn't Columbus and anyway, he was religious, they couldn't explore any relationship. She had to just banish him completely from her mind and get on to the next thing, whatever that was.

It was dark by the time they left campus. The road to town was completely cleared now, and the moon was shining on those few cars still stranded on the shoulders. Arden turned away, not wanting to see Musa's wreck.

Ali's palace was as imposing as Nawaf's. The driver led them into a wing off the main building, to a large living room filled with men and women, a mix of Westerners and Saudis. Arden saw uniforms among them and thought of Johnny. A tall Saudi separated himself from a cluster and came up to them. Ali—now she recognized him as Nawaf's friend from the other night.

"*Ahlan was ahlan*," he said. Welcome. He indicated the long tables of food and drink. "Please, eat," he said in Arabic.

"*Eid de kum mubarak,*" Arden remembered. His smile broadened.

"*Aiwa, Eid de kum aleikum.*" She didn't understand what else he said.

"Last night was the Eid family party, and tonight's for his friends," Evelyn translated. She wrapped her arm round Ali's waist and walked off with him, a sight that clashed noisily with what Arden thought was supposed to be the norm in public. Nobody seemed to notice. They were all laughing, drinking, flirting with each other. The non-Western women did not look like Saudis; they didn't have the thin features she was familiar with in her girls, and their voices were louder than Saudi voices.

"Who are these people?"she asked Grace.

"You heard him, they're friends, they're from all over. I recognize some of them from the other night."

Another Saudi detached himself from the crowd to greet them—Nawaf, his smile as smooth as Arden remembered. "Hello, ladies," he said sweetly. "Can I bring to you glass of champagne?"

That sounded just right. The first sip was cool and tingly and went down deliciously, soothing the burning in her throat. Nawaf sipped too, studying them over the rim of his flute. His eyes narrowed in a deeper smile when she looked at him. He reached into his pocket and pulled out the tip of his pipe, showing her, lifting his brows.

She shook her head, smiling. Kate stepped close to him, and followed his hand with her own, into the pocket. Arden, suddenly realizing why Kate hadn't wanted her there, looked away quickly. She saw a pair of empty armchairs across the room, by a bookcase, and decided she'd just sit and drink. She hadn't had champagne since last New Year's. Grace sat next to her for awhile.

"How do they get this stuff through customs?" Arden asked her.

"*Customs,* are you kidding! It's smuggled across the border, from the north."

"From Iraq? No way."

"Jordan. By the truckload. AWACs find them, let them go."

"Unbelievable. This is so different from what I expected," Arden said. "The disconnect between this little subculture, or whatever, and the rest of their society."

"It's only royals who can act this way, from what I've seen."

"So I get why the others resent this."

"But it's kept private, so it doesn't really matter." Grace shrugged.

"But how can these guys say they're good Muslims?"

"From what I've heard, Muhammad wasn't against wine, just over-indulgence. And relations between men and women were stiffened up by the Wahhabis." Wahhabism was the type of Islam practiced in the Kingdom, a strict interpretation whose rigorous observation was monitored by the ubiquitous mutawas. "The original Bedouins didn't have this separation. The women worked alongside the men, in fact I'm pretty sure they still do. The community couldn't have thrived otherwise."

"But then why all these restrictions and punishments now?"

Grace leaned forward to say quietly, "The royal family's in trouble here. They let our military in to protect them during the Gulf War. There was a lot of resentment against royals before, because of parties like this, their frequent travels to the West, their acceptance of modern technology like satellite TV, what have you, but now it's really intense. So they have to let the mutawas crack down, even though they keep themselves immune by hiding this kind of behavior."

Arden recalled Faisal's comment about American troops on the road to Makkah, his anger about the destruction of Eridu to create an air base. She'd been paying more attention to his looks than his politics. How *stupid* this infatuation had made her. "Can you just grab a bottle, Grace? I feel like getting drunk."

Grace laughed, and took a bottle from the nearby table. "Why?"

"I fell for the wrong guy here."

"But you don't meet guys. You only came to one party."

Arden spilled the story.

Grace's eyes grew wide—the 'spud stud,' as Evelyn referred to Faisal, was a legend of suave since his museum lecture. "He's fascinating." She poured liberally into Arden's glass, so it foamed off the top.

Arden mopped at it with her sleeve. "He's off limits."

"Then let him go. There are plenty of fish in the sea here. Just look around. You're pretty, Arden, go pick another one."

"But I don't want any other one."

"Then," Grace said, filling up her own glass and draining it giddily, "you're dumb. This is a fantastic dating opportunity for a single Western woman, and there's no point in mooning over some Saudi who doesn't want you. There are so many others, not Saudis, no risk. Or if you have to have a Saudi, pick a prince."

"There's no one else like him. He saved me in the storm today." She took a big gulp, trying to swallow the scratchy rawness in her throat.

"Of course he rescued you, he felt responsible for you. Anyone would do the same. And you'd've felt equally grateful. It's human nature." Grace refilled their glasses. "But he sounds religious, Arden, so there's no way. Unless you're going to convert, and somehow I don't see that happening." She smirked at the way Arden was draining her wine.

Arden blinked dryness from her eyes. "I'm not sure if it's religion, really, or just caution about the rules here. He just got back so maybe he's being overly careful. But Nawaf and Ali don't care about rules."

"They practice temporary marriage. And don't forget, they're royals."

"I really don't understand this."

"You don't have to, Arden. Don't worry about it. We're here for a year, just visiting, so have fun while you can. Because once we're back in the States we're back to the dry life of academia, don't you remember? These guys are a lot more interesting than academics." Grace waved her hand at the party. "They're journalists from all over, diplomats, wealthy businessmen. Any of them would take your mind off Faisal tonight."

"Oh don't say his name!" Arden moaned. She knew she'd had too much champagne.

"Get over it." Grace laughed. "Go enjoy yourself. I plan to." She swallowed the rest of her wine, and stood, adjusting her skirt. "Just watch me."

Sure enough, she made her way across the room and entered into a conversation with a lively group. An American reporter Arden recognized, from his photo in the local newspaper, paid particular attention to what Grace said, and soon they were in a discussion alone.

TWENTY-TWO

S O IT REALLY IS THAT EASY, everyone hooks up except me. She might well have sat all night had Johnny not come to collapse in the armchair vacated by Grace.

"Hey there."

"Hi Johnny."

"I know you, I gave you a ride the other night, but I forget your name."

"Arden."

"Y'all a southern gal?"

"Hillbilly. You're not in uniform now."

"Nah, I'm off duty tonight." His dimpled grin took in the empty bottle. "Looks like you're off duty too, hillbilly."

"I'm so off duty you can open that bottle you brought, soldier." She sat up straight. "Sorry, Johnny. *Pilot.*"

"Fighter pilot."

"Fighter pilot and defender of the faithful."

"Whoa, don't go that far, that's not the deal here. They don't want to hear that."

He filled her glass. "You're on a tear, huh. How come?"

"It's dumb."

"Most reasons for gettin plastered are."

"So I'm not saying." She leaned forward. "Tell me about you instead. How'd you end up here, Johnny?"

"Not much to tell. Grew up kinda hard, buncha bullshit, Air Force was the quickest way out. I'm from a small family, just my mom and sister and me. You?"

"Just my mom and sister and me too. My parents split up when I was young."

"My Dad died early, cancer." Johnny's mouth twitched to one rueful side.

"Sad."

"Yeah it was, for my mom. She had a rough time of it. One reason I was bound to be independent, help her out some."

"So what d'you think of the Kingdom?" She found herself mouthing the same thing Saudis did; like Americans, they were always curious to know what foreigners thought of their country, and, also like Americans, they optimistically expected superlatives because of what they'd built out of 'wilderness.'

"This place is a trip and a half."

"Like how, for you, Johnny?"

"Like they give our gals a hard time, they aren't allowed to socialize like y'all. Mutawas freak if they come out in uniform. And there's a lotta double standards here, from what I can tell. Just look at these parties. Anytime you got one set of rules for some folks, not for the others, there's gonna be trouble."

"There's trouble here already I think."

"You betcha. This's a real dangerous place for us; I mean, the military. Fanatics wanna kill us, think we're propping up the regime. And they hate it that we're around Mecca. You remember, last year, Hesbollah blew up our barracks in Khobar. On the coast. Fuckers."

"What about the Saudis around here, they're not fanatics are they?"

Faisal hated seeing Americans around Mecca. But he couldn't be a fanatic. He was an academic, an intellectual, Western-educated. His mother was American. He spoke perfect English.

"Well, Nawaf is a real sweet guy. My Mom loves him." Johnny's smile was affectionate. "Know what he did? Sent her a gold piece, from his family, something rare. They had it for centuries."

"Centuries," Arden marveled. "Wonnerful."

Johnny's brows rose. "No more for you, babe. I'll bring you a soda, you can tell me what's buggin ya."

She drank the soda thirstily. Her throat felt so sore, must be some sand still stuck there. When she coughed she felt it deep in her chest. She must've gotten some in her eyes too; they itched unbearably.

"So whassup, hillbilly Arden?"

"Iss nothin."

"Young gal like you, I'm guessin homesick. Or maybe love trouble."

"Love sucks."

"*Oh* yeah. Tell me all about it, babe." His grin was teasing, flirtatious.

She let herself smile back. "He's all wrong for me."

"But you want him *so* bad."

"He's a Saudi."

Johnny laughed. "And you such a honky!" He flicked a lock of her pale hair. "I knew you liked em. Whyn'cha just marry him, you know, for a night? They can do that. Get im out of your system."

Oh sure, she could just see suggesting that to Faisal! "He's conservative. Seriously."

"Then you're seriously screwed." His grin grew wider. "Cept technically, you're never gonna be. Not by him anyhow." He leaned toward her. "Give it up, Arden. Affairs with Saudis? Trouble like that you don't need. Unless it's just a temporary-marriage royal hookup."

She blinked back sudden tears. Her eyes felt so hot.

"Oh bullshit." He leaned further toward her, his face so close she could see the navy flecks in his eyes. "You just need another kinda guy."

He ran the back of his hand lightly down her cheek. His touch was soothing. She watched his smile deepen. She realized, at once, how cute he was, and how hungry she was for an affectionate touch, after yearning so long for Faisal's. *Well, why not?* "Pick up that fiddle and dance right where you are," wasn't that how the song went? Faisal certainly didn't want her, she might as well have someone who did. Grace was right.

"Come on, pretty gal like you, you deserve some lovin." He started to smooth her hair back from her temple, and the steady stroking, on her aching head, was hypnotic. "Why wait on someone can't give it to ya?"

"Johnny ... this isn't a good idea." But she didn't move away.

"You need a distraction, darlin, me too."

"From what?"

"From all this. Come on, let's distract each other."

"Okay, Johnny, wha' the hey."

He stood, and took her hand. He seemed to know his way very well around the palace. Walking with him, she had a flash of knowing this was the wrong thing to do, the wrong way to erase Faisal, but a stubborn, defiant part of her, the part fueled now by rejection and alcohol, kept her hand in Johnny's. He led her to a secluded bedroom, closed the door behind them, helped her get her dress off. She welcomed the feeling of him surrounding her. She'd forgotten the intense pleasure of full-length skin on skin.

She had the wit to at least ask him to use protection. Then she gave him as much as she could, but Faisal would not be banished. He seemed to be there with them, white sleeves folded, watching in disapproval. Arden twisted in Johnny's arms, trying to get Faisal's face out of her mind.

Pretend, a wicked voice told her. *Pretend this is the one you want.* She closed her eyes and imagined Faisal's strength against her, imagined it was his tongue she suckled, imagined tangling her hands in his long hair. She remembered how he felt that afternoon as she'd held him so tight, how his heart had pounded next to hers and how his gasp of shock had felt like excitement, before he'd pushed her away. Sudden heat rushed and she strained against Johnny until she achieved a guilty, grateful release.

She fell back, drained, and Johnny fell with her.

"See, honey," he sighed. "Now we're distracted."

THE AIR IN THE ROOM, or the lack of it, woke her wheezing for breath sometime in the night. She sat up, holding her throat, thinking she had to find a bathroom, get a drink of water. She turned to the boy beside her, wanting to wake him, but then she realized that what had woken her was light, not thirst. A light came from the door, which a ghost was opening. She pulled back, breathing even harder.

Not a ghost, a white-clad figure. Of course. Saudi Arabia.

She dragged the sheet up and watched as the figure left the door open, just a crack, and approached her.

Nawaf.

He smiled, held a finger to his lips. As if in a dream she saw him bending toward her, white headdress drooping. So suddenly that she could not react he reached for the back of her head with one firm hand and leaned to kiss her quickly with the same warm, hashish-tasting mouth she remembered. He drew back, still smiling.

He walked around to the other side of the bed where Johnny lay and bent to kiss his lips too, so gently that Johnny didn't wake. Then he lay down next to Johnny and sighed, deeply, as if finally finding a comfortable place to rest. He wrapped an arm around the sleeping pilot. Something in the hushed dim scene reminded her of Jesus and the disciples, was it Judas's kiss? Johnny didn't look like Jesus but Nawaf was a dead ringer with his thin ascetic face and long robe. But that didn't fit. Jesus was Jewish, not Bedouin, right?

She was probably hallucinating; this must be champagne-induced fantasy. It was actually kind of sweet. She felt very strange, like the time she took acid with Paul and ended up sleeping on the porch roof. But at least then she'd been able to breathe.

"*Ya Nawaf. Moya, min fadlak.*" Water, please, she said in Arabic. Nawaf leaned up to look at her, and then reached back for a bottle of water on the nightstand next to him. He opened, handed it to her, watched as she drank it all down.

"*Enti kwayisa?*" he whispered. Are you okay?

She nodded. She lay back next to Johnny. Nawaf's slim warm hand found hers and she held onto it, closing her fingers around the comforting palm. Concentrating on holding on helped her breathe again. She and Nawaf fell asleep with their hands linked over Johnny.

TWENTY-THREE

ARDEN'S OWN WHEEZING pushed her awake.
Each breath was dragging as if pulled by blood red, needle-sharp wires strung through her chest and cutting into her throat. Her eyes were so sore she could barely open them. *What a horrible hangover.* She staggered to a door that led, she was glad to see, to a bathroom. The shower steam helped ease her breathing and she drank the hot water even though she knew it wasn't potable, but her throat still hurt when she came out. It was way too cold, they needed to adjust the A/C. She wrapped herself in the top bed sheet and lay down, to catch her breath and warm up.

Some time later, someone was shaking her shoulder. She pried her dry eyes open. It was Nawaf, perched on the bedside like a slender wingless angel, a look of pity on his narrow face. He put a cool hand on her forehead.

"I am sorry you don't breathing good," he said softly. "We take hospital."

She tried to sit. Behind him were Evelyn, Ali, and Johnny, with the same grave expression. *Who died,* she tried to say, but it hurt to talk. The burning in her eyes forced them shut.

"Help me wrap her up, I'm getting her out of here." Johnny's hands smoothed her hair back as he spoke above her. She felt a blanket drawn around and relaxed in its warmth. Johnny held onto her and they shuffled through the palace out to his Jeep. Nawaf and Ali helped her in and stood watching as Johnny drove away.

"Ali wanted to get his own doc to come look at you here, but I didn't think that was a good idea. Might bring up some awkward questions. I got someone I can call." He clicked into his mobile phone. "Hey Colleen? Johnny here." He listened for a moment and then laughed. "Yeah, yeah. I know. Hey listen. I got a situation. Girl I know, from the university, she's having an asthma attack. I'm bringing her to the hospital, you're on duty now, right? Can you meet us there?"

He wove through the morning traffic at such speed she thought they'd both die in a crash before reaching the hospital. If she was being punished, if she went straight to hell for having sex with one man while in love with another, at least hell would be warm; even when she didn't even believe in hell. The cold inside her seemed to increase with every block. Her teeth were chattering.

It cost such effort to breathe, she held onto each little wisp of air like a drop of water pearling onto the desert flowers she'd seen yesterday, glistening lightly on the side of those lovely yellow cups. Then it was as if the rain covered her again, soaking through until her skin was cold and her body started to shake. This was unlike any hangover she'd known. Her lungs burbled with uncontainable coughs. Had she smoked with Nawaf last night? Nawaf who looked like a Bedouin Jesus?

"Last night," she croaked. "Nawaf."

"Hang on hon, we're here. My friend Colleen's a nurse."

"Nawaf loves you."

"I love him too, he's my bro. Hold on to me." He was lifting her out, walking with her held beside him as he went through double glass doors.

"Can't you just take me home, Johnny," she pleaded weakly. "I don't even know if I have my insurance card." She couldn't handle some long wait in a crowded emergency room with a bunch of dispirited sick people.

He laughed. "This ain't the States, hon. You're in the Kingdom, in the King's neighborhood. You don't have to worry about insurance. Ali'll take care of this."

A wheelchair slid under her. "There now, and isn't it just your luck I'm on duty here today." It was a sweet feminine Irish lilt. "I'm just hooking you to some oxygen, it might sting a bit but then we'll have you breathing clear again. Ready?" Arden felt a pinch in her nose, and a rush of air that knifed through her chest. She winced at the pain, and shrank away from it into sleep.

When she woke she was in a hospital bed. She had a tube attached to her upper lip, and cool air was filtering into her nose. A large TV hung down from the ceiling and its remote control attached to the bed. She clicked it on—*The Waltons*, with Arabic subtitles. She watched in a stupor as John Boy successfully engineered the refinancing of a neighbor's farm with the local crusty banker. It was nice the way they all said goodnight at the end. She recalled Nawaf's tender goodnight kisses to her and Johnny. Had that really happened? A wave of exhaustion pulled her under.

Then a pretty red-haired woman was fiddling with the tube under her nose. Arden twisted away from the discomfort. "It's all right Arden, I'm just taking it off. You'll still feel a bit wheezy, but you'll be able to breathe on your own now." She wrapped the tube up and put it into a rolling cart. "I'm Colleen, the day nurse. You're a teacher here, I take it? That must be interesting."

"The English Department. My ID should be in my bag," she remembered.

"Yes, the admin took care of all that, and we've let the university know you're here. You've a lovely name. I know some Ardens in Ireland as well."

"There's Irish in my family. Way back." Her voice was hoarse and strange.

"Are you able to tell me what happened? Johnny thought it's asthma, but you've got rather a high fever as well, so we've put you on antibiotics. The doctor's having a look at your chest X-rays and then she'll be in to talk to you."

"It was the khamseen."

"You were out of doors in the storm yesterday? How could that be?"

"I was stupid."

"Don't be too hard on yourself, we're foreigners here, we can't know all the dangers." Colleen smoothed the blankets. "Only, I do want to make sure it wasn't a drug reaction? Sometimes at parties here, you don't know what you're getting?"

Startled, Arden said, "All I had was champagne."

"You're sure no-one slipped you something."

"No."

"It's just that you arrived here wrapped up in blankets and nothing else, so I did wonder, although I know Johnny's a decent chap. You're sure nobody did anything to you that you didn't want?"

Arden felt heat rushing into her face. Did she have to admit to having sex with Johnny? "No, I'm fine." How embarrassing! Especially since she had the confused impression that Johnny knew Colleen well, maybe even intimately. He was probably quite a player in the expat community, why not, he was fit and eligible.

"We'll have a chat, later, about risks here. What to avoid, that sort of thing." Colleen smiled. "We'll just have your supper brought, and you can rest a bit."

Arden turned the TV back on, and watched *Little House on the Prairie*, happy to lose herself in the pioneer risks of the Old West instead of talking about hawaja risks in the New East. She couldn't bear to examine, just yet, the implications of what she'd done with Johnny. She got the dad mixed up with Little Joe from *Bonanza* but tried to follow the thread of the story.

She was annoyed when the program was interrupted by the entrance of a young Saudi woman in gray hijab and coatdress under her lab jacket, looking the epitome of cool efficiency.

"Hello, I'm Dr. Al Abboud." She had an English accent. She looked at Arden over slim half-glasses and glanced at the chart she was holding. "Your X-rays show some lung shade, just a slight pneumonia, so we'll keep you here until the fever's gone."

"*Pneumonia?*" Arden stared at the doctor. "Jesus H. Christ."

"Peace be upon him," Dr. Al Abboud replied, not seeming to realize Arden was swearing. Muslims referred to Jesus as a respected prophet. "It's a limited congestion. We got you at the beginning, so you should have a good recovery."

"But I haven't been sick!"

"The nurse says you were out in the storm yesterday? It happens quickly. You call it valley fever in your country, I think. We see a lot of this after a khamseen. If sand gets into the lungs it can cause an infection."

"Faisal was right." Saying his name gave her a sinking feeling.

The doctor eyed her. "We've got you on penicillin so you'll feel better soon. Perhaps go home tomorrow. I'll check on you in the morning."

Arden turned her attention once more to the TV. Now it was some musical with Indian actors, dodging coyly around a copse of trees, like the ones she'd hidden behind that day across from the mosque. She felt her eyes closing again, against her will.

Sometime later a tray was rattled in by a shy little Asian woman. Supper was a thin soup with a few lonely noodles floating on top. Arden pushed it away after a couple of painful swallows and lay back.

How she wished for her banjo, or a good book! She should call someone, but who? None of the sheikhas could get to the hospital on her own. And it wasn't as if Dr. Zafeeyeh, or Sayeed, God forbid, would know how to get some romances for her to read. Easy tears pricked as she thought that Annie or Mom would know exactly what to bring. She could at least ask for an English Koran. She read some every day. She especially enjoyed the poetry of the suras, parable-like nuggets of counsel for daily life.

The ringing phone on the nightstand startled her.

"Hello?" she said cautiously.

"Hey babe, how ya doin?"

"Johnny! Thanks for calling me!"

"We wanted to come visit, Ali and Nawaf and me, but we thought we'd better let you sleep. We're sending some presents."

"Hey, Johnny, can you send some books?"

There was a silence, as if he did not know what to make of such a request. Then he said, "You need your schoolbooks? I'll tell Ali to drive some of the gals at the U to bring em. He'll do anything, he feels so bad you got sick in his house."

"It's not his fault. I breathed in the khamseen dust yesterday, is all. That's what made me sick. Tell Ali I had a good time at the party."

"Yeah, that *was* a good time." Johnny's chuckle seemed to leap into the room. "We'll do it again when you get better."

Now it was her turn to be silent.

"For fun, darlin, nothin heavy. I like you, but I like just about everybody." That made her laugh, relieved. "Here's Nawaf, he wants to say hi."

"Hello, Ahden, I am hoping you will be very good."

"Hi Nawaf. It's sweet of you to call. Thank you."

"Johnny and I, we flying tomorrow night, we going far. Maybe we can see you before we go."

"Where are you going?"

"I can't to say *you!*" Nawaf's soft laugh filled her ear. "I don't tell to anyone."

"Nawaf. When you go, take care of Johnny."

"Yes. Always."

"We're outta here, but you rest up, okay?" It was Johnny again.

"Be careful. Look out for Nawaf."

"Course, babe, I'm his copilot! See ya."

She hung up. She was glad Johnny knew her connection to him was strictly casual. It made her feel less guilty. She wondered if he realized how powerful Nawaf's attachment to him was.

144

Energized by their call, and hungry, she swung out of bed. She took some riyals from her purse. There must be a vending machine where she could buy some chocolate. They didn't sell Hershey's in the Kingdom, something to do with distribution rights, but she could find another kind.

TWENTY-FOUR

S HE VENTURED DOWN the hallway, glancing at the
quiet patient rooms with caution, mindful of where
she was and how little she wore. The hospital gown
would not have met the muttawas' approval and she
clutched it awkwardly round herself. At the end of the
hall she saw what appeared to be some kind of sitting
room.

Nothing could have prepared her for the sight of
Leila, whose face was uncovered, and Faisal, sitting in a
lounge marked "Families." They must be visiting a
relative. She approached them quietly, padding barefoot.

Faisal saw her first. His face lit up in a wide
unguarded smile, which told her they were here for her. A
wave of affection swamped her equilibrium and she
staggered to sit next to Leila.

"*Ya* Miss Arden!" Leila reached for her and held her
in a hug that felt so good, so right, Arden closed her eyes
and rocked with Leila as she would have with Annie.

"How did you know I was here?"

"I heard from Eyman. Your friend Grace is her other
teacher. We were just waiting for the nurse to get your
room number."

"Thank you," she whispered. "I was getting lonely,
and hungry." A mischievous imp within her relished the
concern narrowing Faisal's eyes.

"Hungry!" Leila repeated in shock. "*Wullahi*, we'll
take you away from here! They can't not to give you
food."

146

"I was just going to find a chocolate bar. I have some riyals. You can tell me where the vending machines are."

"You need real food, not chocolate," said Faisal. "What's your prognosis, anyway? What are they keeping you for?"

"I have pneumonia." The imp inside was gratified to see his dismayed frown.

"The khamseen. I'm so sorry, Arden. Leila can take you back to your room, and I'll get you something to eat."

"*Ya* Faisal, we should take her to our home. We can look after her."

"We can't look after pneumonia."

Oh give it a try, Arden thought, *I'd love to stay with you.* An untimely wheeze crept out. She covered her mouth, but not before Faisal heard her. "You shouldn't be up."

They each took an arm as if she needed help getting to her room. Brother and sister looked at the supper tray in distaste. Leila muttered in Arabic, "This is not food. I will tell them." She took off, presumably toward a nurses' station Arden hadn't seen.

She felt shy, alone with Faisal, confronted with the object of her desire in this intimate setting. She got into bed, as modestly as possible, and pulled the covers up. Faisal prowled around and looked into corners as if checking for cleanliness.

"Arden, I should have judged the weather yesterday. If I'd known better, we would never have gone out in the storm. This is my fault."

"No it's not."

"I should have told you about the dangers. People underestimate the dust."

"You didn't know I was going to get out of the car." Her voice was hoarse again.

He shook his head. "I'm *supposed* to know better."

"You saved my life, *ya* Faisal," she whispered.

"What did you say?" He came to stand next to her. The fingers of his right hand held a short string of worry beads. She reached for its dangling end.

"You saved my life," she repeated. "*Ya sadiki, shukran.*"

"*Afwan,*" he responded automatically, *you're welcome.* She pulled the small marbles close, entwining his fingers. If she could bring his hand to her cheek, his warmth would ease the cold inside her. His mouth tilted up in what looked like an inadvertent smile, but he tried to pull his fingers away. They were twisted tight in hers with the beads.

Faisal jerked his hand free and the string snapped. Little balls bounced, clacking, around the slippery floor, and he watched them scatter with a look of disbelief. "*Ya salaam,*" he exclaimed quietly. Just as he turned to look at her, Leila returned with Colleen.

"What's this all over the floor?" Colleen looked at Arden in confusion. "Is it a necklace? But you weren't wearing any—"

"Worry beads," Arden croaked quickly.

"Mmm." Colleen looked at Faisal closely. "You're from the museum, sir, I recognize you." Her tone was suspicious, as if his beads were an archeological intrusion into the sterile hospital environment. He kept his head down.

Colleen turned to Arden. "Your friend seems to think we're not feeding you, Arden. Only it's just, with the throat you've got, a light diet is recommended." She looked at the watery soup. "It is a bit unappealing, I must say."

"I was hungry. It didn't taste good."

"Had you not eaten breakfast, then, before Johnny brought you this morning."

She shook her head, not daring to look at anybody's face. *Busted!*

"Well, I'll not stand in this lady's way, should she want to bring you another meal." She looked again at Faisal, curiously. "Sir, I suggest you go with your sister, so as to respect everyone's privacy. The cafeteria is just down the hall, I'll show you."

Faisal and Leila returned with a shwarma sandwich and a Pepsi. "We have to go, the visiting hour is finished, but we'll come back tomorrow night," Leila said.

"I'll be going home tomorrow."

"That seems too soon," Faisal said, eyeing her critically. How horrible did she look to him? She drew the covers up.

"But if you are here I will bring some of the girls, they will like to see you, if that is good," Leila told her.

"Of course it's good!" She had a sudden thought. "Do you have anything I can read? Or is there a hospital shop, I can get a book? Can I get an English Koran here?"

"Faisal, what is that English book you brought?"

"It's archaeology, Arden, I don't think you'll be interested."

"Of course I am, but I won't take it if you're reading it."

"*Ya* Faisal, give her the book," Leila told him with some impatience.

With obvious reluctance, he lifted a slim paperback from his long cloak pocket. It was called *Dilmun*. He handed it to Arden.

"You can discuss together later, as we do in the class," Leila said. "We like to bring you another gift but the shops are closed."

"Arden, goodnight," Faisal said abruptly. "Leila, I'll meet you downstairs."

"I think my brother is tired from Haj, he is different since he came back," Leila said in an apologetic tone after he left. "Usually he is very friendly."

"Maybe he's shy in front of me. I'm a stranger. I'm a woman."

"No, he isn't shy to women, like most of Saudi men. He has too many girlfriends, in America."

Oh naturally, in America. "He's a Hajj now, so maybe he's being more strict."

"He is being not like himself. I'm thinking he is sorry he came back here. It's so different the life, from California. My father wants him to get married too soon."

"Married!"

"Of course. My family is finding my husband and arranging Faisal's wife at the same time. All of my cousins are being examined. My father's wife Aisha is in hurry now to get us from the house." Her smile lessened the harshness of this statement.

"I thought Faisal's taking you back to the States for grad school."

"We find husband for me, and wife for him, who don't mind to go to America."

"You can have a double wedding," Arden proposed sadly. She closed her eyes, bruised by the topic and even by Leila's company, suddenly. The light touch on her shoulder, though, was welcome.

"Good night ya Arden. We see you tomorrow."

"Thanks Leila. Goodnight."

TWENTY-FIVE

THE SANDWICH WAS HOT, dripping lamb juice, stuffed with onions, tomatoes and spicy meat. She wished she could enjoy it, but only one swallow scraped her throat so badly she could not take another. Even the Pepsi stung, going down. Discouraged, she lay back and stared at the ceiling.

What a fool I am! How *deluded.* She'd behaved like an idiot with Faisal. Add Nawaf and Johnny to the list; nothing but mistakes with men here! She'd allowed the strangeness of this setting to shake loose her common sense. Or, more accurately, she'd behaved as if she were on the prowl in Columbus. And this was no Columbus. She'd never been on the prowl there, anyway; she wasn't the flirtatious type. Looking for hotties in bars had never appealed to her.

Her relationship with Paul had been easily physical, but not inflammatory. His increasing lack of ambition, even in getting his poetry heard, had started to annoy her, echoing too much of what she feared was her own inertia. A year into their relationship, he was like a brother: easy to leave.

Earlier, in college, she'd had several boyfriends like Johnny, liaisons of proximity or convenience. She picked only the mild ones. The safe ones. Nothing to tie her down.

No one had ever generated the shortness-of-breath, sweaty-hands, tongue-tied heat Faisal aroused. But it was just chemistry! Just his eyes, which probably hypnotized every person who saw him. Well, and his smile. His long shiny curls. His smooth-looking skin. Or maybe it was just the storm? The rain. The flowers. The vulnerability he'd caught her in, when they first met near the hilltop mosque.

The direct American way he spoke freely and looked straight at her. The devout Arabian way he prayed. His flowing robes and headdress, even. Strip away that mystique, wasn't he ordinary? Good-looking, sure, but ordinary: she pictured him in khakis and a polo shirt, short-haired, reading the paper at Starbucks, talking about the latest Pearl Jam concert or pottery in New Mexico, instead of the Ubaid or desert weather ...

He was not ordinary.

She'd never seen such eyes in such a face.

But she hated feeling this needy! She wasn't used to it. She didn't know why she was acting like such a fool, for the first time in her life, in this risky place. She'd even broken his friggin worry beads. She could see one now, in a corner.

She dragged herself out of bed to pick it up and roll it around in her palm. It was a lovely greenish-blue, with white streaks, a perfect little Earth in her hand. She could almost see a miniature Saudi Arabia in its eastern swirl, with a teeny Riyadh, and a dot that was his Land Rover driving away from her right now, driving away to his separate future while she sat here on the cold hospital floor. She held the bead tight, pretending she could feel his warmth still imprinted there.

She tossed the bead away and it rolled under the bed. She stumbled into the small bathroom and turned the shower on so that she could cry without the noise frightening the other patients. She clutched a towel and wailed into it, pressing it tight against her face.

A knock on the door made her jump.

"Arden, it's Colleen. I'm just leaving your medication on the table here."

"Okay," she choked out.

"Don't stay in the steam too long, it will only aggravate your lungs."

Was she this annoying with every patient, or just with Johnny's squeezes?

"You've been sent a big bouquet of flowers, it's ever so lovely, only the scent might make it difficult for you to breathe, so we've kept it outside at the nurses' station. I brought in another package for you."

"Please bring the flowers." Arden put strength into her voice.

"But you're sounding very congested, I really think it's best—"

Arden opened the door and glared at her. "I'm congested because I'm crying."

Colleen stared at her in dismay. "Whatever can be the matter?"

"Nothing." Arden ripped the package open; a jewelry box containing an obviously expensive, useless gold bracelet. Nawaf. She tossed it onto the nightstand, got back into bed, clicked on the TV. *Abu SimSim, Sesame Street*, entertainment at its finest. She turned the volume up and tried to ignore Colleen, who came to stand next to the bed.

"Arden. I know you're in pain."

"I'm sorry," Arden muttered, ashamed of her outburst. She turned off the TV. "I'll be better soon, and then I can get out of here." She swallowed her medication to prove it, but the liquid burned her sore throat.

Colleen studied her. "If there's anything else bothering you, we could talk. I've a lot of experience with young women here." Colleen picked up a stray bead and held it toward Arden, pointedly. "And how violent their men can be." She put the bead into the jewelry box, obviously thinking they came from the same source.

"No, he's not—he didn't break them. I did, by accident. He's trying to do the right thing."

"What right thing would that be?" Colleen's voice was wearily dry, as if she'd heard many grim variations on this theme.

"He knows it's dangerous for us to have any kind of relationship in the Kingdom. I should stay away from him."

"He isn't staying away from you though, and you alone in bed half dressed. I thought he was an honorable fellow, someone you knew well, not one to leave you crying your eyes out in the bathroom!"

"I wasn't crying over him!"

"Somehow I don't think it was our Johnny, though." Colleen sighed, and sat down in the chair next to the bed. "This women's ward has seen its share of desperate trials. A lot of them inflicted by men."

"Nobody inflicted anything on me. I got myself into this."

"In this country, where we're all totally dependent on men for our well-being, I'm hard put to see a woman suffer and not know who's to blame. You may have gotten ill on your own by being outside in the storm. But you can't be breaking your heart over some Arab in a nightdress without his collusion, by Jesus."

"Peace be upon him."

"And don't give me that. You're an infidel like the rest of us white women. Believe me, handsome as may be, they're not worth it. Some have AIDS, you know. They don't know it, and getting tested here is a scandal for the average person, so their women come in ailing. And their babies too, of course." Arden looked up, horrified. "They go on sex trips. Full of sickness, some of them."

"But that's totally against Islam!"

Colleen continued, "They've ways to rationalize their behavior. I'm just wanting you to know, in case you've a mind to go after your man. Who's conservative, you say, he must be a devout Muslim? Let's see how long he can keep that barrier between you, if you're determined to break it down."

It hurt to imagine sex trips, AIDS, dying babies and unknowing wives. It hurt to contemplate how lost this society was, if their men wandered abroad in search of titillation, while at home upholding a rigid sensuality-crushing standard. How sad to imagine Leila's or Maha's or even Feiruz's future husbands vulnerable to that kind of craziness. Leila deserved a husband as innocent and as impassioned as she was!

But who was she kidding? She herself was as vulnerable as any young Saudi to random lust spells. She'd had Johnny, when wanting Faisal. But that was her right, wasn't it? To have anyone she chose, if she could not have Faisal, the realist, who saw no reason to risk involvement with her in this frightening place.

Arden swallowed again, feeling her throat constrict as if closing on a boulder that scraped all the way down, feeling her eyes brim with too much reality. "Do you ever just let people sleep?"

"Yes." She smoothed the blankets over Arden. "You've drunk a very peaceful night there along with your antibiotics, doctor's orders, and I promise you'll dream well."

"Give me that bead and I will."

"You're hopeless." But she pressed the bead into Arden's hand. "At least, tell me you'll take precautions." She frowned until Arden nodded. "Make him get tested."

As if.

Her fingers slowly picked out "Maid of Constant Sorrow" on the blanket and moved on to "Bluer Pastures" as the tranquilizing effect of her meds drew her into sleep.

TWENTY-SIX

A RDEN WAS STILL clutching Faisal's bead the next morning. Its circular impression on her palm reminded her of the old *Princess and the Pea* fairy tale.

What was she thinking, crushing on an unattainable man like some all-wet helpless victim?

She'd come here to advance, not regress.

She opened her hand, letting the bead roll away. She heard it bouncing and had to smile at the nurse's quizzical expression.

Dr. Al Abboud, noting Arden's still-high temperature, advised another night's monitoring in hospital.

The sunshine pouring through the window was hot and bright again, the few days' clouds dispersed, rain forgotten, arc of sky as blue as the gaudy island-dotted Mediterranean she'd glimpsed on the plane coming to the Kingdom, so many months ago. It was the right weather for reading about ancient Bahrain, and she passed most of the day pleasantly immersed in *Dilmun*. Every so often a nurse came to take her vital signs and make her walk the hallway.

Late in the afternoon she was roused from her reverie by the arrival of Eyman, Maha and Leila. They presented her with an embroidered silk abaya and hijab, and an assortment of Chanel bath products. "We also brought for you English Quran, Miss, and Nora Roberts," Maha said, grinning, aware of the humor in this juxtaposition.

Nora Roberts, Alhamdulillah!

"We miss you at the class. We had to spend the time at the Language Lab and it was very boring." Eyman pouted. "You have to come back soon."

"She must rest for a long time. My brother says the pneumonia take months if she don't be quiet." Leila pulled the blankets up to Arden's chin. "We don't stay to make you tired, Miss, we only saying hello."

"I wanted to bring chocolate but she don't let me." Eyman shot a teasing look at Leila. They looked so sweet in their black, a trio of designer-cologned, French-manicured Singing Nuns. Arden reached for their soft hands.

"I'd love chocolate," she said hoarsely. Her throat was still closed.

"Tomorrow," Leila promised. "We leave now so other friends can visit."

"Other friends?"

"The American, the one with his, how is it?" She conferred in Arabic with Eyman. "His uniform. He drove Miss Grace to see you. We met them in the lobby."

"He is very cute boy, Miss," Maha said mischievously. All the girls giggled.

After they left she thumbed through the Koran. She'd left off where Muhammad was addressing questions seventh century Christians might ask about Islam. He covered key aspects of Christianity; wisely conceding the Virgin birth, putting a bit of spin on the Resurrection, but staunchly refuting that Jesus was God's son or that there was a trinity of God. Islam only admitted one God. Arden concurred: the final erosion of her Christian belief, in her early teens, had been the mystical idea of the Holy Trinity. The local Episcopal minister hadn't satisfied her skeptical curiosity.

She closed her still-tired eyes after a bit. It seemed logical to ponder religion in this culture, where life was structured around faith. The automatic adherence to prayer calls, the reference to Allah in every figure of speech, the ritualistic way people behaved with each other, even the calendar, which was based on the *Hejirah*, the date of Muhammad's flight from Makkah, and not the Anno Domini: all was evidence of unshakeable belief.

She was curious about the strident-sounding calls to arms against infidels, both in the old Koran and in the fundamentalist movement erupting around the Middle East. She didn't know enough, from a historical perspective, to deduce if the *jihad* alluded to in the Koran was just a reflection of the early struggle for tribal unification around Mecca, or was a more universal tenet of Islam.

She heard the door but didn't open her eyes. Grace and Johnny, no doubt. "So what do guys you think?" she asked. "Is the *jihad* warrior thing just a historical twitch or does it have validity today?" She figured they would have an opinion. Islam was inescapable as a topic of expat discourse in the Kingdom: everyone was fascinated.

The low laugh that greeted her question made her eyes fly open. Faisal was walking in with an armful of glossy books. The sight of him thrust blood through her at such a rush she felt faint. Her hands tightened on the covers.

"Validity, I think, but do you really want my opinion?" He sat in the chair next to her, smiling, setting the books on his lap. "I brought you some books." He held them up one by one: desert flowers, like the ones they'd seen, desert wildlife, Saudi antiquities. They were beautiful. But he was too close. His scent enveloped, giving air and simultaneously taking it away. She tried to take a deep breath, to focus on the books, but she could only gasp, and that made her cough.

He leaned over and took her cold hand into the warmth of his. Could he feel the pulse leaping in her wrist? She absorbed the sight of his long light eyes and wide mouth. He closed her hand firmly around something he'd put there—a short string of worry beads. He let go and leaned back, exhaling shortly, eyes widening slightly as he watched her, as if backing off from something too hot to touch. She could barely hang onto the string.

"You seemed so eager to have my beads yesterday. You can figure out your own mantra, *ya* Arden, with each bead, or make up a song. It'll help you get well."

She tried to speak normally. "Mantra? Now that sounds like California. *Ya* Faisal." She let his name linger as she fingered the beads. They were green with little white swords and palm trees imprinted on them—the Saudi flag. Cute. She slid them back and forth, tentatively. "*Shukran.*"

"*Afwan.*" He stood. "You rest. I just came to drop off the books." He stacked them on the table. He seemed so far away in his long white headdress and gray cloak, a figure from the dream of nomadic prehistory she'd been lost in with *Dilmun*. She didn't want him to go. A fold of his thick embroidered cloak brushed against her hand as he turned, and she took it between her fingers and closed her eyes.

She heard his soft laugh. "No, *ya helwa,* you can't have my *besht.*"

She stumbled on his words—*helwa* meant sweetheart, surely? Was he joking? He'd used the same word with Leila, she remembered. But *besht* could only mean his cloak. She opened her eyes. She didn't want him to make fun of her.

"We didn't talk about *jihad.* I have serious questions."

"I have serious answers, when you're well." He laughed again. "Who did you think you were talking to? That Irish nurse?"

"I thought you were Johnny and Grace. They came to see me, Leila said."

"We met. Johnny had to leave. He says he'll call you when he gets back from his mission. He wanted to make sure you got the flowers?" He looked around the room and saw the huge bouquet Colleen had finally brought in. "Nice."

As she stared, wondering what he thought of Johnny, and of her, his smile faded.

She saw his pupils expand, darkening the green as he stared back at her. Dust motes hovered in lazy paths of late afternoon sunlight between them. The hospital sounds from the hallway ebbed. His shoulders rose once, then fell, and he lowered his gaze to the floor. She looked from his eyes to his hands, clasped in front of him, knitted together so tightly that his knuckles looked pale.

Grace's arrival broke the spell. "Oh, Faisal, you're still here. Johnny wanted me to give you this." She handed him a card. "He says call him in a week or so."

"Thanks." He glanced at Arden once more. "Goodbye. Have a good rest."

"Thanks for the books, *ya sadiki*."

When he had gone Grace said, "He took a risk, coming to see you alone." She looked at the books and smiled. "He must like you, Arden, in spite of being religious."

"It doesn't make any difference," Arden said slowly. "He has to get married soon. Leila told me. It's being arranged."

"Married! Jeez, Arden, you better not go there. You know the punishment here for fooling around with a married man? Execution! Talk about losing your head! Jeez!" She put the books under the bed, as if to hide the evidence of Faisal's visit, and frowned at Arden, leaning close. "Drop this guy. Just *forget* him."

"I know." But she could not help asking, "Did he and Johnny … get along?"

"Thick as thieves in the lobby, as if they'd known each other forever. Johnny speaks good Arabic, can you believe it?"

"What did they talk about?"

"Politics." Grace shrugged. "Johnny was glad to meet a regular Saudi. He doesn't get to mingle much with civilians. I think they were making plans to meet up again."

Arden sank back. What difference could it make if they became friends? Faisal was lost to her anyway. She'd best put him away, like a strong bluegrass woman would, in her favorite songs.

TWENTY-SEVEN

*F*AISAL'S HAIR RIPPLES BLACK *on her pillow as his chest rises and falls with peaceful breaths. Arden leans as close as she wants and he does not pull away or stiffen or even stir. She traces with her finger and mouth the outline of his features—long eyes, sharp nose, supple lips. She lies on him, head to foot, skin to skin. Her bare feet fit on top of his, heel to toe. She wraps her arms around him, recalling the gesture from Nawaf with Johnny, and rests with her face pressed under his chin. She touches the pulse on his warm throat with the tip of her tongue. Sleeping with him is bliss. Belonging. Comfort.*

Arden jerked awake. Her heart was pounding and her T-shirt was damp. She coughed. Five in the morning again, *damn.*

She sat up and hugged her knees to her chest. *I'm doing fine,* she told herself, *I'm doing a good job and learning the language and feeling at home. I'm paying off my debts. I'm doing just what I came here to do.* She repeated this to herself every morning; his suggested worry-bead mantra. But after six long weeks since last seeing Faisal, she still could not shake him from her psyche.

She swung her legs over the side of the bed and set her feet on the floor. She looked at her long toes splayed on the industrial-grade carpet and she saw them once more superimposed on his feet in her dream.

"Snap out of it." She took her shower, dressed, and went to the kitchen to make coffee. Some time later Ruth appeared. They'd been roommates since Arden's illness, at the behest of Dr. Zafeeyeh.

161

"Good morning, how are you?" Ruth was nicely fussy with Arden, making sure she ate well and rested.

"*Alhamdulillah,* and you?" Practicing Arabic was a way of distracting herself.

"You're still not sleeping." Ruth's gray eyes narrowed in concern.

"I'll sleep during the holiday."

"It's not too late for you to go back for Christmas."

"To the States? It's too far, too expensive."

"I have a friend at Royal Jordanian Air. We could still find a cheap flight to New York from Amman for you."

Arden managed a smile for Ruth. "Nah."

"You aren't homesick?"

She thought for a moment of Ohio at Christmas: gaudy colors, noisiness of carols made meaningless by repetition, cheap stuff foisted on frantic consumers, snarling mall crowds, dirty snow, excessive spending. Only Christmas Eve was special, holding hushed joy. It *was* a lovely story, after all, full of hope.

"I've made my home here."

Arden had thrown herself into work. She was helping to organize the Girls' College Film Club. She was also now on the planning committee for next year's curriculum. She had a solid feeling of being part of the college, a feeling that gratified her deeply since it was the first time she'd made a real effort to be included in a working community.

She stayed away from the all-weekend royal parties to avoid reminders of her reckless behavior with Johnny and Nawaf. She sent money to pay off her loans. She re-read *Dilmun*, steeping herself in ancient Bahrain; she read the Arabic newspaper, feeling linguistically accomplished yet still bored by the content; she read the Koran, still puzzled but increasingly intrigued.

Throughout, Faisal was infused, a backdrop in the tapestry of life she was trying to weave for herself in what she now thought of as her adopted country. She wondered how his adjustment was progressing, whether he liked his potential wife choices. She wondered what he would think of her observations of his society.

Her constant dreams of him were so painful.

She dreaded the emptiness of the upcoming break.

"I know we haven't been very close, Arden, but if something's wrong, we could talk about it," Ruth said, bringing her attention back to the kitchen.

Arden shook her head.

Yearning for him churned in her stomach, dragged her breath, and made her aware of the thinness of her skin. If she hadn't vowed to make more careful choices, she might have wished to transfer her longing to someone who could receive it—Johnny, or even Nawaf, or Ali—anyone in their circle, where relationships seemed to form, melt and re-form as easily, as promiscuously, as multiplying amoebas. Evelyn was now on her third prince, Ali wrapped up in someone else.

Johnny had called when he and Nawaf had gotten back from their mission, making it clear he'd like to see her again. She knew what that meant, and had demurred. "What, didja get your raghead?" he'd asked, amused.

Her glum silence made him laugh.

"Honey, get over it! Bird in the hand, babe, but I ain't waitin on ya."

"I know. I'm in kind of a different place now anyway."

"Like how?"

"I want to be a really good teacher here. Be an example for the girls, if I can."

"Good for you," Johnny answered slowly. She was pleased to hear the respect in his tone. "I guess we won't see you at the parties."

"You won't see me. But no hard feelings, okay?"

"Never."

Seeing Leila in class was a constant reminder of Faisal. She tried to overcome it by treating Leila very gently, very kindly, and then of course the others thought that was unfair. Leila had invited her for tea several times. Basking in Leila's warmth and humor in their kitchen was a bittersweet experience. She'd been disappointed, and relieved, that Faisal wasn't there. She had not asked about him.

She'd agreed to go to Leila's again after classes today. No wonder she dreamed of him. She wouldn't run into him at their house, though, it was the last, short day of class before the break. He'd be en route to his Ain Qanass dig.

"I'm fine," she repeated to Ruth now, pouring another cup of coffee. "I guess it's just taking awhile to get over being sick."

"You could cut back on your activities. Have an evening to rest sometimes."

"I like being busy. It keeps my mind active."

"I did that when I first came. It frightened me to be alone in my apartment downtown, so I overbooked myself with all kinds of things." Ruth smiled. "I was easily spooked by the Kingdom in those days."

"I didn't feel spooked here except a couple of times by the muttawas," Arden said. "I thought I'd like getting to know these people."

"The Saudis."

"Sure. I thought they'd be interesting." In truth, as much as she felt steeped now in the gentility of the people here, and as much as she was enjoying her involvement in the college, nobody in particular interested her anymore.

"I remember feeling that way too," Ruth said. "When I first went to Jordan everyone seemed fascinating in the beginning."

"Really?" The few Jordanians Arden had met in the Kingdom seemed aggressive and aggrieved, jealous of their wealthy neighbors. There was an ugly expat joke about how the 'noggin knockers' had struck oil by tapping their foreheads on the ground in prayer. Saudi luck was considered unearned by every other Arab country.

"It wore off," Ruth said. "Have you heard about the sojourn curve?"

Arden shook her head.

"It's a classic study of foreign students in the U.S., but it applies to everyone who lives in a different place for some set period of time. There's a U-shaped curve that describes the experience—at first, it's like a honeymoon phase, everything's intriguing and the native culture feels very seductive.

"Then, after acclimation, there's a deep let-down period where life gets difficult and the culture becomes impenetrable, even if the language is easier to understand. In fact, knowing the language well makes the experience even more depressing because it's understood that it's real life, not just a vacation or visit.

"Finally, when the sojourn nears its end, there's an intense re-engagement of the surrounding culture and an almost frantic embrace of it." Ruth sighed. "That's when people make their mistakes."

"Like what?"

"They fall in love, get married, drop out, sign up for new degree programs, get illegal jobs, overstay their visas, all kinds of life interruptions and changes, not *all* mistakes, I suppose, for the ones who make a go of their choices."

"So that's just, culturally induced, like brainwashing?"

"An avoidance of the life they're supposed to return to."

"Life in the States is such an enticement for lonely foreign students?" Like the uncle that Eyman had mentioned during Leila's party, imprisoned in his apartment for fear of the city at night, and of some of the students she remembered, now she'd had time to recall, in Columbus, who'd seemed permanently bewildered by the pace and brusque nature of American society.

"Or any country so different from one's own. It isn't geography, or the quality or comfort of the experience. It's the sojourn itself. They studied Peace Corps workers too, and found similar patterns. Even the barest Third World hut became a place to cling to, once leaving it seemed imminent."

"Strange," said Arden.

"It could be that some of this curve may be affecting you, Arden, now?" Ruth asked hesitantly. "You seem so much less cheerful than when I first met you."

"For sure, it feels like the honeymoon is over." That much she'd admit. "But I think I'm just tired. It's been a *long* semester."

At the bus stop a number of the teachers held covered dishes, contributions to the classroom parties held to celebrate the end of exams. Arden took her banjo, finally giving in to the girls' insistence that she play again, and the case dragged on her shoulder, heavy with the reproach of a long-neglected friend.

The last three Christmas Eves, she and her sister's boyfriend Kyle, a guitarist, played carols in her Mom's living room, under the tree, and Annie sang harmony. *Shut that memory out.*

She could not, however, refuse to play "Jingle Bells" when the Intermediate girls demanded it that morning, after she went through her folk repertoire for them again.

"How do you know this song?"

"Too many of our families study in America, they know the Christ-mas," Khadijah said. Arden had to smile at the sound of a proper Saudi princess belting out "dashing through the snow." And wouldn't you know, Khadijah even remembered what a bobtail nag was, from "Camptown Races." Arden taught them a couple of other secular numbers. They liked the references to snow and Santa Claus, and asked about his genesis. Her own laughter felt unused, but welcome, as she told them all about it.

TWENTY-EIGHT

A RDEN WAITED FOR LEILA at the gate when classes were over. She waved goodbye to the other students she recognized, and smiled her thanks when they called out, "Merry Christ-mas, Miss!"

Some had given her gifts, tokens of thanks and acknowledgement of the Christian holiday, which she found touching: she'd never been aware of Eid when teaching Arab students in the States. She remembered the early discussion with the expats about dominant cultures and thought, not for the first time, that Western culture really was the dominating one in the world, even here.

The only girls left in the empty schoolyard were the unfortunate ones whose rides had not yet arrived. They sat around on the benches under the bougainvillea, chattering and complaining. The stranded ones.

Maha had written a funny piece about this in the student newspaper—it was a veiled plea for driving privileges, but so cleverly written that it slipped past the censors and had enjoyed approval amongst the students and a number of teachers.

Arden wondered, with some amusement, whether she was being stranded now. Was she supposed to meet Leila somewhere else, or had Leila just forgotten about their tea date? Should she try calling their house? The admin here would have the number. She could beg Dr. Zafeeyeh for a ride back to campus; she would surely lend a driver.

Arden walked over to the low building where the college offices were housed, but they appeared to be empty. She was getting a little nervous. If she couldn't

167

find Leila or Dr. Zafeeyeh, what would she do? Ask for a ride from one of the last stranded ones? She did have one emergency number—Sayeed's, of course. He'd told them he was their last resort after all resources of the Womens' College were exhausted. She hoped she wouldn't have to call him.

She heard voices coming from behind the last closed office door. She hesitated outside for a moment. It sounded like, yes, it was Leila, she recognized, even in Arabic. But her voice was distorted with emotion of some kind. Arden leaned closer to the door, heart pounding. Leila sounded angry.

She knocked without thinking. The door opened. Dr. Zafeeyeh stood there, scowling, such a surprising expression that Arden didn't know what to say.

"Miss Arden." Leila's teary voice came from within the room. "I am sorry, that you waiting so long for me."

"What's wrong?"

Dr. Zafeeyeh asked Leila sharply, in Arabic, "Do you want her to know?"

"Aiwa." Yes.

Dr. Zafeeyeh sighed. "Come in, Miss Armstrong. We've had an unfortunate incident, I'm sorry to say. Although it has nothing to do with your department."

"Unfortunate—what?" Leila asked.

Dr. Zafeeyeh ignored her. "This girl's exam results came in today, as did everyone else's, as you know."

Arden nodded. She'd done her share of what was called invigilating, a British expression for supervising exams. The college went to extreme measures to prevent cheating, with rigorous standards for timing, seating, noise control, even lighting during the finals. It was an exhausting, nerve-wracking set of days for everyone involved. But Leila was a good student; she'd earned her A in Arden's class. What could this be about?

Dr. Zafeeyeh fixed Leila with a severe look. "We suspect, after a careful study, that this girl might have had an—irregularity—in her science exam."

"No! It isn't true!" Leila's voice cracked with anger. Arden walked over to put a hand on her shoulder.

"Dr. Zafeeyeh, what makes you think so?"

"Her score was much too high for the average, much higher than any other girl and in fact, higher than the boys' score also."

So? "Maybe she's just really *good*."

"Miss Armstrong. Your devotion to your students is well known. But in this area, you are unfamiliar with how things work. It's possible she saw the exam ahead of time."

"What!"

"Her brother is on the science faculty. Perhaps he was able to obtain it for her."

This was unbelievable. "Leila. Does Faisal know about this?"

Leila shook her head. "They don't let me to talk to him. He is probably still outside the school, waiting for me."

"Dr. Zafeeyeh, I met her brother, some time ago. Perhaps I can speak to him—"

Dr. Zafeeyeh's face grew even darker. "You are a young single teacher. You cannot be seen outside our college talking to a strange man alone!"

"Of course not. Excuse me, I wasn't thinking." Arden did think then. "I have another idea."

"Yes?"

"Let's have the science teacher test her individually, to see if she knows the material. Not from the exam. Independently." She went on, as if elaborating from long-standing pedagogical experience, putting an arrogant tone into her voice. "That's how we handled similar cases at the university where I held my last post. We found it to be a thorough method of testing real knowledge."

"Miss Abdul Aziz," Dr. Zafeeyeh said to Leila, "You may tell your brother that I kept you here. Then please come back. You will go with Mrs. Hamdi." She called for her assistant to accompany Leila.

Once the girl was gone, Dr. Zafeeyeh said, "Your conclusion is the same as mine, in this. It is the way we save face here."

Arden frowned her bewilderment. Save face?

"This is the worst part of my job." Dr. Zafeeyeh sighed heavily. "We can't have a girl scoring higher than the boys. It's just not done." At Arden's gasp, she continued, "Yes, I know. You think we're terrible. But we have to fight so hard, here, to keep our little autonomy. We're at risk every exam time, since the girls' scores keep rising to where the boys' are. Close, is not so bad. But to have a girl do so much better—we can't allow. The men won't allow, actually.

"So, we have the girl tested separately. If it isn't the same exam, she can get whatever score she likes." She sighed again. "We do it often. We redo entire exams."

"But did you have to humiliate her that way?"

"She already has the reputation of a rebel. If she knew why we can't let this score stand, she would protest so much that she'd get into much worse trouble than just taking another exam. You may find this cruel. I am doing it for her protection. I want her to finish her degree here, not to be expelled in disgrace."

Arden could not even begin to express her dismay. She kept quiet.

Leila returned in a few minutes. "He will wait," she said.

Dr. Zafeeyeh called the science department, but there was no answer. She turned back to them.

"Miss Al Ansary, this score will not stand. We will re-examine you after the break. If you choose to review the material, so much the better. We'll give you another chance to prove yourself." She looked at Arden. "Miss Armstrong, your support of your students is appreciated. I hope you rest during the next two weeks. Goodbye."

Arden followed Leila. Once outside, she hugged her tight. "I'm so sorry you had to go through that, honey!" The endearment slipped out without caution.

"Thank you, Arden, I knew you will be on my side. I never cheated in my life."

"It's so stupid!" Arden bit down hard on the inside of her lip to shut herself up. She did not want to blurt to Leila the entirety of the altered scores policy.

"Please, don't tell to Faisal. He will be so angry to her."

"How did you explain your lateness? And he must have seen you were crying."

"I told him that it's a woman's troubles. I told to him you were helping me."

'Woman's troubles' could be much more alarmingly misconstrued than school troubles. "You don't want to tell him the truth? You know this isn't your fault at all."

"I can't to say they think I cheat. Please, don't say anything."

"Okay. You're the boss." But this must be common knowledge at the university. Faisal wouldn't want Leila to be the victim of it; he needed to be told what had happened. Maybe she could get him alone to talk.

TWENTY-NINE

THEY VENTURED OUT TOGETHER. Arden paused when she saw a bearded man behind the wheel of the familiar Land Rover. Only after climbing in did she recognize Faisal's eyes; the rest of his features were completely altered by facial hair. Another man, also bearded, sat beside him. As was customary, neither turned to acknowledge the women.

The men were listening to some kind of speech, an Arabic exhortation. Arden saw that in fact, it was a tape, which Faisal popped out as soon as the women were settled. He replaced it with Nirvana. "Smells like Teen Spirit" tore out, its snarl rendered incongruous by the setting, as they sped past ministries lined up like wedding cakes. The man next to Faisal, apparently not a Nirvana fan, frowned coldly.

"Your brother looks different," Arden whispered to Leila.

"He changed so much since Haj. Now he is going to new *masjid.*"

"New *masjid?*"

"A different mosque. All they talk is political, all the time. It is very boring."

Arden kept her eyes down so she would not be tempted to look at Faisal. In spite of her worry about Leila, the sight of him squeezed longing around her chest as tight as her highest banjo string. What would they do if she reached forward to encircle his shoulders with her arms, to run her hand under his headdress to touch his hair? A scandal, disgrace, a hasty exit visa, *wullahi*; still, the image would not go away.

Faisal drove into a neighborhood of a type Arden had not seen before in Riyadh—old, unpaved, with twisting streets barely big enough to allow the Rover to pass. She noticed only one beaten-up looking street sign. Heavy mud brick walls seemed to lean in on them. Faisal turned into a courtyard where a cluster of mangy-looking goats scattered as they slowed to a stop. He got out with his companion and they walked together to a rusty metal door. They stood for a moment, talking. The looming buildings shadowed the men's faces. Faisal's formerly open expression was obscured by his beard, but Arden saw the flash of his smile as she watched him.

Leila nudged her. "Arden, don't look at them. The new people Faisal is meeting, they are very hard, you say, very consertive?"

"Conservative," she corrected automatically.

"Even more than Wahhabis."

Arden couldn't imagine any sect stricter than Wahhabism. "So he's more religious now?"

"Not Faisal, but these others men they are very strange. I don't know all they talk about, I don't see them together often. But I hear when he is driving me and they're with him. I don't like them. It isn't good, what they are talking."

"What do you mean?"

"I don't like to tell you. It is dangerous, they speaking like this in the Kingdom."

"How'd he get mixed up with them?"

"Some of them he knew before, some he's knowing from the new *masjid.*"

"So they're what, anti-government?"

"We can talk later, maybe. Faisal is coming back. He left that other man here."

Once in the Rover, Faisal turned to smile at them, and the warmth in his eyes shot through her like electricity. "Arden, how've you been?" His gaze narrowed slightly on her. "You still sick? You look a little … tired."

"You look a little hairy." Her hand flew to her mouth, to shut it, but brother and sister both laughed.

"I might take it off before my expedition."

"Ain Qanass."

"You remember." He smiled again, glancing at her in the rearview as they turned slowly out of the courtyard. His white teeth flashed against curved lips, set off by the blackness around them.

"Of course." *I remember everything.* She dropped her eyes and made herself sound authoritative. "You'll have to give another lecture when you come back, Faisal. All of us at the college want to hear about the excavations."

Leila said, "Yes, you can arrange with the English Department too. The girls always enjoy Faisal talking."

She suddenly thought of how other women saw him—in video classes, at the museum. And girlfriends, she assumed, back in the States, who'd been free to enjoy his smile, his kisses, his hands on them, his laughter in the morning. She pushed away these hungry, toxic, useless visions.

When they pulled into the long circular drive, Leila said, "We have surprise to show you." Arden could not imagine what she meant, but when they went inside, to the kitchen, she saw a little fake Christmas tree standing on the island, resplendent with twinkling lights and shining colored balls.

This was an astonishing surprise to see in a Saudi home.

It was nearly impossible to get Christmas-related items in the Kingdom. A few cooperative shopkeepers hoarded decorations and cooking ingredients, and expats passed around their bedraggled plastic trees to close friends when their contracts were up. Like urban legends, the trees seemed always to have existed: no one could remember how they'd actually acquired them in-country. Leila's expression was so expectant of Arden's pleasure, as she looked at her, that Arden had to smile.

"It's beautiful, Leila! This calls for a song."

Arden took out her banjo and perched on one of the barstools at the giant island. She stroked a few notes, getting into minor key, and looked up at Leila. Strumming with slow care, she sang the loveliest carol she knew, hoping its religious significance would not offend.

"What child is this, who, laid to rest, on Mary's lap is sleeping ... "

The silence in the room resonated with the last note. When she looked up, both were watching her with the same serious expression, Leila sitting rapt at the island, chin in hand, and Faisal leaning against a far counter, arms folded in his cloak. Maybe they thought it was a kind of prayer.

Time to liven things up. Arden launched into a rowdy version of "Deck the Halls." She would have done the Wassail song she loved, about the devil taking whoever didn't provide enough ale for the Wassailers, but it might be a little bawdy for good Muslims. Still, if they liked Rage and Nirvana, how offensive could a Christmas drinking song be? Never mind. She was supposed to be a model of rectitude.

"Do the one about always," Leila told her.

"I thought you didn't like love songs." She didn't want to sing that in front of Faisal. But she'd do whatever it took to make Leila smile tonight.

"It's not love song like most others."

She tuned to the key for "I Will Always Love You," the haunting Dolly Parton classic. She got through it by concentrating on the tricky chord changes, watching her fingers and singing deeply.

"Do the black hair song."

"Leila, you're in a romantic mood tonight," Arden said, hoping to tease her out of it. But Leila insisted. The old folk song was one of the class favorites, of course. She'd changed the gender to suit the girls' fancy.

Leila added a good contralto:

Black, black, black is the color of my true love's hair,
his face is something wondrous fair,

175

and the sweetest eyes of any lands
I love the ground on which he stands …

When she closed her eyes she could sing to Faisal directly, pouring out the weeks of yearning and this flush of renewed ardor. She peeked at him when the song was over. She wasn't sure if she was relieved or disappointed to see that he wasn't watching her. His head hung down, the fronds of his headdress drooping to his waist. In the silence that followed the music she heard clicking and saw his hand worrying a set of beads. He must have gotten a new strand since she'd broken the last ones.

Leila was also staring at the tile floor. Arden wanted to break this contemplative mood before it engulfed her. "Aren't we supposed to be having tea?"

Faisal turned on the lights above the island. He pocketed the beads, undid his cloak, rolled up his sleeves, and washed his hands at the sink. Leila joined him.

"When Leila told me you were coming, I thought maybe you'd like to make cookies with us," he said. "Winter breaks with my mother, these last few years when I was at Berkeley, she always made cookies at Christmas. She sent us the tree and cookie things this week."

Arden let the banjo slide gently to rest against the island. He'd been thinking of her, as kindly as Leila did, he wanted to make Christmas cookies with her. She was glad their backs were to her so they could not see the tears that welled up at his words. She wiped them away quickly, but not quickly enough for Leila, who turned just then.

"Oh, Arden, we're making you sad for your home? You are wanting your family now at the Christmas Eid?"

"No." Her voice quavered, but she said, "You're making me feel this is home too, you're like my family to do this for me."

"We feel the same. We wanted you to come to us, didn't we *ya* Faisal."

"Absolutely." He smiled directly at Arden, and his look of frank affection dried her tears. He handed her a rolling pin. "We needed your help in the kitchen."

Faisal assembled ingredients and utensils on the island's granite surface, and soon they were each rolling out dough in separate spaces. Faisal's mother had sent sugar decorations and cookie cutters in seasonal shapes, and Arden had to explain to Leila what the reindeer signified and how a snowman was made. She sang "Rudolph" and "Frosty."

Faisal corrected her description of snowman construction technique, insisting that the body could be created without rolling balls of snow.

"Oh like you'd know? You had snow in California?"

"We went to Aspen some Christmas times, I know about snow."

"Sure, to ski in, not to build from."

"I won the snowman contest one year. Actually it was a snow lady." The gleam in his eyes allowed her to laugh at him outright.

"Your brother is not as religious as he looks, Leila, even with that long beard," she said playfully. Joking with him was like being able to breathe again. Leila looked from one to the other of them, grinning. Arden played "Winter Wonderland" while the cookies baked. Faisal made tea.

"Can you do "Amazing Grace"?" he asked, as the kettle whistled. "That's my mother's favorite."

"Of course. But you have to sing too, I bet you know the words." She played the old hymn, and sang, and he joined in with a decent tenor when he turned from the stove. They watched each other, finishing with a little harmonized flourish.

"Faisal, if the archaeology thing doesn't work out for you here, I think we should take our show on the road," she told him. "Leila, you'd pay to hear this, right?"

"I didn't hear him singing in English before. I will pay. Faisal, it is sad you didn't bring your guitar here."

"You play guitar?" Another reason to love him.

He nodded.

"But you don't have it with you?"

"I left it at my mother's. You know how we are, here, about musical performances." Wahhabism frowned on it.

"Nobody ever gave me trouble about playing my banjo in class."

"You're a Westerner," he said, with a charming shrug.

They sat in the den off the kitchen and argued about whose cookies were better looking, better tasting, when they ate them. Arden felt relaxed enough to curl up in a corner of the sofa, feet tucked under her long skirt, head resting back as she watched their sibling banter. Their warmth was profoundly soothing after these dry weeks; she felt it creeping into her rigid limbs and loosening her tight nerves. If she could spend more time with him, easy like this, maybe she could shake off her pining. Maybe she would get used to him, like a brother, if she saw him often.

"Thank you," she told them some time after the teapot was emptied. "I needed this so much."

She realized how they resembled each other as they looked at her again; their large eyes differed only in color. Their compassionate expressions were the same.

"I'm sure it's hard on you to be away from family this time of year," Faisal said. "I remember my first year at college in the States, trying to fast for Ramadan in the dorm before I knew there were other Muslims on campus. It was lonely." He looked at her closely. "Are you sure you're recovered?" he asked. "You look tired."

She felt heat flush her face. "Thanks for asking. I'm okay."

"I want you to come to my engagement party," Leila said. "It's next month."

"I'll be glad to come! When did you decide? Who did you finally choose?"

Sister and brother shared an amused glance.

"I didn't decide," Leila said, "but I agree to accept. He is one of my off-cousins, one of the few that I would consider to marry."

"One of the *very* few intelligent ones," Faisal said.

"Is he kind? Is he ..." Arden hesitated, not sure how far she could go with this. "Is he attractive, to you? Is he interesting as a person? Is he funny?"

"She's so picky," Faisal told Leila. "One out of four would do." Arden smiled, taking his teasing as another sign of his ease with her.

"I didn't see him since we were children, so I don't know is he attractive to me right now, but Faisal met him too many times to exam him for me. And I saw his video, and I talk to him on the phone."

"Do you like what you know? Will he be a good friend to you?"

"He will be good. We both like mathematics. He's going to study in Indiana next year, and I might apply there too."

"That's next to Ohio!" Arden sat up, thrilled. "*Wullahi!* I'll come see you!"

"*Wul-la-hi*," Faisal imitated Arden's inflection in soft, amused mimickry, as Leila jumped up.

"I will bring to you his picture. He's a handsome boy, you will see."

THIRTY

ARDEN LOOKED OVER at Faisal after Leila left, wanting to emphasize and prolong their new familiarity, but she wouldn't discuss the Womens' College until they were well away from Leila's possible hearing. "She seems happy about this."

"It's one of the reasons I came back. I didn't want her fixed up with some idiot. He's younger than she is, so he'll let her be strong. And we won't let him take other wives." His laugh was short. "Don't give me that look. You know it happens sometimes."

"So, Faisal, how about you? Did they find you a wife yet?" She said it lightly, but he did not smile. He looked down as if deciding how to answer. Maybe the topic made him uncomfortable, since it was really none of her business. She leaned forward and chose another. "Tell me about the new mosque you've found."

"Leila told you?" His wary frown suddenly reminded her of Sayeed. She could see how drawn his face was behind the beard. He had lost weight in these weeks, as she had. "What do you want to know?"

She attempted to neutralize his unexpected reserve. "I'm getting pretty interested in religion. I read the Koran every day."

"And you're finding ... what?"

"I've wondered how Islam could be so widely interpreted by so many groups. It seems so straightforward to me."

"How?"

"It seems to me that Muhammad—peace be upon him," she remembered to say, "wanted to bring prosperity to the region by getting the tribes together around Mecca, tribes which worshipped different idols, by revealing his own belief in one deity. He thought that would enlighten people, and get them to behave as a community."

"That's how you read it?"

"He knew that if the fighting stopped, there would be a better chance for economic and social development in the region. Monotheism was a simple solution."

"So you conclude Islam was a political creation."

"Political? No, profoundly spiritual. The tribes were enlightened by their belief. It provided structure." This was what she found so appealing. "I like that Islam is so clear-cut. That's why it seems odd, to me, that there *are* so many different interpretations. I mean, it seems like these interpretations, all over the Islamic world, are the real political creations. Ways of manipulating people."

"There are different interpretations within Christianity too."

"It's a matter of faith."

"But some Christians put more emphasis on your Trinity idea, or Mary, for example. What kind of Christian are you, Arden? Catholic, Protestant?"

"I stopped accepting that whole story a long time ago, actually," she said slowly, realizing it was a bittersweet revelation in this strange new Christmastime, watching for any sign of disapproval on his face. In the Koran, people without religious belief were considered unclean. It was hard to tell what his expression was, under the heavy beard; his emphatically religious aspect was daunting.

"You're not a believer?" His tone was mild.

She admitted cautiously, "No. I think this is all there is, no omnipotent guy on a cloud watching out for us, no afterlife in Heaven if we behave a certain way." She watched his slow nod. "I guess that makes me an infidel in your book."

"It makes you a seeker for new ideas, if you found Christianity confining. You're studying the Quran. Maybe you'll find what you're looking for. We're all seekers, *ya* Arden." He smiled, a smile not so much of approval, she realized, as she might have expected from a conservative proselytizing Muslim, but of understanding.

"So, Faisal, you know what I think, now tell me about your new mosque."

He just looked at her, smile fading.

"You can be straight with me. You know from Leila I keep confidences."

"I know that from you, Arden. But are you sure you want to talk about this?"

"I want to talk about how things are going in your life."

"The people I'm meeting ... see some things as I do."

"What are you seeing?"

"Too much I don't accept."

"Politically."

He nodded.

"So ... is this a new feeling? At the museum, you seemed to be okay with government and oil support of the digs."

He shrugged. "Early days. I was trying to adapt."

"But then you found out about the air bases during Haj. I get that made you mad, maybe made you anti-government, but Faisal, excuse me for being so direct, why would you want to bite the hand that feeds you?"

"Maybe I'd rather feed myself. What we're too dependent on can destroy us." His mouth twisted in a bitter little smile. "I know this concept is alien to Americans. You're so used to freedom of expression, it's inconceivable to you that others don't have it."

"But I thought Wahhabism doesn't lend itself to free political expression," she said, recalling a phrase she'd read in the newspaper, wondering if she'd understood its Arabic correctly. "I read King Fahd believes democracy isn't appropriate to this region, that the people are like—" she broke off, remembering how she'd been surprised by the word that she'd so far associated, actually, with Christianity. She chose her conclusion carefully, aware the discussion was approaching dangerous ground. "The leader is like a shepherd, for his flock? That he guides them."

"You mean King Fahd's mouthpieces." His contempt was obvious. "What's left of him since his stroke isn't capable of leading. The assumption is we're as stupid as sheep, that even a disabled king is wiser than the people."

Cold chills raced up her spine. It was common to complain about bureaucracy, but nobody was supposed to criticize the monarchy, not out loud, not even in their homes, nobody. It was the worst heresy. "But ... you don't think so?"

"We're fully capable, with some education, of governing ourselves."

"So, is this why you joined the new mosque? They agree with you?" She reached to understand. "But if they're religious, don't they share the monarchy's view of Islam?"

"They do. They believe democracy is a threat to Allah's divine sovereignty."

"So then ... you don't agree with them either? Even though you're wearing their beard?" As if he were adopting a disguise.

He took out his string of beads and studied it. Purple, she saw, deep and even as the sky above Bethlehem had purportedly been on that long ago Christmas eve. He clicked through them, one by one, was he praying? Counting? He suddenly looked up at her through thick lashes, a look that felt as intimate and perilous as touch. But his smile was not a smile, she saw, under his beard, it was a tightening of the lines around his eyes and mouth that could signify pain as much as pleasure.

"Have you heard our expression about friendship, Arden?"

She shook her head.

"We say, the enemy of my enemy is my friend. We use it to learn algebra." He studied her then as if she was far away, or perhaps behind glass, from someone else's collection—a curiosity. He seemed to be lost more in his thoughts than in her face, despite his close inspection. Finally a wry expression gently lifted the corners of his mouth, the soft mouth she was so thirsty for, but did not warm his eyes.

She wanted to bring him back from that distant place. "Faisal."

Now his eyes focused deeply on hers. "You've been in the Kingdom awhile now. Do you still *love* everything?" His tone told her how naïve he thought that was. "I've known Americans who think they're living in some kind of movie here, and we're the exotic natives in funny costumes. Is that what you love, is that how we seem to you? Like the Arabian Nights?" It sounded mocking as he mimicked a sexy-sheikh pose, flinging out his headdress, hand on hip. Who had insulted him like this?

"No, Faisal, that's not who you are to me."

She felt too defensive, now, to tell him how his culture had been seeping in as her Arabic improved, as she kept up with her Koranic reading, as her enjoyment of the girls grew and her college involvement deepened. She'd felt, at times in the last six weeks, that she could flow right into their society as if born to it. Maybe she *was* still in the honeymoon period of her sojourn, as Ruth described this morning and as Faisal's sarcastic expression seemed to conclude, but the attachment felt genuine.

"So what *do* you see?" he asked.

"Politically? There's definitely hypocrisy. One way of behavior for royals, another for ordinary people. But I don't see any outward resentment, I don't see any unrest or demands for democracy. Most people seem happy here. My girls *will* find a way to drive, eventually, but they care more about getting real jobs than voting."

"That just shows you how fucked up things are. They don't realize they'll never get one without the other."

Wow. He said "fucked up."

"Of course you'll never see unrest. We've mastered oppression to a degree you wouldn't believe. It's even worse since the war."

"But there's so little crime, Faisal—"

"You buy that hype?" He gave a cynical laugh. "Terrible crimes are committed here, but if the perpetrator's identity is an embarrassment to the regime, or the crime itself, for that matter, it's completely covered up. It happens all the time."

"But there *is* social progress, and people aren't poor." Khadijah's most recent speech had been on the charitable society she and other socially aware princesses had founded, to build a shelter for battered women and what she called 'girls who are mothers but not wives,' a radical concept in the Kingdom. That had to be a sign of significant activism. "You should be impressed by the way social awareness is growing here. There's reason to be optimistic."

"Of course social awareness is growing. Our per capita income's dropped by half in the last ten years, and our population's exploded. There are too many idle kids with no skills and nothing to do. They're not educated, even the ones at our school. We have a lot of problems to solve."

"Yes," she acknowledged. "But people seem so devout that it appears to make up for the challenges—"

"Blind devotion can be an escape."

Now he sounded like a Marxist! "Faisal, you're devout too!"

"Individually, yes, but my society, spiritually speaking? We're in great pain."

"But you've got Mecca! The guardians, right, you're in charge of the whole deal? It's like living in the Vatican, how can you be in pain? You have the hotline to Allah!"

"It's not about Makkah," he said impatiently. "That's just a symbol. Besides, an enemy militia is the guardian now, not Muslims."

The way he said 'enemy' jolted her. "Faisal! You're talking about *Americans*. We aren't your enemy! We're

185

here to protect you." She remembered Johnny. "I mean we're teaching you to protect yourselves."

"We could have done that without you, we have *mujahedin*."

"Inside the Kingdom?"

"Some few here, some in Afghanistan. You trained them during their war against the Russians," he clarified. "Many of us would have been willing to defend our country without American help."

"Didn't you need it?"

"You were *forced* on us. You don't belong here anymore. Your presence makes it so much harder for those of us who want freedom."

Stung by the directness of his words, she stood. "That's not fair! I know you're angry about that base they're building—"

"*You're* building."

"But your country *invited* us to come for Desert Storm! And as far as I'm concerned, personally, I'm doing the best I can to be a good teacher. I'm working harder here than I ever did in the States, and I'm liking it more. And the girls like me."

He stood too, and put a hand on her arm. "I'm not talking about you personally, *ya* Arden. I want you here. In the Kingdom and in my family's home. You've been a good friend to Leila. *I'd* be a better friend to you, if circumstances allowed."

His touch was warm, and in his expression was the tender admiration she'd been longing for. She stared at him, trying to recall her point. He was so close she couldn't think straight. His eyes reminded her. "*You're* part American."

He dropped his hand. "I know there are so many Americans who came here to teach, and build, and learn. I appreciate that." He stepped back. "But the U.S. military has to leave. We need to manage our own development."

"How are they stopping you?"

"They're keeping this corrupt regime in power."

"But that friend of mine, the guy you met at the hospital, is a pilot, and he and his buddies are building your air force, along with your own royal family."

"Johnny. Prince Nawaf." His laugh was derisive. "They're deluded! I've talked to them. They have no idea how they're being used."

She could see no good coming from a deeper friendship between Johnny and Nawaf and Faisal, and she could see no way out of this uncomfortable conversation. She wished to recapture the moment just passed, when he said he'd like to be a better friend. But he was on the other side of the room now, a distant look replacing the sweet one, his arms folded as if to keep her away.

THIRTY-ONE

IT WAS A WELCOME DISTRACTION when Leila came back into the room and handed Arden a photo of a comely youth in a headdress.

"He's handsome! You'll have to bring this to class, the girls will be jealous."

"They saw his picture already, but they aren't jealous. We have too many handsome men for every girl here." Leila's smile was mischievous as she looked from Arden to Faisal. "Even Faisal is handsome when he doesn't have beard, don't you think so Miss Arden?"

"Uh uh, I'm not going there." Arden laughed. She didn't want Leila to discern her feelings for Faisal.

"I think she's going back to campus, *ya* Leila, it's getting late. I'm getting some stuff upstairs. We can leave in about twenty minutes." He left them.

"Thanks for the cookies," Arden told Leila. "My Mom will be glad when I tell her. She's a real Christmas fanatic. She doesn't like the idea of my being alone here."

"Next year I will meet her, I hope."

"She'd love that. I'm very happy for you, Leila." She spoke quietly then. "I want you to know, I'm not letting this exam accusation go without a fight."

"No, Miss Arden, I want to forget it after the second test."

"You can. I won't."

Leila turned to fiddle with Arden's banjo. "Thank you for the music. Faisal didn't hear any banjo before. I could see that he liked very much."

"Oh, he probably heard it in the States, but didn't know what he was hearing. He was there a long time." She fastened her abaya, deciding to say more. After all, Leila had opened the topic earlier. "I'm surprised he's so anti-American, actually, Leila. I'd have thought, after living in California for school, and having an American mother—"

"He worries she is too free."

"Really."

"He loves her, of course, she is very friendly and beautiful, with hair like yours. She is full of life. Very good artist, she makes the silver jewelry. But she lives like hippie woman. She even uses drugs." Arden glanced away. "He doesn't like to see her with a boyfriend."

"She's American. It's a different culture. Didn't he date, too, in the States?"

"Date?"

"Have girlfriends."

"Yes, every time I visit him, he has different girlfriends. But, you know, he is a young single man."

"So older single women aren't allowed to have a boyfriend?"

"But she is his mother. Do you like to think your mother has a boyfriend?"

"Actually, my Mom doesn't date much, but that's just because there aren't many available men for her in Columbus." At Leila's surprised look, she clarified, "My parents are divorced."

Leila walked over to the window, which looked onto a stone courtyard. A small lit fountain was playing in the middle. Her wide, mobile mouth, so much like her brother's, flattened into a line as she stood there. "Faisal doesn't like his wife. He is arguing with my father and stepmom Aisha all of the time." Arden felt an implosion inside, as if her heart were collapsing into her stomach. "It is my only sadness, now. I don't understand what is happening to him."

"When did he get married?" Arden managed to ask, feeling herself age as she stood, right there in the Al

Ansary den. Why had he not told her, when she'd asked him just now? "I'll have to congratulate him."

"He didn't marry yet. He refused to have the engagement party. Her family is very angry to us. I'm glad they are in Jiddah, not in Riyadh."

"Why doesn't he like her?"

"I don't know. It is the first time he isn't talking to me like my brother." Leila turned to her, with the determined look Arden recognized from class arguments. "I like to ask you a favor."

"Anything."

"I like to ask you, talk to Faisal about what is happening to him now. He isn't used to Arab women, he is used to American, since he was eighteen he lived mostly in America. He has a good respect for you. He thinks you are brave. He was asking me how are you all the time, after you got sick. He might talk to you."

"He doesn't really know me, Leila, and it isn't my business."

"Ready to go?" They heard Faisal call as he came back into the kitchen. Leila kept her eyes on Arden.

"Talk to him, for me. Please."

When Faisal came into the den, fastening his cloak, they saw he was once more clean shaven. He handed Arden her scarf, but it drooped ignored in her hand as she stared at the change in him. The shape of his face was newly, sharply defined, and his eyes stood out like sculpted searchlights. He looked somehow more Saudi than when she'd first met him; he had lost the tan of the breezy hilltop, and the cheer of the museum. He looked more like the typical narrow-featured Nejdi man indigenous to Riyadh. There was a sternness she had not seen in him before.

Even more surprising than his new face was the appearance of an older man behind him, a man who was so clearly their father that Arden beamed at him, in a way she knew was not appropriate in the Kingdom, but that she could not contain.

He didn't seem offended. He came right up. "I've heard so much about you, Miss Armstrong. It's good to meet you. I'm Othman Al Ansary." His English was as easy as Faisal's, his smile as infectious as Leila's. He had her sparkling brown eyes.

"*Asalaamu aleikum.*" As the visitor, she knew instantly that she should have let him say it. She knew better, at least, than to offer her hand.

"*Wa aleikum a salaam!*" He laughed, and looked at his son and daughter. "You didn't tell me she speaks perfect Arabic."

"Thank you. I appreciate the hospitality of your home."

His eyes were shrewd, evaluating whether she was a fit companion for them even as his words flowered further. She was glad her abaya was straight. "This is a lucky friendship. You're all part of the university we built in the middle of the desert, Miss Arden, you and both of my children."

"These two are my favorite people in the whole Kingdom," she said, looking at Leila and Faisal. "My good friends here." Leila grinned at her. Faisal smiled. "As for the university, sir, I'd be honored to discuss it with you. At length."

"I see why Leila likes you," Othman said, smiling. "I hear an opinion already, I think? We'll have you come to a real dinner soon. Not cookies! We can discuss educational progress in the Kingdom." This was an enlightened invitation—an unsegregated gathering with ideas on the menu. Arden had been to a number of dinner parties at other students' homes, always only with women. She understood, now, how it was that Leila and Faisal were so comfortable expressing liberal thoughts.

"No, Baba, boring," Leila said. She winked slightly at Arden, to signal silence. The test score issue was obviously still on both their minds.

Othman ran an affectionate hand down his daughter's long black hair. "Any other topic then, *ya helwa*. You can do all the talking. As usual."

191

Arden and Faisal both laughed at this.

"You found your electric," Leila told him. She touched his smooth cheek. "Is better. You don't look like imam anymore."

He shot an amused glance at his father. "No imams in our backyard, eh Baba."

"Good luck in Ain Qanass, ya Faisal." Othman said, in Arabic that Arden understood. "Drive safely. Find a lot of pots."

Faisal enveloped them both, his cloaked arms spread like wings as he embraced them. "Don't worry." He went on in Arabic. Arden's throat tightened as she watched them, touched by their closeness and by his ease in expressing love.

THIRTY-TWO

IN SPITE OF THE BURDEN of Leila's request, and the burden of Leila's exam, in spite of the knowledge that he was supposed to be someone else's husband now, Arden couldn't suppress her excitement at the prospect of the long drive alone with Faisal. She could not suppress the urge to sit as close as possible, leaning her elbows on the seatback dividing them to talk in the intimate darkness. This might be the last time she'd be able to.

"*Ya Hajji* Faisal." She loved saying his name. "You think we'll run into another khamseen?"

"*Ya sheikha* Arden. I don't think so. It's a clear night."

"Too bad. It was fun playing cards. You still have some candy bars back here."

"Have one." Have whatever you like, his tone said. Perhaps he also felt the whiff of last-chance freedom between them.

She inched forward and patted his shoulder, as she would have done with any friend, knowing that was clearly breaking the barrier between them but reasoning he'd broken it first tonight, with his light touch in the den. "I had too many cookies. Faisal, thanks for including me, to bake with you and Leila. I'll always remember your kindness."

He sent her a quick sideways smile. "Thanks for your singing. That's what they call bluegrass? It's nice. Play some more."

"Mostly it's what they call folk music." She took out her banjo and found the notes after a little fiddling.

193

"Black, black, black is the color of my true love's hair, his face is something wondrous fair, and the sweetest eyes of any lands, I love the ground on which he stands."

She played "You are my Sunshine": the words reminding her of how she'd awoken that morning: *"the other night, dear, as I lay sleeping, I dreamed I held you in my arms, but when I woke I was mistaken, and I hung my head and cried."*

She played "Pack up your Sorrows," "Wild Mountain Thyme," and "Barbara Allen," songs the girls enjoyed. She closed her eyes and poured her heart into singing for him. Faisal drove at an almost leisurely speed, letting other drivers swoop past.

They rode in silence for a time after she finished. She wished the drive would go on forever, she wished for another storm, anything to delay their eventual parting. She wondered how to broach Leila's topics.

"*Ya Hajji.* Look at the moon." The moon was sailing full and yellow overhead, its orb at the largest, early stage of the evening, illuminating the dunes and the stars, which shared its splendid space as a backdrop of lustrous sparkles. "Will you stop so I can see the desert at night?"

Without hesitation, he pulled over far past the shoulder.

The air held a freshness that was surprising in such dry environs. She took in deep breaths of the clean scent.

"Let's walk a little, if it's safe here. I have something important to tell you."

"Oh?"

"It's kind of awkward." She started walking, and he joined her.

"Yes?" he said quietly, watching her. A tiny smile played on his lips. She wondered what he was imagining. She wished she could choose a sweeter subject, one leading to romantic conclusions; she was exhilarated by the sense of opulent possibility in their easy companionship and in the wide moonlight.

"It's the university. Remember we talked about hypocrisy, earlier?"

"The ... university?" He sounded baffled by her choice of subject.

"Did you know girls aren't allowed to score higher than boys on the same test? That they make the girls retake tests if that happens?"

"No. I didn't hear this before. How do you know?"

"Apparently it's pretty routine. The Womens' College Admin says the men insist on it." She looked at his profile as they walked. He was frowning.

"There are many crazy rumors. It isn't what Baba thinks, the academic life here. But it's my first semester, and I don't teach a girls' subject. I don't know if this is true."

"It's true."

"How do you know?" he repeated.

"Leila was accused of cheating on a science test this afternoon. That's why we were late. She was afraid to tell you, in fact she made me promise not to talk about this. Dr. Zafeeyeh even had the nerve to imply that you might have given her the test, Faisal. She said it right in front of Leila. I couldn't believe it."

"Dr. Zafeeyeh?" He stopped. "What was your conclusion?"

"I suggested the science teacher examine her separately."

He nodded slowly. "Thank you. That was wise. It allows them to save face."

"You're thanking me? That's what she did! You *agree* with her?"

"Of course I do. I understand how they think."

"How should we explain this to Leila? She didn't want you to find out, but I felt it was important for you to know—"

"I don't want Leila to know she was accused only because of this nonsense about keeping the boys' scores higher than the girls'."

"Why on earth not?"

"She'd raise a fuss, you know her, she'd get herself in terrible trouble." She couldn't believe she was hearing tired resignation in his tone. She'd expected him to be outraged. "I don't want her to know why this happened."

"So you think being accused of cheating is less dangerous to Leila, ultimately, than knowing where this injustice comes from?"

"Believe me, they'll never mention cheating publicly, in relation to a Saudi. It's better for Leila, now, to let this go."

"Dr. Zafeeyeh already mentioned it to me! You want to cover this *up*?"

"She needs to graduate in June so that she can leave here. I can't let this get in her way. It was hard enough finding that one decent cousin for her."

"But this is as bad as the politics you were talking about!"

"It's part of the same corruption, the same repression, like the censorship issue," he agreed. "But I'm not going to hold up Leila's progress at the university." He frowned at her. "I want her out of here with her degree and her husband, settled safely."

This seemed a strange way of putting things. "I think Leila deserves to know how this happened, and that she's not to blame." She stared at him, aggrieved and disappointed by his lack of support. "This thing has *got* to change, if not for your sister then for the others. I thought you of all people would agree with me. But maybe it's not important to you, since it's just about college girls. Not about ... revolution."

She started walking again, fast, away from him. It was tough going. The ground was uneven, hard on the small ridgetops and alarmingly soft in the valleys. Her irritation increased with every summit. When she reached the top of one bony ridge, she bent to pick out a chunk of sand. She threw it down the other side, unsatisfied as it disintegrated in the air without impact. She tried a few more, and was equally frustrated. Weren't there any rocks in the desert?

Faisal spanned the distance between them in a few long strides. "Here, like this." He dug into the sand and came up with a heavy clump. He handed it to her. "Try it now."

She flung it with all her might and it smashed, splashing the duneside opposite them. He handed her another. That one, too, was heavy enough to draw out her anger.

"You need some pillars," he told her. Was that a smile?

"Pillars?"

"You're trying to stone the devil." Yes. He thought this was funny.

"I'm trying to stone this—this bullshit about men and women here." She hefted a menacing handful and measured the distance between them.

His reaction was unsatisfying. He held up one hand as if to ward her off, but pulled his face straight as if to contain, and could not, a spilling out of laughter. Once it was out, he leapt up the dune sideways so he could laugh freely out of her reach, his draped figure shaking. Under other circumstances she would have enjoyed his loss of control. She considered him a moment, thinking of the lovelorn weeks she had passed dreaming about his eyes. She felt a thrill of pure hostility. She hurled the sandball at him.

Her aim was true. It hit him square on the head, hard enough to knock off his *aghal,* the black rope anchoring his headdress. The falling sand pulled the rest of his headdress off. He clutched it, still laughing, spitting out sand and shaking his hair. He sat down on the side of the little dune, elbows on the robe pulled taut against his knees.

She decided not to toss another.

"I won't let this rest. I'm going to take this up as high as it can go."

He finally looked up, dusting his hands. "I appreciate your loyalty to her."

"Then why are you laughing at me?"

He grinned again. "I'm not. It's just the way you looked, *ya* Arden, trying to stone the devil without stones." He laughed once more.

She waded up to him, hiking her long skirt to climb. It was hard going. She sat near him and then lay down, linking her hands behind her head for a pillow, and she looked up at the sky.

THIRTY-THREE

THE MAGNIFICENCE OF STARS fell on her like a wave, like an enormous wave crashing down with boisterous strength. The constellations she'd admired, lakeside summers near Columbus, were a little different-looking in this generous Eastern sky. The Big Dipper seemed elongated. Orion's Belt drooped past the frame of her vision. Closing one eye, she raised a finger to trace its trajectory, to try to connect it to where she thought the North Star should be. She pictured Saudi Arabia on the globe, and pieced together the equatorial countries encircling Earth. The Kingdom, for all its heat, was still way north of the Equator. So, then, the North Star was right over there …

"Which one are you looking for?" He was lying back now too.

"The North Star."

"There." He pointed, but she couldn't follow. They were all so bright.

"Where?"

He took her hand. His was warm, a little sandy: his arm was strong against hers as he lifted their linked hands toward the sky. Her awareness of him came back in a swoony rush she tried to ignore. He moved her finger to the star which, she now saw, was even brighter than its fellows.

"I've never seen such stars. They're incredible."

"This is nothing. We're still so close to Riyadh. You should see them in the Rub Al Khali. The Empty Quarter."

The very name held a fascinating chill. "What's it like there?"

"Empty." They both laughed. He lowered their hands to the ground between them, but left hers loosely in his, almost as if he'd forgotten they were joined. He stared upwards, still. "No, not really empty. It's very beautiful. The sand is almost red. It's the cleanest place I've ever seen, the quietest. And there's life, if you know where to look."

"Do you go on digs there?"

"No, I just go camping sometimes. People passed through, but nobody lived there long enough to leave anything interesting behind."

"I wish I could go."

He turned his head to her and smiled. He was so close she could see, in the moonlight, individual grains of sand clinging to his luxuriant black curls. She looked at them; she could not look into his eyes. "I'd show you so much, if it were possible, *ya* Arden, I wish I could. I really like the way you enjoy things here."

"Oh." She swallowed. "Well. I like you too. *Ya* Faisal." Her palm felt suddenly sweaty, but she didn't want to take it from his.

"You're a good friend to Leila. Thanks for standing up for her." As he continued to look at her, he stopped smiling. "You'll get in trouble if you pursue this test score issue, you know, you already dodged a bullet with Al Issam once."

"I don't care. It's outrageous. The others will think so, too, when I tell them."

"Let me talk to the guys in the Science Department, see what evidence I can get. But I have to warn you, you're taking a risk. We get rid of troublemakers here. We send them away. Or worse."

"Let em try."

He scooped sand between their palms with his still-joined hand. "You're going to use this again? It'll take more than sand."

"So what will you be using?"

"What do you mean?"

"You and your new mosque people, Faisal, what are you going to use to change things here? To stone your devils?"

He turned his face to the sky again without answering. He rubbed the sand between their hands with his palm. She wondered if the stimulation was intended to distract her. His touch felt natural and she rubbed back, instinctively. "Leila's worried about you," she told him. "She's afraid your involvement with these people is dangerous."

"I know."

"And she's afraid it might be distracting you from ... settling down." She didn't want to say more than that, in spite of Leila's request. For one thing, he hadn't welcomed her probing his engagement before, in the den. For another, she wasn't willing to give airtime to the competition. If she didn't talk about other women in his life, she could pretend they didn't exist.

"Leila still thinks of me as the kid she knew when we were growing up here. I have different priorities now. We can't always do what our families want." He shifted away to sit up. He shook out his headdress and sifted sand from his hair. She watched as he folded the cloth back on top of his head and stood. "We should go. It's late." He looked around at the ground near his feet. "Do you see my aghal anywhere? It's like a round rope?"

Arden felt it suddenly, under her calf. She'd thought she was lying on a little ridge. She pulled it out, rose, and stood in front of him. She hit it against her hip like a tambourine, loosening its sand. "Even if your priorities changed, Faisal, you should still listen to the people who worry about you. People who care about you."

He reached for the aghal, but she held it back, seized by a playful impulse. "Let me put it on you." He stood still, eyes down, as she pulled the braided rope tightly onto his head, the way she thought it was supposed to go. He winced.

"Too tight? Here." She pushed it up a little higher so that it just rested on the cloth of his headdress. It didn't seem heavy enough to hold the fabric down by itself, but Faisal nodded. His headdress was the thick red-checked woven kind worn, she supposed, in winter. The lines around his eyes seemed to crinkle then, just a little, as if her fussing amused him. Encouraged, she smoothed the long sides of his headdress down onto his shoulders. Her hands lingered on his upper arms, unwilling to let go. She felt his breathing quicken.

She felt the victory of his cloaked arms slowly surrounding her, tentative at first, in an embrace that grew more defined as his arms confirmed their hold. She reached around his waist, not clutching him tight as she'd done after the khamseen but just linking her hands loosely over his cloak. She rested her head on his shoulder and breathed him in deeply, feeling the pain of her ache for him dissipate as quickly as the rain had in the desert. The relief was so powerful she could have slept right there, lulled by the strong thudding of his heart.

She felt his chest rise and fall, heard him swallow. She lifted her face to look at him. The expression in his eyes was hidden by the shadow of his headdress as he looked back. A moment's contemplation passed between them. Then he brought one sure hand up to thread his fingers into her hair, under her scarf, and wrapped his other arm around her waist, pulling her close. He took her mouth into the kiss she had imagined so often, a long, slow, warm kiss she would have gladly drowned in. A few grains of sand were still on his tongue and he rolled them into hers as if they were sugar. They clung, swaying, before he pulled away, dropping his arms and looking down. She clutched her abaya around herself and shivered. She could barely stand up without him.

"*Ya* Arden. *Ya salaam.*" He shook his head. "I was afraid of this, with you."

"You're afraid of one hug, Faisal, one kiss?"

"You know it isn't enough. This is—just the beginning."

His quiet admission gave her the courage to say, "Then let it be the beginning."

"It's complicated." The desire she heard in his soft voice gave her hope, but it did not alter the conflict in the way he lowered his tone. "I like you, so much." He reached to grip her hand once, firmly, and let it drop. "But it wouldn't be fair to you, Arden, a beginning between us. I have ... obligations."

The Jiddah woman he was promised to. Of course he would do the honorable thing for his family, in the end. She couldn't extend herself in the face of this discouragement. She looked at the sand under her feet and toed a channel, digging back and forth. Slippery grains fell into the channel as fast as she tried to rub it deeper, erasing the little chasm she was trying to create between them. He watched her.

She did not know how long they might have stood like that, possibly until the next khamseen swept over to bury them like a couple of Dilmun figures, but their stillness was shattered by the roar of a jet fighter overhead, and another, and a third: the nightly F15 reconnaissance run from the nearby Prince Sultan Airbase. The desert shimmered with rumbling vibrations.

Faisal spat his contempt to the ground beside him, with such force she was instantly shocked out of her melancholy. "Let's get out of here."

She followed him, staggering and stumbling over the dunes back to the Rover. He did not help her, he was far ahead, anger and frustration apparent in his stride. She knew he was angered by the F15s, but she hoped he was as frustrated as she was by the brevity of their moment.

He confirmed it. "I'm sorry, Arden. I didn't intend to get into this with you."

"I'm sorry too." He could not possibly know how deeply she felt this. "I don't think you realize how—"

"Yes, I do." But he drove in silence then, like one of his immortal young countrymen, peeling around curves and shuddering over traces of sand on the highway, oblivious to danger. They reached university housing in less than half the normal time. He screeched to a halt in the parking lot that served both their buildings.

"Have a good expedition," she told him quickly, opening the door.

"I'm not leaving for a couple of days. But thank you." He turned to look at her. She could see that his smile was strained. "I'll walk you to your apartment, Arden."

As soon as they got out, another vehicle pulled up next to the Rover in the parking lot. Arden, leaning in to retrieve her things, heard Kate's and others' voices. She turned, and realized with dismay that Johnny, in his 'raghead' disguise, was following Kate and Grace. She froze, clutching her banjo case, as they all met.

"Faisal! Good to see you again. I didn't get a chance to properly thank you for the video lecture you gave my senior seminar. It was excellent."

"My pleasure, Kate."

Kate went on, "This is my colleague Grace—she was also at your museum tour—and our friend from the base, John Jackson."

"We've met. *Ahlan, ya* Grace. *Keefak, ya* Johnny." How're you doing?

"*Kwayis, Alhamdulillah, ya* Faisal." Fine thanks. Johnny whipped off his headdress and reached to shake Faisal's hand. In the light from the streetlamp Arden saw the green in Faisal's eyes seem to sharpen to ice on the insignia revealed under the pilot's sport coat. He smiled at Johnny as they shook hands.

Johnny then moved beyond him to give Arden a bear hug and a noisy smack of a kiss. "Arden! We missed ya, babe!" He rocked her a little way away from the others. Her case swung from her shoulder and bumped him. "A banjo, dang, you *are* a cracker."

He shot an amused glance at Faisal. "He's your guy? He's not religious."

"What?"

"I've talked to Faisal plenty this month. He's cool. Not orthodox," he whispered, pulling her back into the little group.

"We heard your buds out there," Faisal addressed Johnny, slipping into a vernacular that startled Arden in its friendly familiarity, after his anger in the desert. He tilted his head skyward. "What kinda payload you packin on those things these days?"

"Fuel efficiency? We're lookin at all the options, but it ain't easy. You guys like to go too fast." Johnny grinned. "Just like on the highway, *ya sadiki*."

"So how far can you fly before you have to refuel?"

"It ain't much mileage, I'll tell ya."

"But you said you got a long way on your mission."

Kate rolled her eyes as the men discussed jet engines. "Isn't *this* typical," she said. "Get a couple of alpha males together, and no matter how different they are, suddenly it's all about machines." She surveyed Arden. "You and Faisal, hmm," she murmured. "That was sneaky."

"If he's *single*, Arden," Grace whispered, staring at Faisal and Johnny with narrowed eyes, "you could bring him to the New Year's party."

Johnny was apparently issuing the same invitation. "Music, good food, fun people, it'll be a blast. You should both be there, ya Faisal."

Faisal said something to him in Arabic, low, and Johnny laughed. He wrapped an easy arm around Faisal, and the two of them leaned into one another, exchanging smiles, looking like a State Department propaganda photo: "Yank pilot befriends local sheikh."

"This guy's gonna fit right in," Johnny told the women. "You shoulda brought him around before, Arden."

Faisal's gaze connected with Arden's when she looked at him again, and one of his eyebrows lifted slightly. His expression seemed to say, if you can't beat em …

"Will you be here New Year's Eve, Faisal?" asked Kate. "What about Ain Qanass?"

"We're leaving Friday after noon prayer. I'm not sure if we'll be back by your new year."

"When are you taking me to the desert, *ya sheikh*?" asked Johnny. "I told some of the other pilots you'd show us the Empty Quarter, after we talked about camping last time. Would you be able to go right after New Year's?"

"Sure, for a few days."

Johnny looked at the Land Rover. "We can take turns driving."

"It's a deal," Faisal said. He clapped Johnny's shoulder. "Tell your guys, and I'll call you." He turned to Arden, who was still holding her briefcase and banjo. "Let me help you with those." He took the briefcase and nodded to the Westerners. "Merry Christmas, *ya sakideen.*"

"And to all a good night," Kate said, dry.

THIRTY-FOUR

H<small>E WALKED HER</small> to the little promenade between their buildings, away from the parking lot. "Which building is yours, Arden?"

"This one." Curious, she said, "It's interesting you and Johnny have gotten friendly, I mean, since you're so anti-military?"

"Not on a personal level, I told you. He's just doing his job. And I'm educating him on what that really means, here. He's a good boy. I like him." He glanced at her. "You and he are pretty friendly too." There was a question in his light tone.

She took a moment to answer, afraid of sounding defensive. Her relationship to Johnny was none of his business, but she didn't want him to guess how intimate it had been. At least, to her, sex was intimate. To Johnny it was just a form of exercise. But she had a feeling Faisal wouldn't see it that way, especially after the heat of their kiss; even though he was promised to someone else. "Yeah, he's a friendly guy," she said, keeping her voice casual.

At her apartment, he took the banjo case so she could get out her keys and open the door. Ruth greeted them. Her eyes grew wide at the sight of Faisal, and her hands flew to her uncovered hair. She looked at Arden, confused.

Faisal immediately looked down and stepped back from the doorway.

Arden, remembering the proprieties that should be observed, tried to alleviate the tension with introductions.

"This is Dr. Al Ansary, from the university. He gave me a lift from his sister's house, she's my student. Dr. Al Ansary, this is Ms. Hamad."

"*A salaamu aliekum*, Madame."

"*Wa aleikum a salaam.*" Ruth's face relaxed as she looked at him. "I know you from the museum."

"Yes, I'm with the Department of Antiquities."

"Would you … like to come in, and have some tea?"

"Thank you, Madame. That is very kind."

"Please, sit down." Ruth went into the kitchen.

Arden said quietly, "You don't have to stay. She's just being polite."

"So am I," he whispered. "It's what we do." He sat down on their couch and surveyed the blank room. "You just moved in?"

"Sort of." It was disconcerting to have him right here, in her living space, where she'd awoken that very morning with the dream of him. She sat across from him. "We were assigned to be room-mates just a month ago. We haven't really had time to make ourselves at home."

"The year is almost half over."

"I'm signing up again."

"In spite of the test score situation?"

"Maybe I can make a difference for the girls."

"Don't be so sure they'll ask you back, if you make waves." His smile lessened the hard words. "Remember I told you, we don't reward bothersome people."

"I'm already on the curriculum committee to plan next year. We'll be evaluating the English materials for boys as well as girls. It's a start. And I was just asked to help out at the U.S. Information Agency, to monitor the English language proficiency tests. I'm supposed to do a test tomorrow, as a matter of fact."

Ruth heard this last, as she came in with the standard tray. "Arden, the TOEFL administrator called, he left a number so you can arrange your ride to the USIA with their driver tomorrow morning."

"USIA?" Faisal said. "I use the library there all the time for research. I can give you a ride, if you like."

"Thank you," she told him, confused. If he didn't want to deepen their relationship, why was he offering to drive her? "That's very kind, Dr. Al Ansary, but it's not necessary." She didn't want to use his first name in front of Ruth.

"I'll be happy to take you, Ms. Armstrong. I'm looking up schools for my sister. Since she'll be in Indiana next year."

"Indiana University is a good school," Ruth said. "I went there."

"Bloomington?" Faisal asked. "That's where her husband will be going."

"Good choice," Ruth said. "It's a beautiful campus, lots of activities she could get involved in. There's a large Muslim community."

"Good to know," he said, leaning forward. "I've worried about her being in the States. It can be such a judgmental society toward Muslims. She's very idealistic."

"Bloomington would be a positive introduction." Ruth and Faisal smiled at each other.

Faisal put down his cup, and stood. "Thank you, ladies, for your hospitality. Miss Armstrong, I'll be outside in the parking lot at seven thirty for you, okay?"

"Okay, Dr. Al Ansary. Thanks again."

His smile was courteous, but when Ruth turned into the hallway, to see him out, he looked back at Arden and gave her a little wink; just like Leila's.

As he walked to their door Arden could see only his back, the long flowing headdress and heavily embroidered cloak. She wished she could strip the regalia from him. It was too much a symbol of all that prevented their closeness. It made him appear so separate, like any strange Saudi man. She might not know him at all, in spite of the ecstatic harmony of their brief union in the desert, in spite of his continuing friendliness. It was a lonely feeling.

Ruth must have noticed her bereft expression, for as soon as she closed the door behind him she said, "Arden. I have a story for you. Stay there; I'm bringing more tea."

Arden leaned back, beyond tired from the long day and the evening's emotional turmoil. She took off her abaya and blazer and put up her feet. She felt too depleted to even tell Ruth tonight about Dr. Zafeeyeh and the test scores. She'd tackle that tomorrow. Ruth had been here a long time; she would know about it already, probably, and she could advise Arden how best to handle it. She stared into the hallway where he had gone, as if an afterimage might remain.

"I can see now why you're still sick." Ruth poured them both a fresh cup.

"What do you mean?"

"He brought you here, alone? It's totally unheard of, you know, it's a huge risk. The way he looked at you. The way he jumped at the chance to be with you again."

"He's just ... trying to be helpful."

"Seven thirty in the morning on the first day of Winter Break is a lot more than being helpful. And he's waiting for you during your test? And he's leaving on a dig the day after? Come on, Arden. I'm not so old I don't remember being in love."

"We're not in love." Arden was frightened by the words' power, spoken aloud. "Anyway, he's not." It was just one kiss, she thought, already nostalgic. She wanted to be alone, to lie in her bed and re-live its magic, savor the thrilling feeling of his hot mouth on hers, his warm hand in her hair, his arm tight around her waist. She wanted to remind herself it had actually happened.

Ruth's stern voice interrupted her reverie. "I won't bother to warn you how dangerous these relationships can be here. I know you're probably not going to be dissuaded from your path; I remember how it was. Nobody could tell *me* anything. I knew it all." Ruth sipped tea.

THIRTY-FIVE

"WHEN I WAS AT INDIANA, in the mid 60s, I was a sorority girl." At Arden's surprised look, Ruth smiled. "Hard to believe, huh? I didn't keep up with fashion since then, but in those days we thought we were the very definition of style. We felt bold wearing miniskirts.

"We lived in a big, pretty house on campus. My sisters were such fun. My biggest problem in life was getting my hair to behave and choosing which frat boy to go out with on weekends.

"That all changed when I was a junior. I was a bright student, and one of my second semester classes was an advanced philosophy seminar. The first day of class I noticed the most handsome boy, dark haired and kind of sultry looking. Turned out he was a grad student from what he called Palestine. He wasn't my type, he wasn't a crew cut blond football player in madras, but I found myself looking forward to those classes, just to be near him."

"So, did you ask him out?"

Ruth smiled again. "We didn't do the asking in those days, we just gave subtle hints. But he was Muslim—I didn't know anything about that religion, although he explained it in class—so my hints toward him fell on deaf ears, or at least I thought. Then one day he asked if I'd like to come to a party he and some other Muslim friends were having to celebrate Eid.

"He was even better looking up close, and so polite, and his friends were fun. The women showed me how their food was made. Everyone got a kick out of teaching me some Arabic. They seemed so sophisticated to me, with their strange music and foreign cigarettes and talk of politics.

"At the end of the evening, he walked me home. We sat for awhile on the big front porch swing—this was late April, and all the flowers were blooming, the air was filled with them—and I took his hand. To me, that was just a friendly flirtation, but it was a big deal for him. He started talking about how marriage between us wouldn't work, how he had to go back to his country and contribute, how his family already had a girl picked out.

"I was flabbergasted. All I wanted, really, was to make out with him. We didn't even have sex back then unless it was a serious boyfriend. Only a few of my sisters had gone all the way, as we called it. I told him it was okay, we didn't have to get married just to kiss. I thought I was pretty with-it, I liked feeling kind of racy in those days. And I'd never felt such a pull toward any boy. The class was three times a week, and I'd just get over studying the curl of his hair, the brightness of his eyes, his beautiful skin, and I'd have to see him again."

She looked long at Arden, with a wry smile.

"I guess I must have been persuasive, because we ended up making out on the porch. He was the most exciting guy I'd ever kissed, partly because I was so attracted, but also I think because this was real passion for him and not just another notch on some belt he had in mind, like a lot of the frat brothers. He was careful with me. He told me he loved me and that he'd try to arrange things with his family.

"I wasn't thinking he was serious, I just wanted to date him, but sure enough he called his family and somehow got their okay to get married. Since my parents weren't there he asked the sorority housemother to sit with us for his proposal. She must have realized how unprepared I was for his announcement, because she wisely advised us to have a long engagement. Girls got engaged all the time, and it didn't always mean marriage.

"But it certainly meant that sex was less of a taboo in my culture and, it turned out, in his." Ruth's smile grew warmly reminiscent as she looked down in private memory. Arden smiled too, for the dark boy and pale girl in that long ago sweet-scented spring. "We became lovers. We had one magical month, before the Six Day War."

There was a silence, and then Ruth went on, "He had no word of his family in Gaza, so he decided to get to the refugee camps being set up in Jordan.

"I'd never known such craziness—he and his friends were all frantic, trying to find real news, and at the House we were putting on the big graduation dance and cramming for finals, and I was trying to steal time to keep our love alive. By then I was completely attached to him, terrified that he'd go off and I'd never see him again. I was able to convince him to at least take his finals so he could get his degree.

"He left. He promised to stay in touch. I went to the dance with a blind date and packed to go home to Indianapolis for the summer. I had a job lined up as a nurse's aid.

"I wasn't paying attention, I was so overwrought by missing Yousuf and trying to get news from the Middle East, but one of the nurses who worked with me saw how sick I got every morning."

"Oh no," Arden murmured.

"Yes. I'd lost track of my periods. In those days it was really hard to get an abortion, even if I'd wanted one, so there was no way out. I decided I'd go to Jordan and look for him. I figured I could teach English to support myself, his friends had said there were Americans who did that in the Middle East. My family thought I'd become some kind of hippie—I didn't tell them I was pregnant, because they were pretty religious—so essentially I just ran away. I got myself a passport and booked a flight to Amman.

"This was the time when a lot of young Americans were wandering around the world, and I met some nice

213

Jewish kids in Amman, idealistic commune types who'd been en route to kibbutzim in Israel and gotten stranded by the war. Through them, I found a job as a waitress at an Amman hotel. They served as a kind of support group for me while I was working and looking for Yousuf and getting bigger and bigger. We lived in a ramshackle apartment. The neighbors were incredibly hostile, they all thought it was free love and drugs day and night.

"I couldn't find Yousuf. Eventually I met someone who knew which camp his family had fled to, and I was able to finally meet his mother when I was about six months along. As soon as she saw me she knew what had to be done. She arranged for a marriage ceremony in his absence. I went to live with her and her sisters before the baby was born. My Arabic was still limited, but they were so kind to me. I could tell she appreciated my determination to find her son.

"Life in the camp was pretty awful, even worse than the crummy Amman apartment. I couldn't keep my waitress job since I had no transportation. I felt like a burden to the sisters, but they somehow found a way to keep us all fed. The clinic at the camp was run by the UN. That's where my son was born. I called him Yousuf.

"He was just a few weeks old when the news finally reached us. Yousuf had joined a guerrilla group who were sneaking into the occupied zones for raids on Israeli soldiers. They called themselves freedom fighters. It seemed so strange to me—he was a gentle philosophy major, not some brutish warrior! But his family was very proud. They wanted their farm back, and they really believed they'd get it, in time. They thought the world would be on their side.

"Not too long afterward, we heard that Yousuf and his group were killed during an ambush in the Negev, the southern desert. It stunned me, but I was so beaten down by new motherhood in the camp, and I hadn't seen him in nearly a year by then, so it didn't have the impact on me that it had on his family. They were devastated. I realized that to them, he'd been a real person who represented hope for the future, but for me he'd just been a kind of fantasy.

"His mother understood that somehow. She sat me down one day—by then I was fluent—and told me to go back home to America. She saw how sick I was, anemic and with a deep kind of depression, now we'd call it post-partum, but back then, I thought I was grieving Yousuf. She knew I wasn't. She knew I needed to leave.

"I finally agreed with her, once she made the argument that I could be more of a help to them if I finished my degree and got a good job. She said I'd have to be like little Yousuf's dad, and provide for the family even if I had to live away from them. It's common all over the Middle East, you know, in the poor countries outside the Gulf. She said an American woman was strong enough to do that.

"I knew her argument made sense. I wanted to take baby Yousuf but she couldn't let him go. It would be like losing both sons, she said, and I'd be free to concentrate on work without him.

"I got money from the U.S. Embassy to fly back to Indianapolis. I was lucky to still be in good standing at the university, so I could borrow money to pay for school and keep on as a senior. I held down two waitress jobs and went to class in between. Of course I couldn't live in the sorority, it was too expensive, and I had nothing in common with the girls anymore. The world was changing anyway. Vietnam, drugs, and new music were making kids think about different things than hairdos and who was getting pinned."

"But you were lucky to be back in the States at all," Arden had to insert.

"I didn't feel that way." Ruth smiled sadly. "I didn't feel part of student life. I was sick with missing my baby son, so I threw myself into work. I looked at my classmates and thought that although we were the same age they were like children to me. Their naïveté disgusted me sometimes. I became pretty judgmental."

Her smile told Arden that she knew she still was. "I started looking for jobs in Jordan. I found a girls' school outside Amman that needed an ESL teacher. My second trip was so much easier than the first. I felt like a heroine coming to rescue the family. We were able to find a little house, I made sure I fit in well at the school, and Yousuf grew into a happy and beautiful boy. His grandma never gave up her hope to return to Gaza, but she was grateful not to live in the camp. The sisters found suitable husbands. Life worked out.

"Basically, I lived there ever since, at least until Yousuf needed money to get married, seven years ago. That's when I came to the Gulf. I visit them whenever I can. Yousuf works for the UN Refugee Commission, still trying to improve conditions for Palestinians in Gaza. I have two little grand-daughters, Suad and Lilya."

"And your parents?"

Ruth laughed. "I saved up enough to bring Yousuf to see them when he was about four. He came for regular visits after that, and they actually ended up helping pay his way through college—Indiana U again. Full circle."

Arden stared at her now-cold tea. "Ruth," she began, "I think you've been very brave, and I'm glad there was a happy ending, but I don't quite see—"

"What it has to do with you." The travel clock on the coffee table ticked the late hour. "I think ... I see myself in you. You're more attuned to this culture than the others, I don't know why, maybe because it's your first sojourn outside the States. You're sincere in your efforts to understand this society, the language, the religion."

Ruth considered her cup before continuing, hesitantly, "You know, Arden, choosing to fall in love can be a way to alleviate a stressful situation."

At Arden's puzzled frown, she elaborated. "I've seen it here, fairly often. Saudi men seem remote to us, and we're not allowed to know them, but they control every aspect of our lives. So to get close to one, to become intimate, is a way of making them familiar and of lessening that feeling of helplessness we all suffer from in the Kingdom. If we can control a love affair we think we've regained a measure of autonomy and belonging too. And of course, if we make them our lovers they become like us, not alien, not frightening."

Was she speaking from personal experience, Arden wondered, studying Ruth. The older woman shook her head. "No, Arden, I didn't fall in love here. Saudi men symbolize too much repression, to me. But it's happened to other American women."

"Faisal's not—"

Ruth smiled. "I know. Dr. Al Ansary *seems* like a different kind of Saudi. I'm just cautioning you to be careful. The attraction between you is obvious. I'm sure he finds your openness toward his culture very appealing."

"Not appealing enough to explore a relationship," Arden said. She could not contain her wistful sigh. "He's supposed to be engaged."

Ruth sat forward, alarmed. "He's engaged, and he's seeing you alone? That's bad, Arden. You'll be the one who gets in trouble, not him. Engagement is like marriage here. You know the punishment for adultery?"

"He said he had obligations and it wouldn't be fair, to me, for us to get involved." She felt the gloominess of this sink deep, and bit her lip.

"I can see that hurts you, but he's wise not to take advantage. I wonder why, though, he's driving you alone tomorrow. You know if you get stopped, as an unmarried man and woman alone, you can be arrested."

"He's a good Muslim, Leila says, they wouldn't stop him."

"Leila thinks he walks on water." Ruth frowned. "I hope he isn't going to change his mind about the two of you. These things can end horribly in Riyadh if you're not careful. Broken hearts are the least of it."

Arden decided to bend the vow of silence she and the sheikhas had taken, when invited to the first Bell party. "I know of Saudis and Western women having affairs."

"Sex with princes doesn't count, except for the diseases and unwanted pregnancies." Ruth laughed at Arden's gasp. "It's no secret—those palace parties go on every year until the crackdowns during Ramadan. We're lucky the admin and students don't have a clue, they aren't part of Western gossip here. But Dr. Al Ansary isn't a royal, Arden, so he can't protect you.

"Anyway, I remember how it felt, being in love with a compelling person from a serious culture. The consequences can be permanent. If you were to get involved, if he weren't engaged, think about how it would be to live here, married to a Saudi."

"Married." A lifetime of looking at him, touching him, talking with him, freely.

"Relationships between non-royal men and women here can only end in marriage or expulsion, or worse. Be very careful when you're alone with him. He doesn't look at you as if he's attached to someone else. That's dangerous."

THIRTY-SIX

IT WAS TOO COLD to wait in the parking lot. The winter air had a thin, icy dryness that seemed to slice right through the cotton and silk Arden was wearing. She walked quickly to Faisal's building, hoping the neighbors wouldn't be up to watch and criticize at this hour on a winter weekend, the first day of break.

Faisal answered the door, looking down at his watch. His glossy hair was uncovered. "*Ya sheikha*. Am I late?"

"*Ya sheikh*, I thought—can I wait here? It's cold outside."

He glanced out at the hallway. He opened the door wider, to let her enter, and closed it quickly behind her. He did not repeat that she shouldn't be there.

"Can I ... have a cup of coffee?" She could smell that he'd made some. She glanced toward the kitchen. He went in and poured her a cup. She followed.

She leaned against the counter and sipped. He stood still, she could see the bottom of his thobe. Her bravura fled as his silence lengthened, and she finally looked up at him.

She wasn't prepared for the measurement in his eyes, as he'd looked at her in the den last night, as if she were a sea on a far planet, seen through a telescope. As if she needed to be identified. There were dark circles under his eyes and she hoped it meant he'd lost sleep over her, as she'd lost over him, reliving last night's kiss.

He took a step toward her but stopped, ran a hand through his hair, let out a tired sigh. "I'm so confused around you. I forget where we are. Who I am." He

219

reached into a cupboard for a commuter cup and poured coffee into it. "Let's get you out of here."

"You're not—" she gestured to his bare head.

"Yeah. See?" He turned back into the hallway and walked down to the bedroom.

Waiting in his living room, she saw piles of rucksacks heaped in a corner, and maps spread out on the coffee table. Ruth was right—his offer to drive her this morning, in the midst of his dig prep, was beyond courtesy. As she pondered, she looked at his maps, topographical close-ups of Afghanistan, Pakistan, other new post-Soviet "stan" countries. The Afghan map was the most detailed, marked with red circles. She sounded out the Arabic names. "*Kahbool. Kahn dah har. Mazar ee shah reef.*" He must be planning his next expedition.

"*Ya* Arden?" His soft voice startled her. He stood at the door, flipping his headdress back with one hand, holding his cup with the other. "Come on."

On the road, she started a conversation that she intended to keep friendly, so the nervous vibe between them could dissipate. "So, are you ready for tomorrow?"

"Yes. I have to call everyone in the group, make sure they're ready too. I always end up being the most organized one."

"It would be interesting to go on a dig with you sometime. Not here, I know that can't be, but somewhere else. In one of your groups."

"You'd do well. Leila says you never lose your cool."

Only around you, she thought. "She sees me at my best. I love teaching here."

"Teaching here is bringing out the worst in me," he said, to her surprise. She'd imagined he'd be popular with students. "I can't stand the narrow-mindedness I hear from some of these boys. They're hopeless."

"But you can challenge their thinking, get them talking, get them to see other views, even within the parameters we have to honor here. Isn't that the purpose of universities?"

"In a more open society, maybe. Here, it's a lost cause, unless you're a religious fanatic. They're the only ones winning young people over with teaching these days."

She studied his smooth face and saw as if superimposed yesterday's heavy beard. But she also recalled Johnny's comment: "He's not orthodox." Still, how would Johnny know, from a few phone conversations? "Well, Faisal, aren't you one of them now?"

His eyes, in the rearview, were narrow as he glanced at her. "They have the power to change things here. They're the only ones with that ability, so they're the only choice."

"They're going to change things through religion? Isn't the Kingdom already just about as religious as a society can get?"

"Not for everyone. You said last night, there's such hypocrisy. And you're just an outside observer. It's worse than what you see."

"So you want some kind of—theocracy—that's even *stricter* than this?" She could not even begin to imagine it.

"It's not about what I want, as an individual. Anyway, that would only be a temporary first stage, one step toward what needs to happen here, one step of many that will eventually improve the chance for us to form a real government."

"Oh yeah, like in Iran? *That* really worked out for democracy."

"Of course we will learn from the Iranians' mistakes."

"You're serious," she said slowly. "You *are* talking about revolution."

He laughed. "You never heard me say that."

"That's dangerous here, Faisal, Jesus."

"Peace be upon him."

She didn't know what to think. His disillusionment puzzled her. As far as she could see, he had an enviable position in his society. He had a great job, a solid family, he was devout, there was no reason he couldn't rise as high as he wanted to in the Department of Antiquities or the Ministry of Education, even if he wasn't a royal.

She wondered what had made him grow this unhappy, so quickly after his return. She thought of his fury at the base being built on the archeological site. Was that enough to so deeply embitter a member of the privileged class? Maybe it was also related to the disagreement about the wife his family had chosen for him? She didn't even want to think about that today. Obviously he'd resigned himself to his marriage, in spite of their kiss and his admitting he felt confused. She changed the subject. "Are you planning a dig in Afghanistan next?"

"A dig?" He looked startled.

"Your maps."

"Ah, you saw them."

"I thought you must be organizing your next trip."

"I've been thinking about ... doing some research in Afghanistan."

"Did the Ubaid get all the way up there?"

"There was trade, of course, but the Ubaid themselves pretty much kept to the Eastern coast. Traders came through Persia to get to the Gulf, to Bahrain, then they met the Ubaid."

"Is Bahrain as much fun as people say?"

"Fun?" he asked, as if he'd never heard the word before. Of course he wouldn't be sneaking out of the Kingdom for alcoholic R&R at the resorts.

"I mean, the beach."

"I don't know that side of Bahrain. I go to the Dilmun areas."

"I'd like to see those sites. I loved reading it, thinking about how development occurred in stages. Fire, tools, worship, art."

"You should visit the sites in Bahrain, Arden. You can still get a tour during this upcoming break."

"I'd rather go with you."

His smile appeared. "*In sha'allah.*" God willing: the all-purpose phrase here.

They were in downtown Riyadh now, near the section where most ministries were. "USIA, let's see, it's over here behind your embassy compound."

They passed a grand building, heavily barricaded, with alert-looking Marines standing guard. Arden felt a pang when she saw the bold-colored American flag rippling in the breeze. "Old Glory."

He glanced at her. "You miss it?"

"I haven't, really, so far."

"Even now? Christmastime?"

"I had my Christmas last night, making cookies. How about you, Faisal, do you miss the States?"

"I miss my mother. And Berkeley, sometimes, my Profs and classmates, since email isn't the same. And the beauty of Big Sur."

She would have liked to ask him more about his mother, she'd been intrigued by what Leila had said about Faisal's relationship with her, but they were pulling into a gated parking lot.

They went in together, past the main reception desk where Arden got directions to the test site. It was odd to see Christmas decorations, to be surrounded by English again, to speak to a Western woman in a short skirt behind the desk, to see the portrait of a beaming Bill Clinton, almost a year into his second term, hanging on the wall. In official portraits, Saudi dignitaries did not smile, and Arden studied her President, thinking of the different kind of message a big genial grin sent.

"He looks so friendly."

Faisal looked at the picture. "Americans usually do, at first."

The registrar behind the desk, hearing this, frowned at him. "Can I check your ID, sir?"

Faisal showed her his driver's license, looking at her with the most charming smile Arden had ever seen him produce. She watched, annoyed and amused, as the clerk responded to his direct warmth with a flustered smile of her own.

"You've been here several times recently."

"I'm helping my sister apply to schools."

The clerk's gaze lingered on him. "Please sign in, then, thank you sir."

Arden signed with him.

Once inside, Faisal turned to the nearby hallway. "I'll be in the library, through there, where the college catalogues are."

THIRTY-SEVEN

AFTER THE TEST, she found him at one of the computers, just before the noon prayer call sounded through the building. There was a prayer room set aside even here in the embassy compound. Faisal went to pray, along with other visitors and employees.

She invited him to lunch to thank him for bringing her to the USIA. With the money she'd earn from supervising the TOEFL, she could afford it. The only restaurant she knew in Riyadh was a Danish place where Sayeed had brought the teachers. The restaurant was as quiet as Arden remembered it, but was now decorated for Christmas, a novelty that made her halt at the entryway, taking in the twinkly lights and colorful Danish ornaments.

They were seated in a discreet high-walled booth in the family area; it was assumed they were husband and wife. The booth was constructed so they had to sit fairly close together.

Faisal loosened his cloak. "I like this place too," he said. "How did you know about it?"

"Sayeed Quraishi brought us to lunch here after we got our contracts signed." It seemed so long ago.

"Sayeed Quraishi," he repeated. "I've met him a number of times."

"What do you think of him?"

"He's decent, honest. A bit self-important."

"He seemed all-important when we arrived." Arden smiled, remembering. "He seemed to have such control over us."

"He does, actually," Faisal said. "He's very well connected. He'll be the one who can get you out quickly, without problems, if you protest the grading policy. Or if you ever have any other kind of trouble here. If you can't reach Prince Nawaf, get Quraishi."

His serious tone made her sit up straight. "You really think I might get sent out because of that?"

"It's possible," he said slowly. "Especially since you're already on Al Issam's radar. I'd like to tell you to drop it."

"Why?"

"Because you to want to stay here, in peace."

"I'll get other teachers behind me, and not just the Westerners, they can't send all of us out. The censorship thing we can't change, maybe, but this—this we can do."

"I like your attitude."

They shared the mixed grill and a pitcher of Saudi champagne. He told her about the Ain Qanass expedition, and she told him about the Film Club. They agreed that Leila's husband would work out. They argued about long engagements; he was in favor and she was against.

She dared to say, "I hear you're giving your family a hard time about yours, Faisal."

"I'll never accept an arranged marriage."

"But then why ... " Confused, she began again. "But your family has someone already picked out for you. And you picked out someone for Leila."

"Leila always had the right to refuse, Baba and I made sure. And I have that right also. My father's been brainwashed by his new wife. It's not his idea. And it certainly isn't mine."

"I thought you had to comply, to be a good son."

"She's just trying to settle an old score with some of her people in Jiddah, and she thought matching me would do that."

"So ... you're not a good match?"

"Not now," he said, looking down. "I told you last night, I have obligations."

"I thought you were talking about your family's expectations. Your engagement."

"Now it's my turn to ask about you," he said smoothly, shifting in the booth so that he faced her. "Tell me about Ohio, your family."

"It's a short story. I was born in West Virginia, moved to Columbus when I was ten. My parents were divorced when I was little, like yours. I have a younger sister Annie who's getting married soon, like yours. I grew up, I was a communications major in college, I taught ESL for awhile, I came to the Kingdom so I could meet you, *ya* Faisal." She tried a flirtatious smile. Why not, if he wasn't taken after all?

And he sure is smiling too. "I thought you came for riyals. And adventure."

"Oh yeah." She grinned. "This lunch is an adventure, isn't it?"

"Tell me more. How did you learn to play the banjo?"

She talked about living with Uncle Munro, who had worked in a coal mine all his life, whose love of singing the old-time bluegrass tunes was cut short by lung disease. She told him about Aunt Patty, the carpenter, who had built their little frame house high in the breathtaking Smokies, reached by a torturous series of muddy switchbacks cut into the rock. She told him about the way the cabin seemed to perch on the brim of the earth, occasional cloud wisps dreaming past, and the way the spring flowers seemed to float from their branches into the air around them, as if swaying to the ringing tones of the banjo Uncle Munro was teaching her to play.

"The colors," she remembered. "The sweetest lilac, that's like a light purple? And yellow forsythia, kind of like what we saw after the storm in the desert that day, and dogwood," she tapped a finger on his sleeve, "white as your thobe. It was as close to heaven as I've ever been, except for that time with you after the khamseen. The scent of lilac was miraculous."

"*Alhamdulillah,*" he murmured softly. His gaze held the wonder she'd seen in him, after the khamseen, when she'd shown him her hands. She was brought back to Riyadh, and the Danish restaurant, but she was falling over the edge of his appreciative regard. "I can see that little girl with the banjo, barefoot, on the porch, in the mountains. It sounds so much like my mother's place in Big Sur."

When the waiter brought the bill, Arden reached to take it, and tucked her credit card into the leather folder. "I wonder if you've ever cut your hair," Faisal said after the waiter left. He lifted one finger to touch an errant strand escaped from her scarf. "I don't think you've lost the innocence of that time, have you Arden. It shines through you."

The waiter reappeared, with a regretful expression. "I'm sorry, Madame, but your card has been declined. Have you another we could try?"

Her American Express card, so new, she thought, already in trouble? When *had* she sent that payment? Arden frowned, biting her lip, trying furiously to recount backwards. What terrible timing! What a mood-wrecker!

"I'll take care of it." Faisal reached into his cloak pocket and pulled out a handful of riyals. "Your scanner must be malfunctioning."

"I'm sure that's it, sir."

As the waiter walked away she didn't know where to look, what to say. She could feel a fiery blush spreading over her face. How humiliating. She was even more immobilized, then, by the feeling of Faisal's hand on hers, on the seat between them. He squeezed gently. "Happens all the time here in the Third World, you know," she heard his low voice. "Can't rely on the machinery."

His gallantry allowed her to laugh a little. "I guess it's all the sand, huh."

"It creeps in," he agreed. He took his hand away and asked, in the same quiet tone, "How bad is your financial situation, Arden?"

His soft voice and level gaze held her still, unable to look down and avoid the subject. She found herself spilling out the story of the student loans, the credit cards, the mounting minimal payments that had threatened to bury her in debt and that had, ultimately, led her to pursue a job in the Gulf. She finished quickly, hanging her head. What would he think of her now, just after she'd glimpsed how entranced he'd been by his vision of her innocence?

"If you need money, let me help you." There was no judgment in his tone. "You know money isn't one of our obvious problems."

"I couldn't accept. It wouldn't be ethical."

"And is it ethical for these card companies to use your need against you in charging interest? In Islam we don't believe in interest. To us it's like gambling. We loan where it's necessary, and we repay as possible, in an honest fashion. You wouldn't have gotten in trouble like this in the Kingdom."

"Next time I'll have the good sense to be born in Riyadh." She smiled at him. "After the revolution, of course."

"Shh." He laughed a little. "You know Muslims don't believe in reincarnation. There's no next time. You had your chance, and you were born American."

"I blew it," she acknowledged, with a cheerful shrug.

"You were lucky, Arden, much luckier than you probably know."

"I'm starting to feel attached here, though," she confided. "I feel like I could fit in. My Arabic's getting pretty good, and I love the students. I want to stay on."

"What about the cultural restrictions on you?"

"They seem normal to me now. Different than the States, of course, but normal, for here. I accept the differences."

"In spite of that kid whose ball hit you by the masjid?" He grinned.

"He brought you," she told him simply.

He glanced down, this time only for a moment, and when he looked up the hard lines of his newly-shaven face were soft with affection. "*Ya helwa*," he murmured. "Thank you for that."

They sipped their coffee in a short silence, before he continued, "But what about the university's hypocrisy, Arden, how do you accept it?"

"I want to change it! The girls deserve to participate in their society, and have their contributions appreciated. But I love so much that's here, in spite of that."

"You're in an isolated bubble," he said gently. "You're seeing a tiny slice."

His cynicism took her aback, again. "It isn't tiny," she insisted. "What I'm seeing, Faisal, are people who really live their faith, who respect each other, whose sense of family, and kindness, is just amazing. Don't you think they're good Muslims like you? I'm surprised you don't seem to see this too."

"I did, when I was young. But I can't blind myself to what's wrong here now. Being a good Muslim is irrelevant. Islam's being twisted."

"Well, it sounds like your religious fanatics are twisting it too, aren't they?"

"They're a means to an end. They'll be temporary."

"I guess I still don't understand why you're so angry," she said slowly. "What was so different here, when you were younger?"

"The war you call Desert Storm tore off the mask," he said simply. "The collusion between the royal family and the American government is obvious in a way now that might have been possible to ignore, before. Now we all see what an impediment it is to any kind of political progress here."

"Or maybe you're just seeing it, for the first time, as an adult."

"I wanted to come back in '91, I wanted to join the military, but Baba insisted that I stay in school, in America. I had to obey him then."

"He was right. That would have been a waste. You can do a lot more building for progress here as an archaeologist, and a teacher, than as some kind of soldier!"

The sadness that drew down his features as he looked at her seemed out of place with his laugh lines. Then he shook his head as if there were no point in further discussion. "It's too late."

She did not know how she could refute him, although she believed he was wrong. She felt the weight of his conclusion move between them as heavy as regret. "I wish you didn't feel that way, Faisal."

"I wish I'd met you before." He spoke almost as if to himself.

They shared a look that, for her, telescoped the room onto his face, as if there were some kind of vacuum that drew all extraneous sights into just this one set of features. His gaze dropped. She saw his shoulders rise and fall in another long sigh. He turned her hand over and deliberately stroked it, running the tips of his fingers in a slow circle around her palm, just barely touching her skin. She shivered, caught between arousal and confusion, between the eroticism and lightness of his touch.

He spoke, but his Arabic was too low, too fast for her to understand. He moved his hand away, to push himself out of the booth. He flipped his headdress and stood.

"Let's go, *ya sheikha*, let's go for a drive."

THIRTY-EIGHT

OUTSIDE, THE GLARING SUNSHINE and azure sky contrasted with the restaurant's dim Christmas ambiance, lightening the mood between them as they got back into the Land Rover and lifting it further when they reached the open desert. After asking what she wanted to hear, he put on Green Day. He rolled down the windows at her request, so she could smell the air, and she laughed at the way his headdress flapped wildly in the wind. Grinning, he tore it off and threw it to her in the back seat. She put it on and made her mustache face in the mirror at him, liberated by the sight of his tossing hair and the sound of his tenor as "Good Riddance" blared through the speakers about something unpredictable but, in the end, right.

She *was* having the time of her life.

"Faisal, can we stop and take a walk?"

"Not today. See the way the sand is shifting, if you look closely on the ground?"

Indeed, she could see a constant movement, an activity just above surface level.

"Even in a small wind, the air picks up the stray grains and throws them around."

"How will you manage in Ain Qanass?"

"We'll wrap up, and go slow, and dig deep. We'll pitch strong tents. We're concentrating on just one site, so we won't move."

"I'll miss you." She took off his headdress and folded it over and over.

"Thank you." Too soon, they were approaching the campus. Faisal turned the music down and reached for his headdress, which he arranged, one-handed, on his head.

"Will I see you again like this?" she ventured.

He glanced at her in the mirror. But they were at the gatehouse and he had to talk to the guard. Arden shrank back, pulling her scarf over her face.

She repeated, as they wound around to the parking lot, "Will I see you?"

He looked at her again, eyes narrow. "How much of a risk-taker are you, Arden?"

It did not strike her as a rhetorical question. She remembered Ruth's statement last night, about a compelling person from a serious culture. Could she tell Faisal how she had longed for him, for so many weeks, in spite of the risks? Didn't he already know? "I think you know." She looked into his eyes in the mirror. "You've known all along."

His brows pulled together briefly and a corner of his mouth twisted. He pulled into the lot. He turned off the ignition, but then sat still. She heard beads clicking.

"I'm so thirsty, Faisal, can't we have some tea?" She knew he could not refuse.

"Tea?"

She smiled. "You'll make some for us, and we can talk more. Just as friends. I need your advice about this grading thing."

He turned around then, leaning his arm over the seatback, to stare at her, his question clear. She lifted her chin and stared back, answering as openly as she dared.

After several moments he nodded. "Come to me. I'll go first, and you can follow, if there is nobody around to watch you. At least we can talk in private. Just as friends," he added, stressing the last word.

As she trailed after him at a discreet distance through the deserted courtyard, feeling as silly as a bogus spy in a bad movie, she imagined every window glaring down at her. She used a different entrance to his building than he did, and a separate stairwell. She felt a mixed thrill of subterfuge, fear and physical excitement as she stood in front of his door at last. When he opened she thought she saw her own emotions crossing his face. He stood for a moment, arms folded, blocking his hallway. His outfit looked formal suddenly, and her abaya and scarf felt similarly awkward, as if they were in costume, in that same bad spy movie. She shifted from foot to foot. He didn't move.

"Tea?" she prompted.

"Come on." He walked into his kitchen and she watched as he went through the ritual. She took the tray into his living room, moved papers from the couch once more, and they sat side by side. She asked him about his posters, just to get her mouth moving, and he pointed out the differences in photography, as desultorily. This topic quickly ran its course, and they were left without words. She shifted close, glad to be rid of words, but he straightened away from her.

He put his cup down and fixed her with a look of such intensity that she feared, with a deep sense of impending regret, the finality of whatever pronouncement he might make. His eyes seemed to examine every thought she'd ever had.

"I'm not free to explore this, Arden. I can't give you what you deserve."

"When you said that last night, I thought you meant your engagement."

"No."

"Because I'm an infidel then," she muttered. She looked down and scuffed her toe on his carpet. "I know what a good Muslim you are."

To her astonishment, he laughed. "That wouldn't stand in my way."

"Then ..."

"You can't tell anyone this." He took her hands in his, firm as a longtime lover's, holding still, looking for her assent. She nodded. "I'll be leaving the Kingdom soon."

"Your research project in Afghanistan? Maybe I could visit you, during the summer," she suggested, as if their relationship were a foregone conclusion. She'd heard that 1997 Afghanistan wasn't a safe place for Westerners, but people thought that about Saudi Arabia too.

Faisal lowered his head and studied their joined hands. His expression, when he looked up, was even darker than in his den last night, black pupils erasing the light from his eyes. "Arden. This isn't about archaeology. You know my opinion about the political situation here, you know I'm involved with the people who are going to change it."

Fear flashed through her as swiftly as lust, covering her skin with the same shiver. "Those religious fanatics."

"They're one way," he agreed. "There are others."

"Couldn't you try to—work the changes from within? There must be people, educated, who have the same opinion? The same complaints?" She thought of her brightest girls, the ones who would, she was sure, determine a different future for themselves here, in their quiet way.

"I thought that, when I came back. But people are afraid to act, or they're disorganized, or they're ineffective. There's too much argument and not enough power. This has to be done outside the Kingdom." He took his hands away. "I don't need to tell you more. But it's not safe for me like this, to stay here indefinitely. Not safe for my family either, and not for you if you're close to me."

"Not safe? You mean because of the spies?"

"Secret police."

"So they'd what, arrest you if they discovered these plans?"

"Arrest, no," he said softly. "I would disappear."

"Then let me come with you, if you have to leave!" Even as she exclaimed, she knew this sounded absurd. She couldn't just follow him willy-nilly to some revolutionaries' hide-out, in some undetermined spot in the world. Some wasteland in Afghanistan? She couldn't even get an exit visa. And they weren't a couple, anyway, not yet and maybe not ever from the way he was talking.

"There's no way, *ya habibati.*" He watched her. "Anyway, do you really want that? Are you willing to risk so much for a ... a boyfriend?" Amusement lightened his tone as he smiled. She sensed him wanting to let her down easily; slipping away.

"I don't want a boyfriend, Faisal, I want you. I never felt this way. I never acted this way. I tried to get you out of my mind, all these weeks. I can't. You're who I see, since the day we met. I'm just—lost."

The words spilled as if knifed out—seeds draining from a stabbed hole in a sack, lying unsown on the desert floor without rain—into the silence that greeted her confession. She stared at the intricate pattern on his carpet, a series of geometric greens and blues against deep maroon.

She felt his hand touch her shoulder in a gesture so light she didn't know what it signified. Sympathy, perhaps, embarrassment? She knitted her hands together, still looking down, half expecting him to rise and usher her to the door.

"I know." When she looked up at him his eyes were inviting, warm with an unexpected, teasing license. "Of course, I know. And now you know why I've been fighting it. But if we both get lost? Don't you care what happens after?"

"No. I don't care."

He did not move any closer, his cloak barely touched her abaya, but his hand slid slowly from her shoulder down her back.

After wanting for so long, she was finally free to put a hand on his face. She touched him, her palm lingering over his brow, cheek, chin, and the sudden smoothness of his mouth. She outlined his lips with one finger and slid inside. His teeth closed on her knuckle and his tongue flicked her fingertip, hard and explicit. She scraped her finger out, aroused as never in her life, watching his green eyes darken with a hunger that matched hers, wondering what he might do next, not caring what he might do next as long as it brought them together.

He stood, took her hand, and walked her down the hallway to his bedroom. He sat on the edge of his bed and held her in front of him. He undid her scarf and abaya with the deftness he had shown during the storm. He unbuttoned the front of her shirt and slid it slowly off, his warm hands clinging to her skin, his warm tongue following.

Ferocity flooded her. She hooked the aghal circling his head and flung it like a Frisbee. He laughed as she tore at his headdress, snatched the little yarmulke-like cap on the top of his head, and sailed it behind the aghal. She had waited so long to get her hands on his thick, slippery curls, and they felt so good she had to close her eyes and clutch his head to her waist, tight, so that her fingers could savor the sensation.

Then she finally brought his face up to kiss, a greedier kiss than last night's had been, both of them freed now from any constraint. She pushed him back on the bed and tugged at his cloak and thobe impatiently, struggling, as he laughed again, with the unfamiliar, voluminous layers of cloth. The cloak alone must have had eight yards of fabric! Just as she finally found the buttons on his thobe, the prayer call sounded.

Faisal squeezed her hands before he sank to the floor, to kneel by the bed. The soft chanting he joined in, eyes closed, did not take him away. She sent up her own little prayer as Faisal stretched beside her on the bed again, after the final notes faded. They threw themselves into each other, into the holiness found in another kind of worship.

It seemed as if eons passed before she could even open her eyes. She twisted her fingers further into his sleek hair, pulling his face to her cheek. She felt his lips press on her chin and his teeth followed. The sharp pressure stirred her breath. She turned her mouth slightly, to meet his, and was lost once more, lost and found again, so easily. The light on his bedroom walls gradually faded from cream to yellow, to gold, to pink, to blazing peach, gilding their bodies with the changing colors.

When the light was only a soft gray, Faisal roused himself to bring in a tray of cheese, apples, and biscuits with a jug of water. Arden felt it was the first time she'd ever eaten and drunk. The water tasted as delicious as wine, the apple as fresh as the one in the Garden of Eden must have tasted to Adam and Eve. She held hers out for Faisal to bite. His slow smile acknowledged the reference as he complied.

"But you're not Eve. She was darkness, you're light."

"She was the mother of all of us, if you believe that, so we share her darkness."

"You're right, of course, *ya helwa*, but you are still light."

"Not all the way through." She wanted to work up the courage to tell him about Johnny, and maybe even about Nawaf, when the time was right. She should do that before they all met at the party next week.

He put his hand on her cheek. "You're light to me, Arden." It was a terminal erasure of all that was past.

He made tea again, and they put on two of his thobes, and sat entwined in his living room to watch the moon rise. She braided the ends of two locks of their hair together, yellow-white looping up into blue-black, finishing in a tight love knot. "I'm staying here with you tonight."

"No, *ya habibati*. I still have to call my group, and finish packing. If you stay I won't even be able to stand up tomorrow, let alone lead the dig."

"You could hold the dig in the desert right here. You could sit and direct them."

"I'll tell them to dig in the playground outside. In the sandbox. They could uncover some ancient Legos."

After their laugh he looked away from her, at the desert out the window. "I can't stay here much longer, after Ain Qanass." She sat up straight too then, and the braided hair yanked at her temple. "But now there's you," he said, as if continuing an argument. "I knew that being with you would make this harder."

She understood, now, why he had been so hesitant to seal their relationship. She stared at him, chewing on her lip. She didn't want him to leave the room, let alone the country. She didn't even want to unbraid their hair. She felt her eyes beginning to water. "Why can't you just be a good archaeologist here? Why isn't this enough?"

"I tried, Arden. I did."

"Maybe you didn't give it enough time."

"I'm sorry, *ya helwa,* I should have turned from you, so you could turn from me."

She blinked away a tear. "I don't want to turn from you. We belong together."

"Even if we don't know when, or how?"

"I told you, Faisal, I don't care. Come into the kitchen with me. There's something I want to do."

They walked in step to the kitchen, linked by their wrapped arms and the joint braid. She found a scissors and clipped it off, freeing them from each other. She sliced the braid in two, and put one half in his monogrammed thobe pocket. He put his hand over it. "I don't need your hair, to remember you in Ain Qanass. You'll be in the air. You'll be behind my eyes." He unlooped the Q'uranic sura he wore around his neck, a little silver tablet on a chain, and put it around her neck. "This is only the first of so many gifts I want to bring you."

"Just bring yourself back to me."

Somehow she tore herself away from him to use his shower, somehow she dressed. Somehow she said goodbye to him, and made her way across the dark courtyard to the apartment she shared with Ruth. She tried to arrange her face so that she looked normal. She couldn't arrange her thoughts.

THIRTY-NINE

ENTERING THE APARTMENT she and Ruth shared was like coming home, because of Ruth's story, told the night before. She'd confide her own story now. It was probably written all over her, whether she wanted to confess it or not.

Ruth was in the kitchen, making tea. A box of Christmas cards was open on the table, envelopes spread out, and an address book. "Oh, how'd you find cards here?"

"I got them during Haj, on my trip to Jordan." Ruth turned to Arden. "Want a cup? I never got around to making dinner."

"Sure. Thanks." Arden draped her abaya over a chair and sat at the table.

"So, how'd the test go?"

"Uneventful."

"You were there a long time." Ruth must see something, as she studied Arden over the rim of her cup. Usually they never questioned one another's comings and goings.

"We love each other," she said simply, and the telling seemed to liberate a huge whoop of joy inside her. She laughed.

"But you said he was engaged?"

"That's all over," Arden declared.

"But here, in the Kingdom? It's risky for you to have a relationship with a Saudi, Arden, this is what we talked about."

240

"He won't be around for long," Arden said. She couldn't tell Ruth about his politics, of course. "He's going to be doing a dig in Afghanistan for awhile."

"Afghanistan! There's nothing left there."

"It wasn't quite clear, actually, just where it would be. I'll go visit him there, or somewhere nearby. We didn't finish … hammering out all the details."

"When he comes back to the Kingdom, you'll have to decide to either marry him or break it off." Ruth looked at her for a moment. "You know this, Arden."

"Well, we didn't really talk about marriage just yet. I mean, I'm telling you because, because of the talk we had last night."

"He knows it has to be kept secret."

"But he's for real, Ruth, he loves me. We'll be together once this is sorted out."

"What needs to be sorted?"

What didn't? The enormity, and the danger, of her allegiance was just beginning to settle in. "Well, if we did decide to get married, we'd need to tell our families," she began slowly, thinking aloud. "And they might be … surprised." She wondered what he would do about his spurned fiancée in Jiddah, whether his dad and stepmother would assume Arden had broken them up, and resent her for it. She wondered if Mom and Annie could get visas to come here for a wedding.

Or maybe they should get married in the States, so his mother could be there too. He could get a job at some university there, certainly, even apply for political asylum, if it came to that. "Our sisters are both getting married soon, so those are probably enough family events for this year, I'm sure."

"So it may be some time before a wedding is even possible."

"Yes, unless we can just have a quick one? Like, a justice of the peace type thing?" A number of Arden's friends, back home, had needed quickie weddings.

"I hope you're using protection."

Arden looked at her blankly. Protection? No. They hadn't. And she'd never even thought of Colleen's insistence on his getting tested. But Faisal wasn't some kind of risky partner! She was sure they shared caution about that. Of course, she'd had Johnny. A sinking feeling came over her. She had to tell Faisal about Johnny. He had to know before he was sucked into the royal groupie circle. If he'd be around that long? How imminent was the danger for him here, anyway? She realized there were too many questions she hadn't asked.

"Arden? Were you careful, at least?"

"I guess we hope Allah will protect us." She fingered the sura around her neck.

"And I'm sure you have that on good authority." Ruth smiled.

"Faisal's pretty devout. He prays. He only cut off his beard for the expedition."

"He usually wears a beard?"

"Up until yesterday."

"But Arden, you know, that tends to be a sign of fanaticism here."

"He's not really into all their ideas," she lied. "He's just trying it on for awhile."

"How will your mom feel about this? Won't they worry that he's a Muslim? A foreigner?"

"She'll think he's wonderful," she declared. Columbus had never produced anyone like Faisal. She couldn't wait to tell Annie. "And he's not the kind of dour religious guy who never has any fun. Didn't you think he was interesting, and friendly, when he came here last night? Don't you think he's so handsome?" Like all new lovers she wanted to hear her love praised.

"I always liked him, Arden, when we met at the museum. He's very personable. And his English is flawless."

"His mother's American."

"She lives here? Did you get a chance to meet her?"

"They're divorced. She lives in California."

"Did you meet his father?"

242

"Once," she said, uncertain of when and how these wedding meetings would take place. She wondered how Leila would feel. Happy, she hoped, they'd become very fond of each other. And what fun it would be to live near her in the Midwest! Arden's thoughts stumbled suddenly. She'd been fantasizing living with Faisal in her old Columbus house, locked in the bedroom for days on end, emerging to sit on the porch and play music. She'd envisioned herself in jeans and him in his robe and headdress.

Foolishness.

But if he could work out some kind of compromise with his political conscience, they could make their home in Riyadh, and visit Leila during the summers. They could live right here on campus. They'd take weekend camping trips into the desert, and make love outside under the stars. He'd teach her how to find old pots, and she'd teach him how to play the banjo. They'd pray for rain, in Arabic, along with the King on the radio. Or, no. Not with the King.

"We didn't ... really work out the family stuff." This was nothing but the silliest fantasy, after all. He'd never even mentioned marriage. She had no idea, really, what she'd let herself in for. Out of steam, she looked down, and let the long wings of her hair cover her face.

But Ruth sounded pleased, her voice holding a touch of nostalgia as well as a hint of worry. "If I can help, I will. If you need someone with you, to meet his family eventually, so you don't appear to be alone."

"Thanks." Ruth's rectitude would make her a powerful ally with a Saudi family.

The phone rang. Ruth answered, handed it to Arden, then went to her room.

"Faisal?"

"I shouldn't have made you go, *ya habibati,* I want you with me," he said. "I can't even concentrate on packing. All I see is you."

"I could come back, I could be there in two minutes."

243

His low laugh melted her. She sank onto the couch, clutching the receiver as if it were his hand. "I know, I wish it too, but we wouldn't sleep. I can't just blow off this excavation. The group's been counting on me for months."

"I miss you already. Can you call me while you're gone? Or I'll call you."

"My mobile won't work. Nobody's built a cell tower out there. We only have a satellite phone, for emergencies. But I'll call you as soon as I come back."

"Are you crossing the Empty Quarter?" The name still frightened her.

"We'll be northeast of there. Don't worry, I know the terrain."

"I can't wait to see you again! Will you be here for that New Year party?"

"Tell Johnny I'll call him. I think I'm supposed to take him camping that week."

"Faisal." But this was not the time, nor the way, to confess. Maybe she could make Johnny swear to silence before the two men spoke again. He'd do that if she asked.

"Arden. I'll see you everywhere."

FORTY

THE NEW YEAR'S EVE noise level at Ali's palace made it hard to think. Madonna blared from the multiple speakers, followed by Lyle Lovett. Arden took a moment to appreciate his band's smooth fiddling before she moved to the champagne table to take a cool flute. She relished the first tingly slide. Was there anything more festive than a swallow of New Year's Eve bubbly? She toasted her own future and wished Faisal were there to toast along; she'd find him some ginger ale if he didn't want alcohol. She'd love to dance with him to the swingy Texas two-step number. The way he moved, she'd bet he was a great dancer. Breaking free of long skirts for once, she'd worn her favorite Western style shirt that night with tight blue jeans, and her kickass boots. She took a couple of dance steps.

She hadn't heard from him during his dig, but hadn't expected to. She pictured him tooling in his Rover up and down calm golden dunes, blue sky backdrop blazing, or hacking methodically at a patch of promising-looking rubble, eyes intent, or sleeping deep, untroubled, dreaming of her, under the stars, his animated face calm enough for her to cover in kisses. She'd love to creep into his sleeping bag beside him. What was that naughty old song about midnight at the oasis and sending the camels to bed …?

She took her champagne over to the table where Grace was filling a plate.

"You're looking so much happier than the last time you were here, Arden, does that mean Faisal's coming?" Grace gave her a sly look.

Arden could not suppress her smile. "I'm a goner," she confessed. "I've been having wedding fantasies."

"You'd *marry* him?" Grace's dismay was so sharp that Arden was alarmed, as if it were contagious.

"In a heartbeat," she said defiantly.

"Arden, think about it! You'd marry a Saudi? You'd live here permanently, convert, wear a veil, never drive again, have you really thought about what it means?"

"We probably wouldn't live in the Kingdom."

"How could you have a normal marriage in the States? No housemaids there, you know, you'd be the one doing all the housework, all the childcare—these guys don't believe in any manual labor either. You'd never even get him to shovel the snow."

Arden thought of the way Faisal dealt with the khamseen. "He's different. Anyway, maybe we wouldn't live in the States either."

"Most Saudis want to live in the Kingdom. I have to introduce you to some of the Club ladies, they know a couple of American women married to Saudis, the ones allowed to come to Club meetings. It's like house arrest. The cage is nicely gilded, Arden, but basically you'd be a prisoner for life. I mean, would you raise a *daughter* here? Jesus! Think about it!"

"Faisal's different," Arden repeated.

"He's probably worse. Kate said he was wearing a long mutawa beard when he video-lectured her B Section. You know what that means."

"That was just a kind of ... phase."

Grace studied her, hearing the uncertainty in her voice. "You don't really know, though, do you. You can't have gotten to know him very well."

"I feel like I've known him all my life."

"That's lust."

"No."

"Sure it is, don't you feel that way with every new guy you're hot for?"

"I didn't feel like this before."

Grace sighed. "I forgot how young you are." She put her plate down and patted Arden's shoulder. "I don't mean to rain on your parade, but I just don't want to see you hurt, or making some huge mistake. I hope you'll take some time to think about this carefully."

Arden nodded, deflated by Grace's disapproval. She was sorry, now, that she'd said anything to her, even though she wanted to share her excitement.

"Of course I understand the attraction, we all know he's totally sexy. Kate's mystified by how you got to him. By all means, enjoy him, if you can be careful. But I wouldn't take any talk about marriage seriously. They all think they have to say that. And he's religious, so he might even mean it."

Arden didn't answer. She'd already said too much.

"On another subject, Arden," said Grace, "I'm glad to know you're looking into the grade discrepancy issues here. Evelyn and I both agree, it's a scandal. We're willing to meet with Dr. Zafeeyeh whenever you like, after the new term gets underway. And I'm sure Kate and the others will support you too. One of the Egyptians was telling Evelyn that it's gone on for years in the Medical College! Can you imagine?"

"It's about time somebody shook this up. They're crazy to think it can go on indefinitely," Arden said. "We need some higher-up involvement, can you think of anyone who can rally the men?"

"I'll ask George for some heavy-hitting old timers."

"We need Saudi men so Dr. Z. won't feel beleaguered. Faisal said he'd lobby his colleagues in science."

"Wow, good for him!" Grace exclaimed. "He's willing to stick his neck out on this? He must not care about keeping his university job."

Arden sidestepped. "He's an idealist. I might even get his father on our side."

Leaving Grace with a group of consular workers, Arden went in search of Johnny. She had to ensure his discretion. She might not know Faisal in the way Grace thought she should, but she could be pretty sure that under his easygoing veneer he was an Arab man, and that meant he wouldn't like the idea of her being with other men. He'd known, surely, that she wasn't a virgin, but she recalled the gentle way he'd stopped her from discussing her past.

Johnny was carousing in the game room with a bunch of other off-duty pilots. She could see from the crates of empties that they'd been drinking plenty of beer. Even Nawaf was drinking beer. She had to smile at the sight he made, aghal rakishly askew, chugging a Heineken and lounging a little lopsidedly against the pool table where Johnny was lining up a shot.

"Yellow, side pocket." Johnny aimed, thrust, and stood, grinning and accepting Nawaf's hand slap as the ball flew into its target. They both saw Arden at the same time. Nawaf lurched toward her, Johnny swaggered, and they enveloped her in an affectionate embrace, rocking her between them in a testosterone-laced sandwich.

Nawaf stroked her hair as Johnny kissed her wetly, sliding his hands into her back jeans pockets and pulling her close enough to feel his erection. She didn't flatter herself it was for her. The atmosphere in the room was loose and rowdy and she imagined all the pilots were anticipating a night of revelry with the women enjoying the action at the pool tables and pinball machines.

"Lookin good, babe, got any for me?" Johnny said, husky. "To celebrate 1998?"

"And me," Nawaf said into her ear. Arden got the distinct feeling they'd shared girls before. She'd suspected it, that night she'd spent here sleeping with them: their way of loving each other without having to confront it. She twisted away.

"Cut it out, guys, I'm taken."

"Oh yeah, Faisal called me. He said he'd be here, I gave him directions."

248

"Faisal?" asked Nawaf.

"The archaeologist. You remember, we met for coffee that time. He knows the desert, he's cool, he said he'd take us camping this week."

"That one want see the planes, always talking *seeyaseeya?*" Politics.

"Yeah," Johnny said, saluting beyond Arden's head. "Here he comes, *ya* Nawaf."

Arden turned, apprehension flooding through her, and watched with her heart in her throat as Faisal made his way through the crowded, smoky room to where they stood. Nawaf's arm was still around her waist. She elbowed him aside and he staggered and stared at her, aggrieved, as Faisal reached them.

"Happy New Year, *ya sadiki*," Johnny clapped Faisal on the back. He laughed at Faisal's unsmiling regard. "Don't worry, man, we're just keepin her warm for ya." He gave Arden a little push toward Faisal. "She's all yours."

Oh Johnny, shut up, Arden told him silently. She could feel hostility emanating from Faisal like a leaking can of mace, hissing toward the three of them.

Nawaf laughed too then, in comprehension, and spoke to Faisal in a rapid low Arabic that had Faisal's gaze turning, cold as glass, back to Johnny. Faisal smiled, although it was not an easy smile. He answered Nawaf, nudging Johnny, and they all laughed.

Arden knew raw male jostling when she saw it. She walked quickly out of the game room, adrenaline racing. She'd witnessed enough bar brawls, and fights amongst her West Virginia cousins, to recognize the signs. Faisal's dislike of the royal family and the U.S. military, the shock he'd have felt at seeing her entwined with the men, and the beer inside Johnny and Nawaf, made for a combustive mix. Good, she thought as she stopped in the bathroom to wash out the taste of Johnny's kiss, let them beat each other bloody. If Johnny and Nawaf thought so little of her that they were willing to mislead her lover, and if her lover was so easily misled, why then—

She shook her head, looking at her panicked expression in the mirror. No. She'd let herself in for their worst assumptions by her own behavior, with each of them. It wasn't their fault if they thought little of her. But why shouldn't she pick and choose her partners, just as men did, even in this rigid society? Why the hell not?

And if Faisal assumed the worst of her? Appearances were certainly not in her favor. Blinking back tears, she gulped some champagne to ease the congestion in her throat. *Fuck it.* She would find a way to smooth things over with him. She straightened her hair, drank some more. She rolled her lipstick on, carefully.

She went back to the main salon and attached herself to a group standing by the dessert table. Someone handed her another glass and she held it, trembling still, in spite of her determination to stand up straight and not to fold, feeling cold perspiration trickle in an unpleasant little rivulet down her back. Her great-looking shirt wasn't lending her any more courage than the champagne she had already downed; in fact she felt undressed, suddenly, without her abaya.

Kate walked up to her, smiling, holding her own flute. She wore a lavender silk caftan, embroidered in turquoise, which seemed to float around her.

"You look beautiful, Kate." Her voice was surprisingly steady.

"You too, Arden, those straight lines suit your height." She took a sip, surveying Arden. "Did Faisal find you? He came in a few minutes ago, looking for you."

"He's just … saying hi to Ali."

Too late, Arden realized that Johnny wasn't the only one whose silence should have been secured, if she wanted to preserve a façade of innocence. They'd all been there that morning, they'd all witnessed Johnny covering her nakedness with blankets before bundling her off to the hospital. Of course, she thought, eyeing Kate and trying to gauge her level of friendship, it didn't matter now. Faisal's conclusions would have been completed in the instant he saw her squashed between Johnny and Nawaf.

"So the two of you are together now? You and Faisal?"

Arden nodded.

"Just remember, he's not a royal. You'll have to be very careful."

That he wasn't a royal was the least of it. But everyone had to weigh in with their advice. She must look so clueless to the older teachers, she realized suddenly. "I know."

Kate continued to study her.

Faisal approached unbloodied, unflustered. There must not have been a fight after all, at least not a physical one. He smiled at both of them. "Good evening, ladies, it's almost midnight. Everyone's getting together in the atrium for a toast. Shall we?" Like some genial English gentleman in a smoking jacket he offered an arm to each. He gave Arden's hand a brief squeeze as if the scene in the game room never happened.

"I missed you," she told him in a whisper. "I'm sorry about—back there."

He glanced at her. "We'll talk."

Her heart sank. Her head was spinning with alcohol and anxiety, a nauseating mix. She stumbled and he tightened his grip on her hand, trapping it to his ribcage. If she could move it up just a little she'd feel his heartbeat, but his arm was like iron.

In the atrium Ali had fixed a huge glossy sign in English and Arabic and French, saying 'Happy New Year 1998.' The pilots had brought blowers and party hats from their commissary, as well as multicolored '1998' balloons, which floated around the room amongst the tall palms and twisting vines adorning the indoor fountains.

The high ceilings and marble walls and floor made the crowd's excitement level seem to rise in an echoing bubble of party chatter, disembodied, as if it would burst on the ceiling, pierced by the chandelier, in a confetti shower of flirtations, challenges and witticisms that would then float down to mingle with the balloons and settle on the shoulders of those other than the intended recipients, a crafty party game.

It must be the champagne, Arden thought, that made this scene so uncomfortably surreal to her. She wished only to be in his room again, making amends to him, for Johnny and Nawaf, the only way she could think of, with her body. But he was gregarious; he greeted many of the guests. They knew him from the museum, of course, anyone who'd had a tour there over the years when he'd been visiting from Berkeley, or since his permanent return. The women's eyes, and some of the men's, loitered on him.

It was obvious, though, everyone who said hello was surprised to see him at the party. Their glances immediately flicked to her and back again, as if surmising she was the reason for this digression from his normal reserve. Certainly they made an unusual pair, she in her jeans and boots, wild hair foaming almost to her waist, he in his immaculate robes, aloof and regal.

At midnight, Ali had arranged for a short fireworks display on the lawn outside the atrium. Parabolas of brilliant light seemed to cascade down into the room as everyone shouted "Happy New Year" and toasted and kissed.

Faisal lifted his glass to Arden's, and took a healthy swig, before wrapping an arm around her, a public display of physical affection so surprising she didn't expect it. His swift kiss was too quick to be enjoyable but she felt herself responding nevertheless, felt her arms creeping up to try to reach into his hair under his headdress. But he quickly moved her away from him with one firm swing. He drank again, deeply, and exchanged his empty glass for a full one on a nearby tray.

"I didn't know you drank," she said timidly, unsure of how to defuse his anger.

"There's a lot we don't know about each other."

"So, Faisal, how was the expedition?" asked Kate, who was still standing beside them, watching their interplay.

"Not as productive as we'd hoped, Kate," he said, turning toward her.

"You didn't find the pearl fishing evidence?" Kate's smile was sympathetic and, Arden realized, professional, as if they were on a level of civil discourse quite separate from the roiling waves of mixed emotion crashing back and forth unspoken between Arden and Faisal.

Arden extricated herself completely from his hold on her arm and straightened herself. She looked at him directly, keeping her eyes free from apology. "Did you find any awls, any borers?" she asked.

"Not enough to make the trip feel worthwhile," he answered, meeting her even gaze with his own. "Not enough to leave here for."

Kate's little smile was a concession. "Well, Happy New Year, you two," she said lightly, putting her glass on the table behind them.

The sound of throbbing Arabic music started in the other salon, and everyone drifted slowly in as if charmed. The band was a group of wild-looking men who played the same kinds of instruments Arden remembered from Leila's Eid party. Nawaf, Ali and a few other Saudis were standing near them, swaying slightly to the rhythm. Faisal left her to join them. She felt her tension rise as he put a hand on Nawaf's shoulder, but the prince turned and smiled, and put an arm around him. Soon Faisal was swaying along with the line of men, whose number grew as the music's volume called them in from many rooms of the palace.

Then the men were dancing, not just swaying, stylized and in unison. Their eyes were half-closed, their feet sure as they stepped back and forth, inscribing slow circles, thobes billowing soft bells around their sandaled feet. The power and dignity of the dance held the Western guests motionless, respectful in their acknowledgement that for them, this was as rare a sight in the Kingdom as desert roses. The men looked timeless, like figures on Faisal's sherds, as they swung, and the music was somber, deeper than the high-pitched sexual thrumming that the women's dance had been. It sounded to Arden like a hymn.

She'd been right—Faisal was a good dancer. He was bewitching, in fact, in his line of brothers, in the solemn cadence of their graceful flow. She fell in love anew as she watched him lead them in a kind of slow crack-the-whip across the room. His hands rose in a fluid arc above his head, and the others' hands followed. He caught Nawaf's hand in his, and the others linked hands too. When a couple of pilots, grinning, tried to join them, Faisal pulled them in and showed them the steps.

How could Faisal seriously contemplate leaving this culture when he fit into it so effortlessly? Did he realize how much it was part of him? She wondered if he understood how, if his political ideals led to revolution, the community fabric here would tear apart into shreds that would never heal.

When the music ended, those left in the audience, mostly women, cheered loudly. Faisal remained in the center of the dancers, his arms around Johnny and Nawaf, all laughing.

"By noon tomorrow," she heard another pilot tell Faisal as the crowd around them dissipated. "Can you come pick us up at the base?"

"*La, ya* Faisal, come my house first, so I can get you ID from my father," Nawaf said. "Too many question, if you go to the base by yourself. They don't let you in."

"Okay guys, Nawaf will bring him in," said Johnny. "How about supplies?"

"I have plenty left from my Ain Qanass dig."

He had just returned, yet he was planning to leave. Maybe he wanted time away, to reflect. She turned back to the atrium, to get another glass of champagne. She needed to swallow the melancholy that rose in her throat at the thought of his second departure.

Then he was next to her, his smile thin, but genuine. "Let's go."

Outside, the air was quiet and cold, clean-smelling. They passed a few workers bringing in the fixtures for the fireworks display, and Faisal murmured hellos to them in Arabic, and gave them some bills he pulled from his pocket.

"*Shukran, ya sheikh*," they thanked him.

"You're giving them a tip?"

"I'm sure putting on a fireworks display is outside their normal job description," was his dry response. "Remember, this is not their new year."

FORTY-ONE

FAISAL'S ROVER WAS as filthy as after the khamseen, and when she climbed in back she had to move aside bags of equipment. He had not even unloaded, she thought, her heart swelling like a sponge, he must have showered and come straight to the party to see her. Just in time to witness her being mauled by Nawaf and Johnny.

She lifted a couple of backpacks to put them in the trunk behind her, and then jerked them up in fright when she saw what was in the trunk. She knew rifles. This one was a .303 Enfield, a lethal old beauty. What was he doing with a weapon, forbidden for personal use in the Kingdom? Had his revolution started? "Damn," she said aloud.

Faisal looked back to see what she was doing. "Don't worry, it's not loaded," he said. "You can put those in the trunk, but be careful, they're artifacts. *Shukran.*"

"Jesus Christ."

"Peace on him," he said absently, pulling out of the driveway.

This was an inadequate response. "Is it part of—what you're planning here?"

"Of course not," he said, cool eyes meeting hers in the rearview. "One old rifle wouldn't even begin to make a difference."

She pushed her thoughts past the violence this implied. "Then what's it doing here?"

"I always take one on our expeditions. We never know what might be out there."

She could not imagine what threats might face an archeological expedition. What desert animals needed this kind of power? Snakes? Wild camels?

"Bandits," he clarified. "Sometimes we need to scare them off, near the border."

"Let's do some shooting on the way home," she said on impulse. Maybe some target practice would help him let off steam. They could blow away a couple of sand dunes.

"You've had too much champagne for me to trust you with my Enfield."

"I'll sober up in the desert air."

"How'd you learn to shoot, anyway?" Then he smiled suddenly.

"Uncle Munro," they both said together, and shared their first laugh since his return.

"Yeah, he taught me. I'm not bad."

"*Ya salaam*, Arden, I like everything about you. Everything but this. How could you go with those fuckers back there!" He muttered to himself in Arabic. Sounded like some strong cursing.

The tension that mention of Uncle Munro had dissipated—a typical phenomenon, in her family—sprang back and seemed to thicken the air between them as they got deeper into the desert. She kept quiet. He'd have to get it out of his system, and she'd have to let him.

It wouldn't be helpful to point out that he'd befriended those fuckers, and was in fact taking them camping as if they were all the best of buds. Besides, there was no explanation that would bridge the cultural divide between them, on the subject of casual sex; it was obviously too deep to be broached in any mood but cold sobriety. And he was right, she was full of champagne. She sighed and stared out at the blackness.

"I know I have no right to be angry," he said suddenly. *Damn straight*, she thought, relieved and impressed that he could admit this right away. "Johnny told me you were with him before you and I—before. I lived in the States, I know how Americans behave, I don't blame you. But I hated seeing their hands on you." He added in Arabic, his voice low, "*Ahebek.*" I love you.

"I wanted to tell you about Johnny, but there didn't seem to be the right time," she said, apologetic. "It really didn't mean anything." How lame that sounded.

"Don't tell me, Arden, please. I won't let this come between us. I just need some time." He drove in silence then.

I should tell him to stop, Arden thought. *We can walk together and talk about this. After all, I'd feel the same way if I met some girl he'd slept with. Oh Faisal.* Just as she thought this, he pulled over off the road. He sat for a moment, not looking at her, and then got out of the Rover. She saw him climbing away across one of the little rises. Should she leave him alone to walk it off? She hated his being hurt. She hadn't even said "I love you too." *Ya salaam.* She had to do something!

She turned to look again at the rifle. It was, indeed, unloaded, but a box of shells sat right beside it. She could load it and pull off a few shots, in the other direction from where he was of course, just to loosen things up a little. She wanted to shock both of them out of this funk. She leaned over the seat and moved the backpacks aside, reaching for the ammunition.

One of the packs yawned open and she saw, with a rise of wondrous fear, that the bag was full of bones. Ancient bones, for sure, but still. She sank back into her seat, eyes searching the dunes for him. Then she took a breath and turned slowly. She had to look again. *They look like skulls! No,* she corrected, as the clouds peeled away from the moon, *they're pots, and broken bits of pots. Of course.* That damn rifle had put scary thoughts in her head.

All desire to shoot left her as she sat waiting. The moon was a slice of what it had been last week, the night he'd first kissed her, that seemed so long ago now. I love you too, ya Faisal, she told him silently, seeing him approach from beyond the rise, I'll never hurt you again, I'll follow you to the ends of the earth. She realized he must have gone to pray. She loved that he sought peace that way. His face was serene as he opened her door. He climbed in beside her to wrap her into the embrace she needed.

Soon he got back into the driver's seat, soon they reached the campus, soon he let himself into his apartment, soon she followed. He met her just inside the door and folded her around him as if she were another cloak. They moved, locked together, making their way to his bedroom.

As the heat of their night passed she felt her need for him grow rather than lessen. The more the ache inside her was soothed by their loving, the more frantic she became. Finally he turned on the light beside his bed, leaned on one elbow, and studied her. His hair was tousled in ebony tangles to his neck, his cheekbones and lips flushed an exhausted rose that made her want to taste there again, his eyes were heavy-lidded with fatigue and satiety and, still, desire; so beautiful she could barely stand to look at him.

"Talk to me, love," he told her in Arabic. "Tell me everything. I'm here. I'm listening." He stroked her hair back with soft fingers.

She had nothing to say. She stared at him with a sensation of sinking helplessness, a crushing realization that the more she had him, the more she wanted him, and that was a damned uncomfortable place to be. She leaned over him to turn the light off, and then stretched out full length on top of him. She felt his tired chuckle shake his chest. She clung to him. She felt more lost lying on him than dreaming of him in her own bed, but she did not know why this should be, now that he was so completely hers. A few of her anguished tears trickled onto his neck, and he rubbed them from her cheeks and rolled her to lie next to him.

"If you don't talk to me then sing. Can you sing "Amazing Grace" again?"

Was there anything she could not do for him? She sang.

"Do you know the song called "Lay Down your Weary Tune"?" he asked then. "An old recording my mother has. It reminds me of Big Sur. It sounds like your music."

"Tell me about your mother."

"Caroline. She's wonderful," he said. She heard the smile in his voice. "You will like her. She'll think you are ... she'll love you as I do. I want you to visit her in America."

"Leila thinks you don't approve of her."

He laughed, still stroking her hair. "I had issues when Leila and I visited there one time and she had a guy living with her. Caroline gave me a big lecture, saying it was none of my business, but I noticed she never had another live-in when I stayed. Leila, though, is living in this culture, she believes in its standards."

"Which do you believe in?"

"I don't even know. I lived both standards but in separate ways, do you see, for too many years. But Leila will decide for herself, soon now, what is the right." Weariness was loosening his grasp of English, Arden realized, amused; weariness and love.

"Do you sing for me, *ya habibati?*" He pulled her close to him. "Please."

It was a hymn to natural beauty. Although one of the loveliest of Bob Dylan's songs, it had a mournful undertone that bordered on resignation, and a martial air that made it sound like the song a sad soldier might play on the eve of battle. She was surprised to hear Faisal ask for it.

"*Yullah, ya* Arden, I'll sing with you," he mumbled in Arabic.

Perhaps it was the singing, and perhaps it was the advent of dawn, like the drums of dawn in the song, but she felt released from her intense anxiety of the night. She could only manage half the verses before succumbing to the warmth of his skin under her cheek and the steady beating of his heart. He kept on singing for awhile, his gentle voice whispery, his accent making the words uniquely his own. He was a pretty good singer, she thought as she drifted off. He kissed her as he sang the word 'banjo.'

"I'm sorry to leave again so soon," she heard him say softly some time later, when she thought she was already dreaming. "I wish I could stay with you forever."

"Stupid camping trip," she muttered.

His arms tightened around her. She wrapped herself around him like seaweed around a rock, drifting in and out of sleep as waves of love washed them ever closer.

FORTY-TWO

THEY DID NOT RETURN.

Three days into the week, Arden got a call from Kate, who had a pilot friend on the base wondering how long the camping trip was supposed to have taken. Faisal hadn't given any detailed itinerary but Arden certainly didn't expect them back yet. They'd wanted him to take them to the Empty Quarter, after all, and that was a long journey even with all of them taking turns driving. Arden thought they'd be lucky to do the trip inside of a week, realistically.

"They didn't have a week, Arden. Apparently a couple of them only had three days' leave. Even Johnny and Nawaf only had four." Kate's voice held a hint of worry.

"Well, then, I guess they'll be back tonight. Or tomorrow."

"Faisal didn't tell you anything more specific."

"He said ..." Arden tried to remember. Their morning after had been a mad scramble to get her out of his place before the neighbors were awake to witness her departure, and they'd shared only a hasty farewell kiss at his door after they woke up. There had been no time for coffee and conversation. "He said he'd get in touch with me soon."

"So, didn't he call you?"

"They only have a satellite phone, for emergencies. They don't use it unless there's an accident or something." She pictured it as he'd shown it to her, sitting on the table in his empty living room, a bulky black box with a handset attached to the side.

"He doesn't have a mobile number we can call?"

"No, there's no service out there."

"Uh-oh, those guys are going to get in trouble, for them it's like going AWOL or something. I hope Faisal cooked up a good excuse for them." Kate chuckled.

"The pilots must have been desperate for a vacation, I can imagine."

"Maybe they just went over to Bahrain," Kate suggested wickedly. "Checking out the casinos."

"Ouch!" It was bad enough that her missing him was already so visceral. Kate's teasing was salt on her wound. "Don't even say it."

"Probably found some beach bunnies."

"It's too cold for the beach," Arden told her firmly.

The next day, Nawaf's cousin Ali called her. Hearing him, she thought he was Nawaf, and cried, "Hi! It's so good to hear your voice! Where are you guys?"

"Hello, Miss Ahden, I am in my home, this is Ali."

"Oh. I thought—"

"Does Faisal call to you?"

"No, I haven't heard from him."

"Miss. My cousin Nawaf. His father need to know what habben to his son."

"Well, I suppose they got delayed somehow, maybe a khamseen?"

"No, is not time for khamseen. Nawaf is late now one day for flying. This doesn't habben before. You have the phone number where we can call to Faisal?"

"His mobile doesn't work there."

"Give to me anyway, please, and give to me the number of his family, if you have? If you don't have, of course we find them."

Arden obliged, stirred by Ali's clipped tone. He sounded unlike himself. He sounded angry. She was beginning to wonder if she should feel angry too.

"Ali, here's his family number, only it's just that—I only have it because his sister is my student. They don't know that Faisal and I, we're ... close. I don't want his family to hear about me from anyone but him, or me, okay?"

"I understand. I won't to speak about you to his family."

"And if you hear from Nawaf and Faisal, could you let me know?"

"Yes, Miss Ahden."

"Thanks for the wonderful party you gave, that was really—" he had hung up.

Arden wondered how she could call Leila without making the girl suspicious. How could she possibly ask if they'd heard from Faisal? She couldn't. She'd see Leila in class tomorrow, though, and maybe she could casually work in a little dialogue about 'what your family did on break.' Leila would tell her, wouldn't she, if there'd been any mishap, any strange desert delay? She looked, blankly, at the phone in her hand, which was bleeping its 'hang up now' signal. She put it in its cradle and went to find Ruth.

"I'm starting to feel a little anxious," she said. Ruth listened, and thought for awhile. This was a quality Arden had come to appreciate in her new friend. She waited, hoping Ruth's explanation would be sensible.

"You said he had a satellite phone?"

"Yes, I saw it before they left, a big funny-looking thing."

"Something like that, used for expeditions, probably belongs to the Department of Antiquities. They must have the number."

"Yes," Arden said, grateful. "How can I get it?"

"I don't think you can. I think you should tell Ali to get it." Ruth's eyes were serious. "I think you should call him back right now and tell him."

Arden dialed *69 and was forced to ask the person who answered, in Arabic, if she could speak to Prince Ali. As she waited, the song about fabulous Prince Ali Ababwa, from Disney's *Aladdin* cartoon played, hysterical and unwanted, in her mind.

"*Ahlan.*" Ali's sober voice came on. Arden was so flustered by his tone that she started speaking to him in

Arabic before getting tangled over 'satellite phone.' Ali listened to her repeat Ruth's suggestion in English, and hung up again, after an abrupt thanks, once she had finished.

"Now what?" she asked Ruth, who was sitting next to her.

"Now, you wait," Ruth said, and the sympathy in her voice was not possible for Arden to stay and listen to, because if she needed sympathy there must be a terrible reason for it, and she would not accept any terrible reasons right now.

Arden went into her bedroom and finished getting her wardrobe ready for the start of the new school term. She sat on her bed, considering the top she'd paired with her outfit for tomorrow. She'd finally put aside enough riyals for the gold necklace she'd been craving, she was going to buy it at the souk next weekend.

She didn't realize hot tears were staining her carefully laid out suit until Ruth's gentle hand touched her shoulder. She turned and clung to the other woman's side. Ruth stroked her hair.

"I'm sure there's a perfectly good explanation," Ruth said quietly. "You remember, you told me how the khamseen came up that day, how sudden it was and how it stalled traffic for hours." Her touch was soothing. "You also told me he was equipped for any emergency, that he wasn't even ruffled by the storm. He's an old pro at the terrain, I'm sure, Arden."

"He even had his rifle." Arden sniffed.

Ruth's hand stilled on her shoulder. "His what?"

"He even had a rifle, a nice old Enfield, in case they ran into a bandit."

Ruth's voice, above her, sounded a little distracted then, as she resumed her patting. "Then he's prepared for every possible contingency."

This thought let Arden get the sleep she needed to work the next day.

In the Intermediate class, she looked anxiously for Leila, but the girl was not there. She mustered the energy to get through the lesson, somehow. She called Leila's number on her mobile as soon as she was alone in the classroom.

"*Ahlan.*" It was a man's gruff voice. Othman, or some driver or servant?

"Please, Leila?"

"She can't speak right now," the man said in Arabic.

"I am her teacher. Please tell her—" Arden ran out of words for a moment, wishing she could go to Leila, sure now that an emergency was indeed underway. "Tell her I want she feel good." She cursed her pitifully limited Arabic.

"Miss Arden? This is Othman. *Assalamu aleikum.*"

Pain bloomed in her chest and spread to her throat. She could not answer.

"Miss Arden? It's kind of you to call. I'll tell Leila you send your regards."

"*Wa aleikum asalaam,*" Arden said. "I hope she feels better soon."

Othman said finally, "She's not sick, Miss Arden. Faisal is missing. He took a group to the Empty Quarter, and they haven't returned." Othman's concern was audible. "Apparently they were expected back days ago."

"I'm so sorry." Arden bit her lips together.

"I don't understand it," he sighed. "He had an Iridium phone, it had a GPS, I don't know why they haven't found the signal. They can find them at the bottom of the ocean. On the moon."

"GPS?"

"Global Positioning System. It tells exactly where the phone is located, on a satellite grid. Very powerful."

"So then, they can find him?"

"Antiquities hasn't been able to pick up the signal. They're sending a crew out today."

"I hope they'll find him soon."

"Thanks, Miss Arden. We hope so too."

Sometime during her next class, Arden realized she couldn't keep up the pretense of normalcy anymore. She plugged a long dialogue sequence into the language lab, for her girls to memorize, and went to her little shared office. She sat at her desk.

Grace was there, doing lesson plans. "Any news?"

They all, of course, were waiting to hear. Grace's foreign correspondent friend had gotten wind of the story and was keen to interview Arden and the others, an interest he did not realize would never materialize in the Kingdom. Women did not appear in the news, and the teachers had been warned, sternly, to never talk to the press.

"His dad says Antiquities is sending out a search party."

"But isn't that a good thing?"

"They can't get any signal from his phone. It has some kind of thing they can tell where he is, except they can't." She put her head in her hands, thinking of the wicked wind, the twisting sand, the choking dust. She thought of how he'd saved her and wondered who, among those airmen he'd taken, would know enough about the desert to save him now.

She pictured Johnny staggering in the alien half-light of killer dust pluming off a monstrous, mountain-sized dune, losing his way down the enormous slope, fighting gravity like the warrior he was and defeated by it as only a fighter pilot could be, as he wheeled and spiraled in the shifting soft grains. Air, he could master. Ground was his enemy.

She pictured Nawaf, sweet Nawaf, his mouth filling with sand as he called after Johnny to come back, come back *ya habibi*. She didn't even know the names of the other boys but she could almost hear their cries as they tried to make order out of chaos, as they had been trained so well to do.

Suddenly she was filled with fierce anger. "They were so *stupid!* They would all have been so hungover, that morning! What the *fuck* were they thinking!"

"Was Faisal hungover?" Grace asked fearfully.

Arden's sigh came from deep in her lungs, from confusion she hadn't known was there, buried since the

New Year party. "He had some champagne, I don't know if he was used to drinking, but if he had any doubts he should have postponed their goddamn trip!" She coughed. "Maybe he was trying to prove how macho he was."

Grace shut the door. "Just how macho was he?"

"He saw Johnny and Nawaf being overly friendly with me. Maybe he was still angry about that, wanted to show them what a stud he is, or something, some kind of desert cowboy." She hated to think of that rifle, its cold gleam summoning homicide. Oh Jesus, peace be upon him, let Faisal not have given in to that wicked temptation.

"I think it was the other way round," Grace said slowly. "I heard Johnny and the other pilots, even Nawaf, insisting on going out right away, in the game room that night at the party. They wanted to take advantage of their New Year leave."

Arden's fury was spent. She mopped her face with the inadequate Kleenex Grace handed her from the office box. When Grace went to class she made a call she had never made before.

"Dr Zafeeyeh? This is Arden Armstrong, of the English Department. I'm feeling really sick, I think it's the stomach flu, and I think I'd better go home. I'm sorry to leave the students in the lurch like this." She listened for a moment. "A driver? I'll wait for him at the gate." She scrawled a note for Grace, with her lesson plan for the rest of the day, and bundled up in her abaya and scarf.

It was a beautiful, sunny day, with the blue sky as pure as she'd ever seen it. The air was crisp, just at the edge of cold, and the scent of newly blooming jasmine was sweet as she waited by the deserted gate. It took more than forty-five minutes for her name to be called, barked over the annoying intercom, and she hurried outside, feeling every bit as harassed as her students always said they were, after waiting half their lives for rides someplace. She reviewed in her mind the correct way to tell a driver, in Arabic, the directions to the desert housing compound.

There was no need to give directions, however. The driver was Sayeed Quraishi.

"Hello again, Miss Arden," he said as she settled herself in back.

"Sayeed, it's nice of you to give me a ride, how good to see you." And, surprisingly, it *was* good to see him. His sober young face reminded her of a time when she'd been free of care here, when her worst worry was having to share a flat. That seemed frivolous now. "How are you doing in this new term?"

"*Alhamdulillah.* And you? Did our arrangement with Miss Ruth work out?"

"Sayeed, I have to thank you for getting us together." She smiled at him in the mirror. "She's become a good friend."

His smile was still shy, she noted. "That is good news. And your classes? You are enjoying them?"

"I love them," she said simply. If he continued in this kindly vein she might lose it again, she thought, and turned to the window, away from his gaze in the mirror. She brought a Kleenex to her mouth.

The long ride out to the desert campus seemed littered with reminders of Faisal—this was where they'd waited out the storm; this was where they'd first kissed; this was where he'd thrown his headdress off, grinning; this was where she'd been freaked by the sight of his pots in the trunk—something snagged on her memory then, something small but significant, if she could see it more clearly ...

But the fragment was gone. She stared out the window, hard, as if she could see all the way to the Empty Quarter where they were hidden.

Sayeed looked at her. "Is something wrong, Arden?" She shook her head, but when they stopped at her parking lot he turned to face her before she got out. "Let me know, if you are more sick. Be careful."

Too late, she could have told him. It was much too late for her to be careful. She went to bed and drifted into a kind of stunned sleep, haunted by dreams of trying to pull Faisal out of the sand. When the phone rang she sprang awake, sure it had to be him. She was disoriented by the American man's voice on the line.

"Miss Armstrong? This is Prescott Montgomery, I'm with State."

"State?" She tried to quickly clear her muddied mind. *State of what?*

"The State Department. Would it be convenient for me to pay you a quick visit?"

"Why?" Was it the test she'd given at the USIA? They were run by the State Department.

"I just have a few questions, regarding the expedition that's gone missing." What connection could there be, between the camping trip and the State Department? She'd met a guy from State at one of the parties, a quick-witted upper-class type who'd deflected the expats' questions about his work with smooth jokes. "We're not spies," he'd smirked. "We just cover them."

"Okay," she told Prescott Montgomery. "I'm in—"

"We know where you are."

FORTY-THREE

PRESCOTT MONTGOMERY WAS A COOL, watchful man in his forties, with keen gray eyes that surveyed every inch of the bare apartment where Arden let him in. He studied her, too, from her head to her toes, taking in the abaya and scarf she wore, as if she held the key to some door he was trying to unlock.

"You're wondering why I'm here."

She nodded. She'd fixed tea before he came, and covered up, as if she needed some sort of protection against official inspection.

"I'm interested in knowing more about Dr. Al Ansary. We've been asked to help in the search."

"Dr. Al Ansary?" Why would he ask *her* about Faisal?

"You brought him to the USIA last week. He listed himself as your guest in the register."

"He drove me, as a favor."

"Have you heard from him since they left?"

"No, but he wouldn't have called me."

"Why not?"

"For one thing, they only had this satellite phone, it was—"

"We know." He was watching her face. "How well did you know Dr. Al Ansary?"

Why was he using past tense? "He's my student's brother."

"But you brought him to the USIA?"

"He was looking up schools for his sister in the library."

"And using the internet to send e-mail."

271

Were USIA visitors not supposed to e-mail prospective schools? How else would they get information? Why did he make it sound like suspicious behavior? "He was probably downloading applications. I was doing a test there. I was in another—"

"We know."

His tone made the cold beginning of fear tighten her. "I think you better tell me what this is about."

"Actually I was hoping you might tell me."

"Tell you ...?"

"Tell me what your relationship was, and what you might have known about his plans. Tell me so you can help us find the Americans he took."

"He took them camping."

Montgomery's clear eyes had the look of someone who had seen combat, a look that came from a faroff cold place. "They didn't go camping."

"What? How do you know?"

"Antiquities went looking for their GPS, their phone he used, and they found it."

"Where?"

"Sitting on a table in his empty apartment, in the building next door. The police are still over there. I just left them."

Arden's hands stiffened around the teapot. She felt a rushing in her ears, a flood of icy water that cascaded through her body. "No." But of course this was true, this was the thing she had forgotten—the big black box had been in the Rover's trunk next to the bags of pots the night of the party, and sitting alone on his table the next morning. But so? Of course he'd had to unpack everything from the first trip to get ready for the second. He'd have done that, she supposed, while she was still sleeping. Her throat tightened. "Maybe it wasn't working when he tried to use it that morning. Maybe he left it behind on purpose."

"Maybe because he had no intention of being located."

She could only stare now, a stare he returned, until his terrible conclusion settled inside her with the cold press of truth. "That's what you think."

He nodded, still watching her face, evaluating. "Leaving it in his apartment, disconnected, was his joke on everyone that he knew would be looking for him."

"And you think I—you think maybe I have some idea of what really happened."

"A connection's established. We have the evidence at the USIA, and the missing prince's cousin says you two were together the night before their trip."

"We were all at the same party, he just gave me a ride home—" Why was she hiding her relationship from this man? Americans wouldn't care if she was with a Saudi. She straightened up. "We're in love. We might get married."

He shook his head. "Not on this planet. But thanks for your honesty." He stood, and went to look out at the courtyard. "Can you tell me why he might have done this?"

"You think he took them away on purpose?" That didn't make any sense. If he needed to leave, he'd go alone. Those pilots would just get in the way.

"We think they've been kidnapped, yes. Those were four of the best pilots in the Kingdom, one of them close to the throne. The Saudis and the U.S. Air Force are furious. Anyone connected to this is feeling the heat, and it'll be turned on you if you have the slightest inkling of an idea about this that you don't tell me now, while you still have the chance to be questioned as a free person."

She dug her nails into the space between the seat cushions to remind herself of reality. She knew they were in a familiar quiet white apartment, prayer call sounding wistfully outside, tea cooling on the tray. His words sounded the false, the unreal note.

"I think I am entitled to a lawyer?" she heard her own voice say faintly.

"This is the Kingdom." His smile spread, wolfish, as he turned away from the window. "You don't get one."

"You're my government here. As an American, I would think—"

"As an American, I wonder if you're thinking about those brave young men he spirited off like some goddamn pied piper, thinking they were going camping."

"But what makes you think he kidnapped them?"

"We have his e-mails."

Arden clasped her hands together. "What?—what did they say?"

"Don't you know?"

She shook her head, meeting his scrutiny.

"We know he had correspondence from outside the Kingdom. E-mailing from the USIA was his way of avoiding the Saudi firewalls, the censors. It's unlimited access there in the library. He'd done it before, we found his screen name."

"He was finding schools for Leila!"

Montgomery just looked at her.

"He only went there as a favor to me! I took him out for lunch afterwards!"

"Under the circumstances, I'd say that was damn big of you," he said, dry.

"But this doesn't make sense. He's *friends* with Johnny!"

"John Jackson? How do you know?"

"You're making this all sound so sinister. I don't see, logically, that he could have done this by himself." Against their will, four of them? Was he that strong? Of course, she remembered, he had the rifle. But who'd be driving? And why, why would he ever do such a thing? How could it possibly further his cause of political change here?

"We think he wasn't alone."

"But where would he take them?"

"Maybe Yemen, maybe Pakistan, maybe Afghanistan."

"*Afghanistan?*"

Montgomery frowned. "There's a terrorist organization, Saudi-based, that moved its operation to Afghanistan last year."

"No." Faisal's group was religious, not militant. She could not believe this. But she suddenly remembered his comment about the Enfield, the comment she hadn't wanted to hear too closely: *One old rifle wouldn't even begin to make a difference here.* "You're saying ... he was one of them?"

"We don't know. We can't read his e-mails at the USIA, they're encrypted, but we can tell there was correspondence to Sudan and Afghanistan. Not, presumably, countries where his sister would be applying to schools."

Her abject slump at these words must have told him all he needed to know. His voice was grave. "The Saudis want you arrested. I can tell them you were an innocent bystander, so to speak, that you didn't connect him to the pilots on purpose. We can stall them for awhile so we can get you out of the Kingdom. But if they don't buy the story, they can come after you. We won't be able to help you. You're a Saudi employee here."

"I can't leave the Kingdom." She stared up at Montgomery. Where could she go? "This is my home now," she told him, but her voice sounded insubstantial, wispy with wishful thinking, even to her. He looked at her with an expression that, on a softer face, might have resembled sympathy.

"Tough break, but it's best you get a grip. The Saudis want to question you. Come with me, and we'll hold the discussion in my office at the embassy."

"Right now?"

"Right now. If they come here it's their turf, I can't protect you at all."

She looked around the living room as if there should be some reason to stay. "Can I get my banjo?"

"No, Ms. Armstrong, I'd rather not let you out of my sight." The polite way he phrased this was ultimate, the door slamming shut on her last glimpse of what had been.

"Can I at least make a phone call?"

He shrugged, and gestured to the phone.

She dialed Sayeed's mobile number as if her fingers knew he was the one person who could help her now. "This is Arden. I need your help."

"Do you need an ambulance? Security?" His voice, though alert, was an oasis of calm. "I see you're calling from your home phone on campus."

"No, nobody's hurt, but I have to go to the State Department, of the … " she floundered, as if speaking of a suddenly foreign country, "the United States, at the U.S. Embassy in Riyadh, and I'll need some good advice." She looked at Montgomery. "Can I have a friend meet us there, a university official?"

"I need a background check on him."

Sayeed, hearing Montgomery's voice, asked, "Who are you talking to, Arden?"

She tried to explain, but she had neither voice nor heart for coherence. "I'll just wait for you there," Sayeed said finally. "They'll let me in, they know who I am."

"Would you tell Ruth, please?"

"Yes."

"But not Dr. Zafeeyeh, not yet, please?"

"No."

"Thanks, Sayeed."

FORTY-FOUR

THE INTERVIEW WITH the Saudi intelligence agents went quickly, with Sayeed there to translate where necessary, and to lend her what passed for moral support, as a representative of her employer. He frowned as Arden talked about what she knew of Faisal, and how well she knew him, but she was too stunned to feel embarrassed by Sayeed's disapproval.

There was little to tell, after all. When she described for them the locale, as best she could remember, of the strange little goat-inhabited neighborhood where Faisal had dropped off his fellow fanatic, even the most suspicious-looking Saudi smiled at her recollection of the goats.

She would not let their assumptions simply pass unchecked into truth. "But that doesn't mean he kidnapped them. You have to know, Faisal wants to improve his country. He believes in *democracy*." She addressed this touchstone word to Montgomery, whose expression remained unmoved. "He's an idealist," she insisted.

"Oh, an *idealist*," Montgomery repeated, drawling. His upper lip twisted into mockery bordering on insult. "Idealists like him get Americans killed."

She shook her head in emphatic denial. "He's a very good Muslim, sir," she entreated the suspicious-looking lead Saudi interviewer. "He doesn't want air bases erasing the Kingdom's valuable archaeology." How she wished she could plead Faisal's case in Arabic; she thought it might make all the difference here.

"We are all good Muslim, Miss," said the lead Saudi. "We all wish to improve the life, for every Saudi people and for others people in the world." He looked at Montgomery. "If she shares his idea, I don't want her in the Kingdom."

Sayeed spoke up. "It will be easier to watch her here than in America. If he contacts her, we can know." As always, the mantle of authority settled easily on his slender frame. The others nodded slow agreement.

Arden wondered if they assumed she didn't understand or if they thought, as men, that she could simply be ignored. "What if I don't want to stay?"

Sayeed's answer was cold. "You cannot break your contract without reason. We don't give you the exit visa." The eyes of every man focused on her; she felt a swell of oppressive claustrophobia that bordered on panic. The sensation stiffened her resolve.

"I'm in the embassy now," she reminded Montgomery with what she hoped was a fierce stare. "I can stay right here. I can ask for asylum. I can call home, and tell the story—"

His dry laughter interrupted her. "There's no such thing as asylum for someone who collaborates with a terrorist. Remember, three of those pilots were Americans."

"But you know I didn't. You know ..." she stopped. She recalled Faisal's saying that any crime could be covered up here. Now she saw how easy it was to manufacture one too. She was completely powerless in the Kingdom. And she could not get out without an exit visa. She folded her hands tight on the table and stared down at her knuckles, willing her face to betray nothing of her dread.

"You will keep teaching until the end of your contract term," Sayeed told her. "I expect you to do a good job. If not ... then we ... find another place for you," he ended delicately. He probably meant prison. This was not as shocking as it seemed. Westerners were jailed routinely, for a gamut of offenses—drinking, causing traffic accidents, being an unmarried couple in a car, eating in public during Ramadan, violating contracts. Usually the sentences were short. The Riyadh Women's Club made regular visits to jailed women, to take food and books.

The lead Saudi eyed Arden. "She is in danger if she stay here," he told Sayeed quietly, in English. "If he contact her through his helpers. She is in danger from them."

Montgomery's impatient shrug dismissed this. "There can't be many here."

"There are enough. Look, how this was too easy for him."

"Like a goddamn pied piper," Montgomery muttered.

Sayeed looked to Arden to explain the reference; and, as odd as she found the setting, she told them of the magical musician who rid the town of Hamlin of its rats, and then of its children when he was not adequately paid. She remembered the narrator Scheherazade, of *One Thousand and one Arabian Nights*, and wondered if she could change their conclusions by spinning more tales.

"We did not receive demand for payment." The Saudi lead took the story literally.

"It's early yet." Montgomery rose, heavily, to his feet, and Arden saw in his weariness a certain defeat. He'd been expecting her to illuminate the ending of this story, she realized, and she had confirmed for him that it would not be satisfactory. "But we won't recognize demands, anyway, that's our policy. Brass is gonna hate this."

Montgomery shared a sober look with the lead Saudi.

The interview concluded. It was agreed that a prominent archaeologist like Faisal could not be linked to any kidnapping. The official story? The Empty Quarter group had gone missing, presumed lost. A tragedy. Arden's and Faisal's shared history would vanish under a swirl of sand.

"Thanks for being so open, Miss Armstrong." Montgomery said, after the intelligence agents left. "You made it easier for us, and for yourself. Keep in touch."

He put his card on the table between them. She didn't want to touch it.

Sayeed picked it up. "She will," he told Montgomery.

THE RIDE BACK to campus seemed endless. She fingered the sura around her neck, the only tangible link she had to him now, other than their whimsical little braid, tucked inside a baggie in her purse.

Sayeed's mouth tightened as he watched her in the rearview. "I am sorry for the bad that happened to you here."

"Oh no, it wasn't bad." Her whisper was thready.

His eyes widened. He didn't speak to her again. She didn't listen when she heard him talking quietly on his mobile, even when he said Ruth's name.

The ghosts of Johnny and Nawaf, if they were ghosts now, seemed to dance on the highway just in front of her, a jaunty mirage whose dissipation did not erase their images even as Sayeed drove through them. Two other figures hovered behind them, shimmering, faint with small glints of insignia on their pockets. She could not see Faisal at all. Her fingers closed tight around the sura. She didn't even know what it said.

RUTH OPENED THE DOOR, her face a mask of grief. Grace, Evelyn and Kate crowded behind her, all wearing the same expression, awed in their disbelief that tragedy could have invaded the fantasy that had been their life in the Kingdom. He'd been right about that, she thought, they'd lived in a bubble.

Sayeed pulled Arden aside just before she entered. She looked curiously at the way his hand restrained her arm in blatant physical contact; but he did not withdraw it, and this more than anything confirmed for her that they were outside the rules now. He glanced beyond her at the women gathered. "I told Ruth, only, about what happen to you. Tell those others not to speak of this to anyone, if they want stay here. We don't let this story to be told."

She looked into his black eyes. Couldn't he explain, make this scenario understandable, show the omniscience he'd seemed to have in the beginning? Even though she was now in a sense his hostage, she was afraid suddenly to let him go. He might be her last link to discovering the truth. He returned her stare, deeply, the longest look they'd ever exchanged. She could see that he found her both dreadful and fascinating, and that his new obligation to watch her closely might not sit as comfortably on him as he'd conveyed during the interview.

"Please do something for me, Sayeed."

"What is it?"

"Tell me what this *sura* means?" She took it from her neck. He studied it for a moment. Her assumption, that he knew the Koran perfectly, was correct.

"It is sura 12, 111. It speaks about the old, the pre-history." He translated slowly, peering closely at the tiny script. "*Bismillah a Rahman u Rahim,*" he began, as was done before a *sura* reading. In the name of Allah, the magnificent, the most powerful:

> "*In their history it is a lesson, for men who understand. It is not a fiction story, but a confirmation of living scripture. It is a detailed explanation of everything, and a guidance and mercy for believers.*"

He looked up with his fathomless eyes. "It is good sura for archaeologists. They look back." He held her gaze a moment longer. "Not for *mujahedin*. They have to look forward." He handed the tablet to her and then turned away. His back, walking off, looked just like Faisal's would have.

RUTH HAD MADE TEA, of course, and they clustered around the pot as if it were a fire and they tribal women with herbs to burn, to ward off the evil spirit that had come to threaten them. Ruth, ignoring Sayeed's threat, had told them the story. Evelyn lit a cigarette, unheard-of for women in the Kingdom, but nobody objected.

"Here's my problem with this scenario," Kate said, as always getting straight to the point. "From what I could see, which admittedly isn't as much as Arden might have seen, Faisal had everything to lose. He wasn't some wacko with an axe to grind. He was at the top of his game in this society, and he threw it all away. *If* he really did this."

"If we can trust anything Saudi intelligence says," Ruth said. "Or the U.S. State Department."

"If he could actually plan this kind of thing, and carry it out all alone," said Grace.

"If we'll ever really know." Evelyn tapped her ash on the side of her saucer. She slanted an inquisitive look at Arden.

For some reason Arden was picturing his apartment as she'd seen it on that harried last morning. What was it that kept coming to her? Not just the satellite phone, not just the sight of it on the bare table—that was it, of course. His apartment had been empty, cleaned of every trace of him. The books, the papers, the maps, the posters on the walls, even the carpets. She'd been startled by the starkness in the light of morning, she remembered, but he'd dismissed it with a single shrug.

"Semester cleaning." He'd smiled. "Didn't you see how the place needed it? They came while I was gone. They'll paint this week, put it all back." He'd walked her to the door with arms that had felt so strong, so supportive, and that she now thought were probably firm with the intent to get her out of there.

He could have said he'd be doing research on the moon and she'd have believed him, as long as he was looking at her with his beautiful, deceitful eyes or touching her with his soothing, treacherous hands or speaking to her in his soft, lying voice.

But she didn't *want* to believe that! She didn't *want* to think he was deceitful. Yet she could not ignore the damning evidence of that scoured apartment. Seeing it again in her mind's eye made her feel a hundred years old, with a hundred years' worth of bitter memories and only the certainty of death ahead of her.

"He left," she muttered. "He had no intention of coming back." She recounted, her voice shaking, how his apartment had looked.

Grace said at last, in a tentative voice, "Maybe in a way it's just as well he left, before you could get even more involved? I mean, if you'd actually married him, you'd be considered an accomplice."

"Or you'd have to live in exile, in some cell, with other terrorists," Evelyn said.

"What will you do if he gets in touch with you?" asked Kate.

"He can't." Anguish strangled her voice. "He'll know they're watching me." Besides, why would he want to get in touch with her? She'd been a brief pleasure and then an inconvenience. "I don't want to hear from him anyway." She shook her head, fiercely, willing tears away from her eyes and throat.

"He must have realized the compromising situation he put you in," said Kate. She and Evelyn shared an outraged look. They seemed about to expand on this topic.

Ruth stood then, and picked up the tray. "I think Arden's going to need a little time alone, to process all this." It was the signal for the others to leave.

When they'd gone Ruth gathered Arden into her arms and rocked her while the broken sounds of loss echoed in the empty room.

After sunset Ruth persuaded her to put on a whole-body hijab, for privacy, and they went walking together like Saudi ladies in the evening air. The sprinklers had just been turned off and the grass and hardy blossoms gleamed wet in the lights. They walked up the hill and stood on top, across from the mosque, and gazed through their scrims to the swells of ochre sand where the first stars were emerging low and bright in the violet sky, to the south, above the Empty Quarter. Then they walked slowly back home, leaning on each other's arm for balance and, more, for comfort.

FORTY-FIVE

ARDEN WAS NOT ABLE to give in to the profound sickness she felt at his betrayal and disappearance. Her sickness was overshadowed by the changes in her Kingdom life.

It started with the phones in their apartment—every time they made a call, a little clicking noise signaled that the line was being tapped. It continued when they realized someone was coming in for regular searches. Whenever she and Ruth returned to the apartment after time away, it was apparent that their things had been inspected by unknown hands. And her letters from the States were obviously opened and read. Most of the letters from home were about Annie's upcoming wedding, and she couldn't bring herself to describe to her family what had happened and why they should be circumspect in what they wrote.

At school, Dr. Zafeeyeh seemed to look at her in a different way, and Arden wondered in her paranoia if Dr. Z. had heard a rumor about her affair with a Saudi. She didn't perceive any new attitude from her students, at least, but she missed Leila terribly. The girl had not returned to school; the family was presumably in mourning. Arden was working up the courage to go and visit them.

The other teachers pulled away from her, as if they thought her situation was contagious. Grace told her they would take up the girls' test score cause without her since they weren't sure how Arden's dubious status, in Sayeed's eyes, would compromise the possible results. She learned from Kate, with a sense of bittersweet satisfaction, that Faisal's Science Department colleagues had willingly cooperated with the grade investigation. But she missed walking around the campus with the *sheikhas,* missed their camaraderie on the bus, and missed their collegial discussions, although they hadn't gotten personally close. Now they were merely polite.

A terse letter arrived from the USIA. She would not be administering any more tests there; no explanation was included.

Arden found solace in Ruth, the only person who understood how she was suffering. She tried not to lean too hard; she didn't want to tire Ruth with her lamentations, but she was soothed by the sympathetic look in Ruth's eyes which made explanations unnecessary.

They tried to make light of their surveillance. Arden thought once, with a pale shade of her former whimsy, that she should leave a little note for the spies. There was something peculiarly protective in being so closely observed when so many were distancing from her. She minded the spying more for Ruth, whose dealings with Palestinian refugee organizations were now further exposed and perhaps compromised. Although the Saudis gave lip service to supporting the Palestinian cause, their actual aid was tempered by U.S. attitudes.

"We're used to it," Ruth told her in a wry tone when Arden apologized for bringing down the heat on them both. "I've suspected my communication was overseen from the beginning. I've always been really careful here."

"How did you stand it? For so long?"

"I need this job," Ruth said simply. "There's nowhere else I could make this kind of money and still be close enough to visit as often as I do."

"That's why you never rock the boat."

"Never." Ruth smiled. She had not joined in the *sheikhas'* demands for grade reviews. She said, based on long knowledge of Kingdom practices, that they were wasting their breath and compromising their contracts for nothing.

She remained skeptical toward the conclusion that Faisal had kidnapped the pilots. "I don't think he betrayed you, Arden. He never struck me as flighty. Remember that if he was seen as a political threat, they'd concoct *anything* to discredit him," she told Arden firmly. "I've learned to question every Saudi story I hear."

There was relief in this kind of reassurance. But Arden could not adopt Ruth's measured assessment. Her feelings were too unruly, running out of her like water from an overfull sponge, no boundaries to contain hurt. Like a newborn, she felt herself imprinted onto Faisal, unable to separate love from reason. She didn't know what to think, or even *how* to think, anymore.

SEVERAL WEEKS PASSED. Arden plodded through gray days lit only by her affection for the girls and by her friendship with Ruth. She took consolation in continuing to read the Koran, although it shed no more mystical light on her circumstances than it offered for any other; its advice was tersely practical. She could surmise that any imam here, hearing her outpouring of grief as if at a Catholic confession, would merely raise a dry eyebrow as if to say 'what did you expect, love without marriage brings only tragedy.'

She didn't, finally, have the nerve to visit Leila and Othman, even though she knew this was rude cowardice. But she was afraid the spies would follow her to their house, and she didn't want to compromise Faisal's ability to communicate with his family, should he be able to in some way. She'd made a lame excuse when the girls had asked her to go with them, and they'd eyed her for the first time with disapproval.

One Thursday morning she finally got onto the ladies' weekend shopping bus again. There was a new women's bluegrass band she'd read about, The Dixie Chicks, and she wanted to see if their CD had made it into the Kingdom's bootleg souks.

But, standing inside one of the glassed-in music shops, she knew her outing had been a mistake. The

Pakistani clerk was putting on a request from two Saudi youths conferring with him. When the music started all three of them nodded their heads, grinning, in time to the distinctive, contagious beat: Smashing Pumpkins, "1979." The music stung; it was what she'd heard in Faisal's apartment when she'd gone to pick up Evelyn's skirt. Before, Arden would have found the scene funny and charming: the way the clerk's gleaming black hair shook gently to and fro in unison with the youths' bobbing headdresses, sharing their enjoyment of Western music, which they might not even understand. Now she looked at them blankly, registering that it was an unusual little Riyadhi vignette, of the sort she'd have earlier enjoyed.

She left that shop and went into the next one. She stood in front of the "American Country" section, flipping idly through recent releases. Her interest in finding the CD had fled, but she couldn't get back on the bus for another hour at least. The music blaring here was "Hold Me," a sprightly Fleetwood Mac number. Its lush harmonies and upbeat piano tempo irked her even more than hearing the Pumpkins next door. It was stuck on repeat while another Paki clerk hummed along happily.

I just can't stand music anymore. Love songs, sad ones, Arabic, alternative, even her beloved bluegrass—all recalled Faisal to her now. It seemed the only musical taste they had not had in common was Phish. And a little Phish went a long way, especially in Saudi Arabia with no easy source of weed as accompaniment. She moved back, intending to leave the shop, but she bumped into someone behind her.

"*Ma'asif,*" she murmured in apology to the tall veiled woman.

"*Ma'alesh,*" was the soft response, never mind. The woman put a gloved hand on Arden's wrist. Surprised, Arden looked at her. She was tall, slim, beautifully covered in an embroidered black silk hijab. Only the most conservative women wore gloves, to ensure that not a speck of skin showed, and such women rarely came alone to the souks, certainly not to buy bootleg CDs nor to befriend strange Westerners.

The woman moved closer, and Arden got a whiff of perfume. She sniffed, frowning, confused. Not perfume, she realized in a breathtaking swoosh, *aftershave.*

Fleetwood Mac crooned about slipping a hand inside a glove.

"Ahden," the figure said in an undertone, "I am Nawaf." The grip on Arden's arm tightened under her elbow, holding her upright when she would have slumped in shock. "Don't speak now, we walk together from the shop."

The winding melody followed them outside, asking how the singer was going to manage with no damage. Through her sense of spinning reality Arden could feel Nawaf's strength as he propelled her along the street with one hard arm linked tight in hers, holding her beside him companionably, as women often strolled together. As slight as he looked, there was iron in his wiry body.

He made a convincing woman—he had the swaying carriage, the fluid walk, the hesitancy in peering out of his veil. He must have paid close attention to the women in his family. She stared at him, trying to detect his expression, but his mesh was very thick, as befitting a conservative lady. Perhaps he had been hiding like this all along, haunting the souks for his own strange reasons, perhaps there had been no desert trip and it was all an elaborate fiction—

She stopped short and jerked her arm from his. *"Nawaf!"* She hissed furiously, "We thought you were kidnapped! Where's Faisal?"

"Stop," he hissed back, clutching her arm again. "We are ladies, walking. We don't standing up in the souk and talking loud. Come." He guided her down a side street, into a nearby alley. "We talk inside." He led her to a brilliant white Humvee and opened the back door for her.

The vehicle was customized to carry royal Saudi women. Its windows were heavily tinted so that no-one outside could see in the backseat, and there was a shaded partition separating them from the front. They were alone, as secluded as ancient maharanis in their curtained howdahs. Nawaf flipped back his face veil and wiped his forehead with the back of his hand.

"I don't know how ladies wear this," he muttered. "I don't like. Is too hot." He reached into the armrest and took out two bottles of water. He handed her one, unscrewed the other and drank from it thirstily.

Arden felt heat race into her face as she watched him.

"I know you are surprise I come to you like this, *ya* Ahden. I don't have no other way. The Security telling Johnny and me don't see you, don't talk to you or any others teacher. They waiting for Faisal to find you. But I know he don't never find you here."

He plucked a shopping bag from the Hummer's back storage and dropped it in her lap. "Faisal tells me, give to you. I don't want help him, but Johnny tells me yes, I should to bring you. So take this from Faisal and thanks to Johnny."

She clutched the bag. The object inside felt like a CD. "Did you go camping?"

"We go, yes, we saw al Rub Al Khali. Faisal is good guide. We laughing every day. But I am all the time having big argument with him. After four days I tell him, leave my Kingdom. We take him to village on the border, of the Qatar."

He drank again while she stared, aghast.

"He want change my country," he snapped, countering her disbelief with a glare of his own. "I'm telling to him he's so stupid to talk to me about this changing, don't he know my family? I don't have interest to change anything. The people is happy here, they love the King, they don't be hungry, they don't be angry. They are good Muslim." He fixed Arden with a sudden suspicious frown. "Why you love him too much?"

She could not answer. Her back and arms reverberated with chills that chased each other around her body, in spite of the heat that was mounting inside the still vehicle. She pictured Qatar, on the edge of the Empty

Quarter and just as desolate. How would Faisal possibly have survived?

"His road is bad." He studied her. "He make a big enemy, fighting my family."

Her voice finally emerged. "So you ... *banished* him?" This sounded so old fashioned she wasn't sure it could be accurate. But Nawaf's shrug told her he didn't understand her anyway. "You sent him away?" she asked, louder, accusing.

His teeth gleamed. "He's lucky I don't kill him."

His comment flew past her struggle to comprehend. "But everyone thought he took you. All of us, your father too. Even your cousin Ali."

"Ali now knows the truth. He keeping quiet like all of us."

"But what about his phone, I mean the Antiquities phone? In his apartment?"

"He don't have any phone with him. There can't be phoning, not from al Rub al Khali, we all know this. Nobody of us bring phones."

"Oh Nawaf! *Ya salaam*, how could you just leave him!"

"I'm telling to you, he is lucky I let him alive!" he exclaimed. "I don't want him here! I say, *ya* Faisal, you make a war against my family, next time we meet you are my enemy, and I make trouble for all who help you here. Even you, *ya* Ahden." He gave her knee a little pat. "We get Security to frighten you, to see do you know his plans, his others bad people."

"So all that with Montgomery, all that was just a lie? Did Sayeed know?"

"Nobody of them know except some of secret police. They do what I tell them."

"How did Faisal leave things with you?"

Not understanding her, Nawaf indicated the bag. "He told me to give you."

"No, I mean, what did he say, when he left?"

"Faisal thinks he give his life to Allah." His laugh rang out, full of amused incredulity, in the closed air. "Allah will give him to me and my planes."

She heard how faint her reply was. "Maybe he'll change his mind."

"Too late for that." He gestured to the bag. "I only bring because you were my friend. My man was looking for you in the souks so I can to find you. I know how is the love, *ya helwa*." He nudged her cheek with the back of his gloved hand, a glitter in his eyes swimming up and away again quickly. "Johnny asks me, tell you the truth, bring to you the CD. But after today I don't see you. If you come to me I don't know you."

"But Faisal didn't commit any crime."

"He want change my family? You should think he is like dead man." He eyed her for a moment. Then he pulled the veil over his face—an impatient, conclusive gesture. "Go now. I don't want them find me with you."

"He's not a criminal," she repeated helplessly. "You're all safe, they don't need to watch me anymore, not now. *Ya* Nawaf, *min fadlak*, please, you're the only one who can help me." She grabbed an appeal. "If Johnny was in trouble like this—"

"You crazy, you think I am helping you find him?" His sharp breath drew in the cloth in front of his mouth. "He's enemy of Johnny too! Faisal hates America, you should know this *ya* Ahden! Your Faisal is dead if I see him again."

She knew better than to argue. But she would not let this go without a final fight, the least she could do for Leila. "I will be quiet about this if you do something for me."

"No." He reached across her to open her door.

"It will be good for your family."

She had his attention. "What thing?" he asked, suspicious.

"Change university policy. Let girls have high exam scores if they earn them."

"What? I don't have nothing to do with university."

"You can do anything. Obviously. I will keep quiet, if you make it happen."

"Nobody believe you. But if you talk I don't let you to stay here."

"I'm ready to leave, but I will tell everyone unless you fix this. And I'm still a teacher, so if you don't change it, I will know, and I will tell the truth about Faisal. His family will believe me." She wondered if that was true.

Nawaf slumped back against the seat. He pulled his veil aside for another drink of water. "Why I am doing this thing? Counting girls' marks at school? What reason I'm giving to my father and uncles?"

Arden had planned the grades campaign, even if she hadn't been able to execute it directly, and its arguments sprang to her mind just in time. "Because, your country needs good workers. You need to have girls be as educated as boys so they can work as teachers and doctors for other girls. You must know about the Five Year Plan."

"Five Year, yes, I know."

"So you know that having more Saudis work, than people from other countries, is important. So girls have to be trained to take jobs like mine. Then you won't need so many foreigners here."

He kept watching her.

"Besides, it looks bad for the Kingdom to have girls always getting low grades. It's an image problem. And you look like a hero if you change it."

"That is only thing I do more for you."

"I could make you let girls drive, too ... you know the Americans won't like to hear how you made a story about pilots being kidnapped. You know they could make trouble for you."

"*Emshi.*" Go. He dismissed her, and Americans, with a royal wave.

SHE DIDN'T DARE tell Ruth about her meeting. Once in her bedroom she opened the bag. It was a dusty and battered CD, she saw with crushing disappointment, a collection of Bob Dylan songs covered by a folkie named Tim O'Brien. The last one was "Lay Down Your Weary Tune." Like she'd want to listen to that now. As she put the box away she felt its scratched plastic cover buckle. She opened it with frantic fingers. Folded smoothly inside the lyrics pages was a letter. Her pulse quickened at the sight of its bold strokes, a handwriting she had never seen but that spoke aloud:

Arden my love,

You won't hear from me again until you choose to, once you're away. I'm so sorry to bring this trouble to you.

I don't want to leave you, but you know I was ready to leave the country. Nawaf is nudging Allah's will along by insisting on my departure now. I am going to Afghanistan to investigate a community that shares my views. But I hear they are more oppressive toward women than even in the Kingdom. It would be dangerous for you to visit me.

When you return to the States this summer you must find my mother, Caroline Ullmsted, in Big Sur at her shop, called SilverSword. You can tell her the truth. I will write you, through her, with an address where you can contact me.

I will let Leila and Baba know about me, somehow.

I'll find a way for us to be together, if you still want. But if you can't write to me this summer, I understand. I expect nothing. You already gave me so much, with your love. I hold you in my heart forever.

Your Faisal

There was some Arabic writing below that, which she could not read. She sat with the letter in her hands, tears rolling and sinking into its cheap paper surface, melting his handwriting. She crumpled it into a tight ball, small enough to be safely flushed down the toilet. She was still sitting on her bed, hours later, when Ruth called her to supper.

FORTY-SIX

It was bewildering to be bombarded, in June, by the color and noise and violence of American life. During her first week back all outings, all transactions, all TV and radio programs, produced a cacophony that rang as jarring as it was lively.

American voices were loud, people were enormous, laughs were public, and clothing was eye-poppingly colored. Some things were colorless: the currency was small and monotonous, coffee was bland, spices meager. It was strange taking public transportation again, such as it was in Columbus. Traffic was tame, however, and routines were adhered to rigorously, so the noise level lowered for her somewhat in succeeding weeks.

Arden missed Saudi Arabia with a passion that astonished her, since she'd endured her last months there with increasing distaste for the country. She searched for Muslims, for Arabic, for evidence that people from that part of the world had ever ventured over. She found little trace. Once she saw a Middle Eastern-looking clerk in Walmart, with ALI on his nametag, and she startled him by effusively greeting him in his native tongue, smiling as she would never have dared in the Riyadhi souks.

Her debts were paid, and she'd saved enough to float for a few months cheaply while she decided what to do next. She figured a solution would come to her, once she'd visited Faisal's mother.

Her friends sensed she was deeply changed, and after five minutes of her fending off stereotypes—"Didn't you feel oppressed there, as a woman?" "Did you see any camels?" "Did you meet any sheikhs who own oil wells?" "What were the harems like?"—conversation tended to dwindle. She would not confirm their preconceptions, and, strangely, they weren't interested in hearing anything else.

She told no one about Faisal.

She didn't know if she *could* talk about him, even to Annie.

She no longer shared the concerns of her peers. She didn't watch *Friends*, was not crazed by the fledgling dotcom revolution, and didn't care about hooking up in clubs. Drinking wasn't fun anymore and she found she'd lost her taste for pot. She didn't bother to reconnect with Paul.

ARDEN WAITED, now, outside the Big Sur bus station. The scent of pine was intoxicating, as was the rush of fresh air sweeping over from the Pacific Ocean across Highway One. She was waiting for Faisal's mother. Caroline—she pronounced her name Caro-lyne—had told her they could meet at the bus station, since directions to Caroline's place were confusing.

Arden was glad to buy a cheap ticket to California, glad to flee the familiar, yet unwanted, congestion of Columbus and the tight quarters at Mom's. This week in Big Sur was her gift to herself for surviving all that had come before.

The drive down Highway One from San Francisco was the first time Arden had been alone since leaving the Kingdom. She drank in the wild beauty, the silence, grateful for the road's sharp twists, which forced her to concentrate on driving. She felt the tension of the last months begin to dissipate, in the gusts of Pacific wind rocking her crappy little rental car, even as she wrenched the steering wheel on the narrow road.

She'd thought her anxiety and sadness would never ebb. But now, in the sharp coastal sun, so different in clarity from the Kingdom light, she thought she could glimpse a vista just over the horizon that promised an ease of sorts.

She knew that visiting his mother was the reason for her spirit's lifting. She needed to see at least one person who had loved him too, before she put him behind her forever. Leila had not returned to school at all. Leaving his sister and Othman behind, without speaking to them again, was a heavy regret. One more of so many.

The bus station was attached to a little convenience store, manned by a proprietor who didn't look like a clerk, with his many piercings and his wool hat pulled down low over blond dreadlocks. She studied him discreetly through the open door. She was still not used to looking at men directly, nor having them look at her again. And they looked, openly, but the gazes did not hold any mystery for her.

She shifted on her two-person bench. Not a bus had passed in the twenty minutes she'd been sitting there. The unusual clerk stepped outside and was eyeing her as if he might be about to start a conversation.

Then a tall, jeans-clad woman strode up. She was striking, with a striped woven poncho, huge silver hoops hanging from her ears, bright blue polish on her short nails. Her skin was tan, deeply lined, her long hair silver-gilt blonde, and as she approached Arden her eyes shone an unusual green: shallow river water.

Arden could not speak. Tears obscured the sight of his eyes once more regarding her. Caroline sat down. Her perfume was something expensive, dense and musky. After some moments Arden wiped her cheeks and looked at his mother again.

Faisal's eyes held her with matter-of-fact appraisal. She could have been standing again in his living room, but she was here in Big Sur at the bus station. "Caroline."

"Arden."

Both nodded, then Caroline said, "Let's get out of here." Her voice was deep, but with a hint of music behind it. "I'm in the red bug, follow me, hmm?"

"Not fast," Arden warned her. "I'm pretty Midwestern on these mountain roads."

Caroline laughed, low, and it sounded so much like Faisal that Arden winced.

"Ready?" That look again, challenging.

Caroline drove slowly enough for Arden to follow without too much trouble, even though her rental car had no pickup in climbing the long hills. She was reminded of Uncle Munro's place as they wound higher and higher up the sides of a deep canyon. She got glimpses of ocean far below, as well as a river glinting on the other side, but didn't dare look too closely. She had to shift to the practically non-existent second gear at one point, wondering if it were possible to slide backwards down the canyon. But Caroline pulled off into a tiny wooded drive, *Alhamdulillah,* and Arden slunk her rental behind as if to its final resting place.

"I don't think this shitty little thing's going to make it back down the mountain," she said, unfolding herself from the driver's seat, slapping the vehicle's side.

Caroline's laugh rang out. "Come on in. Need help with your bags?"

"I didn't bring much." Her banjo and one backpack: after the Kingdom clothing strictures, life in jeans was perfectly simple. She hoisted her bag onto her shoulder, and followed Caroline into a neatly made long log cabin, of a workmanship her Great-Aunt Patty, the carpenter, would have appreciated.

"I'm putting you in Faisal's room." Caroline indicated a long hallway.

Arden's backpack thumped to the floor.

"What? I thought you'd like to see where he stays, when he's here. He loves it up here. I thought you'd get a kick out of seeing all his stuff."

"I do." Arden nodded, tears clouding her vision again. "I will." She stood still.

Caroline surveyed her. "I've been waiting for you since February."

Arden sank onto the nearest couch. "February!"

Caroline sat next to her. "I got a letter mid February. Typewritten, no return address, postmarked Pakistan. Nothing personal, so I know he didn't send it. It told me to expect a package for you, from him. That you might get in touch." She studied Arden for a moment. "I haven't heard from him, or been able to reach him, since right around Christmas. His father told me he's gone missing in an expedition, which seems pretty fishy to me. I don't know why Faisal had something sent to you here."

"He didn't know my address in the States. But we were ... together."

"I figured that." Caroline's scrutiny narrowed. "But—in *Saudi Arabia?*"

"We met through Leila. I was her English teacher there."

"Leila's coming to visit me with her new husband later this summer, before her grad school program starts. So, tell me, you got involved with my Faisal—in the Kingdom! That took some crust. And then, what?"

Aching, Arden told her of Faisal's banishment, and watched as a mixture of horror and relief dawned on his mother's face.

Caroline concluded, "He was anti-Royal, but he didn't kidnap any pilots."

"The secret police let the Americans think he did, to get their support to spy on me and anyone he was meeting with. To track down his emails at the embassy. I don't know how the State Department took it when the pilots showed up later, unharmed. Nawaf probably engineered some plausible lie. You remember, there's no real news allowed there."

Arden still found it hard to believe that sweet young Nawaf had proved so Machiavellian. She had not underestimated his power, however: exam policy had been altered, according to a memo sent from Dr. Zafeeyeh. Girls' scores were no longer pegged to boys'.

Caroline said slowly, as if thinking aloud, "In a way it's a very Saudi story. I remember how things work, in the Kingdom. I couldn't stand it for more than a couple years. I met and married Othman here, and I committed to give it a try." She looked up at Arden with the beginning of a smile. "Faisal chose the wrong tribal guy to lobby for democracy." She snorted. "He thought he was at a *majlis*." *Majlis* was the weekly open forum the King held, to hear opinions and grievances from ordinary citizens, a holdover from the old days.

Arden nodded. She had concluded as much, in her many months of pondering.

"Where do you think he is?" Caroline asked. "For sure he got out of Qatar okay."

"I'm afraid he ended up with that creepy Taliban bunch in Afghanistan."

"Oh Jesus Christ."

"Peace be upon him," Arden felt compelled to say.

"He'd never stay with them. They're destroying the archeological artifacts."

"But where else can he go? He's been labeled a terrorist, by us and by them."

Caroline got up and began to pace, showing a contained energy like her son's. She went to the window. "Who saw you come from the airport? Never mind, you wouldn't have noticed them. Nobody followed you up here, though, that's for sure. I guess we're alone for the duration."

"You don't seem very surprised."

"I've been afraid of something like this. His last years here, since the Gulf War, it was all revolution, all the time. I hadn't heard such incendiary stuff since the 60s, only it was coming from a bunch of Arab fellows with beards who refused to shake my hand. In my own house! I made him get rid of them." She turned, frowning. "I thought he was going to settle down when he finally went back to the Kingdom for good. He was so eager to make his Haj. He was very serious about Islam, and about his archaeology."

"They were everything to him, when I met him."

"So what the hell happened?"

Arden sighed. "They turned one of his dig sites into an air base. So we could get at Iraq more easily. Or Iran, whichever."

"We?"

"The U.S., Saudi Arabia, you know. Our special relationship."

"Oh yeah. I know that one." Caroline shifted closer on the couch. "Now I want to hear about your romance."

Arden relayed the short history, from the first day on the hilltop to the last goodbye, in the empty apartment that, Arden now knew, had been indeed readied for cleaning and not for a final departure.

"He was excited about doing more excavation work there," Caroline said sadly. "And he wanted to make sure Leila's marriage was solid."

"I never saw her after Christmas," Arden said slowly. "She doesn't even know about us, or any of this. Neither does Othman. They were told he was lost in the Empty Quarter. At least, as far as I know. He might have been able to get in touch with them, somehow."

"Well, I sure won't tell write or call with the truth about his plans to leave. They don't need the heat over there, or the stigma. When Leila comes here I can talk to her." Caroline stood up from the table. "Come on, let me show him to you as he was here."

They walked down the long hallway, which was hung with dozens of photographs. Faisal as a bright-eyed baby, Faisal as an impish-grinned little boy, Faisal as a teen, sexuality smoldering in the smirk he gave the camera— "One of his girlfriends took that one," Caroline said— Faisal playing soccer, holding a guitar, in cap and gown, on skis, behind birthday cakes, on top of mountains, in front of caves. In every picture he was smiling.

The panorama of his California life was sweet, and painful, for Arden to view. She wanted to stay, learning his milestones, and she wanted to turn away. The last hung photograph was Faisal with a group of bearded men in Caroline's living room, obviously a candid and unwanted shot, because the men were scowling and covering their faces. Faisal's grin was teasing, his face beardless, as he would have looked when Arden met him, had he been smiling then, had his long hair not been covered by the headdress.

"That was before he went back last September. See those thugs behind him in the photo?" Caroline shook her head. "They were humorless. So unlike him. I couldn't see the attraction, and it bugged me to watch my bright boy falling under their influence."

"The enemy of my enemy is my friend," Arden murmured.

"Whatever. That mumbo jumbo never cut any ice with me, no matter how he tried to explain it." Caroline's voice hitched a little. "I hoped he'd settle down. He was a fine scholar, and he'd be a great husband, a great father. His dad and I agreed on that. I thought he could have a life in the Kingdom."

"I guess he thought so too, at first."

"I should have just let his dad keep him there, instead of coming back to me each summer. The more you travel, the more fucked up you get, I've come to believe."

Arden nodded slowly. She understood arriving at that point of view.

"I'll let you put your stuff away and open the package—it's in there, on his bed. Then we'll go walking. I'll take you to his favorite place on the canyon."

His room was as alive as if he'd just left it—posters, magazines, bright Bedouin weaving on the bed. Arden sat on the edge, pressing her lips against emotion.

Inside the box, wrapped in a protective nest, was a pot like those from his last expedition, and a letter folded on top of it.

Ya Arden,

Of so much that I wish I could give you, this comes from the best of me. If you want to, write to this POB number in San Francisco. I use a network of people to forward my mail. I left Afghanistan when I realized I could not agree with that group.

We can find a way to be together again if you choose. If not, dear heart, I will understand. I keep the memory of our love always.

Your Faisal

Her tears splotched on the mellow surface of the pot.

She wanted to hurl it against the wall and watch it shatter into the million pieces he'd left of her, shards that could not be put back together without so many scars that the original was forever altered. She was not the woman who fell in love last September. She would never be that woman again.

CAROLINE LED HER up the canyon to a lookout where the wide sweep of the Pacific, raging in afternoon sunstruck glory, swelled in a glassy green arc.

"This was where he'd come to play guitar. He liked that religious song about the weary tune. It was written here, you know, when Dylan was visiting Joan Baez."

They started singing together, and the sound was tossed over the cliff by the rushing wind.

Throat too tight to sing any more, Arden watched the roll, break, spray, subside, for as long as it took the earth to wheel a little further away from the sun. She could almost hear the early prayer call wafting from across the far oceans, the farther deserts.

She stared into the green water as if she could look once more into his eyes. She closed her own eyes against the sight and prayed, hard, for peace.

Author's Note

I lived for five years in Saudi Arabia. I treasure the memory of my time in the Kingdom for its open-hearted people, from whose unique history I learned so much.

ACKNOWLEDGEMENTS

My thanks go to: My mother who gifted me with rich, deep, strange stories and the wanderlust that has inspired my own travels. My sister whose lively imagination peopled our childhood with fabulous characters and whose love of reading inspired mine. My husband who always encouraged me and who has fascinating stories of his own. My children who allowed my writing to eclipse any notion of home cooking (apologies to my hungry eldest son who wanted me to add more scenes of people eating barbecue). My writing collective—Julia Buckley, Elizabeth Diskin, Cynthia Quam—who shepherded my work from the beginning, who are the best editors, publicists and critique partners any novelist could hope for, and without whom I would never have finished a manuscript. Wells Street Press for helping me get from manuscript to publication. Other writers and artists whose generosity has moved me: Karen Osborne, Sam Reaves, Kathi Baron, Marilyn Brandt, Erica O'Rourke, Jennifer Stevenson (the latter three from the august ChicagoNorth Romance Writers of America). Columbia College Chicago for Story Workshop. Cherished friends: aDOORables, NapaGals, YaYas, and Ann L to whom I declared my first novel 'finished' years ago after writing THE END and running to her house all aglow. Snaps to Mary H with whom I cooked up the idea to get serious about writing on a napkin in Canada. The Oak Park community whose support has so nourished my family and me during my illness, especially Mary, Fran, Beth, Elizabeth, Kathryn and Kathy. Finally, pulmonologist Benjamin Margolis and Sherrie Majdic, and oncologist Philip Bonomi and Irene Haapoja, whose care has granted me time. Special thanks and love to Sue.

ABOUT THE AUTHOR

Award-winning writer Emma Gates was born in New York. She earned a BA in Spanish/Latin American Studies from Indiana University Bloomington, and an MBA with concentration in Arabic/Middle Eastern Studies from Thunderbird. She worked for three years in Mexico and five in Saudi Arabia. She is an international business and telecoms specialist currently living near Chicago with her family and a pair of inscrutable cats.

PLAYLIST

I often listen to music while I write. Sometimes I choose from the era I'm writing about, from my own collection, but sometimes my favorite radio station provides inspiration which can creep in to inform the story ambiance (shout-out: WXRT Chicago).

Thanks to my brother, who always shared the best music, and to my children who gave me the great compliment of saying how much they like my musical taste. Thanks to the artists whose brilliance so greatly illuminates my life.

Worlds Apart – Bruce Springsteen
Jerusalem – Steve Earle
American Boy – Steve Earle
Camptown Races – Stephen Foster
Union Maid – Woody Guthrie
You Look Like Gold to Me – Ben Harper
Sert al Houb – Mohammed Abdu
Kiss Me, Kill Me – U2
Shine on You Crazy Diamond – Pink Floyd
Wish You Were Here – Pink Floyd
Welcome to the Machine – Pink Floyd
Corduroy – Pearl Jam
Maid of Constant Sorrow – Stanley Brothers, adapted
Bluer Pastures – Dolly Parton
The Water is Wide – trad. English
Down in the Valley – trad. American
Jingle Bells – James Lord Pierpont
Smells like Teen Spirit – Nirvana
What Child is This – William Chatterton Dix
Deck the Halls – trad. Welsh
Gloucester Wassail – trad. English
Rudolph the Red-Nosed Reindeer – Johnny Marks
Frosty the Snowman – Walter 'Jack' Rollins and Steve Nelson
I Will Always Love You – Dolly Parton

Black is the Color of my True Love's Hair – trad.
American (adapted by the author)
Amazing Grace – John Newton
Winter Wonderland – Felix Bernard and Richard B.
Smith
You are My Sunshine – Jimmie Davis and Charles
Mitchell
Wild Mountain Thyme – Francis McPeake
Barbara Allen – trad. English, Scottish
Pack up Your Sorrows – Richard Farina
Tonight, Tonight – Smashing Pumpkins
Good Riddance – Green Day
Private Conversation – Lyle Lovett
1979 – Smashing Pumpkins
Hold Me – Fleetwood Mac
Lay Down your Weary Tune – Bob Dylan as performed
by Tim O'Brien
Peace Train – Yusuf/Cat Stevens